PEN…

THE P…

Michael Innes, in priva… Stewart. Educated at Edinburgh Academy and Oriel College, Oxford, he has been Student of Christ Church, Oxford, and Reader in English Literature at the University of Oxford.

He has published many novels—including the quintet *A Staircase in Surrey*—and several volumes of short stories, as well as books of criticism and essays, under his own name. His *Eight Modern Writers* appears as the final volume in *The Oxford History of English Literature*, and he is also the author of *Rudyard Kipling* and *Joseph Conrad*.

Under the pseudonym Michael Innes, Dr. Stewart has written broadcast scripts and many crime novels.

THE

PAPER THUNDERBOLT

by

MICHAEL INNES

Within the navil of this hideous Wood,
Immur'd in cypress shades a Sorcerer dwels . . .
And here to every thirsty Wanderer,
By sly enticement gives his baneful Cup.

COMUS

PENGUIN BOOKS

PENGUIN BOOKS
Viking Penguin Inc., 40 West 23rd Street,
New York, New York 10010, U.S.A.
Penguin Books Ltd, Harmondsworth,
Middlesex, England
Penguin Books Australia Ltd, Ringwood,
Victoria, Australia
Penguin Books Canada Limited, 2801 John Street,
Markham, Ontario, Canada L3R 1B4
Penguin Books (N.Z.) Ltd, 182–190 Wairau Road,
Auckland 10, New Zealand

First published in the United States of America by
Dodd, Mead and Company, Inc., 1951
Published in Penguin Books 1987

LIBRARY OF CONGRESS CATALOGING IN PUBLICATION DATA
Innes, Michael, 1906–
The paper thunderbolt.
(Penguin crime fiction)
Reprint. Originally published: New York:
Dodd, Mead, 1951.
I. Title.
PR6037.T466P36 1987 823′.914 86-30425
ISBN 0 14 01.0089 X

Printed in the United States of America by
Offset Paperback Mfrs., Inc., Dallas, Pennsylvania
Set in Times Roman

The characters, places, incidents and situations in this book
are imaginary and have no relation to any person,
place or actual happening.

CONTENTS

NOTE

IT IS PROPER to inform the reader that the internal economy of the Bodleian Library in the University of Oxford, as described with some particularity in the ensuing romance, is entirely the fruit of fancy. And, more particularly, those subterranean regions in which the climax is set, although frequently vouched for by reliable persons as bearing a general correspondence with what is here imagined, have never come within the purview of the author, whose common occasions have familiarised him only with that which lies above ground-level. He is very conscious of being seldom charged with any large adherence to the *actual,* and he begs acceptance of the postulate that, if there be (as assuredly there must be) a *real* Bodleian Library laid up in Heaven, its foundations unquestionably rest upon such immensities as are rudely figured in this insubstantial tale. And be it added that the author, contemplating his finished and fugitive performance and realising one odd consequence of the Copyright Act of 1709, is constrained to murmur with a wholesome awe certain lines of old Samuel Daniel, similarly circumstanced three hundred and fifty years ago:

Heere in this goodly Magazine of witte,
This Storehouse of the choicest furniture
The world doth yeelde, here in this exquisite
And most rare monument, that doth immure
The glorious reliques of the best of men,
Thou, part imperfect work, vouchsafed art
A little roome.

THE PAPER THUNDERBOLT

PART ONE

ROUTH IN AN INFERNAL REGION

. . . involv'd
In this perfidious fraud.

PARADISE LOST

1. There was a wait in the bank. Routh's inside felt empty, flabby. His own patter nagged in his head. *No need whatever for a deposit to secure delivery. Our senior sales manager knows your standing in the community, madam.*

Routh shifted his weight furtively from one foot to the other. He glanced over his shoulder and through the gilded letters MIDLAND BANK LTD at the quiet street. The old Douglas two-stroke was just round the corner. He had to be careful that nobody following him out of the bank rounded the same corner and saw him mount it. Provided he worked each town quickly and left this one fault on his trail it was alright. You should say *All right.* Remember your education.

But just at present able to offer a few influential customers twenty per cent reduction for cash with order. Again his own glib phrases were spilling aimlessly over his mind. Perhaps that was what he would have to do in Hell: go on repeating these things through all eternity.

The man in front was paying in cheques and a lot of cash. The teller ticked off the amounts that were already filled in on a long slip. *Making only three pounds ten precisely, madam.* If only you had the guts for a hold-up. Smash and grab. Smash the teller's silly face and grab all that. Routh's right hand in his trouser-pocket—the one where the lining was only a big ragged hole—trembled as it touched the woman's mean, creased cheque. . . . And all this for three pounds ten. *Uncrossed and made payable to bearer, madam, if you don't mind.*

It was here once more, the bad moment. The chap in front had closed his shabby leather bag, was having some fool joke, was going. Routh took the cheque from his pocket. The very paper was hot and clammy. He hated banks so, surely banks must hate him. At least they hated these small open cheques presented by strangers. Yet they would never really try a check-up—not then and there. Customers—the small sort that Routh chose for *his* customers—didn't like it. So it's all right, I tell you. Push it over. Remember you're a gentleman. Push it at him. Quietly, pleasantly. Good morning.

Routh saw his own hand tremble. He would remember afterwards—he always did—that it had been with anger, not fear. It was with anger at the pettiness of the thing, at all this for three pounds ten. He knew that, really, Routh was on a big scale, was a being cast in a large mould, would rise to the grand occasion when it came. And it would come. He would carry out a big thing as cool as ice, as cool as Raffles. And his heart then would not thrust against his ribs as it did now. . . . The teller was looking at him.

But it was all right. The man's pen was poised over the signature to scribble. In a second he would say indifferently "Notes?" and flick the petty amount off the orderly piles in his drawer. Don't say anything more. Wait. A normal commercial transaction. Routh repeated the phrase to himself. He found himself repeating it again and again. A normal commercial transaction. A normal . . . The teller had gone.

A big clock ticked on the wall. Its ticking queerly struck in at Routh's pounding heart, fought with it rhythm against rhythm. His knees went wrong, so that he had to lock them, to press them against each other. The bank swayed. All right . . . *all right*. It's happened before. Nothing to do with *you*. The woman has a shaky account, a tiny balance and no arrangement for overdrawing. She's been a nuisance for a long time, and now they won't even honour her blasted cheque for three ten—not if the credit isn't there. That's what he's gone to see. Only hold on.

But what if it's something else? He tried to think about the woman and her cheque. It was the woman with the hare-lip, with the window curtains that had seemed more morbidly secretive than anybody else's in the drearily respectable little road. She had been one of those that open the door on the chain. With that sort, to get in is to triumph. *Our senior sales manager knows your standing*. In a quarter of an hour he had sold the non-existent contraption. *Making only three pounds ten precisely, madam*. Not, he had thought, the bank-account sort. Watching her write the cheque in her gimcrack parlour with its paranoid curtains he had been surprised. *Edges us round the quotas. Thank you*.

Of course she had swallowed it. Staggering, but they nearly all did.

Or had she?

Routh's breathing quickened. After all, one day you'd be caught out. One day you'd meet a trap. More often now you met a woman who knew, who tumbled. It was because of articles in the pocket mags, because of Scotland Yard programmes on the Woman's Hour. Then you had to smile yourself quickly out, make for another town, change for a time the thing you pretended to sell. And one day you'd meet some dim little woman who'd do better, who'd give you a cheque and then call straight round on the police. It might be the wife of a policeman. Come to think of it, there must be plenty. It might be the wife of a local detective sergeant. And perhaps the woman with the hare-lip was that.

There was a sudden cold sweat on Routh. He wrenched his eyes up from the counter. The teller had become the baldish back of a head, and blue serge shoulders shiny in the beam of the bleak October sun. He was whispering into a sort of box or pen behind him. Routh heard the undistinguishable whispering and heard the tick of the big clock and heard still his heart that now had something slack and impotent in its throb like the sea idly pulsing deep in a cave. . . . He knew with a quick rush of lucidity that he had lost his head. There was a sharp relief in knowing, in knowing that now he could only act out the logical consequences of panic. He knew that it was probably still true that the teller was debating whether to pay out three ten when there was only fifteen bob in the account. But he knew it was no use knowing that . . . And then he saw himself.

It sometimes happened with Routh. As if a great mirror were let down from heaven he would see himself as he there and then stood. It happened to him at bad moments, mostly. Backing off a doorstep with his mouth twisted in malice, beaten by a woman that wouldn't buy. Pawing a drab who disgusted him. Cringing in a pub before some drunken bully. And now.

The other Routh was standing beside him, sweat on his brow and with one cheek twitching, his eyes fixed in terror on a blue serge jacket shiny at the seams. The other Routh's left hand had gone to his mouth and furtively he was gnawing at a ragged cuticle. The boy from the good grammar-school hiding behind the second-rate public-school tie. The Army deserter with the Air Force moustache. The outlaw, the bandit, the lone wolf sweating into his soiled vest, having to battle with his knees, his breathing, his sphincter-control in order to bring off a seventy shilling swindle.

Rage and humiliation and naked fear swept over Routh. There was nobody on this side of the counter. He turned and ran from the bank, ran for the two-stroke round the corner.

2. Pulsing sturdily between his calves the worn old engine thrust the miles behind it at a steady thirty-five. Suppose the bank rang up the police and told the story. That would be five minutes. The woman hadn't been on the telephone—he had noticed that—and it would be another ten minutes before they had one of their C.I.D. men on her doorstep. Another five

and he'd have the type of fraud taped and his report back at headquarters. . . .

But the familiar recital of dangers and chances that should have crossed and recrossed Routh's mind like a stage army, tedious and inescapable as a chain of cigarettes, was to-day reluctant to march. Riding blindly across country, he had to keep coaxing it from the wings. The raddled old thoughts that ought to have cut their routine capers effortlessly before his fatigued attention had gone shy like kids being smacked and cajoled through their first turn in panto.

Routh was frightened at this inertness of his fears. He knew that when his own arguing and reassuring voice left him other voices came at him instead—voices out of the past. Daddy's. Mummy's. Darling, darling Mummy. . . . The throttle was full open already, so if they came he couldn't get away from them that way. *Suppose the bank rang up the police. . . .*

Around Routh, this morning of an autumn that had come early held shafts of sunlight through vapour, held dark rich ploughland backed by a dozen greens turning to russet and gold. Already there was a litter and soon there would be a mush of chestnut leaves on the macadam. A leaf caught in the spokes and flipped at the mudguard like the whirr of a flushed bird. Routh rode blind, deaf. What stretched before him was not a high road but a plank, slimy and supple, across a little weir. *Come on, old chap, have a go.* Routh felt Mummy's too quickly apprehensive hand tighten on his own. She could see how difficult the plank was, whereas Daddy's eyes behind their queer pebble glasses saw only the idea of it. Again Daddy was urging him. And he was hanging back. He was hanging back because already, secretly, he had attempted the crossing and had failed. Half-way he had turned giddy and fallen. In a second he had been down in the little pool—down, down, suffocating and with a roaring in his ears, as if someone had pulled the plug on him, or let him out with the bath water. An old man pottering with a fishing rod had given him a hand to the side. Probably he had been in some real danger of drowning.

Come on, old chap. Over you go. We'll come round by the bridge and join you. His fear was irrational. He could only get bruised and wet a second time, could do no more than make himself ridiculous. But the thought of the first time—of the moment that was like a plug pulled—was too bad. He remembered the covert and dripping slipping home, round by the canal with street boys guffawing and in through the back garden. . . . He took a great breath, and did it. He crossed the plank as his parents watched; and turned, exalted. He expected them to wave, to move upstream to the bridge. But Daddy had laid his hand on Mummy's shoulder to stop her. *Now then back again, old chap.* Daddy shouted it as if Niagara were between them. It made him sound mad. Mummy had gone pale. She was wringing her hands, mute like a silent film. And a glint from Daddy's glasses, caught by the boy as he tried to brace himself, was like instantaneous intelligence flashed across a battlefield on a mirror. It wasn't the burden of his own funk he must carry over the plank again. It was Daddy's. And he knew that if he broke under it once he always would.

There had been a man in the next field, turning a machine that chopped up turnips. He had been looking over the hedge wonderingly when Mummy came and pulled him blubbering from the grass. Routh knew now that it would have been no good successfully making that second crossing. For there would always have been another one. That was Daddy's madness. But on the silent walk home, as he peeped snivelling from behind Mummy's skirts, he saw only that Daddy's cheeks held two bright red spots. And that one of the cheeks was twitching.

3. It was a memory that Routh had come to fear as the entrance to a long tunnel of fantasy, worn mercilessly smooth by the constant cramped transpassage of his straightened mind. The injustices, the deprivations, the slights, the cruelties leered at him from their niches. Routh cheated, scorned, mocked, ignored—he hungered after the endless images, but feared them more than he hungered.

Always this engulfing fantasy threatened to hurl him from his safety, from his rational mind's chosen vocation as a petty crook into some unguessable madness. To live by robbing obscure households of half a week's pay: it was the life of measure, of dangerous pride eschewed, of due and wary regard for the gods. Routh of the indomitable will, Routh the planning animal: the danger came when these were thrust aside by the long review of Routh the victim of circumstances, Routh doomed by Daddy, Routh spitefully beaten, Routh unjustly sacked, Routh demeaned and degraded in seedy travelling companies and troops of pierrots on the sands. And as Routh recreated in himself the sense of a whole society with cruel hand outstretched and eager to pull the plug, terrifying hints of hidden and dangerous volitions rose up through his weak anger. His whole body shook like a trumpery room given over to some obscure and vicious brawl.

It trembled now so that the Douglas left a wavy track behind it. The wash of fear that had swept over him in the bank and robbed him of three pounds ten was mounting, and as it mounted was meeting some strange new chemistry full of menace. He could no longer think about the number of minutes it would take for the police to begin enquiries there behind him.

Routh swerved at the side of the road and came jolting to a stop. There was now no dissociated part of him to control the machine. His eyes were misted with tears in which his anger, his resentment, his enormous self-pity welled up and out. That he should have been baulked of three pounds ten was a wrong deeper than any plummet of his mind could sound. At the same time it was a deprivation so squalidly insignificant that the spectacle of his own helpless anger at it was unbearable. The tears released by the sorry conflict had no power to assuage, afforded no relief to the weedy figure astride the old Douglas by the roadside. That figure in its pinched and mannikin stature, was too vividly before him. It seared his vanity. To banish it, to vindicate in himself the generous inches that all the world had conspired to deny: this was the clamant need of his whole being. . . . He looked ahead up the empty road and saw the figure of a woman.

She had overtaken and passed him regardless—a girl in breeches and leggings whom one would have taken at first for a boy. She was whistling. And her whistling picked out, as with a sudden strong accent, the stillness and loneliness of the place. As he looked, the woman turned to her left and disappeared down a lane. It could be distinguished as winding between high hedged banks to a hamlet nearly two miles away. Even more than this stretch of unfrequented secondary road, it seemed a place of solitude and secrecy. Routh slipped from the saddle and pushed the Douglas behind a near-by thorn.

He turned by the sign-post. It pointed to a place with a queer name—Milton Porcorum. He followed the whistling woman rapidly, exalted by the fierce purity of his intention. Beside him walked another Routh, a new and triumphant externalisation, Routh gigantic and terrible, Routh the destroyer. He was ahead. Through this gap, as she came up with it, he would spring.

In fact, he slithered. It was less effective. But the woman pulled up, startled. She was older than he had thought—about thirty, with pale blue eyes and a thin, firm mouth. She was suddenly quite still. Routh gave a queer cry. At his first grab she quivered. At his second she vanished. The woman vanished and as she did so agonising pain shot up Routh's left arm. It was such pain that his knees crumpled beneath him. He was kneeling in mud and his head was going down into mud. He struggled and the pain sickened him.

"Rub your nose in it."

The voice of the woman from behind and above him carried to him inexorably his preposterous fortune. He put his face in the mud and moved it about feebly.

"And now in a bit of gravel."

Throbbing to quickened pain Routh was kneed and twitched across the lane. Again his face went down.

"Rub it harder."

The voice, mocking and excited, ended in a low laugh. Constrained by his agony, Routh did what he was told. He felt the skin of his nose and cheek go raw. He heard a quick controlled intake of breath, sensed skilled hands passing swiftly to a fresh hold, felt the earth drop away from him and swing back with shattering force low in the belly. For a long time he lay semi-conscious and helpless, deeper beneath his nausea than ever child sunk powerless in a chill brown pool. Through his ears passed waves of uncertain sound. It might have been the distant voices of street-arabs jeering at an abject small boy.

4. When at length Routh got to his feet it was early afternoon. His left arm was numb and his face felt bruised and scarified. He fingered over it tenderly with his right hand. His mind was an unfamiliar chaos. Staggering up the lane, he fumbled for a pocket mirror, and had to empty his pocket of slivers of glass. Into one of these, held up in a trembling hand, he peered apprehensively. At a first glimpse he felt a surge of mortified vanity, of fierce resentment. This was an outrage. He had been brutally assaulted. And not as in a clean row in a pub. There had been something dirty in it. What good were the police if they couldn't keep people like that behind bars?

For a moment longer Routh stood halted in the lane, his disordered body swaying slightly as he manoeuvered the now tiny scrap of glass before his face. The damage in point of fact was inconsiderable, for his subjection had been after all chiefly symbolical. Under the mud it looked like three long scratches and one raw patch over a cheek bone. He felt a flicker of returning conceit. Wily Routh. He hadn't rubbed his face in the gravel half as hard as he'd pretended. There was some salve to injured vanity in that. But he needed water.

He realised that he was moving in the wrong direction. The two-stroke was up the lane, behind him. He was following the path that the woman must have continued on. He stopped, scared. She might come again and take him and twist him about. But something told him that the apprehension was unreal. He would not see her again. He went on, remembering that earlier he had passed no water for miles, and guessing that in a very little valley into which the lane presently dipped there would be a stream or spring.

He had come upon a high wall. Blank and curving, it followed the line of a concealed lane with which his own had now merged. It was no more than the sort of wall which, running perhaps for miles round a gentleman's park, speaks in the simplest picture-language of a vanished social order. The great house within would long since have been sold for a fraction of what it would now cost to build this massive outwork. And it would shelter a private sanatorium, an establishment for training bank clerks, an approved school. In all this there was no reason why Routh should feel himself in the presence of something indefinably sinister. Only the wall was very blank and surprisingly high.

And then Routh saw the man.

The appearance of this human figure, sudden and unaccountable, suggested a *coup de théâtre* for which the wall's sinister air had been a build-up deliberately achieved. At one moment the wall stretched unbroken before Routh, every foot of its well-pointed surface void in the bleak and shadowless sunlight. And at the next moment the man was there, an immobile and waiting figure some seventy yards away, with the unbroken stone behind him like a backcloth.

Routh's impulse was to turn and retrace his steps—to get back, muddy as he was, to the two-stroke, and chance finding water for a clean-up later on. His legs however carried him unsteadily and inexorably forward. The man made a very slight movement and a wisp of smoke floated upwards. He was smoking a cigarette as he waited. His immobility was hypnotising. Against the clamour of his every nerve, Routh found himself quickening his pace.

The man was standing in front of an iron-sheathed, stone-coloured door set flush in the wall. His eyes took one sweeping glance up and down the lane and then settled themselves upon Routh. Tall and with square shoulders carried high as if in a frozen shrug, he was dressed in what Routh knew to be a high-class tailor's job in homespun tweed. You could tell he owned whatever lay beyond the wall. But you could tell, too, that he was a townsman. His features were irregular and ugly, but they had the controlled mobility that tells of a mind schooled to work swiftly through complex issues. He belongs, Routh thought, at the top of one of the big-money professions—a leading surgeon, perhaps, or a successful K.C. Boss class. And a gentleman.

Well, that's what *you* are—see? Routh—muddy, dusty, torn, scratched, and with the toes hurting in his thin, pointed shoes—Routh braced himself to fill out the role. A gentleman taking an afternoon stroll in unfamiliar country. That was the formula. And better pass the time of day. *Good afternoon.*

The man made no reply. In his silence the uncertain flame of confidence that had leapt up in Routh flickered and went out. The man was looking at him steadily. He was putting two and two together about the shabby figure now sliding past with averted eyes. But at least, Routh told himself, you *are* past. He isn't really interested. Just keep on steadily. Only you'd better get back to the two-stroke another way.

"Come here."

The words, spoken quietly behind him, had, in his already shaken state, the effect of a needle thrust into his spine. He knew that his only safety was to run, and chance making a race for it. But for the second time that day his legs were powerless, and nothing would race but his own heart. Oddly the world pivoted on him as he stood, and he found himself confronting the man who waited before the stone-coloured door.

The man beckoned, without again speaking. He beckoned, strangely, with a downward pointing figure—as one in a circus ring might beckon at a cowed and uniformly obedient brute creation.

Resentment rendered Routh articulate. "Look here," he said, "—what do you think I am?"

But his legs were carrying him back to the waiting man. The feeble truculence he had heard in his own voice gave him no encouragement to rebel.

"I think you are the ruffian who has attacked a girl in my employment." The man was well over six feet, and he contrived to look down at Routh as at a cur. "I suppose you know the sentence you'd get for a criminal of that sort?"

"She did it. She assaulted me." Routh panted as he spoke. The absurdity and indignity of his words were only emphasised by the element of truth in them.

"Where do you come from? What are you?"

Routh took a quick, desperate glance about him. Somehow he had the impression that this scene was being watched, that the tip of his senses, whether of sight or hearing, had detected some presence that might succour him. But nothing he could now see gave any support to this fancy. So he must face it out. At least these were a sort of questions that he could always answer after a fashion, and he judged it well to do so now. "I'm a clerk, and out of work. I've come down from the north."

"Do you think you're likely to get work in the heart of the country?"

"I'm going through to Reading."

"Motor-bicycle?"

Routh blinked. Very faintly, as if some hatch had been opened deep down in his mind, cunning stirred beneath his rage and terror. There was something queer in the way that, underneath, the brute was interested in him. He resolved in a flash that he must at all costs conceal the existence of the Douglas. He plunged at it boldly. "I'm walking. I've hardly any money left."

"And no possessions?"

"A chap took my suitcase on a lorry. I'll pick it up at the station."

"Let me see your identity card."

"It's in the suitcase. And you haven't any right—"

For the first time the tall man faintly smiled. "A deserter on the run—eh? Your people help you at all?"

He was softening. *Hard luck. Let the poor devil off. Give him a hand. A square meal and ten bob.* It was a stage in the well-to-do man's triumphant detection of petty crime that was familiar to Routh. Automatically he played up to it. "I haven't any people. I'm an only child. My father's in a mental hospital and won't ever get better. My mother's gone to New Zealand with another man. I haven't heard from her for five years."

Routh became aware that the tall man, whose hand should now be going to his pocket, was once more swiftly glancing up and down the lane, as if he too had a momentary sensation of being watched. Then the man's eyes met his. Fear leapt anew in Routh. There *was* something queer about him. That he was softening was dead off the scent. On the contrary, there was some hard design in him. And it was only for a second that Routh thought he understood it. No, the man was looking at him simply as a carpenter might look at a plank which he would presently give himself the satisfaction of sawing into sections in the pursuance of some clearly apprehended design.

But even as Routh grasped this, the man's manner changed. Expression had come into his face. It was an expression of weighed or judicial contempt—a sort of judgment that had been impassively deferred until Routh in all his seediness, weediness and cowardice had been bared before him. He took a step forward and made a movement that Routh momentarily interpreted as the prelude to an ironical handshake. Instead, he slapped Routh's face, paused, slapped it again back-handed. "I don't know about your father being a lunatic," he said, "but I certainly believe that your mother—"

Routh sprang at him, screaming—groped for him through a red haze in which the external world had suddenly bathed itself. When he came to he was on the other side of the wall.

5. "I apologise."

At first the words seemed to come to Routh from very far away. There was a burning sensation in his throat that ran deep down into his body. The words repeated themselves and the tall man swam into focus. He was standing over Routh with a brandy flask in his hand, and looking down at him with an appearance of whimsical benevolence. He screwed the top on the flask and thrust it away in a hip-pocket. "A bit of a test," he said. "Don't take it hard, my good fellow. Something of a test—no more."

Routh, helpless on the grass, wished that he had a revolver or a knife. But hatred and the brandy now coursing in him sharpened his faculties and he realised that he *had* a weapon. Trapped on the wrong side of that formidable wall—it was now a shadowed concavity towering above him and stretching around him—he felt obscurely and paradoxically in control—in control of a situation that as yet he didn't remotely understand. He had only to lie low, and never let his cunning sleep, and he would come out of this on top. He sat up. "You can't do this to me," he said—and his voice was shaky by necessity and plaintive by design. "I don't care who you are. You can be gaoled for this."

"Then it looks as if we are about quits, my friend." The tall man laughed shortly and produced a cigarette-case. "Smoke?"

Routh, although himself shaking like a leaf, observed with exultation a tremor in the tall man's hand. His irrational conviction grew that in the unknown game that had been violently forced upon him he would himself be winner and take all. He had concealed the existence of the two-stroke, and to this for some reason he attached a vast importance. Then—mysteriously—the enclosing wall exhilarated him. He had got inside what hitherto he had always been kept outside of—the world where both honest men and knaves had large views and big chances. Yes, that was it. For good or ill he had left the world of seventy-bob swindles behind him. *No need whatever for a deposit to secure delivery.* He would never say that again. . . . Routh laughed aloud.

The tall man was startled. "What's the matter with you?" he asked sharply. "Want more brandy?"

Routh shook his head. He mustn't do anything unpredictable like that again. But his confidence took another leap. If only ever so faintly, his captor was unsure of himself. He was uncertain, standing there like an arrogant lout over a whipped cur, that he hadn't been precipitate, that he hadn't acted out of turn, in grabbing Routh as he had done. This uncertainty was tremendously important—but tremendously important too was the necessity that it shouldn't be let grow. Routh must be no more than the worthless and pliable lump of clay that the brute designed him for. The one thing that Routh must desperately conceal was any potentiality in himself for making a move or springing a surprise.

The tall man was holding out a match. Routh, swaying, managed to get his cigarette drawing. "What do you mean—a test?" he demanded.

"I think I can put you on rather a good thing." The tall man now smiled easily. And he took without a trace of hesitation the transition from country gentleman and outraged moralist to a world of evidently shady proposals and dubious confederacies. "Only it needs guts. I don't mean that it's particularly risky—nothing of the sort—but it does need a *man*. I liked the way you came at me. It was damned plucky." He paused. "There's big money in what I'm thinking of."

Routh felt his always facile resentment stir in him. He had evidently been graded as of very low intelligence indeed. And yet it *had* been a test. But of what? Whatever had flung him at this swine out in the lane, it hadn't been anything deserving a certificate for pluck. "Big money?" he said—and managed to get quickened interest into his voice. He was certain that if there was indeed a gold mine in his present situation he himself would have to do all the digging. He remembered that at the moment his note was weak querulousness. "And look here," he added, "who are you anyway?"

"You can call me Squire. And now, come along. We'll get up to the house."

Routh got painfully to his feet. He began moving by the tall man's side. "How do you mean?" he asked. "Mr. Squire? Or just Squire—of all this?" And Routh waved his hand at the park through which they were walking.

The tall man looked down at him slantwise. "Which ever you please," he said.

Routh bit his lip. The brute couldn't mask his contempt for a couple of minutes on end. It came into his head that he was going to be in some way enslaved, cast into thrall. Or that he was going to be killed. Very conceivably he was going to be killed in order to supply a body for, say, some insurance swindle. Routh's eyes widened on these conceptions as he walked, and his breath came faster than need be, considering the easy pace which his companion set. But still his mysterious and unaccustomed confidence failed to desert him. It was about him like a borrowed garment, unexpectedly bestowed and of surprisingly good fit.

He puzzled over the kind of racket that could support such wealth as he had stumbled upon. The park was large and there were deer in it. To encounter such creatures outside the Zoo was, in Routh's mind, to be on the fringe of a magnificence positively ducal, and he stared in wonder at the creatures as he walked. He noted that Squire too watched the deer, but with a glance in which there was something faintly enigmatical—something of purely practical reference. No doubt—Routh thought—he eats them. No doubt he's deciding which to cut the throat of and get his teeth into next. . . . And then it came to Routh that the manner in which Squire looked at the deer was precisely the manner in which he looked at *him*. For a moment his confidence dangerously flickered.

They had come to a halt before a tall wire fence. It was the sort of thing that runs round a tennis court to keep the balls in. Only this fence ran off indefinitely in either direction with just the same air of formidable enclosure as the high wall bordering the park. Squire had produced a bunch of keys on the end of a flexible silver chain and was proceeding to unlock a gate. Routh looked at the keys covertly. One of them had already been used on the stone-coloured door behind them. It looked as if the man who would get off Squire's property in a hurry must have that bunch of keys at his command.

"Short cut," said Squire briefly. They went on, and he pointed to a grassy slope on their left hand. "See anything moving?" he asked.

Routh looked. The slope had the appearance of a deserted rabbit warren. "No," he said, "—nothing at all."

Squire nodded. "No more are you likely to. Jerboa."

"What d'you mean—jerboa?" Routh remembered again his scared, sulky note.

"The most timid mammal yet known on this earth. We'll go through here."

Once again there was a high wire fence. But this one appeared to define a paddock of moderate size, across which Squire struck out diagonally. The ground here was uneven and there were considerable outcrops of rock. As they turned round one of these Routh stopped dead and gave a faint cry. There was a lion in the path.

There was a lion standing straight in front of them. For a second it was quite still except for a tail that waved slowly in the air. Then it turned round and made as if to slip away.

"Deilos—come here." It was Squire who spoke. He spoke much as he had spoken to Routh in the lane. The result too was very similar. The lion turned again and reluctantly approached. As the beast came nearer the two men his belly came closer to the ground until he was creeping forward like a scared terrier. Presently he was lying quite still, his great jowl tucked between his paws, and a single eye looking slantwise upwards as if he expected a whip.

"The lion, you see, is prepared to lie down with the lamb." Squire leant forward and tweaked the animal by the ear. "So what about it?"

Routh stared at him. "What d'you mean—what about it?"

"What I mean is quite simple. Get down."

"Get down?"

"Certainly. But perhaps you don't believe that you are the lamb? I assure you that you are. The newest and most innocent of my lambs." Squire smiled—an odd, sweet smile that made Routh shiver. *"Lie down."*

Routh looked from Deilos to Squire—from the unnatural animal to the unnatural man—and was by no means sure which was the more alarming. Was this mad freak before the tamed lion merely a whim or cruel joke by the way? Was it, in fact, a sudden and almost meaningless fancy prompted by Squire's knowledge of his victim's earlier humiliation that day? Or was this sort of thing going to go on, and was the lion simply the first exhibit in a leisured sadistic joke?

Long before he had ceased confusedly asking himself these questions Routh found that he had in fact cast himself on the ground beside Deilos. The brute on this near acquaintance was rather smelly, but took not the slightest notice of him. Squire was looking down at them with his horrible smile. "You must understand," he said, "that I am a magician. If I say 'Abracadabra' Deilos will take no notice of you. But if I say 'Abracadabra' backwards, he will at once change his nature and eat you. Wouldn't you like to be able to change the nature of a living creature at a word?"

Routh made no reply. He felt frightened and ridiculous, but still his cunning didn't cease to work. It worked the more desperately, the more he hated his tormentor. And by now he hated him very much.

Squire's smile vanished. He took a quick, almost furtive glance around him. He stepped forward and kicked Deilos hard on the rump—whereupon Deilos got to his feet with a yelp and padded away. Routh, without waiting to be kicked in his turn, scrambled to his feet. Squire brought out a handkerchief and dabbed his forehead. "We must get on," he said abruptly—and strode forward. They passed out of the lion's paddock and moved downhill, through a stretch of sombre woodland. Presently, beyond a lighter screen of larches, the variously pitched roofs of a large and rambling house became visible.

Routh considered the simple proposition that his companion was insane. It was certainly the easiest way of explaining him. And Squire, if mad, must now be considered as harmlessly mad. For they were at length almost within a stone's throw of a house that must surely be too populous to admit even of a wealthy owner's engaging in vagaries of a markedly violent or criminal kind. On the other hand Squire had already behaved so strangely and unwarrantably to Routh that there was no likelihood of any further trouble being made about the affair with his employee in the lane. Whoever was more or less in charge of Squire would have to hush all that up. Otherwise there would be a row. For some seconds Routh gave himself up to the elaboration of a pleasantly novel fantasy. In would be high-class Sunday paper stuff. Out of the Lion's Mouth. The Frank Story of My Two Ordeals. Exclusive. By Alfred Routh.

The glowing picture faded. It wouldn't really do. For once the police had a grip of him they would uncover a dozen of the three-ten swindles while having him on remand. Still, the fact remained that if Squire were no more than a bit of a lunatic at large he, Routh, was invulnerable. There was so much of relief in this reading of his situation that Routh for some moments inclined to it violently. But if it ministered to the ease of his cowardice it correspondingly thwarted his cunning. There could be very little in it. A bit of bluster before a relative or a doctor, and he might get away with a five or ten pound note. There were far greater possibilities in the idea that Squire was involved in crime or racket in a big way, and that his keeping a pet like Deilos and using him to scare recruits was no more than a streak of casual nastiness such as a master criminal might very properly allow himself.

Or perhaps the suggestion of madness was a sort of blind. For Routh an interpretation of human conduct was always the more plausible if it embodied a large element of deception and fraud. With these ideas he was at home, whereas the notion of irresponsible madness was alarming and disagreeable to him. This being so, he had not gone another fifty yards before entrenching himself firmly in his first conviction. There was something very deep in the situation with which he had involuntarily become involved. And out of its depth Routh with all his wits about him might conceivably fish what, for him, would be fabulous wealth. He was proceeding to entertain himself with some details of this beatific vision when he and his conductor rounded the larch spinney and came full upon the house.

6. He had often enough seen such places from the road, but never before had he come so close up to one as this. Squire's house—if it was indeed his—was very large, and Routh knew that it had grown up over centuries. The chief architectural feature of the side at which he was directly looking was an affair of high Corinthian pillars running up past three storeys of windows to a blank entablature and pediment. All this, he saw, was not of stone but of some stuff that needs to be painted. It was, in fact, painted dead white, giving an impression that Routh supposed to be American. But to the left of this was warm red brick enclosing mullioned windows and rising to a succession of gable-ends behind which stood tall Tudor chimneys. Beyond this again, and running off at an angle, was a wing that had at some date been heavily Gothicised, and that now lurked behind meaningless buttresses and groaned beneath improbable battlements. These vagaries account for about half the building, the rest of which was a solid Georgian.

Routh's awareness of all this was intuitive rather than technical. The effect, as of several houses backing awkwardly into each other, was for a moment as disturbing to him as some horror glimpsed in a doctor's medical journal in a railway-carriage, a monstrous birth of twins or triplets fantastically conjoined. But he told himself that once more he was unprofitably fancying things. All the more tangible suggestions that the condition of the place evoked were of prosperity, serenity and cheerfulness.

Well-kept lawns and gravel walks, tall dark hedges trimmed to severe perpendiculars, a few broad beds of massed chrysanthemums: these seemed to speak of a taste in gardens that was mature and good. There was a wide shallow terrace now steeped in sunshine and serving as promenade for half a dozen miniature poodles of expensive appearance and extravagant clip. Several french windows were thrown open to the air, and gave upon expanses of turf or paving so lavishly equipped with garden furniture of the elaborated modern sort, that the effect was of handsomely equipped drawingrooms tumbling out of doors to breathe. Nor was the placid scene without its congruous humanity. A five-year-old boy, sturdy and flaxen-haired, was playing with the poodles. And on a lawn directly below Routh and Squire a company of ladies and gentlemen were enjoying a game of croquet.

A variety of impulses jostled in Routh. Here were half a dozen demonstrably sane persons, engaged in one of the mildest of civilized pleasures. Would it not be best to seize the chance of rushing forward, throwing himself upon their mercy, and claiming their protection from the abominable Squire? For whatever was the truth about Squire he was certainly dangerous, and the shadowy possibilities of financial exploitation which he represented lurked amid hazards quite out of Routh's common line.

But even as Routh debated with himself this course of action, he became aware of a further bewilderment in his situation. The croquet players puzzled and alarmed him quite as much as Squire did. The sharp *clop . . . clop . . . clop* of wood upon wood as a military-looking man with a grey moustache achieved a brisk break was obscurely frightening. If Squire was patently sinister and his house indefinably so, then this spectacle was like a calculated effect designed to enhance the fact. The croquet-players were disturbingly enigmatical. Routh didn't trust them. After all, in an environment which made the lion mild was it not very conceivable that a croquet-player upon being appealed to for protection might simply swing his mallet and dash one's brains out?

But on all this there was only a moment for reflection. Squire swung round a wing of the house and the croquet-players disappeared.

7. Routh now lost his bearings. Continuing to skirt the main building, Squire led the way into a walled garden and out again, using a key each time. Beyond this lay a kitchen garden, empty except for a bent old man culling cauliflowers, and they passed on to a sort of narrow alley of which one side was formed by a high beech hedge and the other by a long, low building of modern appearance and indeterminate length.

Presenting to the world nothing but a succession of frosted-glass windows, this building ran slightly downhill, so that the level dropped as by broad, shallow steps. And presently Routh caught a glimpse of its other end. It had been run out from the house as far as it could go—to the margin, in fact, of a small lake. In the middle of the lake was an island, seemingly entirely occupied by a large, blank and improbable temple. Although such fantasies were unfamiliar to Routh, he guessed at once that there was nothing out of the way in it. Much odder was the fact that this ancient absurdity was now directly linked to the new raw wing he had been skirting by a wooden bridge—a bridge lightly constructed but entirely enclosed, so that it was, in fact, a species of tunnel, relieved only by a few small windows.

But all this Routh only glimpsed. For Squire had stopped before a door near the end of the building, unlocked and opened it, and pushed Routh unceremoniously inside. He locked the door from within, while Routh took stock of a long, bleak corridor.

"Well, here we are."

In Squire's voice Routh again caught a momentary note of uncertainty. He derived what comfort he could from it in a situation that he increasingly disliked. His isolation with the alarming Squire appeared to be complete. There was not a sign of life down the length of this narrow corridor. There was not a sound from the succession of rooms they were now passing. A modern monastery must be like this—the kind in which you take vows to keep your mouth shut. The unlikely comparison, floating through Routh's mind, increased his uneasiness, for there is a whole popular mythology of the hidden horrors of the cloister. Forty Months in a Flagellant Order. By the Author of A Short History of Torture (Illustrated). Momentarily overborne by these new imaginings, Routh looked about him in the expectation of seeing walls hung with scourges and a floor dripping blood. But the walls were pervasively blank, and on the floor of the long corridor was nothing more remarkable than a thick, green rubber that deadened every sound.

"And you can wait here."

Squire was unlocking and opening a door. Routh looked at him warily. "What d'you mean—wait here?" he demanded.

"There'll be an interview."

The words were perfunctory, and Routh sensed that they were quite meaningless. He made to back away. Squire grabbed him, swung him effortlessly off his feet, and pitched him through the doorway.

"An interview with my colleagues, my dear fellow, quite soon. Did I say we were magicians? Alchemists would be a better description. You will no doubt make yourself as comfortable as you can."

Routh picked himself up in time to see the door closing and to hear a key turn in its lock. It was his first confused impression that he was in a small kitchen, but in a moment he realised that it was a laboratory. He recognised it—as even the most ignorant can now recognise virtually any material creation of man—from the cinema. There was a bench, a sink, an affair with various gas burners and a small flue above. There were rows of bottles behind sliding glass doors. The only moveable furniture was a high wooden stool. The room was lit through a large, barred skylight.

Routh surveyed the unfamiliar place. *Alchemy*. That was what Squire had said—that he and whatever confederates he had were alchemists. It meant chemists, scientists. A sense of vast illumination came to Routh. Now he understood.

He had puzzled and puzzled over the racket that could sustain a place like this. There had been a time—he believed—at which a really big operator on the black market could have lived like this if he had wanted to. But nowadays that line of country was said to be not nearly so good. No! Routh knew what he had found. He had found the people who forge the fivers.

8. Like Galileo in the dungeons of the Inquisition, resistlessly imaging the majestic pageant of the planets circling round their sun, Routh crouched in his odd prison and stared out, round-eyed, at the brave new world of his discovery. Not Cortez on his peak could have been more exultant. For in that criminal world upon the inglorious fringes of which Routh habitually moved no current conviction is more compelling than this: that every authentic five-pound note has its identical twin, the creation of forgers so scientifically skilful that all the answering science of the Royal Mint, the Bank of England, and other institutions and persons unspeakably august, is powerless to crush the racket. As far as five-pound notes go, there is twice as much paper money in England as there ought to be.

Routh leapt down from his stool. He, who had only that

morning failed in the prosecution of a familiar seventy-shilling swindle, now brushed greatness. Not far away was a man who—although he had indeed knocked Routh senseless, obliged him to grovel in the dust beside a tame lion, and incarcerated him in an unattractive laboratory—was in all probability at the very head of Routh's profession. His instinct had been vindicated. Let him now but behave with sufficient ruthlessness and guile, and he might leave his baser self behind him for ever. All his frustrations, all his baffled hopes and cheated appetites were stirring. Those impulses which had led him into his inglorious exploit in the lane roused themselves again and roused themselves far more effectively, since they were now bent upon a design far more potent in its appeal.

Routh prowled his prison in a fury, convinced that just beyond its walls lay spread the power and the glory—an absolute command of wealth, and hence of all the kingdoms of the earth. Had he encountered Deilos again at this moment, the creature would certainly have taken him for a dangerous beast of prey.

He placed the stool on the bench, and from the shaky perch thus constituted he examined the skylight. Some of the panes opened outwards and upwards for ventilation. But the whole thing was securely barred and meshed. He went round the walls and cupboards, tapping and scratching; nothing appeared to give the slightest hope of escape. The innumerable bottles on the shelves fascinated and alarmed him. His ideas on chemistry were vague. He believed that if he mixed enough of these stuffs together on the floor there would certainly be an explosion that would blow the roof off. But what would be the good of that if he were himself maimed, blinded, perhaps killed? There seemed no resource but the poor one of making a row. That might frighten them so that they would turn him out. And then perhaps he could put some screw on them from safety.

Routh approached the single door of the laboratory, having now in his head no more than this inglorious notion of thumping on it. But as his eyes fell on the keyhole he stopped and stared. The thing was almost incredible. But there could be little doubt that behind that keyhole lay no more than a very common lock indeed.

From his earliest years Routh had been an amateur of keyholes. They constituted perhaps his nearest approach to a disinterested love of knowledge. And it so happened that this interest had broadened itself with the years. A keyhole had become for Routh not merely something to peer through or listen at; it had become something to fiddle with. And this substantial process of sublimation seemed likely to stand him in good stead now. Frequently he had beguiled the tedium of lonely nights in cheap lodgings by teaching himself, on the strength of such professional hints as he had picked up from inebriated cracksmen, to pick the simple locks that such accommodation commonly provided. And with such a lock, strangely enough, he was confronted now. He could confidently look forward to being on the farther side of it within ten minutes.

Routh fished from his pocket an innocent-seeming twist of wire. As he made his first exploratory thrust at the keyhole he felt the blood course more warmly in his veins. Reason would have told him that only the most slender of advantages was opening before him, and that in this inexplicable establishment he was likely to remain as helpless a puppet on one side of a door as another. But with the sense of power that had again leapt up in him reason had very little to do. The Tables Turned. Routh Hits Back. The theory which he had formed as to the nature of Squire's racket had stirred in him feelings that were avidly acquisitive and predatory. The treatment to which he had been subjected had filled him with malignity. Now his head was swimming slightly with the sensation of fresh scope given to these emotions. But his hand remained so steady that only a very few minutes passed before he was standing, tense and listening, in the long empty corridor.

Close on the right, three steps led to a higher level. Much farther away on the left, several steps made an answering descent.

He remembered the appearance of this long annex from the outside—how it dipped down as by several shallow flights to the level of the little lake. So the house lay on his right, while on his left the building ended in the odd covered bridge leading to the ornamental building on the island. Routh took a gulp of air, swung left, and walked rapidly and noiselessly forward.

Most of the doors leading off the corridor were open. But at this in itself he felt no alarm, since he was intuitively certain that at this hour the whole place was empty. Pausing to reconnoitre, he discovered that this long wing was given over to a series of laboratories, for the most part intercommunicating, and the majority being considerably larger than that in which he had been imprisoned. It occurred to him that there was more opportunity in these than in the corridor to lurk or dodge if anyone did, in fact, appear. He therefore made his way forward as much as possible by this route.

What he saw he saw only vaguely, since he was without a basis of technical knowledge to sharpen his observation. In one room the benches were crowded with complex units of glass utensils and rubber tubing and little bright sheets of metal connected by innumerable wires; these, articulated into a skeleton by sundry steel rods and clamps and brackets, had to his view the appearance of grotesque automata designed in mockery of living things. Another room looked like his idea of a telephone exchange. A third was given over to what seemed a huge pin-table—the kind on which valves light up and the score is progressively shouted at you as the meandering balls make and break one electrical circuit after another.

Routh had only such popular analogies upon which to draw. It was the more to the credit of his underlying astuteness, therefore, that a purely intellectual conclusion presently forced itself upon him. At a first blush these large evidences of scientific effort appeared abundantly to confirm him in the persuasion to which he had recently come—namely, that here were the people by whom the five-pound notes are made. But now a sense not only of the scale but of the variousness and elaboration of what lay around him suggested that even this impressive conclusion was inadequate. Or, if Squire indeed made the five-pound notes, he had some deeper and more grandiosely scientific plot or project in hand as well.

Routh's mind had just halted baffled before this conception when he became aware of voices somewhere ahead of him.

9. "I tell you he's no more than a little rat of a deserter living on his wits."

Routh stopped dead. He recognised the tones of the detestable Squire.

"Very probably. But it's dangerous and unnecessary, all the same. This is something far too big to have you acting on these sudden impulses. What do you suppose the Director will say to such a story?"

"He ought to be damned grateful—and so should you. You know that I've brought in capital subjects before this."

The voices were coming from behind the closed door of what Routh guessed must be one of the last rooms in the building. They were heard the more clearly because this door too had a keyhole. Routh's ear was pressed to it.

"And—what's more—you seem to be in an uncommonly foul temper."

It was again Squire's voice. And Squire's voice had gone sulky. In a flash it came to Routh that Squire was by no means the boss of this mysterious place. He was talking now to somebody with whom he was on no more than equal terms—if even that. And they both had above them somebody called the Director. The word conjured up a vague image of striped trousers, a gold watch-chain, a silk hat.

"I'm certainly not feeling any too sweet. And in a moment I'll tell you why." It was now the other man who was speaking—and his voice, Routh realised, was far more coldly formidable than Squire's could ever be. "But first let me tell you this. We just can't afford the risk of people disappearing on our doorstep."

"But you'd find him, I tell you, so devilish suitable. A craven little brute capable of moments of real fury. You've often said—"

"Never mind what I've often said. If I've said anything at all to you, the more fool I've been." There was sharp anger in the second man's accent. "And now go and turf the fellow out. He hasn't seen anything, I suppose?"

"Nothing at all. Or only poor old Deilos. I couldn't resist having a bit of fun—"

"I lose all patience with you, Squire. Something extremely serious has happened. And now you come in with this distracting nonsense. What have you done with the fellow?"

"Locked him up in number eight. Blue with funk. You can have him when you want him."

"I don't want him. But no more do I want him going out and gossiping about what goes on here. Will nothing make you realise what we're on the verge of? Power such as has never been wielded on this earth before. All the gold of the Incas wouldn't buy a tithe of it. And all that you—"

Routh started so violently that he hit his head on the door-knob and lost the conclusion of the unseen speaker's sentence. The astounding conclusion towards which his mind had already been unconsciously moving had flashed upon him in an instant. Alchemists don't make five-pound notes. Alchemists make gold.

All the gold of the Incas . . . Routh had read about them—a vanished folk in America whose very fish-kettles and chamber-pots had been wrought out of solid gold. And the alchemists had wanted that sort of wealth. They had messed about, pretty well blindly, with chemicals and crucibles, hoping to make something they called the philosopher's stone—a substance that would turn to pure gold a million times its own weight of base metal. And now these people, substituting science for magic, were on the verge of doing just that . . .

Routh again pressed his ear to the keyhole. The missing of a single sentence, he felt, might be fatal to his own power to exploit the terrific possibilities now opening before him.

"Look here, Squire—you may as well know just how the matter stands. The stuff has gone inert again. I'm completely held up."

A low whistle conveyed the invisible Squire's first reaction to this announcement. "That's bad," he said—and Routh thought that he heard malice in his former captor's voice. "The Director won't like it at all."

"It's not in the least out of the way, and the Director understands perfectly. I have command of almost nothing, you know, in a pure form. The position is just as it is with those growth-inhibiting stuffs they play about with. You, Squire, wouldn't make head or tail of it in technical terms. But put it like this. Put it that you have a host of human beings, some tiny percentage of which constitutes a superbly efficient military force that you are concerned to cherish. All the rest are tiresome and irrelevant camp-followers who can never be of the slightest use to you. *And you don't yourself know which are which.*"

A snort from Squire interrupted this exposition. "It sounds damned nonsense to me."

"It *is* damned nonsense, Squire. Unfortunately it is Nature's damned nonsense, not mine. Well, now—every now and then one of the camp-followers does something quite idiotic—stands on his head, say, or turns a somersault. And at that the morale of your unknown army mysteriously collapses and nearly all your work has to be done all over again. My particular sort of chemistry has some very grand names, you know. But that is what you might call the low-down on it. And the present upshot of it is that to-morrow I go back to Formula Ten."

There was a moment's silence during which it occurred to Routh to substitute an eye for an ear. What immediately became visible through the keyhole was not difficult to interpret. Near at hand a blurred but familiar form represented one of the oddly high and square shoulders of the man Squire. In the background was a green baize door in a wall lined with books. And in the middle-distance was part of the polished surface of a table or desk. On this there was nothing to be seen except a pair of hands issuing from the sleeves of a white coat—fine hands, powerful and with long square fingers exquisitely cared for.

"So you see that I have singularly little use for your tramp, my dear Squire. Formula Ten, I assure you, will occupy me very sufficiently for the next few weeks. . . . By the way, here it is."

For a moment one of the hands on the desk flicked out of Routh's field of vision. Then it was back again, immobile as before. But now between the two hands there lay what looked like a single folded sheet of quarto paper. The effect of this appearance was startling. Squire's shoulder disappeared. Squire's voice rose in something like a surprised and horrified yelp. The owner of the hands answered this with a low laugh. "Yes," he said. "Here it is."

"But you've no business to have it out like that. It's outrageous! If the Director . . ."

"The Director has some very odd ways, I admit. This, I really believe, is the only existing copy of Formula Ten. It is unique—and the basis of the whole effort. How lucky we are to have it! It was got out of Hendrik, I have been told, just before he succumbed to the persuasions that were unfortunately found necessary in his case. Am I right?"

"I know nothing about it." Squire's voice was suddenly husky.

"Don't you? Then how much you must regret not having been present, my dear Squire, on an occasion so much in your line. But—as I say—we were lucky to get what we did. One knows people here and there about the world who would give millions for this, does one not? Or even—come to think of it—a kingdom? No wonder the Director will have it out only under circumstances of the most portentous security. I enter into your horror and dismay, my dear chap. But when I need Formula Ten I fetch it out and mention the fact afterwards."

"I don't like it."

"That reminds me. No more do I like your friend the tramp. I don't like his being brought here, and I don't know that I like his going away from here either. I think he had better be killed at once and the body incinerated. See to it, Squire, will you?"

It is difficult to hear something of this sort said about oneself and not suppose, for some moments at least, that one is simply listening to a rather tasteless joke. Had the full force of the words broken upon Routh at once he would undoubtedly have taken to his heels and run. As it was, he remained, misdoubting and stupefied, during the few seconds in which flight might have availed him. His eye was actually still at the keyhole when that orifice was obscured by what was patently the bulk of Squire advancing to open the door. And Squire, it seemed, was now to be simply his, Routh's executioner!

That men so wicked as these could exist was at once incredible and most horribly plausible. And Routh realised that to be found crouching here would be fatal. It was not merely that the secrets he would be presumed to have overheard must absolutely seal his fate. It was also that in such a situation a passive role is fatal; that to turn the tables upon fortune at such a juncture only action will remotely serve. . . . Routh opened the door before him and marched into the room.

Squire fell back with an exclamation. Squire's companion, seated still at his desk, quite feebly echoed it. Routh had undeniably caught his adversaries off balance. The sense of this enabled him to nod briskly at the seated man and to wave Squire casually back. "Good afternoon," he said.

The words came out with nothing of the anxious calculation that had marked his attempt at a similar greeting in the bank that morning. Had he not always known he would carry the big moment when it came? Routh glanced round the room with the easy command of an important person; with the sort of glance that makes enormous leather arm-chairs propel themselves forward, corks pop, syphons spurt, cigar-boxes fly open. "Director not here?" he asked briskly. "It's really with him that I'd better have a word."

Squire and his companion glanced at each other. At length the seated man spoke. "I don't know you from Adam," he said. "And apparently you don't know me. *I* am the Director."

Routh again gave an assured glance round him. The room went some way to substantiate this false claim. The furniture was handsome, and all round the walls were the sort of heavily tooled books you see in expensive shop-windows in the West End. Over the fireplace was a high-class dirty picture: a lot of naked women lolloping around a pool. Underneath this a bright fire burned in an open grate. Routh walked across to it and warmed his hands. "Nice place you have here," he said. "Plenty of books. Nice picture."

"I fear I have not the pleasure of your acquaintance." Squire's companion was a small man with a high domed forehead and almost no hair. His fine hands still lay passively before him. The rest of him was insignificant and even meagre, as if his body had no other function than that of providing a line of communication between that big brain and those long and powerful fingers. He had bleak grey eyes which he now turned from Routh to Squire. "Presumably this is the gentleman whom you supposed that you had—um—accommodated in number eight?"

"Of course it is." Squire, who had still by no means recovered his self-possession, stared at his late prisoner with mingled bewilderment and malice. "But I can't think how he managed—"

"We learn that sort of thing very early in my crowd." Routh put both hands in his trouser-pockets and chinked the few coins in the one without a hole in it. "But you had no idea of that, had you, Squire?"

"Your crowd?" The white-coated man spoke sharply, and as he did so swung round upon Squire. "Did I understand you to say that your encounter with this fellow was a perfectly casual one?"

Before Squire could reply, Routh laughed harshly. "So your poor friend believed," he said. "Mind you, there's an excuse for him. The idea of attacking the girl and then hanging round until somebody appeared—well, it wasn't too bad, was it? Squire was convinced he had me where he wanted me. And so in I came. Not my own notion, I must confess. Quite a junior colleague, as it happens."

On the mantelpiece behind Routh's head, and just below the dirty picture, a clock was ticking softly. At any moment, he realised, it might begin to affect him as had the clock in the bank that morning; it might begin to pound like a hammer inside his head. And if his nerve went he was done for. For certainly the ice on which he was now skating was paper-thin. That he had fooled Squire from the start was a notion that might now take in Squire himself. But could it conceivably take in this other fellow? Only—Routh saw—if it *attracted* the other fellow. If this egg-headed scientist disliked Squire enough to be willing to see him in a mug's role, then any cock-and-bull story having that effect might convince him for a while. The thing to do, then, was to make Squire look a perfect fool.

"Poor old Squire! Has he told you about my father in the asylum and my mother gone off to New Zealand? It would have made a cat laugh, the way it all took him in. Thought he was getting a waif and stray to keep under his thumb at some of your dirtiest work here. And all the time he was getting *us*."

The clock was still behaving normally behind him. Squire was flushed and his shoulders had gone even more unnaturally high and square. The other fellow rose from his desk and walked away from it. "Haven't you," he asked, "taken on rather a dangerous mission? The colleagues you speak of must be uncommonly obliged to you. It's a pity"—and with sudden dangerous sweetness the egg-headed man smiled—"that they won't be in a position even to send a wreath."

Once more Routh contrived a convincing laugh. "If you ask me," he said, "it's your friend Squire here that's about due for a wreath. If he were with our crowd he'd have been taken for a ride long ago. But as for me—well, naturally I've taken my precautions."

"It's damned nonsense." Squire had taken a stride forward. "The little rat's bluffing. He's simply making fools of us."

"It may be nonsense. But it's a sort of nonsense that requires getting to the bottom of." Egg-head turned his eyes slowly on Routh. "You have a crowd," he said. "You have colleagues. You have come here by design. You have taken precautions to ensure your personal safety. If there is any sense in all this, I am quite ready to hear it." He turned with a sudden flash of temper upon Squire. "And as this whole piece of folly is your responsibility, you had better do so too."

"I tell you, it's all—"

"Be quiet and hear the fellow out. . . . Now then, what do you mean by your crowd?"

"I mean a crowd that knows about *your* crowd. All that science stuff." He jerked his head in the direction of the long line of laboratories he had shortly before traversed. "We know what it's about. We know what you're making. Valuable stuff, I'd call it. We think it needs protection. And that you need protection too."

"Expensive protection, no doubt?"

"You mayn't like the bill, I agree. But it's probably very much in your interest to pay up, all the same."

"I see." The meagre man in the white coat again gave his disturbingly sweet smile. "But suppose we are not interested? And suppose we are minded to give these precious colleagues of yours a little practical demonstration that they rather need protection on their own account? If they exist—which is something I am by no means convinced of—we can certainly make you tell us where to find them. We could then return you to them—or return some significant part of you—just as an indication that we were not minded to do business with them. Don't you agree with me?"

Beneath the unfamiliar Routh a Routh all too fully known stirred uneasily. He knew that one falter meant that he was done for. Conversely, however wild his story, unflawed assurance might yet carry him triumphantly through. "You just can't afford it," he said. "If our lot simply let the truth about you seep out, where would you be? The moment we simply *knew,* don't you see, we had you where we wanted you."

There was a brief silence. Squire and his companion were once more exchanging what was a purely disconcerted glance.

"Perhaps you wouldn't mind telling us what you *do* know? Particularly if I admit frankly that there is a good deal of force in your proposition?" Egg-Head spoke with a new mildness.

"Know? Why, that you have the means of making gold, of course."

"Thank you." For the first time Egg-Head looked really non-plussed. He was staring at Routh as if considering whether here was something really very deep indeed. "And Squire here is a sort of mad Midas? In imagining that he was luring you here it was his intention to transmute you into a full-size statue—the Golden Dustman, perhaps—and exhibit you at the Royal Academy?"

"I don't know what Squire was fool enough to think." Routh spoke almost at random. Had he made some wrong move? Perhaps the concern of these people was not with gold at all. Gold, after all, had been no more than a clever guess. Quickly he endeavored to retrieve himself. "We'll call it gold," he said. "Perhaps we don't know for certain—and then again perhaps we do. But it's certainly something you can't afford to have talked about. And—mind you—I'm no more than a messenger." Routh paused, displeased at thus having demoted himself. "Or say an envoy—that's about it. And what I require now is simply this: a substantial sum on leaving as an earnest of good faith—"

"I beg your pardon? Of what?" Egg-Head had returned to his desk and sat down again.

"There's no need to be funny." Routh's voice rose a pitch. He realised that he was near the end of his tether, and that he must bring the thing off within the next few minutes if he was to bring it off at all. "I'm to have a reasonable sum down. And after that my crowd will communicate with you by means that you will be told about later."

"I see. Well, I think we can settle this matter almost at once. Only we shall first have to consult higher authority." Egg-Head had a new note in his voice; it was almost a note of humour, and Routh was unable to find it reassuring. "As you very acutely suspected, I am not the Director. Squire, will you slip across and explain matters? No, my dear fellow, you need not be apprehensive. I can keep a very sufficient eye on our friend. And although I dislike firearms . . ." Egg-Head's right hand vanished into a drawer of his desk, to reappear again holding an automatic pistol. "Explain to the Director that we shall not occupy his time for more than five minutes."

Squire's departure was by the green baize door that Routh had first become aware of when peering through the key-hole. There could be no doubt that the Director lived, or at least worked, on the island at the farther end of the enclosed wooden bridge. Supposing that there was no delay, Squire would presumably be back with him within five minutes. Meanwhile Egg-Head continued to sit at his desk, his back to the baize door, the revolver ready in his hand, and his eye never straying from Routh for an instant. A minute went by in silence, and Routh became aware that the clock behind him was beginning to misbehave. Looking at those two bleak eyes and the muzzle of a pistol, he found it, in fact, difficult to remain convinced that he commanded the situation. And no sooner was doubt admitted than it grew. Routh realised that he had shot his bolt. When a fresh mind was brought in—and moreover a powerful mind such as the Director presumably possessed—it would be all up with him.

Egg-Head broke the silence. "Do you know, I think you have put up rather a good show? I no longer have the slightest inclination to believe your story, but as an improvisation it is thoroughly creditable to you. You are presumably just what poor

Squire took you for: a mere vagabond that nobody is going to worry about, and regularly in some petty way on the wrong side of the law. That's it, is it not?"

Routh made no answer. He was chiefly aware that his stomach felt bad, just as it had in the bank.

"What I like is the way you really have tried to exploit the situation rather than simply wriggle out of it. I wish we could take you on, my man. You'd at least, one day, be more use than Squire. Unfortunately it's dead against the rules. So you see where you stand."

Routh heard his own faint voice, speaking as if in the air above him. "You can't do that! You can't do *that* to me!"

"Be very sure that we can. And look here—there's no need to drag it out. Take a rush at me, man. I can promise you that your death will be instantaneous."

The room had begun to sway before Routh. Egg-Head's words had been altogether impassively spoken. It was impossible to tell whether compassion, or mockery, or the depraved wish for a moment's mortal excitement had prompted them. It was only clear that the game was indeed wholly up. He was to be murdered.

"You poor devil." This time the accent came through. It really was compassion—compassion tinged with embarrassment at the mere sight of anything so miserable and so shabby and so helpless as Routh. And in Routh it lit a last desperate flare of rage. He felt, without any volition of his own, his whole body tauten to spring. If even with a burst of bullets in him he could get his dying fingers round that throat. . . .

The baize door opened. A split second longer and he would have sprung. As it was, he stared over Egg-Head's shoulder, fascinated. For the door had opened only a little, and what had entered the room was a cat. It leapt noiselessly to the back of a chair close to the man's back. He was totally unaware of it. If only . . . And then the thing happened. The cat took a further leap to Egg-Head's shoulder. It was evidently a familiar domestic trick—but for the moment it caught the man unaware and helpless. Routh sprang. The two men went down together with a crash, struggling for the weapon. Routh had it—and in the same instant became aware of Egg-Head's mouth before him, wide open and screaming. Routh thrust the muzzle in it and pulled the trigger. And the great domed head exploded under his eyes like a bomb.

Routh tried to rise. One of his knees, slipping from the body, grated painfully on a hard object on the floor. It was a bunch of keys, similar to that which Squire had used in coming through the park and gardens. Routh grabbed it and hauled himself to his feet. He must get out. The man who was to have killed him instantaneously he had himself instantaneously killed. The automatic as it emptied itself into the grey pulp of Egg-Head's brain must have alarmed the whole place. Within seconds not only Squire and the Director but everybody in the building—even the people whom he had watched playing croquet—would be about his ears. He had seconds to get out of this house; minutes to escape from this whole infernal region and reach the salvation of the hidden Douglas.

Routh turned to the door by which he had entered. As he did so he saw the cat once more. It was crouched on the dead man's desk with humped back and waving tail. He thought it was going to spring at him. But the cat remained immobile—a great honey-coloured creature with long curling white whiskers. Its two fore-paws lay on a folded sheet of quarto paper.

As if from very far back in time, the memory of what he had learnt about Formula Ten swam into Routh's mind. What lay there on the desk was something that Egg-Head ought not to have had access to except amid the most elaborate precautions for its security, something worth millions. Realisation of his opportunity came to Routh like a great flood of white light. To snatch this paper from out of the paws of the cat might be to wrest unspeakable triumph from what had seconds before appeared defeat and death.

He took a step towards the desk. The cat hissed at him and

bared its claws. Beside himself, Routh turned, caught a poker from the fireplace, and hit wildly at the brute, as if intent to mingle its bespattered brains with its master's. But the cat sprang aside and the poker crashed down on the desk. Routh grabbed the paper and ran from the room.

PART TWO

ROUTH IN FLIGHT

Who would not, finding way, break loose from Hell,
Though thither doomed?

PARADISE LOST

1. The corridor was deserted, and Routh ran for the door that gave on the open air. But even as he did so there was a shout from the room behind him. At the far end of the corridor first one door was flung open and then another; there was a chatter of excited voices; and several white-coated figures appeared simultaneously. Routh bolted through the nearest door on his right. He was back in number eight.

The room was empty. He realised that many of the adjoining rooms were now tenanted, and that his only exit was back through a corridor into which these people were peering or tumbling. But if his plight was desperate his mind was working clearly and swiftly. There was a white coat hanging behind the door; he snatched it from the peg and scrambled into it. From a corner of the bench he grabbed a pair of horn-rimmed glasses—these he had noticed during his brief imprisonment—thrust them on his nose, and ran from the room.

The corridor held at least half-a-dozen white-coated figures, shouting and gesturing. Routh shouted and gestured too. At the same time he pushed his way towards the door he wanted. Squire had secured it behind them on their entry, but there was a chance that it was kept unlocked during the hours that all these people were at work. In a matter of seconds he had reached it and found that this calculation was justified. He flung himself through and banged it to behind him.

He knew that the respite thus gained could only be momentary. Fortunately the row of windows down the long corridor held nothing but frosted glass, and he could not be observed simply by a glance through them. In front of him was the high beech hedge that ran the full length of the long building, and Routh saw instantly that a gap to scramble through would not easily be found. His eye turned apprehensively to the door. It must surely be flung open now at any moment. Suddenly he saw that some half-hearted attempt had been made to embellish the bleaky utilitarian structure with climbing plants, and that up the wall on one side of the door ran a scrap of denuded wooden trellis. Routh grabbed at it and climbed. Within five seconds he was lying prone on the flat roof.

The surface was warm in the afternoon sunshine. Long and narrow, with its row of skylights down the centre, the roof was curiously like the deck of a liner. He was exhausted—so exhausted that he was suddenly afraid that he might go to sleep. But through the roof he could hear a mutter of voices, and presently the door by which he had bolted was flung open from within. He heard louder voices and his body tautened in acute anxiety. It sounded as if two of the searchers were running down the path in opposite directions. Would another of them think of the roof, or spot the fragment of trellis?

The door was shut again, and in the immediate vicinity he could hear no sound. But now in more than one direction dogs were barking, and somewhere on the other side of the house a stable bell was being rung with a will. He knew intuitively that the strange establishment upon which he had stumbled had a well drilled response to such a crisis as had come upon it. In other words, against him, Routh, a whole powerful machine was being brought smoothly to bear. The two-stroke and freedom could not be more than two miles away. But he would have to fight his way out to them through the invisibly turning mesh of this formidable mechanism.

He raised himself cautiously. The first essential was to discover the extent to which his position was overlooked. Ahead of him lay the covered bridge and the island. These were alike invisible, and he was presumably immune from observation in that direction. On either hand was a scattering of tree-tops which represented very substantial protection; here and there were gaps through which, even when he was flat on the roof, he might possibly be spotted from the middle distance; nevertheless the hazard seemed small compared with some through which he had recently passed. He looked behind him—and found a very different state of affairs. As he ought to have remembered, this whole structure projected directly from a wing of the main building. And from the main building it was commanded by more than a dozen windows.

He saw that he must get off the roof at once and run for it. But he was reluctant to descend as he had come, and he therefore decided to crawl cautiously to the other side. In doing this he had to face the risk of making some sound that might communicate itself to people still in the laboratories below. On the other hand he had a strong impression that the farther side consisted of a single blank wall without means of egress from the building. And this seemed to represent one threat the less.

The bell had ceased ringing and the dogs had fallen silent. He guessed obscurely at forces now strategically posted and waiting; at the beginning of some systematic combing of the whole property that would be quietly efficient and final. . . . Then he came to the edge, peered, listened, lowered himself over and dropped.

He landed among grass and pine needles, and picked himself up unhurt. It was as he had thought. The building was nothing but a blank concrete surface running off in either direction. In front of him was an indefinite extent of young fir trees. Among these he made his way at once, for they gave at least the sensation of shelter. In a moment he came diagonally upon a faint path. He wished desperately that he was armed. He wished that he had better understood the operation of the automatic. One bullet would have been enough for Egg-Head, and would have made a mess less likely to remain sickeningly on the memory. With the ability to kill and kill again he might be able to fight his way out.

As it was, as soon as he was spotted he was helpless. He stopped, recalling that he still wore the white coat. He got rid of it, but without managing to feel any the more secure. The little plantation of pines was thinning out and merging with a ragged shrubbery. He left the path and ran crouching forward from bush to bush.

The shrubbery ended abruptly. It was bounded by a path which he had approached at right-angles, and along the farther side of the path ran a six-foot wooden fence. He paused, hesitating whether to try scaling this, or to make what speed he could along the path in one direction or the other. And at this moment he heard voices behind him. He broke cover, ran to the fence, searched it for some foothold. There was none. He turned to his left and bolted along the path.

His heart was pounding yet more heavily. He realised that this was partly because he was running up-hill. If he had turned right he would have been making in the general direction of the little lake, and presumably of a stretch of park beyond it. As it was, he must be moving back towards the house. But to turn and retrace his steps required an effort of will that was now beyond him. He pounded on.

Somewhere beyond the fence on his right a whistle was blown. His fancy depicted a long line of men rising at its summons and moving forward, as if on a field-day. All sense of proportion and likelihood had deserted him; he thought of his pursuers in terms of platoons and companies; had a bomb exploded before him or a shell whistled overhead he would have felt no surprise, nor any appreciable increase of terror.

There was another shout on his left. He glanced in its direction as he ran and saw several figures break from the trees simultaneously. Then, as if he had been a train entering a tunnel, they vanished. A fence like the one on his right had abruptly risen up on his left. He was labouring along what was in effect a long corridor. If they caught him here he hadn't a chance. Not a bloody chance. If only he hadn't emptied that gun. If only . . .

The power of thought was leaving him, as if driven out of his body by the fierce pain of his breathing. If he could remember why all this was happening, it would be all right. If he knew where he was, or why he ran, so vast an accession of knowledge must infallibly save him.

Routh pulled up. There was some crisis and his brain had cleared to meet it. He was at a cross-roads—that was it. In front of him the fenced path ran straight on towards a huddle of buildings. To his left a transverse path led directly to the main bulk of the house. And to the right this same path, unfenced and bordered only by low box hedges, ran through an indeterminate stretch of garden to the park. That was the way he must go. He turned to run. As he did so a man with a gun appeared as if from nowhere some twenty yards ahead, leapt the hedge without looking towards Routh, and then moved slowly down the path and away from him, scanning the gardens on either side.

At any moment this new enemy might turn. There was nothing to do but go straight on, and make what he could of the shelter of the buildings before him. They were, he guessed, stables and places of that sort. The distance was scarcely greater than the length of a cricket pitch. Routh covered it without glancing behind him and found himself in a courtyard that was almost entirely enclosed. To his left was a wing of the house itself—the servants' wing, probably, and distinguished by a multiplicity of small, sparely draped windows. To face them was like a nightmare—the familiar nightmare of being on the stage of a crowded theatre, with no idea of a part and no means of getting off. On its three other sides the yard was a jumble of coach-houses, storerooms, lofts and the like. The only entrance to it, apart from the narrow one by which he had come, was through a broad archway straight in front. Through this one would come, no doubt, to the main façade of the house. Should he dash straight through, and so make for that part of the park which was vaguely familiar to him? This question was answered even as Routh, with the slender mental concentration he had summoned back, addressed himself to it. Suddenly from beyond the archway came a sound that thickened and slowed his racing blood. He remembered Deilos and for a moment supposed that leopards or hyenas were at large in the gardens. Then he realised that he was listening to blood-hounds; that this appalling sound was the deep bell-note of which he had read in fiction. No living creature holds a more alarming place in the popular mind than does the bloodhound; and Routh was now reduced to sobbing with fear. At the same moment he heard voices and steps behind him. There was no more than the angle of a building between some group of his enemies and himself. He was within seconds of being captured.

The yard before him was an unbroken stretch of concrete, and it was quite empty. It looked like an arena cleared for some cruel sport. Routh had a fleeting fantastic vision of himself being driven hither and thither about it in abominable torment. His knees shook. He leant against the wall by which he was crouching, and his hands groped over its surface for something to which to cling. They found a small object, round and hard. It was like a cricket ball. Routh's mind was now scarcely more than a pin-point of consciousness, and he groped to understand the thing's function, to give it a name. But even as he did so it turned under his hand, and a door swung inwards behind him. He staggered back a couple of steps and fell. The door, just clearing his numbed body, swung to and closed. A great sheltering darkness had received him.

2. He lay curled up, his body inert but his limbs intermittently wracked by spasm. All his power of interpreting experience and devising responses to it had left him. He was on the two-stroke, and the smell of hot oil was coming up between his knees. Now between high wooden fences, and now over interminable ribbons of green rubber enclosed in the walls of frosted glass, the two-stroke was carrying him sturdily ahead of danger. . . . *Bang!* Ominously the engine had back-fired. There had

been trouble recently with the timing. *Bang!*

Routh stirred uneasily. *Bang!* What he now heard was the noise of a door being sharply closed. There were voices, footfalls going up and down wooden staircases, the sound of more doors being wrenched open, banged to. They were searching the outbuildings all round the yard.

With his situation reconstructed around him, Routh struggled to his knees. The smell of oil was still in the darkness about him. He guessed that he was in a garage. But it was, he instinctively knew, a large place, and unusually lofty. It occurred to him that somewhere there might be a ladder that would take him to some obscure perch high up in the rafters. A flicker of confidence returned to him and for a moment he had a glimpse of the wily and undefeatable Routh, peering down from this fastness at his enemies vainly searching for him below. He got to his feet and felt about him cautiously. Vague masses, impossible to interpret, loomed around him. Garages, he remembered, often had the sort of pit used to get at a car from underneath. It wouldn't do to go straight into one of them.

Another door was slammed close by, and he heard footsteps more loudly than before. They were coming. Within the next few seconds he must hide himself. He took a further step forward, and stopped with a low cry. Directly before him, dim but distinguishable, hung a pale human face, its eyes on a dead level with his own. He drew back and the face drew back too. It was his own face reflected in a panel of glass. His hands went out and once more found itself on a handle—but this time it must be the handle of a car door. Even as he made the discovery there was a creak behind him and a finger of light shot through the darkness. He had only one possible resource left. He tugged open the door, flung himself through it, and drew it to behind him.

The finger of light was now a broad beam. He tumbled over the seat on which he was crouched and sought to flatten himself out to gain concealment. The thing was roomy. Conceivably it was a shooting brake, for there appeared to be no back seat. But there was some sort of tarpaulin sheet, carelessly thrown down; and under this he burrowed. Once there was an ominous clink of metal, for on the floor beneath the tarpaulin was what must be a heap of metal tools, loosely disposed. He lowered himself cautiously upon these and lay quite still.

There were now at least two men quite close to him. One was talking rapidly and the other was giving monosyllabic answers. It sounded like some sort of briefing. Routh was puzzled, for he got no impression that the place was being actively searched. The voices broke off and in a moment were succeeded by a new sound, impossible to misinterpret. A large door was being pushed back on rollers. At the same time light flooded through the chinks of the tarpaulin. Routh held his breath. An extraordinary possibility, alarming yet carrying with it a wild hope, had flashed upon him. Suppose that . . .

The two men were talking again, and this time he could hear snatches of what they said.

"Surely he can't get far?"

"Probably not. But the devil of it is, he got hold of some keys. So if by any chance he reached the ring fence before the current went on—"

"The current! You don't mean to say they've turned on that? They told me that was only for the greatest crisis of all."

"Get in and don't waste time." The floor beneath Routh lurched suddenly and there was the sound of a door closing. More faintly, the same voice continued. "It *is* the greatest crisis of all—only not just as we've expected it. This fellow is the crack agent of something pretty big. And there's the point. He mustn't be killed. He may have hidden this thing already. Or he may simply have thrown it away. That's why we must have him back alive. Ready?"

"Ready."

"Go out fairly rapidly and then come more slowly in again."

Exultant and trembling, Routh hardly dared to breathe. There could be no doubt about the incredible truth. He was going to be driven straight out of this abominable place—yard, gardens, sinister ring-fence, park, boundary wall and all—he was going to be driven straight out of it in search of himself! The fools—the bloody fools! He lay absolutely rigid. Close to his fingers, he knew, was the heavy wrench or spanner that he would eventually raise to bring crashing down on his unconscious chauffeur's skull. And then, having pitched him into a ditch, he would drive the car himself hell for leather to London. Oh triumphant and all-powerful Routh!

The car was moving. It appeared to be coasting out of the garage. Lying on this hard floor, Routh thought, made the suspension feel funny. He had to brace his body more firmly still so as not to give himself away. But what did it matter if he was in for an uncomfortable ten minutes? Only provided—

The engine burst into life. For a full minute it appeared to race unbearably. Routh waited for the gears to engage, the clutch to be let in, the first swift acceleration that might send him lurching or rolling dangerously backwards. But nothing happened. The sense of something quite unapprehended in his situation possessed him. The whole movement was queer. And under his nose—

He stared again, and there was no doubt of it. Part of the flooring on which he lay was for some reason of a transparent substance—glass or perspex. He could see the road beneath him, studded with cats' eyes. Only the road was green—was as green as the rubber in that endless corridor. . . . His eyes adjusted their focus and he saw what was really there. The two sides of the road were two broad green paddocks. The cats' eyes were the tops of white fencing posts dividing them. Routh, in fact, was suspended in air.

3. The discovery was a terrific shock. Nausea gripped him and for a horrible moment he thought that he must vomit. The line of posts slipped sideways across his field of vision. He stared below him in fascination. The earth had swung round like a compass-card and was now almost motionless. His tired mind, making a conscious effort of analysis, grasped the implication that he himself must be motionless too. In fact the craft in which he had hidden himself was a helicopter.

For a moment Routh closed his eyes. He was awed at the extent of his enemies' resources. But he himself had held out against them now—as it seemed—for hours. And he still had his astounding chance of triumph. He had nothing to do but rise from his lurking place, hit his unsuspecting pilot hard on the head, take charge of the machine—

But at this his nerve failed him. The thought of hanging high in air alone, with a set of unfamiliar and inexplicable controls between himself and disaster—this was something he found he couldn't take. In any case he had better wait. The fellow had been told to "go out fairly rapidly." That meant, presumably, outside the boundaries of the estate below him. He must bide his time until they were outside that formidable stone wall. The moment to act would be then.

The helicopter was moving again. It was passing directly over the house, and not thirty feet above the chimneys. The size and nondescript character of the place were now fully apparent. Routh was aware of a sprawling system of stone and tile ridges, irregularly disposed and alternating with broad, flat expanses of lead. His eye caught the long, low bitumen-covered roof of the building whence his flight had begun; and beyond he had a glimpse of the lake. Then the helicopter passed over the front of the house. Above the apex of the gleaming white pediment that had been his first impression of the place rose a flagstaff. Against this a white-coated man was steadying himself as he swept the nearer grounds with a pair of binoculars. The man looked up and waved as the machine passed over him. Routh drew back nervously, fearful that his lurking face might be discerned peering through the perspex. But already the roof had vanished.

Still he dared not move. He had to master a nervous impulse to get a glimpse of the pilot, to estimate from his manner of controlling his machine the chance of bluffing and intimidating him, to study the skull it might be desirable to fracture at a blow. Crouched still beneath his tarpaulin, he had already chosen his weapon for that—a heavy spanner, straight-ended and about a foot long. In his imagination he cautiously poised it, swung it in air. His breath quickened at the thought of it. He realised, with a strange spasm of moral horror and a dark excitement, that there was a blood-lust in him; that he had killed one man and would willingly kill another. It was part of his new stature, part of the Routh by whom the seventy-bob swindler had been magnificently succeeded. . . .

There was a queer sound in his ears. For a second he was puzzled, and then realised with terror that what he had heard was his own laughter. He had laughed aloud in a malevolent glee—and with the ear of his enemy within three feet of him. He realised a new danger—the danger that he might go lightheaded, hysterical, mad. He lay as still as death, biting hard at a wrist.

The fellow had heard nothing. He would have ear-phones, of course; for he was in some sort of short-wave contact with the people below. Indeed it looked as if he had received instructions to change his course of action. For he was not flying straight out of the grounds as Routh had hoped. He was moving gradually out on a spiral. There was no other explanation of the circular movement of the terrain below. And the helicopter was an incomparable machine to hunt with. It hovered at will. Several times it sank to within a few feet of the ground to investigate—Routh supposed—one or another suspicious appearance. Nothing, surely, could escape observation so miraculously armed—not Deilos, crouched among his rocks; not even the most timid mammal yet known on this earth. . . . Routh frowned into the perspex, obscurely conscious of some unresolved perplexity deep in his mind. But at that moment he saw the ring-fence.

It looked something that a child could leap. But Routh knew

how formidable it was. And if it really held some electrical charge, as the conversation he had overheard suggested, then it was now insuperable. But the enemy was plainly reckoning with the possibility that he had made such good speed before the first alarm spread that he had actually got through it. Grabbing those keys had been a lucky move after all. But for that, they would scarcely trouble to send the helicopter beyond the fence and the wall.

And here *was* the wall. They were actually over and beyond it. Routh trembled at the full realisation of how far he had got—of how tantalisingly near to safety he had come. The fellow was going to circle the park—perhaps to range swiftly over the scanty system of roads and lanes bounding it and running away from it. Nobody could stir on these without detection. While the helicopter was in the air only thick woodland would give secure cover to a moving figure. And of that there seemed to be comparatively little in these parts. Below, everything was bare, still, empty.

Routh's field of vision was restricted, but as the hunt progressed he realised that one suspicious object after another was being spotted, pursued, and then inspected at close quarters. It seemed impossible that so systematic a process would not ultimately succeed, and Routh presently recognised in himself a fresh anxiety so irrational that it appalled him. He was in a fever lest at any moment Routh should be spotted and caught. A swoop upon two lovers couched high on a haystack set his heart beating wildly; his mouth went dry as the helicopter casually followed and hovered over a school-child on a bicycle. Any one of the few figures animating this quiet countryside might be *him*. He bit again at his wrist, fighting this ghastly treachery to his own elementary sense of identity.

And then the astounding thing happened. Once more the ground had risen up to meet him—and this time it was coming nearer than ever before. There was a lane, a hedge—and protruding from the hedge a dark patch oddly like a human leg. It was this that was to be spied at—this and . . . The wild doubt lasted only a fraction of a second. What lay below was the Douglas. And the dark splash was one of the leggings he had kicked off when his first fatal madness of that morning had come upon him.

He was delivered from all madness now. He threw off the tarpaulin and rose. The pilot swung round and his eyes dilated. He threw up an arm and at the same time spoke rapidly into the wireless transmitter slung on his chest. Routh hit him and he crumpled in his seat. The helicopter was about twenty feet up. It suddenly looked a very long way.

Routh scrambled over the unconscious man. A wrong touch on the controls and he might soar again. He peered under the instrument panel and saw a tangle of thin cables and insulated wires. He thrust the spanner among them and twisted it—twisted it with all his might again and again. The engine raced, choked, faded out. The earth rose and dealt the helicopter a single shattering blow.

The machine had landed squarely on its belly in the lane. Routh flung himself on a door and tumbled into open air. He saw the Douglas not ten yards away and he gave a weak, exultant cry.

He turned back to the helicopter's cabin, in panic lest the pilot should have recovered, should be reaching for a gun. But the man was insensible. Routh stared at him and his exultation turned to senseless rage. He scrambled half into the cabin once more and with his bare hands pummelled the unconscious face. Then a revulsion took him. He clawed ineffectively at the body, striving to heave it into a position of greater ease. It was like lead. He dropped back to the ground and ran to the two-stroke.

4. The engine started at a kick. Its familiar rhythm steadied him and he found himself once more thinking clearly. There was acute danger still—and the more acute because he had made a bad slip. If only he had managed to rise behind the pilot quietly and get him unawares—or if, for that matter, the fellow had lacked the guts and presence of mind to make that quick revealing mutter into his radio—the position would be a good deal more comfortable. As it was, the enemy already had a fair idea of what had happened.

There was nobody in sight. But at any moment the situation might transform itself; he was, after all, no more than ten minutes' walk from that horrible wall. His first job was to get on an arterial road and merge himself in some southward-bound stream of traffic. Nobody, he recalled, was going to put a bullet in him from a distance. The swine were determined to have him alive. . . . He shivered, and shoved the two-stroke across the grass verge to the road. His quickest route lay straight ahead. But that way lay the entrance to the fatal lane down which the girl had turned that morning, the lane to the abominable Milton—Milton Porcorum. He could see the mouth of it now. And up there, at any moment, might come some swift-moving reinforcement of his pursuers.

He turned the head of the Douglas and faced the helicopter once more. It lay like an enormous crippled insect, slightly canted over and with its rotor-blades quite still. As he opened the throttle and ducked he glanced sideways into the cabin. With a shock he realised that the pilot had come to. He was in the act of hauling himself up in his seat. For the second time his eyes—now glazed and painfully apprehending—crossed Routh's. Then he was gone. Routh cursed his own folly. He ought to have made sure of smashing the radio. Unless the fellow was too dazed to take in what he had seen, he would presently be reporting the direction in which the fugitive was heading.

Routh rode on, getting everything out of the old two-stroke that he safely could. It was still early afternoon. Yet the day had already stretched through aeons. His head swam and the wheel wobbled. He had to steady himself on the unfolding ribbon of time, steady himself on the unfolding ribbon of road. His breakfast had been a cup of tea and a scrap of toast. If he didn't get something soon he would faint. He had gone for several miles without seeing anybody—not even a distant labourer in the fields. But now a figure was approaching on a bicycle. Again Routh's front wheel wobbled. The figure approached and raised an arm. Routh ducked and shied. It was a clergyman, gesturing Christian brotherhood. *Major Road Ahead*. Thank goodness for that.

There was an A.A. telephone-kiosk on the corner, and beyond it a big sign advertising a road-house farther north. Close by this an old man was leaning on a gate, idly watching whatever traffic went by. Routh, remembering his senseless fear of the clergyman, glanced at him boldly. A shepherd or something of that sort, Routh thought—and rejoiced in the further proof that harmless folk existed. And here, going south at thirty yard intervals, were four lorries with enormous loads of bricks. He would let two pass and then cut in. The shepherd was looking at him with a mild, patriarchal benevolence. Routh gave him a condescending wave and swung in behind the second lorry. The shepherd had put a hand behind his head and was doing something to his stick, cocking it in air. The lorries were travelling fast. Routh opened the throttle. He had gone a mile or more before it came to him that if the old man were indeed a shepherd then he, Routh, was the sheep. The affair on the old man's back was a walkie-talkie. He was reporting on Routh's movements now.

Well, it was just another shock. His own speed, and the cats' eyes on the road, and the hundred telephone-wires overhead, and the thundering lorries that were his bodyguard, and the answering stream of traffic almost without intermission roaring, purring, rattling past on the right: all these things sang to Routh and exhilarated him. Let them lurk at cross-roads and jabber to each other over radios as they liked. They could do nothing. Already he had distanced them by nearly half a county—

Routh braked hard. The wall of brick in front was hurtling

at him. The lorry, which had slowed apparently without warning, now swerved off the road and stopped. The lorry further in front had done the same. On a bare patch of ground a dozen commercial vehicles of various sorts were parked before a small architectural nightmare composed of a Nissen hut and three dismounted railway-carriages clustered round a mean central building of hideous yellow bricks. Along the length of one of the railway-carriages, in white letters rudely painted on a black background, was the announcement:

GOOD PULL-IN FOR TRANSPORT SNACKS DAY AND NIGHT

Routh hesitated only a moment. He must eat soon; otherwise he would pass out. And if he stopped now he could go on with the brick-lorries. Better risk it.

He dismounted, thrust the Douglas out of sight behind a trailer piled high with motor-car bodies, and followed the driver who had been in front of him inside. Two of the railway-carriages had been run together at an acute angle, and their point of junction had in turn been rammed like an arrow into the side of the Nissen hut. The whole place looked like the product of a ghastly accident. There were long narrow tables with benches clamped to the floor beside them. There was at least a score of men in the place. One was asleep and snoring, his head on the table and a straggling mop of hair trailing in a pool of spilt coffee. Most of the others were eating and drinking. In the main hut there was a counter with urns, ovens, and piles of sausage rolls and round doughy buns. Two slatternly girls dispensed the hospitality of the place, engaging in high-pitched and unintelligible badinage the while. It was hot and the atmosphere was horrible.

Routh wavered on the threshold. He hated it. It was dead common and everything looked dirty. It was the level of society he worked long hours, trudging from job to job, to keep himself from being submerged in. But hunger gnawed at his belly. He sidled in and sat down half-way up the carriage, beside the sleeping man. One of the girls was passing. He called to her. "Miss!"

She took no notice. He nerved himself and called louder. "Miss, please!" She turned, looked at him with contempt and moved on.

He realised that the girls undertook only to clear away. You went up to the counter for what you wanted. He rose, stumbled over the legs of the man who was asleep, and went forward. "A cup of coffee, please, and two sausage rolls."

The girl whom he had addressed a moment before looked at him vindictively. She splashed coffee at random into a mug, her head turned towards her companion. "My stars!" she said—and jerked an ear towards Routh.

Routh flushed so hard that the blood hammered in his head. Vulgar little sluts. If they only knew that he was Routh! If they only knew that less than a couple of hours ago he had blown to bits—

The steaming coffee distracted him. He grabbed the mug. It fell from his hand and smashed to pieces on the zinc counter. He stared at it stupidly. "I'll pay," he said. "I'll pay for the mug. Give me another."

The girl looked at him with suddenly much deepened contempt. "Pay!" she cried; "who cares?" She swept the fragments from before her so that they broke in further pieces on the floor. She gave the counter a perfunctory mop with a filthy cloth, thrust another mug in front of Routh as if he had been an animal, and turned to scream some greeting at an acquaintance who had just come in.

Routh took the mug and the sausage rolls and returned to his seat beside the sleeping man. Somebody had turned on a wireless. The hut and its tunnel-like annexes were filled with a metallic voice announcing the composition of next Saturday's football teams. Some of the men fell silent and listened. A few brought pool coupons from their pockets and studied them in the light of this fresh information. A man sitting opposite to Routh did this. He was a great brute with a shirt open nearly to the navel, and his chest was covered with red hair. His thick figures, hacked and grimed, fumbled clumsily at the creases of the closely-printed scrap of paper before him. Routh remembered the fine hands of the man he had killed.

He bit avidly into the second sausage roll. He ought to have got a couple of the buns to go in his pocket. But he quailed at the idea of going up to the counter again. It was a matter of physical size. He hated the thought that any man among them could take him and break his back across a knee, like a rabbit. He imagined it happening; the hairy man opposite taking him by the neck in a rough house; the slatternly girls, roused and bright-eyed, looking on. One of them was flouncing past him now. She was actually carrying a big jug of coffee and a superior meat-pie, oozing gravy, to some favoured male. Other males, without animosity, shouted facetious remarks. The girl flung answers here and there as she moved down the carriage, brushing the close-packed men with her hips. A burly fellow in a boiler-suit slapped her on the buttocks and roared with innocent laughter. Routh hated it, it was so low. The place was full of the smell of human sweat, shot with the meagre smell of weak, stewed coffee. The sleeping man lurched over and a massive shoulder and thigh pressed on Routh. Routh took his last mouthful and wondered if he could keep it down. The carriage, he suddenly thought, was like a monstrous meat-pie stuffed with human flesh, with sweat and watery coffee as a gravy running over.

The man with the red hair on his chest raised his head and looked straight at Routh. It seemed to Routh that there was disgust and hostility in every line of his dust-grimmed face. His mouth moved, as if he were collecting saliva with which to express himself. But instead he spoke. "Heard what was last week's treble chance?" he asked.

"Ninety-eight thousand." Routh heard his own voice automatically replying. "A man and his wife in Swansea. Never filled in a coupon before."

"Gor."

The exclamation, Routh realised in a flash, was offered on behalf of both of them. It involved him and the hairy-chested man in a common response. There was a bond between them—that of their both being awed and disgusted also-rans. Routh felt a lump in his throat. Friendship. Pals.

The hairy-chested man brought from his pocket a tin of tobacco and a packet of cigarette papers. With these his blunt fingers fumbled in apparent hopeless ineptitude as he spoke. "Nearly a hundred thousand quid! And Swansea!"

"They oughtn't to fix it that way." Routh spoke spontaneously, firmly, from mature conviction. "What's the difference between a hundred thousand and fifty thousand, I ask you?"

The hairy-chested man wrinkled his brow in thought. "It's double," he said.

"Don't you believe it. Not to the chap that wins it. Fifty thousand and a hundred thousand are pretty near the same thing to him."

"How d'you make that out, mate?" An unshaven man with a battered peak cap had broken in from further down the carriage.

"Think of the taxation when he's invested it. That's how. Super-tax, he'd be paying, with a hundred thousand quid out at a good rate."

"Super-tax! Well, I never thought of that one." The hairy-chested man leant over to Routh. "Fag?" He had contrived a grubby but reasonably efficient-looking cigarette. Routh took it gratefully and fumbled for a match. "No," said the man, "I never thought of that one. And 'taint right. No—'taint right, that isn't."

"Have a light, mate." The unshaven man was amiably thrusting his own cigarette at Routh. "But it don't apply to them folk in Swansea. Man and wife, they are—and going halves."

"If they're man and wife, they'll pay as one." Routh was prompt. "That's the law." He drew at his cigarette. There was a little circle round him—friendly, attentive. The girl who had given him the coffee as if he were a pig had come up behind him and was leaning both her arms on his shoulders. Only the sleeping man was inattentive. "So what I say is," he went on, "why not make it fifty and then ten fives?"

The hairy-chested man tapped his fingers on the table before him. He was counting. "That's right," he said. "Give you a fair chance, that would."

The second girl had now come up. She leant across Routh and brushed the crumbs solicitously from his part of the table. "My!" she said, "if you're not the one to tell us what to do."

Popular Routh. Condescending Routh. The group grew. The discussion prospered. Routh steered it. The increasing babel of talk roused the sleeping man. His weight came off Routh's thigh and he sat up with a start. He was a lad of no more than twenty and he looked dead tired. The coffee dripped from his hair and trickled down his dusty cheeks. He put up a dazed hand to his head. Something queer and unaccustomed stirred in Routh and he brought out a handkerchief—the spare clean handkerchief that he always kept to put in his breast pocket before ringing a door-bell. "Here," he said, "give it a wipe." The boy flushed and took the handkerchief. Routh trembled with pleasure, and looked away.

Across the smoke-filled carriage he saw what made his heart miss a beat. The men driving the bricks were gone. And Squire was sitting in their place.

5. Vanity, for the moment, saved him. His prospective wealth as the proprietor of Formula Ten; his immediate personal safety as the man who had stolen it: neither of these seemed so precious to him as the esteem of the group of transport men around him, as the admiration of the two sluts now leaning on the counter. It was this that enabled him in a second to control himself—and that even stirred him to an act of sheer bravado. He caught Squire's eye through the haze, and gave him a brisk nod.

The man in the battered cap turned round and stared at Squire. "Friend of yours?" he asked.

"Acquaintance." Routh was off-hand. "Commercial." He

paused to arrest sufficient attention. "Travels in—" And Routh named something that produced a roar of mirth from the circle around him. The sluts tossed their heads in delighted disapproval, and fell to vigorously smearing ill-washed mugs with sopping tea-towels. Everybody turned and stared at Squire, who started to stand up, thought better of it, and sat down again.

But it was only for a moment that Routh was able to enjoy his enemy's discomfiture. The grimness of his situation rolled back upon him. Squire would have a car outside, and no doubt he had brought some of his confederates. How would he plan to capture the fugitive? A horrid possibility crossed Routh's mind. What if Squire said he was mad? What if he maintained to this uneducated crowd that he had escaped from an asylum? Might his pursuers not then simply drag him away screaming, without a soul lifting a hand to prevent it? Routh thanked his stars that he had got into the talk of the place; that he had held forth with such sanity and sagacity on football pools. But it had been a mistake to make that joke about Squire. They had all laughed—but it sounded a bit cracked all the same. And now Squire really was rising. He was coming forward to make his monstrous claim. He had pointed at Routh. . . .

There was a sudden dead silence. Everybody was staring over Routh's shoulder at the main door of the hut. It framed two policemen in the flat caps of a county constabulary.

Just this situation Routh had dreaded for years. He had pictured it to himself with a hundred casual variations—but always in essence the same. The law had caught up with him. The bank had rung the police. The police had contacted the woman. . . .

"Keep your seats, please. Licences first—and then a brake-inspection for all cars and commercial vehicles."

The silence gave place to grumbles, routine profanity, and much fumbling in pockets. Routh gave a long gasp of relief—and then caught his breath as he realised not only the irrelevance of his first reaction but also the immensity of the issue with which this sudden and unexpected appearance of the embodied law confronted him. If he were captured by his enemies, they would first make sure of Formula Ten and then kill him. He was under no illusion as to that. And now that they had made contact with him again, did he really have the slightest chance of shaking them off? Except—and he looked at the two policemen—in one way? Powerful as they were, they were unlikely to get at him in a police cell.

He could give himself up. He could give himself up, here and now, as the man who had committed a score of petty frauds all over England. If Squire and his friends were indeed far on the wrong side of the law themselves, they could not then venture to come forward with any charge of their own.

The policemen were checking the licences of two men standing by the counter. Routh tried to think ahead. If he gave himself up he would be searched, and Formula Ten would be found on him. But it would be incomprehensible rather than suspicious, as likely as not. He could explain it as a system he was working out for playing the pools. . . . His mind was made up. He would hand himself over.

He rose and took a step towards the policemen. The movement revealed to him that Squire had a companion—a burly man with a reddish beard, sitting half in shadow. In a flash it came to Routh that he had, after all, a chance worth taking. Probably there were only the two of them. However numerous his enemies, the hunt must have dispersed them fairly thinly. Outside there could be nothing but an empty car. . . .

He walked up to the policemen, his driving-licence in his hand. "Mind if I get along?" he asked casually. "I've only got a motor-bike. Want to look at the brakes of that?"

One of the policemen, a sergeant, glanced rapidly at the licence, and shook his head. "No need for you to stop, sir."

He was in the open air—and free. Perhaps he could even—Routh glanced rapidly round the yard. There was a police-car, close to the high-road. And there, its bonnet sticking out from behind a lorry, was what must be Squire's—a long, grey, open

Lagonda. The two-stroke was just beyond. He went rapidly forward, brought out his clasp knife, and as he passed the back of the Lagonda cut hard into the wall of a tyre, close by the rim. Then he ran the Douglas out into the road and in thirty seconds was heading south.

He must find another clot of steadily moving traffic. That was the next thing. It would at least give him a breathing-space to think another move ahead. No good trying to make London on the Douglas now—not with their knowing how he was mounted and which way he was heading. Better abandon it and get a long-distance bus for somewhere else. Once break the trail like that and he would be pretty safe. It takes the police to find a man who may be in any one of half-a-dozen large towns. And he had actually had thoughts of giving in! Indomitable Routh. Slippery Routh.

Going all out, he caught up with two furniture vans. As he slipped past the first in order to tuck himself between them he managed to glance into the cab. It contained just what he hoped to see—three hefty men. The two vans together were as good as a bodyguard. If the convoy held to the first decent-sized town he would be all right. He was on A 417. Wantage wouldn't be bad, but Newbury, if he could make it, would be better. Oxford, Reading, Basingstoke, Winchester, Salisbury, Bristol: let him only get on a bus for any one of these and he would be as good—or as bad—as a needle in a haystack, so far as Squire was concerned. It meant dropping the two-stroke—but what did that matter when he was on the verge of fortune?

His mind began to work on the problem of Formula Ten. How could he find bidders for it when he didn't really know what it was about? He could do one of two things. Either he could seek out contacts who would know the right method, or he could take some means—newspaper advertisements, perhaps—of communicating safely with his defeated enemies, and simply sell back to them. This last was the cautious and moderate thing to do. Twenty thousand pounds, say, quietly handed over in one-pound notes compressed into a small suit-case. . . .

The second furniture van was no longer close behind him. He twisted his head and saw it at a stand-still a hundred yards back. He could see, too, a puff of steam from its radiator. Presumably it had been obliged to stop and cool off. He faced forward again and saw that the first van was going steadily ahead. He had better do the same. For a couple of minutes he looked straight before him. When he again glanced backwards the stationary van was no longer in sight. It was hidden by a bend in the road—a bend round which there now swung a long, grey Lagonda.

They had lost no time in changing that wheel, or in their dealings with the police. His best chance was to get in front of the remaining van. He swung out—and as he did so became aware that the front van too was now slowing to a stop. Presumably it was going to wait for its companion. Routh peered in as he swerved past. And his heart sank. Of this van—as if by some special malignity of fate—the driver was the only occupant. He was an elderly man who looked as if he would be of very little use. Routh had just made this alarming discovery when he heard the first throb of the car coming up behind him.

There was nothing for it but to accelerate in the hope of picking up some more effective protection before he was overtaken. He swung round a bend and knew that he was lost. Ahead of him was nothing but a long stretch of empty road. Within a couple of minutes it would all be over. They would simply force him into the ditch—perhaps send him into it with a nicely-calculated glancing blow—and then collect him.

Routh knew that he ought to stop and take to his heels across country. That would at least put the enemy and himself on more or less equal terms. But he couldn't do it. His muscles, if called upon for any such decided action, would simply not obey his will. The Lagonda was coming on very fast—far too fast, he suddenly knew, for the deft accomplishment of what it was after. The driver—whether Squire or his companion—had either lost his head, or—

A grey shape loomed for a second on his right. He was in the ditch with the world tumbling over him and the sound of a great crash in his ears. His consciousness, although momentarily reduced to a mere flicker, registered the knowledge that the crash represented some objective happening in the outer world, and that no impact upon either a human body of a single motor bicycle could account for it. A second later he was sitting on grass, as if at a picnic, and staring past the buckled front wheel of the two-stroke at the Lagonda across the road. Only the Lagonda's back was visible. Its bonnet had gone through a substantial stone wall. Routh found himself laughing weakly. Squire had once more made an ass of himself. And this time, with any luck, to the actual destruction of himself and his companion.

Fear like a cold finger touched Routh between the shoulder-blades and ran down his back. He had heard a sound—it might have been a curse or a groan—from across the road. A second later first one human head and then another rose up behind the folded hood of the Lagonda. Squire and his accomplice were staring at him.

They weren't dead yet. But no more was he. Routh moved his limbs cautiously. He was bruised and shaken, and there was a cut across the back of his left hand—nothing more. And his pursuers, even if equally unscathed, had certainly derived no advantage from the crash. The odds were considerably closer than they had been a few seconds before.

Routh looked up and down the road. It was still quite empty. But it was a substantial high-road, all the same, and it could only be a very few minutes—perhaps no more than seconds—before something came along.

But meanwhile Squire was making to climb painfully over the side of his wrecked car. Routh thought that he had better get to his feet. But this took him longer than he expected. When at length he was standing on the road Squire and the bearded man were standing on it too. They were supporting each other like a couple of drunks. But they looked quite formidable, all the same.

Routh moved off. The effort to get on his feet had taken all his energy. He seemed to have none left to think with. But neither did his enemies. Routh shambled off down the road, and they shambled after him. Painfully his sense of the need to plan returned to him. They couldn't very well kidnap him here and now. The wrecking of their car had dished that. And until they knew that he hadn't cached Formula Ten somewhere on the route of his flight they couldn't bring out guns and shoot him. Or not to kill. . . .

Something had happened to the sounds behind him. There was only one man running. He turned his head. Squire was down on one knee in the road. Routh thought joyfully that he had collapsed. Then he saw that Squire's left arm was up oddly before his face, and that there was something resting on it. A spurt of dust flew up beside Routh's feet. There was a sharp report. Squire had tried to wing him. They'd do that, fake him up as part of their car-accident, and then manage somehow to smuggle him away—perhaps in a relief car of their own.

And still A 417 was wickedly empty. Squire was running again, but presently he would take another shot. The ditch on Routh's left had vanished, and in its place was a grass verge and a low stone wall. Beyond were trees. Routh stumbled to the wall and threw himself over; he blundered his way forward, staggering from tree to tree like a ball on a bagatelle-board. A bullet won't wind its way round a lot of bloody trees. He went on and on. There was silence all round him.

He stopped, not believing it. No pounding feet. His eyes were drawn down to his own feet, which ached beneath him. They rested on a thick carpet of pine needles. The enemy might be quite close, after all; they might be moving up on him in perfect silence. Nor was the cover so very good. This sort of tree was in too much of a hurry to reach the sun. It scrambled upwards with indecent speed, leaving nothing but a spare, business-like trunk behind it. Routh stood for a moment at bay, radiating futile malevolence upon the straight, still presences around him. He hated the wood. It wasn't natural—a place that was nothing but trees and silence. People shouldn't make such places. He longed for the street, for four walls and a roof, for a tough crowd that would see fair play.

Squire and the bearded man were close to him. The silence, as if retorting upon his dislike of it, allowed itself to be shattered by their voices. The sound seemed to be all around him. Wherever he moved it was in front of him as well as behind. If he turned half-left or half-right it was the same. Perhaps it was a trick of the place; perhaps among trees sound always behaved like that. Or perhaps—he thought in sudden horror—he was dying. Perhaps he was going to die of sheer long-drawn-out nervous tension. Perhaps this confusion of voices was simply the decay of the senses before death. He floundered on.

The trees thinned and vanished. In front of him stretched a low stone wall. Surely he had seen it before? What lay behind the wall, however, could not be the high-road, because he was looking directly at the roof and windows of a small, single-storeyed house. It was far from being a substantial refuge; nevertheless Routh saw in it his last hope.

But the wall was unexpectedly hard to surmount. His last vestiges of physical strength were leaving him. When he did get to the wall he could do little more than claw at it blindly. At one moment it seemed an insuperable barrier; at the next he was lying along the top of it, his head swimming. The drop was steeper on the other side. He glimpsed a hard surface beneath him, and in front of him a pale wall, a blank window of the little house. And then he fell. He was aware of pain, of voices, of two obscurely familiar forms bending over him. Hands were laid on his body, and at their touch he fainted.

When he recovered consciousness it was to find himself lying on the floor of a small, bare room. He was certain that very little time had elapsed, and he wondered how his enemies had conjured up this prison out of vacancy. His limbs were free; he flexed them cautiously and then, rolling over on his stomach, managed to raise himself to his hands and knees.

The place was tiny and smelt of fresh plasterwork; it had a single casement window, unbarred. Sudden hope leapt up in Routh. This was simply the tiny house in which he had hoped to find refuge, and it was not his enemies who were responsible for his being in it now. It was not *they* who had laid hands on him. He had been carried in here by a friendly, not a hostile power. But in that case his pursuers must still be close by. He got unsteadily to his feet. Why had his rescuers simply dumped him here? He must find them. He must explain the danger. Routh's eye, proposing to search the bleak little room for a door, fell once more upon the window. Squire and the bearded man were framed in it.

Without consciousness of the movement, he tumbled again to his hands and knees. And so he remained—looking up and out at his enemies, like a cornered dog. Squire's hand was on the window, and it was plain that he could force it in an instant. He was trapped. Only a miracle could save him now.

Routh prayed. He prayed for the miracle that would take him from these implacable men. And as he did so the faces of Squire and the bearded man moved queerly and unnaturally across the window—glided smoothly and laterally away. They were replaced by a telegraph post. And that glided away too. There was a tremor under Routh's body. The little house was moving. It was because he had been on his knees, he thought. Mummy had taught him that that was the right way to pray. *Darling, darling Mummy—*

This time he was unconscious for much longer.

6. Somebody was bending over him. It was the lad to whom he had given the handkerchief to wipe the coffee from his face and mop his hair. Behind him was his companion, the hairy man who had begun the talking about the pools. "I wouldn't 'ave thought it of 'im," the hairy man was saying. "Law-abiding little beggar, 'e looks to me."

"They might 'ave been crooks or they might 'ave been cops. But whichever they was, we didn't 'arf get 'im away from them nicely." The lad laughed cheerfully; then, looking down at Routh, saw that his eyes were open. "That's right, mate. Sit up and take a bit of notice. We must get you out before they check us in. No passengers allowed in these bleeding travelling Ritzes."

Routh sat up. The hairy man stepped forward, fished the remains of a cigarette from behind his ear, and thrust it companionably in Routh's mouth. " 'Ere," he said, "no 'arm in a puff of tobacco in the Louis Cans lounge."

The Louis Cans lounge was the same bare little room in which Routh had lost consciousness. There was the window through which Squire and his confederate had peered at him. Routh got to his feet and staggered to it. He looked out on a landscape of trodden mud, dotted for as far as he could see with prefabricated houses. They were the kind that arrive in three ready-made sections which simply bolt together. He had seen these sections on the road often enough. And of course he was in one now.

The miracle was explained. Routh felt a momentary resentment against providence for not having, as he had supposed, suspended the natural order of things in his favour. "What happened?" he asked.

The hairy man held out a match. "We'd pulled up to fill in the log, mate, when you came tumbling over the wall like a sack. So we nipped out and took a look over, and there was your commercial gent coming after you with a gun, and a nasty-looking beggar with a beard beside him. So we bundled you into Buckingham Palace here, and carried you off under their bleeding noses."

"How do I get away from this?"

"Straight down the Mall, mate." The lad advanced to the window and pointed. "There's a bus service at the other end."

The hairy man had opened a door through which one could drop to the ground. Routh looked at the two men awkwardly.

They looked back at him, benevolent and elaborately incurious. All words of thanks had for him connotations of insincerity, dislike, dishonest design. He could speak none of them. "Hope you win that treble chance," he mumbled. The lad gave him a hand down.

7. Workmen were tinkering at a score of prefabs on either side of him. There were acres of these, laid out in unbroken parallel lines. If you were in an aeroplane, and got your height a bit wrong, it would look like one of those awful military cemeteries. Routh shivered. It would be horrible to live in such a place. It would be like annihilation. You would come to think that you were just like other people. There could be nothing worse than that.

At the same time he envied the workmen their anonymity. He realised that he looked queer among them, a hurrying figure with nothing to do with the place. As far as his eye could see, there were only these workmen, all geared into this ant-like, squalidly-impressive communal effort, and himself, a piece of loose grit in it—something lawless and on its own, slipping through the cogs to an irregular and problematical fate.

There was now a metalled road under his feet. And solitude around him. He stopped, alarmed. The workmen had vanished, because in this part of the new estate their work was done. He could hear their clatter behind him. And far ahead he could see different signs of life: patches of grass and flowers, a scattering of television aerials, washing fluttering on a line. Ahead of him people had already moved in. But round about him there was an intermediate stage in the growth of this mass building: rows of these little houses, blank, empty and unquickened. He felt, just because they were so empty, that anything might come out of them. He might turn his head for a moment and there, standing in each little doorway, might be one of his own hidden fears. It was another tableau that would build itself into his evil dream of the long tunnel.

The empty road in front of him was a regular chequer of sunlight and shadow. Each house cast its identical black cube of shade; and monotonously, just past this, was a shorter finger of shade from the sort of glorified dog-kennel provided as an outhouse. He was near the end of the uninhabited block or belt—he could even see what looked like a main road ahead—when he found himself at a dead halt, quivering like a horse that has pulled up in its stride. For a second he was at a loss to account for his own action. And then he saw. Thirty yards ahead of him, the regular pattern of shade was broken. Between two of the cubes, instead of the expected blunt finger, lay an irregular mass of shadow, as if of something crouched low with an uplifted arm. He dragged himself forward, his breath shortening with every step. He read taut muscles, poised limbs into the enigmatical shape. He managed one more stride. Close beside one of the outhouses was the twisted trunk of an ancient apple tree. Its boughs had been lopped, but through some failure of energy it had not been grubbed out. A few shoots were springing from it. There was reason for it to cast a shadow instinct with life. It was the only thing left alive in all this wilderness.

Routh ran. He almost stumbled over a sticky-mouthed child on a tricycle—an intrepid explorer from the inhabited country ahead. There were voices—kids screaming, women gossiping, a baker's boy shouting at a horse—and gusts of music from the Light Programme. A few men, already home from work or out of it, were pottering about before their prefabs, obliterating what small patches of earth they had under useless little concrete paths and bird-baths. Routh spared them a glance of contempt as he ran. They took no interest in him whatever. Probably they thought he was running for a bus.

And so he was. For straight in front of him was a red double-decker, comfortingly urban in suggestion, waiting at its terminus —its side scrawled with a slogan exhorting the prefab population to National Saving. Routh put his last strength into leaping on the platform, and as he did so the bus moved off.

The upper deck was empty. As he swayed forward and slumped down he realised how done up he was. He realised too that he was still wearing the leggings he used on the Douglas. They made him look conspicuous now he was dismounted, and he hastily tugged them off and bundled them up as he heard the conductress climbing the stair.

"Fare, please."

He fumbled in a breast pocket and brought out a ten shilling note. "As far as you go."

"Hey?" The girl seemed to doubt if she heard correctly. "What d'you say?"

"I said 'As far as you go.' I can't say farther than that, can I?" Routh did his best to import an elaborate facetiousness into his tone.

"That will be one and ten. But you can have the Mental Hospital for a shilling." The girl gave him a ticket, a handful of change, and a long stare. As soon as she had gone away he looked at the ticket. But it had only numbers on it, and told him nothing. He began to keep a look out for a sign-post, a mile-stone, the indicator of a bus coming the other way. The bus might be bound for Witney, somewhere like that. It stopped in a hamlet and a number of people got on. Routh peered down at them anxiously as they mounted. It was three old women and a girl. At least it looked like that. He must suspect anyone, however unlikely, who took as much as a glance at him. It would be the same in a tea-shop or in the places one went for shelter: a cinema or a public library. He might feel the sudden prick of a needle. *Excuse me, my friend has fainted. But luckily I have my car outside.*

But perhaps that was only in stories. Perhaps they couldn't really get you with a drug like that. The bus stopped once more and its upper deck was invaded by a tumbling and shouting crowd of airmen. Most of them seemed no more than lads; they flung themselves on the seats, tossed each other cigarettes, called across the bus to particular cronies from whom they had been separated in the crush, craned their necks to study the conductress when she came up for fares. Here, Routh thought, was the best bodyguard he had found yet.

At last he glimpsed a road-sign and saw that they were running into Abingdon. The name conveyed almost nothing to him. He was sure it wasn't on any main line to London. Not that it mattered, if he had really broken the trail behind him at last.

They were in a market-place, and there was a lot of coming and going downstairs. He got large, vague comfort from the solid mass of laughing and shouting boys behind him. There were only two seats vacant up here: the one beside himself and the corresponding one across the gangway. The bus began to move, and then jerked to a stop again. There was some sort of flurry below. He peered out and saw, foreshortened with a queer effect of comedy, the hurrying figures of two nuns. They skirted the bus, one of them flourishing an incongruously secular-looking umbrella at the driver. Then they clambered on. The bus twisted its way out of Abingdon. Routh dropped into a doze.

When he woke up one of the nuns was sitting beside him, and the second had taken the other spare seat just over the gangway. Queer how they had to go about in couples. As if anyone would think of making passes at an old creature like that. Not that this one was necessarily old, since it was impossible to see her face. Pricked by idle and drowsy curiosity, Routh leant forward to take a peep. But still he couldn't see anything. The nun had an enormous white starched hood. She must feel as if she lived at the end of a tunnel. Routh wondered why such things had been invented. As blinkers, more or less, he supposed. See no evil unless it came at you head-on. That sort of thing.

He thought he might catch a glimpse of the other nun instead. When she turned to speak to her companion it ought to be possible at least to catch sight of her nose. But she showed no disposition to do this. Both of them sat perfectly still. Perhaps they were asleep. Or perhaps just staring straight ahead of them. Or, again, they might be praying. But when they prayed didn't they go fumbling and clicking at a string of beads? Routh's eyes went to the hands of the nun sitting beside him. They were idle in her lap. Suddenly, and just as he was taking this in, she slid both hands beneath the black folds of her gown.

The bus was already airless and fuggy. Routh yawned. He remembered vaguely that giving way to sleepiness was a luxury in which, for some reason, he must not at present indulge himself. He yawned again—and jerked fully awake with a start that almost dislocated his jaw. He had experienced, against the screen of his closed eyes, a vivid image on the idle hands of the nun before she had slipped them out of sight. They were large and hairy hands. They were not a woman's hands at all.

The bus cornered sharply and Routh was flung against the inscrutably shrouded form beside him. What he seemed to feel, through every nerve of his arm and side and thigh, was an unyielding sinewy strength, implacably planted in his path to freedom, poised and ready to—

Like a train running into a cutting, the bus plunged out of clear sunshine and between two thickly wooded slopes. In the same instant the shrouded figures both rose and turned upon Routh. It was a moment of absolute horror. The voices of the young airmen behind him seemed to rise in diabolic mockery. Routh understood that he was in hell. In another instant the bus was again in sunlight, and the hooded shape that had been no more than a silhouette bending over him took on interior form and feature. With a tremendous effort Routh looked it in the face. He saw a wizened old woman with steel spectacles. She clutched an umbrella in one small, claw-like hand. With the other she had been steadying herself on the back of the seat close by Routh. But now, glancing at him and seeing something of what was in his face, she touched him lightly on the shoulder, murmured an indistinguishable phrase and went swaying down the gangway. The second nun was younger and went past with lowered eyes. The bus stopped. Routh glimpsed them a moment later, walking slowly up an avenue towards a conventual-looking building behind a high wall. And the shouting and laughing of the airmen was again entirely human.

Routh fell back in his seat, knowing that fear, unintermitted through all that day, had pushed him to the very verge of madness.

The bus swung right-handed round a corner and descended a hill. Routh found that he was looking down at a gas works. Beyond the gas works, mellow in the misted sunlight of a late afternoon in autumn, were the towers of Oxford. And from these, very faintly, there came the chiming of innumerable bells.

PART THREE

ROUTH AND OTHERS IN OXFORD

Turrets and Terrases, and glittering Spires.

PARADISE REGAIN'D

1. Mr. Bultitude stepped out of the main gateway of Bede's and looked about him in mild surprise. It was true that nothing had much changed since his performing the same operation on the previous day. Directly in front of him the Ionic pillars of the Ashmolean Museum supported a pediment above which Phoebus Apollo continued to elevate the dubious symbolism of a vestigial and extinguished torch. On his right, the martyrs Cranmer, Latimer and Ridley, perched on their Gothic memorial, presided over a confused area of cab ranks, bicycle parks and subterraneous public lavatories. To the left, and closing the vista of Beaumont Street, Worcester College with its staring clock kept a sort of Cyclopean guard upon the learned of the University, as if set there to prevent their escaping to the railway station.

All this was familiar to Mr. Bultitude. But it is proper in a scholar, thus emerging from his cloister, to survey the chaotic life of everyday in momentary benign astonishment. Few, in point of fact, neglect this ritual. Mr. Bultitude, having performed it punctiliously, turned left, rolled sideways to give a wide berth to a plunging young woman in a B.A. gown—Mark Bultitude was a renowned misogynist—and proceeded to propel himself laboriously forward. Mr. Bultitude's form was globular and his legs were short; he had much the appearance of a mechanical toy designed to exploit the force of gravity upon a board or tray judiciously inclined; only he never seemed to enjoy the good fortune of facing a down gradient. In conversation with his pupils, indeed, he was accustomed to refer to Beaumont Street as "that damned hill"; and to attribute to the fatigues and dangers attendant upon tackling this declivity his own indisposition to stir at all frequently from his rooms.

Witticisms of this water, reiterated over many years (which, in Oxford, can be a crucial point) had earned for Mr. Bultitude a notable reputation as a University character. Freshmen would nudge each other in the street and intimate with awe that there was Mark Bultitude. If they were scientists they cherished hopes that their own tutors (who had proved to be insufferably dull) might be persuaded to arrange for their transfer to the care of this scintillating intelligence. If on the other hand they pursued more humane studies, but were sufficiently well-born, wealthy, good-looking or clever to have some hope of making Mark Bultitude's dinner-table, they importuned sundry uncles, godfathers, former house-masters, and others of the great man's generation and familiar acquaintance, to open up some avenue to this grand social advancement. Of all this Mark Bultitude approved. He valued highly his reputation as Oxford's most completely civilized being.

And an infallible index of civilization, he maintained, was simplicity of taste. His present expedition might have been instanced as evidencing his own possession of this quality. For his intention—as he had explained to a mildly astonished porter on turning out of Bede's—was to venture as far as the Oxford Playhouse, where he proposed later in the week to provide two of his favourite pupils with an evening's wholesome entertainment. They were to see a delicious old comedy by Mr. Noel Coward. And he was now going to book seats.

Mr. Bultitude, pausing only to pat on the head the youngest son of the Professor of Egyptology (a serious child who had been spending the afternoon in numismatic studies in the University galleries), moved steadily up (or, as it may have been, down) Beaumont Street, and presently arrived at the theatre without mishap. Having secured his tickets he emerged through the swing doors and stood, puffing gently as from healthful exercise, and contemplating with evident misgiving the toilsome hundred yards of his return journey. In this posture he was discovered and greeted by an acquaintance.

"Good afternoon, Bultitude. Like myself, you are taking a turn in this mild autumn sunshine."

Mr. Bultitude, who disliked having positive statements made about himself in this way, nodded curtly. "Good afternoon, Ourglass. What some take, others give."

"I beg your pardon?" Dr. Ourglass was an obscure man from an obscure college, and understood to be wholly occupied with obscure speculations on Phoenician trade-routes. "I don't follow you."

"Then let us proceed side by side. I was suggesting that, in the vulgar phrase, you gave me quite a turn. You look wretched, Ourglass."

"Wretched?" Dr. Ourglass was dismayed.

"No doubt it is no more than a bilious attack—a passing error of the table. But to a stranger, Ourglass, your appearance would suggest dissipation."

"Dissipation!" For a moment Dr. Ourglass was indignant. Then some fuller light seemed to break upon him. "You are gamesome," he said. "This is merriment." And Dr. Ourglass laughed conscientiously. Bultitude's high accláim as a humorist had often been mentioned in his presence, and he understood that he was now in the experience of it. "Evening is closing in," he said. "But it might yet be possible to take a stroll in the Parks."

Mr. Bultitude soberly assented to this proposition—but with no sense of its bearing any application either to himself or his interlocutor.

"I mean," pursued Dr. Ourglass, rather feebly, "that *we* might take a stroll in the Parks."

The massive placidity and benignity of Mr. Bultitude's countenance gave place to looks of the liveliest consternation and alarm. "The *Parks!* and how do you propose, my dear Ourglass, that we should *get* to the Parks? Have you a conveyance? I see no sign of it."

Although the University Parks might have been reached in some five minutes' leisured walking, Dr. Ourglass was abashed. "Perhaps it is rather far," he said. "And, you, Bultitude, are a very busy man."

Mr. Bultitude, although again disrelishing being thus dealt with in the present indicative, extended an arm more or less horizontally before him, and succeeded thereby in extracting a gold watch from his waistcoat pocket. "Shall we walk," he enquired courteously, "to the farther end of Beaumont Street? Shall we even venture to turn for a few yards into Walton Street itself? . . . My dear Ourglass, you have taken to walking devilish fast —particularly up this damned hill."

Dr. Ourglass slackened his pace. "Reverting to your jest—" he began.

"Ugh!"

Mr. Bultitude's grunt might have been the consequence of unwonted exertion, or it might have been an exclamation of disgust. Dr. Ourglass interpreted it in the former sense. "Reverting to your jest upon my appearance, I am bound to admit the possibility of my not appearing quite in the—um—pink. You, after all, are a man of keen observation."

Mr. Bultitude continued to feel resentment at his companion's fondness for character-sketching. He contented himself, however, with what was virtually an imperceptible movement—that of coming to a full stop.

"And you may have noticed," pursued Dr. Ourglass, "that I am worried. The fact is, Bultitude, that my nephew has disappeared."

Mr. Bultitude, although a man of various information and extensive views, possessed a discriminating mind. That Dr. Ourglass had a nephew was information that he was disinclined to treat as momentous, and from this it necessarily followed that the nephew's vagaries could be of no interest to him. Nevertheless he looked at his companion as if in sudden naked horror. "My dear Ourglass," he said, "were you present when this surprising phenomenon took place? And was any lingering appearance left behind? A smile, for example, as in the case of the Cheshire cat?"

Dr. Ourglass took no offence at this. Possibly he supposed that Bultitude had entirely misheard his remark. Patiently he began again. "I am speaking of a nephew of mine, Geoffrey Ourglass, who came up to Bede's last year to read Physiology. This term he has simply not appeared. You have, perhaps, heard his disappearance discussed at a meeting."

The nethermost of Bultitude's chins contrived a caressing movement across his chest. It held the negative significance which a physically more reckless man would have achieved by shaking his head. "So far this term, I have managed to attend only the wine committee. We discussed the disappearance of three dozen of vintage port. A graver matter, you will agree, Ourglass, than the mere evaporation of an undergraduate, however talented and charming. But have you yourself heard nothing from this young man?"

"Nothing whatever, although it has been his custom to write to me regularly when he is away. A friend, however, claims to have caught a glimpse of him some weeks ago in a place called Milton Porcorum."

"It sounds, my dear Ourglass, as if your nephew, with all the generosity of youth, may be casting his pearls before swine. But let me set your anxieties at rest." Bultitude, as he spoke, laid an arm on his companion's shoulder and exerted an encouraging pressure—with the consequence that Ourglass almost buckled at the knees. "A young man who withdraws into the heart of the English countryside is most infallibly engaged upon one of two ventures. He is writing a play, or he is pursuing a woman. It is true that both activities are singularly futile, and that a young physiologist, oddly enough, stands no special chance of success at either. But at least the first pursuit is never, and the second is very seldom, dangerous. Whether it is a tragedy or a trollop,

Ourglass, you may depend upon your nephew's turning up again as soon as he has completed the last act to his satisfaction. . . . Dear me! We have got to the very end of Beaumont Street."

2. Although expressed with some extravagance, the fact was undeniable. Like stout Cortez in the poem, Bultitude had now toiled to an eminence from which he could survey, on his right, the illimitable Pacific of Walton Street. He eyed it with disfavour, however; took out his watch once more; and then shook his head. "I think," he said, "that we must abandon the more ambitious part of our design. For Walton Street, the hour is too far advanced. It is chill. It lacks colour. We will therefore turn left, Ourglass, and make a little tour of Gloucester Green. We will survey the buses."

They walked for a minute in silence. "This nephew of yours," Bultitude asked abruptly; "is he a schoolboy; or out of the services?"

"Certainly not a schoolboy." Ourglass beamed at this show of spontaneous interest. "And Geoffrey was certainly in the army for a time. After that, he was engaged on some other government work, and his decision to come up to Oxford was quite sudden. I greatly welcomed it, I must confess to you. His abilities have always impressed me—and I hope not entirely as a consequence of—um—avuncular partiality. He might do very well. He might even prove quite a scholarly person."

"Ugh."

Bultitude's ejaculation was occasioned, Ourglass supposed, by the effort of changing course in order to propel himself directly towards his confessed goal of the bus station. "Or if not *that,*" Ourglass pursued with innocence, "Geoffrey might at least enter politics with some chance of becoming a minister. There is our family connection, you know, with the Marquis of Horologe."

"Your connection with Lord Horologe?" Bultitude looked at his companion with quickened interest.

"Quite so. Adrian Chronogramme—as you know, the present marquis—and I were Collegers together. The 1910 election. And Geoffrey's aunt, Clepsydra . . . But, really, I must not bore you with genealogies."

"Not at all—not at all." Bultitude appeared to make one of those rapid social reassessments which even the most finely intuitive Oxford men are sometimes obliged to in deceptive cases. "I am most interested in your nephew. From all you tell me, I have no doubt that he has the seeds of scientific distinction in him. We must find him. We must bring him back. Milton Porcorum, after all, is not an *ultima Thule*. It would by no means surprise me to learn that there is a bus waiting to go there now. Come, my dear fellow—come along." With altogether surprising vigour Mark Bultitude waddled quite rapidly forward.

Ourglass followed, apparently bewildered but much pleased. The celebrated Bultitude, he perceived, had begun to treat him with altogether higher consideration. Perhaps he had recalled that Ourglass was the author of that really very searching monograph on the Phoenicians in Spain. That must be it. And now he seemed disposed to take the matter of Geoffrey's worrying disappearance as a matter of personal concern. He had plunged among the buses like a bather resolved to breast the flood. Ourglass panted after him.

There is nothing exclusive about Gloucester Green. It bears no resemblance to Oxford railway station at, say 9 a.m., when an endless line of first-class carriages rolls in, to bear whole cohorts of the eminent to their learned occasions in the metropolis—nor to the same spot at six o'clock in the evening, when the same cohorts, exhausted by the implacable pursuit of knowledge throughout the day, are smoothly decanted into lines of waiting taxis, to be carried off to a refreshing bath before the further ardours of dinner in hall and long hours of keen intellectual discussion in common-room. Gloucester Green is given over not to Heads of Houses but to mothers of families—massive women for the most part who, having been sucked in from the surrounding countryside by the lure of Woolworths or Marks and Spencer, reappear at this evening hour with bulging baskets, knobbly parcels, and jaded and vocal children brandishing glutinous confections on short sticks. For the more convenient reception of these hordes there has been erected a complicated system of tubular pens or runs, suggestive of arrangements whereby some race of gigantic and reluctant sheep might be driven to be dipped. And in and out between the pens rumble the big, red buses—extruding one horde, gobbling up another, and then winding themselves with altogether miraculous dexterity round several awkward corners before making for the open country. It was into the thick of this animated scene that Bultitude had now plunged.

Engines raced and roared; horns blew; across impenetrable masses of compressed humanity mothers separated from children, and children separated from lollipops, cried out in a dismal and surprising manner. It was a peak hour. The whole place throbbed like a mighty heart, governing with its deep pulsations the converging and diverging streams of red.

"Bultitude," called out Ourglass, "might it not be simpler to enquire at the office? I believe there is always someone—"

"No, no—nothing more fatal." Bultitude was already forcing his way into the thickest of the crowd. "To enquire there, my dear fellow, is invariably a labour *de longue haleine.*" The better to make himself heard he shouted this last phrase virtually in the ear of a large woman in front of him—with the satisfactory result that she gave ground in suspicion and alarm, and thus enabled him to press more rapidly forward. "Always make your enquiries of the drivers—or of the conductors as a second best. Particularly when it's a matter of connections. Know the surrounding counties like the back of your hand." And Bultitude continued to thrust through the press, peering up now at one bus and now at another. Ourglass, impressed by this superior *savoir faire,* laboriously followed.

"Now, here's Burford. I shouldn't be at all surprised—" With the head of his cane Bultitude tapped authoritatively on the wind-screen of the bus before which he had paused. "Can you tell me," he called up to the driver, "if you connect with the bus for Milton Porcorum . . . yes, *Porcorum?*"

The reply was lost on Ourglass, but was presumably in the negative, since Bultitude again plunged forward. Ourglass made a great effort and caught up with him. The quays of ancient Carthage, he was reflecting, must have presented just such a bustle as this. The consideration afforded him mild comfort as he was bumped about.

A bus had just moved in beside them, and Bultitude side-stepped to peer at it. "Abingdon," he said. "No good at all. Chipping Norton would appear to me to be much the most likely thing. . . . Hullo! There's Kolmak—I wonder what he has been doing? You know Kolmak, our Research Lecturer?"

Ourglass looked obediently at the crowd pouring off the Abingdon bus. First came a small mob of young airmen; then a nondescript man, weedy and pale, and with a scratch across one cheek; then, following close behind, the person called Kolmak, whom Ourglass just knew by sight. But already Bultitude had lumbered off and was conversing with another driver; in a few seconds he was back, nodding his head in placid satisfaction. "As I thought," he said. "The Chipping Norton driver knows the place quite well. And there is a connection, should we care to go by bus."

"Should we care . . . ?" Ourglass was somewhat baffled by the speed with which the physically inert Bultitude appeared to be taking charge of his affairs.

"Certainly. We will go out there, Ourglass, and investigate quite quietly. We may avoid scandal. Of course it may mean squaring the girl."

"Squaring the girl?" Ourglass, who now felt himself being propelled gently out of the crush, looked helplessly at his companion. "I am willing to believe that Geoffrey may be engaged in dramatic composition—although I have never suspected him of cherishing any literary ambitions of the sort. But your hypothesis —apparently your preferred hypothesis—of a *girl*—"

"Quite so. We must discuss it." And Bultitude gave Ourglass a soothing—and again alarmingly flattening—pat on the back. "And we might well consult Geoffrey's tutor—Birkbeck, would it be?—in a perfectly confidential manner. I think, Ourglass, that you had better dine with me. I believe Birkbeck is dining. We will plan out what is best to be done."

"Really, Bultitude, you are very kind. But I fear the hour is somewhat late for your putting down a guest."

"Not a bit of it, my dear man. At Bede's our arrangements in such matters are entirely domestic. Have you twopence? I said twopence. I'll slip into this box and give our kitchen a ring."

And at this Mark Bultitude, much as if among his other angelic attributes was that of diminishing his bodily frame at will, contrived to insert himself into an adjacent call-box. He emerged again in a couple of minutes, appearing to dilate as he did so. All his fondness for slow motion had returned to him, and he made several majestic pauses *en route* to Ourglass, much as if the latter had been a beacon on a distant eminence. "Well, that is capital," he said. "We shall meet—"

"I really ought to say," Ourglass nervously interrupted his prospective host, "that this—um—conjectural female—"

"Quite so, quite so!" And Bultitude raised a large, soothing hand—thereby causing Ourglass, now wary, to edge nimbly away from him. "Seven-fifteen in my rooms, if you please. And remember that on week-days at Bede's we don't wash or change." Bultitude paused for a moment to make sure that this parting witticism had sunk in. "And now," he said, "I must address myself to that damned hill."

3. Where Friars Entry narrows to burrow beneath the shops of Magdalen Street two women were edging past each other with prams. The wheels locked. *Zusammenstoss,* Kolmak thought—and then realised that the delay might be fatal to him. *"Bitte!"* he called out in his agitation. One of the women stared. He still hated that stare—the insular stare of the uneducated at any evidence of foreignness. But he smiled politely and swept off his hat. "Excuse me . . . but my bus . . . if I might possibly—" The woman squeezed against the side of the passage—but without any answering smile. Perhaps taking off his hat had been a mistake. And he still hated all the mistakes, worrying over them far more than was reasonable in a man endowed with philosophic views, dedicated to liberal purposes. . . .

As he had feared, it made him just too late. He jumped for the moving bus and missed. The indignant yelp of the conductress chimed with his own exclamation of pain as he fell heavily on one knee. An undergraduate stepped forward and helped him to his feet, slapped at him in a friendly ritual of getting the dust off, was gone before he could be thanked.

Kolmak stood on the kerb, breathing fast. He looked up the broad vista of St. Giles' and saw the bus disappearing. It was a Number 2. There wouldn't be another for ten minutes. His quarry had escaped him. Unless . . . He peered ahead to the cab rank—the one in the middle of the road, in front of the Taylorian. It appeared to be empty. Besides, you could not do such a thing in Oxford. You could not conceivably say to a taxi-driver "Follow that bus." It would be ridiculous. A group of students—of undergraduates—might do it. Then it would be what is called a "rag." But a *Docent* who acted in that way would be judged mad. Many of them, for that matter, *were* mad. But in their own English way. . . .

Caught out by himself in mere dreaming, Kolmak jerked into movement. It was intolerable that he should be baulked in this way. Getting off the Abingdon bus, he had had the fellow virtually in his grasp. And now he was gone again. Was it worth while taking the next Number 2, going as far as the terminus, and then prowling a waste of suburban roads on the off-chance of once more picking up the trail? He joined the queue that was forming again at the bus stop. No—it was no good. There was nothing to do but go back and report failure. As he slipped from the line of patiently waiting people he thought that several looked at him curiously. Perhaps it was "bad form" to change your mind in such a matter. Kolmak walked rapidly off, clicking his fingers—an involuntary gesture to which he was driven when under some burden of embarrassment.

Threading his way through the crowd in Cornmarket Street, Kolmak thought of the Kärntner-Strasse. The jostling around him faded as he walked. He was in the Cafe Scheidl with a girl for a Dansing. Or—what was yet more delightful—he was there alone and had taken his favourite paper from the rack; had carried it, like a flag half-furled about its handle, to where his cup of coffee awaited him, dark and strong under its little mountain of whipped cream, and flanked by its equally delicious glass of the marvellous *Wiener* water. . . . Kolmak thought of the Oxford water, chlorinated and flat, and he shuddered as he walked. Then once again his fingers clicked. He felt abased by this increasing tendency to weak, nostalgic reverie.

Kolmak pushed into shops that were almost closing; he bought food, and stuffed what he could of it into his brief-case. In the *Rathaus Keller* there had been a table prescriptively reserved for a group of *Privatdocenten* to which he belonged. If you kept to the unpretentious part things were very reasonable there. Why, Olli had liked to say, pay extra for a tablecloth? He remembered having been told that they had made Olli's death a very horrible one. . . .

But it was no good thinking of that. Undoubtedly the food in the *Rathaus* Keller had been excellent. And the place had been so snug in winter! Those tremendous Januaries, when the snow had been high along the sidewalks; when one envied the rich their great fur collars and the police the little muffs on their ears; and when he could watch, from his garret at the corner of the Ötzeltgasse, the endless gyrations of the skaters on the *Eislaufverein!*

Kolmak found he had got blindly on his bus. It was really

blindly, because there were tears in his eyes—tears of shame at all this weakness. As if he had not—great God!—something else to think about. And to-night he must go out and dine in the college. He had not done so for a week, and it would probably be accounted discourteous in him to stay away longer. Besides, it was a good dinner, and free. To save one's *Groschen* might make all the difference one day.

The bus was stationary at his own stop. He blundered out—apologising too much, too little; he was uncertain which. In front of him a terrace of tall, narrow houses exposed the absurdity of its Venetian Gothic to a bleak evening sky. Kolmak thought it horrible. The dwellings suggested to him the remnant of some enslaved population, degraded in an alien place. Still, once more he had been lucky. There was, of course, the climb. But had he not a bath, even, at the end of it? And there was an empty room! If only Anna . . .

Kolmak bit his lip, turned from the road into a small garden, and paused under a steeply-pitched porch. This was supported on a massive, stumpy pillar which was just what it seemed to be: a sketch by John Ruskin retranslated into stone by some hand devoid of artistry or care. And you had to go under the porch dead-centre if you were not to bump your head against its trifoliations. What a fantastic race the Victorian English must have been!

Kolmak opened the door and went quietly through the hall. The house belonged to the Misses Tinker, ancient women who had owned some august connection with the University very long ago. Kolmak believed that their brother had been *Rektor Magnifikus*—Vice-Chancellor—something like that. It distressed the Misses Tinker to have tenants in their attics. When they encountered Kolmak coming or going they were disconcerted; and because of this they would hold him in embarrassed conversation when it would have been mutually more agreeable to pass by with a smile. Kolmak knew that when he came in at the front door—or out of the little door that shut off the attic stairs—he ought to bang it loudly. For the Misses Tinker might then remain closeted in their own apartments and he would be able to go by unimpeded. But the bang invariably took more resolution than he possessed. He would close the door softly and tiptoe forward. And then one or other of the Misses Tinkers—who since letting the upper part of their house had taken to going about nervously on tiptoe too—would bump into him in the shadows—shadows that were pervasive since the staircases were lit only by lancet windows filled with purple and blue and orange stained glass, and nervously converse.

It was the elder (as he supposed her to be) Miss Tinker who appeared on this occasion. She was carrying a bowl of chrysanthemums as withered as herself, and her form brushed against him like a ghost's as she came to a stop.

"Good evening, Dr. Kolmak. Has it not been a delightful day?"

"It has, indeed, Miss Tinker. Have you cared to go out, at all?" Kolmak spread out the fingers of his free hand very wide, so that he would remember not to click them.

"My sister and I went out—on foot." It was always an implication of the Misses Tinker's conversation that their pedestrianism was a healthful alternative to calling out their carriage. "We walked round to Norham Road—the sunshine was really delightful—and called on Lady Bronson. You will be glad to know that we found her well."

Kolmak bowed, and there was a faint click—but this time from his heels. "I am most happy to hear it." He restrained an impulse to edge away from Miss Tinker. Because she was a feeble and useless old woman she always conjured up in his mind the image of a gas chamber. It hung behind her now, a frame to the scant wisps of her silver hair. Kolmak tried shutting his eyes—an action which the shadows rendered indetectable. But at that his nostrils took up the evocation. Perhaps the chrysanthemums had a part in it. They ought to have been thrown out some days ago.

"But Lady Bronson's sister in Bournemouth has suffered an attack of bronchitis."

"I am deeply sorry to hear it." Kolmak felt that he might now with decency edge towards the next flight of stairs. Even when he had first come the Misses Tinker had been kind. But they had been relieved when he had become "attached"—when Bede's, that is to say, had thrown some sort of mantle over him. Since then the Misses Tinker had lost no opportunity of introducing him to the other old ladies who constituted their circle of acquaintance. They had also put up the rent.

"And now I must rearrange these flowers. You will find your aunt at home, Dr. Kolmak. Until a few minutes ago I believe she was at her piano. And how delightfully she plays! My dear brother used to remark that only Ger—that only the countrymen of Beethoven really know how to play the pianoforte."

Kolmak backed upstairs, bowing. Did the old woman mean that Tante Lise's playing was a nuisance? He didn't know. Often he was helpless, not knowing whether in things said to him there was some underlying sense, some hint or warning or rebuke given under the form of irony. But at least Miss Tinker was retreating into her drawing-room. He had a glimpse of Morris paper, of spindle-legged tables and chairs, of blue and white china, and engravings after Botticelli and Luini. Probably the Misses Tinker had already begun looking after their brother while Walter Pater's sisters were still looking after *him*. Their drawing-room was in that style.

Kurt Kolmak climbed higher. Now he had indeed to nerve himself. Whether or not Tante Lise was at her piano, he must confess this failure, this pitiable letting slip of—

For a moment he thought that he heard his aunt playing very softly. Then he knew that it was only the little Aeolian harp that she had insisted on hanging up on their "landing"—the fragile contrivance of pine and catgut that he seemed to remember, all through his childhood, discoursing its alternate discords and harmonies at an upper window from which one could see, piercing the sky beyond the Hofburg, the great south tower of the *Stephans-Dom*. He opened the door separating his own domain from the Misses Tinker's and stood for a moment by the little instrument. A light breeze was blowing in through an open window and brushing the strings to a faint murmuring. He glanced out and saw—what never failed to give him pleasure—the fine lines of the Radcliffe Observatory, tranquil upon the evening. On its roof whirled an anemometer, ceaselessly propelled by the same force that was raising the low music at his side. If one looked at the anemometer fixedly, its four rapidly revolving hemispheres had the trick of appearing to slip instantaneously into reverse; to do this without stopping or even slackening the headlong speed of their revolution. And then as one continued to look they would have changed again: clockwise and then anti-clockwise in an impossible alternation. It was an image of life, Kolmak thought—life that one so anxiously scans, and that cheats one ever and anon with some apparent sign of a reversal of one's fate, but that nevertheless bears one uninterruptedly—

"Kurt—you have news, *hein?*"

Tante Lise had appeared in the doorway. He went to her quickly, took her hands, and led her back to her chair. The room that she called her *salotto,* and that was all sloping ceilings and joists awkwardly placed for the head, was crammed with the massive birch-wood furniture they had been allowed to bring away with them. Most of the pieces were so high that they had to stand out from the wall, so that the room would have been a paradise for children to play hide-and-seek in. But, Kolmak thought, there were no children. The attics were as childless as was the faded elegance of the Misses Tinker's apartments below.

"I have little news, *Tantchen.* I had thought to gain a great deal. But I have been clumsy and it has come to nothing. See, though! I have been able to buy some *salami*—and a *bel-paese* too."

She took the food in silence and set it out on the Castel Durante dishes that were a relic of her childhood in Rome. Tante Lise's father had been the most distinguished *Kunstkenner* of his generation—that and an eminent mediaevalist, the friend of Winkelmann. These plates were her only material link with that spacious past. "The police have been," she said.

"The police?" Kolmak's hand trembled as he brought finally from his brief-case a bottle of cheap wine. "For me?"

"Aber nein!" And Tante Lise laughed softly—as she used to do when, as a small boy, he had said some inept but charming thing.

"Then about . . ."

"No, no—not that either. Only about myself."

"But it is intolerable!" Kolmak had flushed darkly. "Do the ladies below, the Misses . . ."

"They know nothing of it. A most polite man came—an official of the police, but in ordinary clothing. I gave him *Funf-Uhr-Tee.*"

"You gave him tea!" Kolmak stared at his aunt in mingled reproach and admiration.

"But certainly. Do not forget that I am required to report myself. This official's visit was to spare me that on this occasion. It was a courtesy, an act of consideration due, doubtless, to your *Stellung*—your new position." And Tante Lise regarded her nephew with affectionate admiration. She had a high sense of what his abilities had gained him at Bede's. *"Jawohl, Kurt, du bist nicht schlecht gestellt!"*

But he saw that her eyes were anxious and questioning, and he sat down heavily. "I do not know that I shall keep the *Stellung*. It may be that I shall seek employment elsewhere."

"Elsewhere?"

"With *them.*"

She sprang up. "Kurt! What can you mean?"

"It may be the only way."

"But you know nothing of them."

He laughed wearily. "That is the point, is it not?"

Tante Lise was silent for some moments. Taking the *salami* to the large cupboard in the eaves that served as her kitchen, she began to cut it into slices, paper thin. Kolmak rose, cleared a table of its litter of music, laid out mats and dishes. His aunt reappeared. "But are you not dining with the *Professoren?*"

He put a hand to his forehead. "I forgot."

"You must go. It is advantageous to become more familiarly acquainted with the other *Professoren.* Moreover it is an intellectual stimulus such as I cannot afford you. Do not hurry home."

Kolmak nodded obediently and went out to wash. It was something to have a bathroom. When he came back Tante Lise was standing before the empty fireplace—and so placidly posed that he suspected she had been weeping.

"Kurt, there are always the police."

"No! Certainly not!" And he made a violent gesture. "A hundred times, no!"

"This man who came to-day. He was not courteous merely. He was kindly—understanding. He would not take a brutal view. . . ."

"You do not understand. There is nothing personal in these things. It is all a machine. Your kindly and understanding man would do what some regulation commanded him."

She sighed. "But if there is real danger for . . ."

"We do not know. We cannot yet tell. Give me a little time."

"And to-day? You hoped much of it."

"I will tell you when I return. Perhaps I have taken too gloomy a view of its failure. Certainly there is one little thing that I have learnt. Yes, I will tell you what will surprise you!"

He was boasting—almost meaninglessly, as when he was a child. "And I must go. They will be expecting me."

"Of course they will." Tante Lise was practised in providing reassurance at this moment. "They looked forward—your colleagues—to your contributions to the discussions. They recognise your great authority in your own field. Remember to smoke a cigar. Whatever your ill-success to-day, you have striven hard, I know; and have deserved it. Shall you be speaking to Mr. Bultitude?"

Kolmak looked at his aunt in surprise. "To Bultitude? I

suppose I may—though he is not always very approachable."

"Then tell him about Uncle Nikolaus."

"About Uncle Nikolaus! But why . . ."

"It is something that I observed about Mr. Bultitude when we spoke together at your Provost's party. Remember I am a judge of men."

Kolmak was uncomprehending. But again he nodded obediently. Then he turned to go.

"Kurt—you are forgetting your robe."

"My gown, Tantchen."

He smiled, kissed her on the brow, picked up the black M.A. gown from a chair and went out of the room, closing the door behind him. The Aeolian harp was still murmuring. He shut the landing window, for the breeze was now chill from the advancing autumn night. The music died away. He peered out, and could just distinguish the tirelessly turning anemometer on the Observatory. But the optical illusion would not work in the dusk.

Kolmak tip-toed downstairs. A door opened below. One Miss Tinker or the other would be there—perhaps, Kolmak thought, she would be remembering her brother, a young don with a gown over his arm, going out to dine with Walter Pater in Brasenose long ago.

4. Routh did not know where his new pursuer had picked him up. He had thought of Oxford as a collection of colleges and a row or two of shops, and as a place where everybody went about in a sort of uniform, so that one might be awkwardly conspicuous in ordinary clothes. And he had somewhere read that there were officials of the University who might stop you in the street and ask your business, and who had the power to have you turned out of the place if they didn't like you. He wished he had got to Reading, which was the sort of town he earned his living in and understood.

But the bus station reassured and comforted him. There was

the sort of crowd in which no one could look at him twice. All the same, London would be better. He might get a long-distance bus from this very spot. He could get off as soon as it reached the network of the Metropolitan Railway—at Edgware, say, or Hendon. After that, and barring extreme ill luck, his safety would be absolute. There were half-a-dozen places where he could confidently go to earth.

First, though, he must get something to eat. He had been through more than any man could sustain on a couple of sausage rolls. If he had had something solid inside him he would never have let his fancy run away with him over those two nuns. Routh looked about him and felt that, except for his empty stomach, he was master of himself. He went over to an enquiry office and learnt that there was a coach to London in an hour. At a corner of the bus station he found a pub that was just right for him—unpretentious but putting on a square meal. He forced himself to eat this slowly, and he drank no more than half a pint of bitter. Nothing had ever tasted so good, and as its warmth coursed through him his mind found release from its late tensions in pleasing fantasies. One of these was particularly satisfying; it presented a vision of Routh rubbing Squire's face savagely and repeatedly in gravel. But presently Squire's head turned into a lion's, and Routh was constrained to believe that he had been dreaming. For a moment of panic he thought he might even have missed his bus. His watch, however, reassured him that it could have been no more than a five minutes' nap. He paid his bill and went out.

He was still sleepy. The evening air had turned chill, so that he shivered. But it quite failed to wake him up. He looked around him, heavy-eyed. The broad expanse of Gloucester Green was now much less crowded, and his glance fell on a man standing near the middle of it and looking towards him. Routh had seen the man before; had seen him just as he got off the bus from Abingdon. There could be no mistake. The man was foreign-looking and noticeable. But of course it might be pure chance that he was still hanging about. Perhaps he too happened to be waiting for the London coach.

At least he could put the thing to the test at once. He walked off and turned a corner. The façade of a cinema, islanded between two streets, was now before him. He rounded this, as if to stare idly at the posters with which the farther side of the building was plastered. And out of the corner of his eye he saw the foreign-looking man, now affecting to peer into the window of a confectioner's shop across the street.

Routh turned, and this time walked away as rapidly as he could. When he had gone fifty yards he looked over his shoulder. The man was just behind him.

Routh knew very well what he ought to do. He was still on the fringe of the bus station, which showed no sign of becoming denuded of drivers, conductors, policemen and substantial numbers of the public. He ought to stand his ground, get on his bus when it came in, and travel on it, as he had planned, to London. There, still moving with a crowd, he would get himself a taxi and vanish. But Routh, as all this revolved itself in his head, walked on. He knew he was being a fool. He knew that he was allowing himself to be driven off his own best line of retreat. But he was powerless to stop and stand. And suddenly the truth of his own position came to him. He was on the run.

They had got him on the run. The battle, essentially, was a battle of nerves—and he was losing. His mind flashed back over the afternoon and he saw the shocking significance of the clean break he had managed to make in the prefab, and in the bus blindly boarded for an unknown destination. If they could pick up so swiftly after a check like that, if they could be on top of him like this the moment he set foot down in Oxford, his defeat seemed fated. They were invincible.

And once more the symptoms of fear began to operate upon Routh's body. The last enemy, he knew, would be sheer fatalism; would be a disposition to turn flat round and walk limply into his enemies' hands. Gloucester Green was now a nightmare to him, and he turned sharp out of it through the first means offering—a lane that narrowed before him and turned into a mere footpath between commercial buildings. From in front came a hum of traffic on what he guessed must be a principal street of the city. If he could dash out there and swing himself upon a moving bus . . .

He broke into a run, swerved between two women who were approaching each other with perambulators, and was on the street. There was only one bus. It was stationary. But the last of what had been a line of waiting passengers were boarding it, and in a moment it would be moving. Routh glanced behind him. His pursuer was hard upon him, but seemed to be momentarily entangled with the prams. Routh ran for the bus and jumped on. As it moved off the foreign-looking man emerged and jumped for it too, but missed and fell. For a moment Routh had the happiness of looking down at him malignantly in the dust. Then the conductress pushed him off the platform and he tumbled into a seat just inside. For the second time within a couple of hours he was trundled off for an unknown destination.

Routh closed his eyes, the better to take stock of his situation. That he had once more shaken off his relentless pursuers seemed too good to be true. Nevertheless it was a fact. The foreign-looking man could hardly have had a car in waiting; otherwise he would surely have taken up the chase in it instead of jumping for the bus. So at the worst Routh had five or ten minutes start. It was not much, but if he used it cleverly it would yet save him. And suddenly he knew what he would do. He would make no attempt to get back into the centre of Oxford. Rather he would keep a look out for a suburban garage—the kind that is almost certain to have a car or two for hire. He would go in, take care to keep out of observation from the road, and ask for a car to take him straight out of Oxford. Hiring a car would be expensive, but he had the money and a bit over in his pocket, and it would be worth it. With his eyes still closed, Routh put his hand to his breast-pocket to feel the wallet in which he kept all his cash.

He seemed to go dead cold all over. The wallet was gone. He must have left it behind him when he emerged so sleepily from the pub where he had fed. There was nothing left in the pocket except the thin fold of paper that was Formula Ten. He had not even the twopence that would buy him a ticket on this bus.

Routh opened his eyes again. Planted opposite to him was Squire.

5. The double shock was too great. Routh gave a strangled cry. The effect of this was unexpected. Somebody sitting next to him took his hand and shook it warmly. And from out of a great darkness he heard himself addressed in a high and quavering voice. "My dear Carrington-Crawley, how delightful of you to recognise me!"

The momentary black-out cleared, and Routh saw Squire leaning forward to listen, and at the same time gazing at him stonily. His hand was still being shaken—with surprising vigour in view of the fact that the person concerned had all the appearance of a centenarian. A second before, Routh had felt that he would never be capable of intelligent utterance again. But now words came to him from nowhere. "But of course I recognised you, sir! In fact I was keeping a look out for you."

Thet centenarian gave a crow of delight. He had a spreading white beard, and his only other distinguishable feature was a pair of bright eyes twinkling behind steel-rimmed glasses. "Splendid—splendid, my dear Carrington-Crawley! Perhaps you even might have time to pay a call?"

Routh took a deep breath. "Thank you," he said. "That is just what I was on my way to do."

At this the centenarian crowed again, dived into a pocket, and produced a shilling which he flourished in the air before him. "My man," he cried to the conductress, "two fares, if you please, to Rawlinson Road."

Routh took a sidelong glance at the centenarian, who was now counting his change. Presumably he was a professor, and in that case Carrington-Crawley had perhaps been one of his students. Anyway, that would be the best guess upon which to proceed. But Routh had the wit to realise that it was little use his calculating and planning the right things to say. He knew far too little about the ways of this place for that. He must simply proceed on impulse, and trust to the result's being as happy as his first two utterances had been. And impulse now prompted him to take the lead. "By jove, sir," he said, "it's a great many years since we met."

The centenarian nodded vigorously. "My dear boy," he chirruped, "I think I am enjoying my years of retirement. I think I know how to use them—to use them, I say, my dear boy—to use them!"

"I'm quite certain that you do."

"But I look back on my final few years of teaching with particular pleasure, particular pleasure, particular pleasure. I look back on them with particular pleasure, I say."

Routh wondered how much the old man was really off his rocker. His voice was shrill and commanding, so that several people turned round to glance at him. But none of them appeared to think him anything out of the way. Even the conductress, on being addressed as "my man," had not shown any surprise. Perhaps he was a well-known character about the place. Or perhaps it was just that his sort were the regular thing here.

"And your own year, now—your own year, your own year. Some remarkable men—remarkable men, I say. Todhunter, for example. A most distinguished career—yes, a most distinguished career."

"Ah," said Routh, "Todhunter—we all expected it of him."

"Expected it, you say—expected it, expected it?" And the repetitive old person turned sideways upon Routh and stared so hard into his face that it appeared inevitable that all must be lost. "Expected it?" The old person's voice expressed extreme indignation. "Expected it of that shocking little drunk?"

Routh's heart sank. "We thought he had it in him, all the same, sir."

"You astonish me." And the centenarian looked about the bus, as if this announcement ought to be of very general interest. "You astonish me, Carrington-Crawley. But, no doubt, you knew each other best, knew each other best . . ." The old person's asseverations died away in a diminuendo, and for some moments he remained silent in what appeared to be a sombre reverie. Routh nerved himself to look again at Squire. The bus was crowded, but he judged it not impossible that his enemy might simply hold it up at the revolver's point and then hustle him into some high-powered car hovering behind. In that case . . .

"When did you last see Carrington-Crawley?"

Routh jumped. "Carrington-Crawley?" he repeated blankly.

The centenarian nodded impatiently. "Carrington-Crawley, I said, Carrington-Crawley. When, my dear Todhunter, did you last see Carrington-Crawley?"

Routh's head swam. "I can't quite remember," he said. "But it was a good long time ago."

"Precisely!" the centenarian was triumphant. "Nobody ever sees Carrington-Crawley. Precisely, precisely, precisely."

There was a silence in which Routh felt that something further was expected of him on this topic. "Of course," he said, "Carrington-Crawley was always a retiring fellow."

"Retiring?" The centenarian was momentarily at a loss; then he broke into a ghostly but unrestrained laughter. "Very good, Todhunter, my dear boy—very good, very good. Retiring, indeed! Tcha! Disagreeable young poseur that he was! But here we are, we are, we are. Come along, along, along, I say, along."

At this moment, and while Routh's ancient friend was preparing to hoist himself to his feet, Squire acted. The seats facing each other at the rear of the bus each had room for three people, and beside Routh a place was now empty. Squire rose, slipped into it, leant across Routh, and addressed the centenarian—and at the same moment Routh felt something hard thrust into his ribs. "Excuse me, sir, but you are mistaken in supposing this to be a former pupil of yours. He is, in fact, a friend of mine who has recently suffered a nervous breakdown, and we are getting off together at the stop after your own."

"Rubbish, sir!" The centenarian had risen to his feet and was regarding Squire with the utmost sternness. "Stuff and nonsense! Do you think I don't know my own old pupils? Do you think I don't know Rutherford here, of all men—a student who was genuinely interested in the *Risorgimento*—in the *Risorgimento,* I say, the *Risorgimento?*"

"You are quite wrong. My friend is nervously disturbed and extremely suggestible. And his name is certainly not Rutherford."

The bus was slowing to a stop. Routh felt what must be Squire's revolver digging yet harder into his ribs, and he was frozen beyond the power of act or utterance. The centenarian, however, proved to have decided views on how this sort of thing should be met. He raised a gloved hand in front of Squire's face. "Rascal!" he said. "Are my grey hairs—my grey hairs, I say—to be no protection against public impertinence? I pull your nose." And suiting the action to his words, he pulled Squire's nose—so hard that the latter sat back with a yelp of pain, to the considerable surprise of a number of people farther up the bus. "And now, my dear Rutherford, off we get!"

Routh's ribs appeared to be no longer menaced. He got to his feet, and found it difficult to refrain from clinging literally to the centenarian's coat-tails—like a child to his mother's skirts when afraid of being left behind in some frightening place. But as he stepped off the bus his wits were working again. Would Squire follow at once? Had he reinforcements in a car or van just behind? These were practical problems. But Routh also wondered how Squire had found him, and why the foreign-looking man had leapt so desperately for the bus if he knew that Squire was on the job.

The centenarian had set off at a brisk pace down a long suburban road. Routh scanned it anxiously. It was quiet, but not too quiet. Three or four young men in skimpy white shorts and voluminous sweaters and scarves were congregated round a small sports car by the kerb. An elderly man was clipping a hedge. Further along, a couple of men were high on a telephone pole, leaning back on leather slings as they worked at it with spanners. And scattered here and there were about half a dozen small boys in dark blue blazers bouncing balls or circling idly round on bicycles. Routh glanced over his shoulder. There was as yet no sign of Squire or any other pursuer. If only he could gain the centenarian's house before—

"And now about the *Risorgimento,* Rutherford. What did you think of Count Fosco's book?"

"I'm afraid I haven't read it yet."

The centenarian made a disapproving noise. "Keep up your scholarship, Rutherford—your scholarship, I say, your scholarship. Busy as you senior officials at the Treasury always are, you should find time for your purely intellectual interests."

Routh declared his intention of reading Count Fosco at the earliest possible moment. It was dawning on him that there were very considerable possibilities in this old man. Although not without abundant vanity, Routh had a tolerably accurate notion both of his own present appearance and of the social stamp he carried permanently about with him. He saw that anyone, however vaguely in contact with the external world, who took him for a senior Treasury official must be pretty far gone. He should have no difficulty, therefore, in continuing to deceive this old fool. There was money, for instance. He now desperately needed that. Well, the old fool probably kept a good deal in the house, and he ought to be able to clear him out of it without difficulty. Unless— And Routh turned to his prospective dupe. "Is your household the same as ever, sir?" he asked. There might well, it had occurred to him, be unmarried daughters, or people of that kind—middle-aged folk still sufficiently in possession of their wits to see at once that there was something wrong.

"Precisely the same, Rutherford. My dear old sister and our dear old housekeeper. My sister is quite blind now, I am sorry to say; and Annie is very frail, very frail. A woman comes in during the morning and does most of the work, yes, most of the work, most of the work."

For the first time for many hours Routh allowed himself an evil grin. This was better and better. If he failed to get what he needed by spinning a tale he could very easily clout the three old dotards on the head and take it. He was playing for high stakes, after all, and need not boggle at a broken skull or two. Particularly now that the stars in their courses had declared for him. Ruthless Routh. He looked behind him. There was still no sign of Squire.

The centenarian had stopped before a small detached villa lying behind a low brick wall from which the iron railings had been cut during some war-time drive for metal. As they walked up a short garden path Routh decided that the house was on the way to decay somewhat ahead of its owner. But what much more engaged his attention was the fact that he had gained its shelter without the observation of his enemies. For he was off the road and still there was no Squire.

"Come, my dear boy, come straight into my library—into my library, I say, my library." Routh was aware of a small gloomy hall, of a passage where his feet stumbled on an untidy rug, and of his protector throwing open a door at the end of it and beckoning him to follow. He was well into the room before he saw that it was entirely unfurnished. The centenarian stood by the single window, which was barred. He had thrown down his hat—and with his hat he had thrown down his beard as well. Routh heard a step behind him and spun round. Squire stood in the doorway.

6. "Put up your hands."

Squire had him covered with a revolver—the same, no doubt, which he had covertly employed in what Routh knew now to have been a grisly comedy on the bus.

Routh put his hands above his head. He was caught. For a moment it seemed utterly incredible. For a moment the ramshackle structure of his self-confidence stood, even with its foundations vanished. And then it crashed. They had got him, after all. For behind him was a barred window, and in front Squire's square shoulders were like another and symbolical bar across the door.

But—oddly—he no longer felt fear. Somewhere in him was a flicker of anger—anger at the cleverness of the thing because it had been cleverer than the cleverness of Routh. Apart from this faintly stirring emotion the moment held a dream-like calm and an extreme visual clarity. He saw that his centenarian stood revealed as an elderly man with the air of a broken actor. He saw that the house was untenanted and indeed derelict. Paper hung in strips from the walls; there were places where the skirting-board had fallen away in tinder; the floor, which lay thick in dust, was loose and rickety from some sort of dry rot—it would be a good spot, he suddenly thought, under which to dispose of a body. But still he felt no terror. Far away he heard a bicycle bell and children's voices, and these mingled with the limp arabesques of the peeling paper and the sour smell of decaying timber in one complex sensory impression.

"Get the van round to the lane at the back—at once." Squire, without taking his eyes off Routh, snapped out the command to his accomplice. And the man went—keeping well clear of Squire's possible line of fire.

As soon as he was alone with Squire, Routh experienced in every limb and organ the flood of fear that had in the past few moments eluded him. For he recognised in Squire's gaze a lust deeper than the promptings of the predatory social animal and the gambler for high fortune.

It was something in the way that Squire's glance moved over him. He was studying the several parts of Routh's body in anticipation of the exercise of a sheer and disinterested cruelty. Routh felt giddy. He shifted the weight on his feet to prevent himself from falling. For a moment he thought that he was really going down—that the power of self-balance had left him. Then he realised it was his footing that was unstable. A floorboard had given and sunk beneath his heel. And his senses, again preternaturally sharp, glimpsed a faint stirring in the dust immediately in front of his enemy. Routh was at the one end of a loose board. Squire was at the other. And the board would pivot half-way between them.

But the revolver was pointing straight at his heart. Surprise must be absolute. And time was short. Routh wept. Without any effort, tears of rage and weakness and terror flowed from his eyes. "You can't do this to me!" he cried—and his arms, still above his head, shook in helpless agitation. "You can't—you can't!"

Squire smiled. He was beginning to enjoy himself.

"I tell you, you *can't* do it—you can't!" Routh was now no more than a terrified and bewildered child. He stamped with one foot—weakly. Then with all his might he stamped with the other. The board leapt up. Squire's evil face vanished within a cloud of dust. His revolver exploded in air. Routh sprang forward and with clenched fist and the weight of his whole body hit Squire behind the ear. And then he ran from the room.

There would be the men working on the telephone pole, the man clipping the hedge, the group of athletes gossiping round the sports car. . . . He was out of the house and had bolted into the road. Directly in front of him, one small boy was tinkering with a bicycle at the kerb. Otherwise, there wasn't a living soul in sight. It was disconcerting. Squire would be staggering to his feet at this moment, and groping in that blessed dust for his gun. Routh had seconds, not minutes, in which to vanish from the landscape.

Although the telephone men had disappeared they had left their equipment behind them: a ladder running half-way up the pole and a litter of stuff on a barrow. Sheer inspiration seized

Routh. He grabbed the stout leather sling in which he had often seen such workers buckle themselves. Then he ran to the ladder —making a gesture as he did so to the small boy; a gesture that was an instantaneous invitation to complicity. He scrambled up the ladder, got the length of stiff leather round the pole and buckled again, and then mounted by the metal cleats to the wires. When Squire rushed from the house a moment later Routh was no more than legs and a bottom, a foreshortened trunk, and an arm working industriously as if at some screwing or tightening process.

Covertly, Routh peered down. It all depended on the boy. And Squire, glancing up and down the road, was talking to him now. The boy raised an arm and pointed. He pointed straight down the road in the direction which Routh and the false centenarian had been taking before they turned into that horrible house. And Squire at once set off at a run. Routh waited until he had disappeared; then he clambered rapidly to the ground. The small boy had placidly resumed tinkering with the bicycle. But as Routh came to earth he glanced up at him. "Excuse me," he said politely "but are you Dick Barton?"

"I'm Snowy. And thank you very much."

"I wish I had my autograph-book with me."

Routh realised that he was being addressed with irony; that the small boy shared, in fact, in the general queerness of the place. "Look here," he said urgently, "how can I—"

The small boy pointed across the road. "There's a narrow path between those two houses. My plan is that you should go down that. It comes out by my school. Hide in one of the form-rooms, if you like. There won't be anybody there."

"Thanks a lot." Routh gave an apprehensive glance up and down the road, and then began to cross it. "You'd better get home, sonny," he called over his shoulder. "If he comes back he mayn't like you."

"Oh, I'm not frightened of him, thank you." The boy's voice, which held a muted and urbane mockery, was succeeded by the composed clinking of a spanner. Routh lost no more time, but bolted for the shelter of the path pointed out to him.

It ran first between two houses and then between long, narrow gardens. He saw the school, and hesitated. But instinct warned him against these empty rooms and out-buildings. Were he the hunter, he would be prompted to range through them at sight. So he went on, and presently found himself in another quiet suburban road. He walked down it, feeling his back immensely vulnerable. It became clear to him that he was fatally without a plan. His helplessness turned on the cardinal fact that he was penniless. There was now no possibility of hiring a car as he had proposed. He was so shabby that nobody would think of driving him a long distance without asking to see the colour of his money first. If he could get back to that pub he might with luck recover his wallet. And working his way back into the city would be no more hazardous than any other sort of wandering. Indeed it was these quiet and unfrequented places that were supremely dangerous. Squire had probably begun a rapid scouring of this whole suburb in his van by now. And if that van came round a corner behind him at the present moment he would have hardly a resource left. . . . Routh glanced nervously behind him. A small closed van had rounded a far corner. From the seat beside the driver somebody was leaning out and scanning the road ahead.

At the same moment a group of people emerged from a side-road just in front of him and walked down the road in the same direction as himself. They were elderly persons of leisurely movement, and they had the air of proceeding to some near-by social occasion. There was a silver-haired man in an Inverness cape and an elderly lady in clothes that were uncompromisingly Edwardian. To Routh, who by this time estimated all mankind simply in terms of potential resistance to armed aggression, they looked far from promising. And now they had paused by a garden gate. At the same moment he heard the van accelerate behind him. He found himself without the resolution to look round again and learn the worst. The group of elderly persons were moving up the path towards a large, ugly house standing in a substantial garden. Routh followed them. And at this the silver-haired man in the cape turned round for a moment and wished him a courteous good evening. He realised that the group was a heterogeneous one, and that not all its members were known to each other. Routh replied amiably, put one hand in a trouser pocket—the pocket that was no more than a jagged hole—and affected an unconcerned stroll. One of his new companions, a man of imposing intellectual features, wore clothes very like a tramp's. His own shabbiness, Routh realised, was something that the conventions of Oxford rendered virtually invisible.

He heard the van stop and its door being flung open. Simultaneously the party to which he had attached himself turned away from the house and passed through a further gate leading to a garden on a lower level. At the end of this stood a large wooden hut. It was being used, Routh guessed, for some sort of entertainment. For on either side of a wooden porch attached to it stood a small girl in fancy dress, handing out what were evidently programmes. At the sight of this Routh's group blessedly mended its pace, as being fearful of keeping the show waiting. In another moment he was inside the hut.

The interior formed a single large room, long and low and bare. Islanded in the middle, something like a score of people had disposed themselves on forms and chairs. The farther end was shut off by an untidy but effective system of curtains. Routh slipped into a seat and glanced at the piece of paper which had been handed him. It read:

DICK WHITTINGTON
PLAY
IN AID OF
DUMB FRIENDS

Routh turned from this to his neighbours, and his heart sank. It was true that nobody seemed disposed to question his presence. The gathering was one of parents and grandparents, uncles and aunts; and in various groups and couples they were animatedly discussing the schooling, athletic ability, artistic talent, physical health, nervous stability, feeding, clothing and disciplining of their own or each other's charges. They all spoke very loud —this being necessary in order to make themselves heard above a hubbub rising from the other side of the curtains. But although an individual voice could be lost, an individual face could not. Anybody stepping into the hut in search of him would be bound to succeed in a matter of seconds.

"You *are* Martin's father, are you not?" A woman beside Routh had turned to him and was looking at him in friendly interrogation.

For a moment Routh stared at her in stupid panic. Then he nodded spasmodically, "Yes," he said, "that's right. I'm Martin's father." He might as well say one thing as another. It must be a matter of seconds now.

"I saw the resemblance at once. May I introduce myself? I'm Elizabeth's mother." The woman laughed charmingly, as if there was a great deal of merriment in this fact.

Routh half rose from his seat. "How do you do," he said—and found even in his desperation a grain of satisfaction in having done the thing rather well. Polished Routh. . . . His eye went past the laughing woman to a window close by the door through which he had entered. He just glimpsed, walking past it, the man with the red beard. So they were all after him. Probably the fellow he had knocked out in the helicopter as well.

"And in that case I have a message for you. Martin wants his part."

"I beg your pardon?" Although still automatically the thorough gentleman, Routh was momentarily uncomprehending.

"It seems you have Martin's part. And he wants it to glance at between the scenes."

"By jove, stupid of me—what?" Routh rather overdid it this time. But what did that matter? He was on his feet and dashing for the curtains. "Give it to him now," he called back. He was just vanishing through them when he sensed, rather than saw, the form of the man with the red beard darkening the farther doorway.

He had tumbled into a midget world of confused and furious activity. A horde of children, none of whom could have been older than thirteen, were making final preparations for their play. Close by Routh, a small boy in a boiler-suit was cautiously testing the cords that were to draw aside the curtains. At his feet a small girl, also in a boiler-suit, was banging at some invisible object with a hammer. In one corner several coal-black savages —presumably of the country which was going to be overrun by rats—were practising what appeared to be a spirited cannibal feast. A flaxen-haired girl in a ballet-dress waved a wand in the manner approved for the Good Fairy; another girl, dressed as a cook, was warming up at the business of banging a ladle loudly inside a metal pot; a boy with a sheaf of papers was rushing up and down shouting "Where's Miles? Miles ought to be here. Has anybody seen that twerp Miles?" And in the middle of the floor Dick Whittington—who was a boy, not a girl—sat in austere distinction on a mile-stone, surveying the scene with the resigned condescension of a superior mind.

Routh took all this in very vaguely indeed. He had no doubt that the bearded man, as soon as he had satisfied himself that the fugitive was not in the audience, would come straight behind the scenes. One or two of the children were staring at him, but the majority were too much occupied to notice. He began to circle the stage, tripped over a welter of dangerous-looking electric wiring, and almost crushed a member of the boiler-suited squad who was crouched over a portable gramophone. He spied a door behind the backcloth and made a dash for it; as he reached it and slipped through he heard an adult voice behind him.

"May I just take a look round, boys? I am the inspector, you know, from the Fire Brigade. I go round all the theatres."

There was a respectful hush on the stage. Routh ground his

teeth and looked desperately about him. He was at an *impasse.* This room at the end of the hut was no more than a storage space; it had no other exit and was lit only by two small windows impossible to scramble through. The floor was littered with costumes and effects, and there was a square wicker basket in which some of these appeared to have been stored. Routh opened it with the desperate notion of jumping in. But he realised that even an incompetent searcher—and the bearded man would be far from that—would throw open the lid as he passed and glance into it. He was about to shut it again when he realised the nature of the single article left inside. He had worked in panto himself and had no doubt about it. If only he had time—

From the stage behind him rose a clear, level voice. He guessed at once that it was Dick Whittington's. "I think if you were from the Fire Brigade you would be in uniform." The bearded man's answer was lost in a buzz of speculation. And then Dick Whittington was heard again, speaking very politely. "If you don't mind, I think I would rather you saw my father."

Already Routh had profited by the delay. His jacket and shoes were off. There was a minute of breathless struggle—the thing was, of course, far too small for him—and then he had bounded back on the stage on all fours, metamorphosed into Dick Whittington's cat. He miaowed loudly; a small girl screamed delightedly: "Miles! Here's Miles!"; he went forward in a series of quick jumps, making his tail wave behind him. Through his mask he had a glimpse of the bearded man, confronting Whittington in momentary irresolution. Routh jumped at him, and rubbed himself vigorously against his legs. The bearded man cursed softly, looked quickly round him, strode into the inner room. Routh could hear him lifting the lid of the basket. Then he was out again and had vanished through the curtains. There was an indignant shout or two, and then everybody appeared to forget about him. The gramophone was giving out the sound of Bow bells, very loudly.

"What are you doing in my cat?"

The mask was twitched indignantly from Routh's head. A red-haired boy stood planted before him in a belligerent attitude, looking him very straight in the eyes. "I'm sorry," said Routh, "I just thought it would be fun to try."

"It's not Miles—it's a man!" The small girl who had been shouting before, now cried out in high indignation. A circle of children gathered round Routh and there was a hubbub of voices.

"I never allow anybody in my cat." Miles, as he realised the enormity of what had happened, was going as red as his own hair. "And you're much too big. You might bust it."

"I'm very sorry." Routh was inclined to think that he had escaped from the frying-pan merely to fall into the fire. He scrambled hastily out of the cat. "I'd better be—"

"And who are you, anyway? And who was that other person?" This was Whittington's voice again, bringing its higher cogency to bear on the situation.

"Yes, who are you . . . Why are you spoiling our play . . . Dick's father should send for the police . . . He's bust Miles's cat . . ." The tumult of indignant voices grew, so that Routh was convinced that some of the grown-ups from the other side of the curtain were bound to come and investigate.

"Oh, he's all right. He's cracked."

It was a new and tolerant voice—and a familiar one. Routh turned and saw that he was being inspected by the young ironist who had misdirected Squire when he himself was up the telephone pole. He was still in his dark-blue blazer. He even still carried a bicycle spanner.

"Stuart knows him . . . Stuart says he's cracked . . . Buck up . . . Tell Miles to get into his cat . . . Stuart's brought a man he knows . . ." And again there was a confused tumult. Some of the children had already lost interest in Routh.

"He works on the telephone-wires." Stuart spoke loudly, being anxious to keep his own sensation in the forefront. "But he's cracked, and thinks he's something out of Dick Barton."

"Telephone-wires?" A new voice spoke from the background.

It proceeded, Routh saw, from a worried boy in glasses, who was swathed in various coils of flex. "If you understand electricity, will you please come and look at this?"

"Malcolm's electricity has gone beastly wrong . . . It's a man who's to help Malcolm with the lights . . . Get out of the way, you, and let the electricity-man past . . . Shut-up all of you—far too much row . . . curtain should be up . . . wait until the man's done the lamps . . ."

Routh was hustled across the stage and found himself inspecting a complex piece of amateur wiring. The worried boy was asking him questions. With an immense effort Routh brought his mind to bear on them. "You should do this . . ." he said. "And *that* terminal should take *this* wire . . ." He had an elementary knowledge of what he was talking about, and the boy's fingers worked deftly at his bidding.

A hush had fallen on the stage behind him. Routh drew further back into the skimpy wings. The electrician was muttering in his ear: "I say, you can stay till the end, can't you?"

And Routh nodded. "Yes," he whispered. "I can stay till the end."

The curtains parted, rising as they did so. It was a neat job that had Routh's professional approval. He stayed his hand on the switch beside him just long enough to scan the little audience.

The bearded man, having drawn a blank, was gone.

7. Apart from Dr. Ourglass, there had been only one guest at High Table at Bede's. As he had been brought in by the Provost, whose introductions were regularly unintelligible, nobody yet knew who he was.

"Provost, will you sit *here* . . . and place your guest *there.*" Elias Birkbeck, who as Steward of common-room had to determine the distribution of the company upon their withdrawing from hall to the privacies of the common-room, peered up from the card upon which he had earlier sketched out the most desirable arrangement. "And, Mark, if you would put Ourglass here on my left, and on your other side . . . now, let me see." At this stage Birkbeck, who was widely known among his fellow-scientists as a man of incisive intellect, fell into a muddle so licenced and prescriptive (for he had been known to avoid it only once, and that upon an evening when he and Bultitude had found themselves at dessert without other company) that none of those now moved indecisively about as by a tyro draughts player was at all embarrassed. Or rather nobody was embarrassed except Kolmak, who unfortunately clicked his fingers. This produced a moment's disconcerted silence, in which everybody stared at him, including Birkbeck, who realised that he had forgotten him altogether.

Birkbeck's confusion deepened. He felt Kolmak to be the only man present whom it would be positively discourteous to slip up on. The further result of this was that he found himself unable even to recall Kolmak's name. His nearest approximation to recollection was first a toothpaste, and then a hair-cream; and the horrid possibility of actually uttering one of these by way of address to a colleague so much alarmed him that he dropped his card. Moreover he had already begun to speak, "And if you . . ." he had said, with an intonation making it essential that some appellative should follow. Kolmak, very well aware of the difficulty, again clicked his fingers. At this Birkbeck had an inspiration. "And if you, Doctor, will sit *here*. . . ." It is always in order to address a learned Teuton as Doctor. Unfortunately Birkbeck's confusion was now such that he pronounced the word as if speaking German. And as everybody was now smiling encouragingly at Kolmak with the idea of being extremely nice to him he was left with the impression that some stroke of facetiousness had been intended. So Kolmak bowed, and clicked his fingers and his heels, and sat down beside Bultitude. When he got home he would recount at some length to Tante Lise the fact that there had been a joke about himself which he had been unable to follow, and she would explain that incomprehensible jokes were an Englishman's way of showing that he wished to admit you to his closer intimacy.

Birkbeck was retrieving his card, with the prospect of much further manoeuvering; the Provost had delivered himself of the long and heavy sigh which was his regular tribute to the futility of this part of the day's proceedings; Kolmak was wondering whether anybody would introduce him to the Provost's guest, who was on his immediate left. But now a group of men who were undisposed of at the farther end of the table fortunately fell into hot dispute—and having done this forgot all about Birkbeck and his card, and tumbled into whatever chairs they could grab, arguing fiercely the while. Birkbeck, thus relieved of further responsibility, applied himself to the task of getting the port and madeira into circulation. The serious part of the evening had begun.

"Plain romancing," one of the argumentative men was saying. "But of course I made no suggestion that I didn't believe it. Children should never be challenged about their fantasies. Nothing more dangerous."

"My dear Basil, how profoundly I disagree with you." A second argumentative man, whose large, pallid face gave him the appearance of something normally kept in a cupboard, stretched out his hand for the madeira as it was about to pass him. "If you really believe your son to have been romancing in this matter, and failed at once to admonish him, you have been watering that which had better wither. You have been conniving, my dear fellow, at the creation of poetry. I am surprised at you."

"But *was* Stuart Buffin romancing?" The third argumentative man, who had the appearance of an elderly gnome, ignored the enquiring Birkbeck to challenge the table at large. "Is not Basil Buffin making one of those rash assumptions for which he is so famous? Is there anything inherently improbable in what the sagacious Stuart reported?"

"Stuff and nonsense." Stuart's father spoke carefully and without vehemence—but only because he was engaged in the delicate operation of draining a decanter of port. "My Stuart's sensational report is simply the product of the cinema."

"What's that about my friend Stuart?" The Provost, who had been talking to his guest, turned to the group at the other end of the table. "What has Stuart been up to now, Basil?"

"It's like this, Provost. Just before I came into college, Stuart arrived home with a most absurd story. He claims to have been involved in an episode of melodrama somewhere in the heart of North Oxford. Something about one chap escaping from another chap by shinning up a telephone pole."

"Dear me! Does he describe the chaps?"

"Certainly. The fugitive was a rabbity type, he says; and the pursuer was a tall fellow with high, square shoulders, brandishing a revolver."

The Provost's guest looked up quickly, rather with the air of a man whose ear has been regaled in some unexpected way. Then he glanced at Kolmak on his right with a non-committal smile.

"And Stuart somehow assisted the first chap's escape. He's quite shockingly circumstantial about it all. The rabbity fugitive, he says, had a scratch across one cheek."

"A scratch!"

Everybody looked tolerantly at Kolmak, whose limited understanding of colloquial English frequently led him into inept exclamations.

"I have no doubt whatever, despite Wilfred Wybrow here"—and Basil Buffin gave a casual nod at the elderly gnome—"that Stuart has been going to too many cinemas."

"And I have correspondingly none that there is another and equally tenable explanation." The pallid man, who was a philosopher named Adrian Trist, reached for the walnuts. "Stuart was not recalling a film *made,* but witnessing a film *making.* It's always happening in the streets of Oxford nowadays. Film units—or whatever they are called—descend upon the place several times a year. They consider that we provide a good *décor.* For my part, nothing of the sort would surprise me in the least. If I turned into Beaumont Street to-morrow and was eye-witness to an atrocious murder, I should know that it was merely part of some horror being cooked up in Ealing, or wherever such things are coined and uttered."

Birkbeck paused in the operation of dissecting a tangerine. "If such an assumption were to become general," he said carefully, "there would surely be some risk of criminal elements actually perpetrating—"

"Quite so. But there is yet another possibility." It was the gnome-like Wybrow who now spoke. "What Stuart Buffin undoubtedly witnessed was an Initiative Test. It is something that the Army has lately thought up to give employment to otherwise idle warriors. Twenty or thirty young men wearing some distinguishing badge are set down, say, twenty miles from Oxford and told to reach the centre of the city without being spotted by a policeman. Naturally they behave in all sorts of *outré* ways, to the delight of the Stuarts of this world and the unspeakable alarm of sundry old women."

"Both Adrian and Wilfred have given their censures with characteristic ingenuity." Mark Bultitude, who had so far been concentrating on the consumption of a large slice of pineapple, looked solemnly across the table. "But I am myself in favour of a real detective chasing a real criminal—or conceivably *vice versa*. After all, why not? There must be quite as many burglaries committed in this country as there are either films concocted or Initiative Tests carried out. Why should not Stuart have judged judiciously of matters which Stuart alone saw?" Bultitude paused to drink a glass of port, thereby refreshing himself sufficiently to tackle a second slice of pineapple. "But perhaps there is more to tell? Perhaps the sagacious Stuart followed—'trailed' would, I believe, be the technical word—"

The Provost's guest looked up again. "Shadowed," he said.

Bultitude stared. "To be sure—shadowed. Perhaps Stuart—"

"Your son followed this man with the scratch on his face—yes?"

Everybody again looked at Kolmak, who seemed this evening to be excelling himself in oddity. The usually retiring *Kunsthistoriker* was leaning forward and eagerly scanning Basil Buffin's face.

"Well, not precisely that. But Stuart claims to have seen the fugitive again quite soon afterwards. And where? Where, my dear Adrian, was this film actor spotted afresh? Where, Wilfred, had your otherwise idle warrior deigned to display his initiative? If we are to believe my Stuart the answer is *inside a cat.*"

Bultitude let a piece of pineapple fall on his plate. "That," he said, "*is* a little odd, one is bound to admit. And who would suspect a son of Basil's of possessing so abnormal a fantasy?"

"A cat?" Birkbeck repeated the word meditatively, as if particularly anxious to conjure up before his inward eye a substantially accurate representation of what it denoted. "I don't know that such a statement makes sense. In fact I am fairly confident that it does not. This boy must have been dreaming."

"Not at all."

Everybody turned in surprise. The speaker—the only person present who had hitherto been entirely silent—was Bultitude's guest, Dr. Ourglass.

"Not at all. For your son, sir"—and Ourglass looked vaguely along the table, being not very clear as to which of the persons at its farther end stood in a paternal relationship to the problematical Stuart—"your son is in a position to bring forward—if only indirectly and through myself—a significant piece of corroborative evidence. As I was walking into Bede's to enjoy an excellent dinner"—and Ourglass looked amiably about him, receiving a glance of large admiration from Kolmak, who judged this to be a particularly happy stroke of courtesy—"as I was walking, in fact, down Bardwell Road I met a small girl of my acquaintance. Her name, indeed, is unknown to me, but we seldom pass without offering each other the time of day. As with all children—or so I should judge—her remarks are not invariably easy of interpretation. And on the present occasion she said something that I had to confess to myself at the time as leaving me wholly at a loss. But the very unintelligibility of her words only served—or so I believe myself able confidently to assert—to make them the more memorable, at least for the time." Ourglass paused, having for the moment a little lost himself in the pursuit of all this precision. "In short, what the child said was this: *'There was a man in Miles's cat.'* The assertion is, I confess a wholly mysterious one. But it does serve to corroborate the otherwise frankly somewhat unconvincing asseveration of—um—Stuart." And Ourglass, presumably feeling that he had acquitted himself not ingloriously on this the first occasion of his dining in Bede's for a number of years, took a modest sip of madeira and followed this up by making careful approaches to a grape.

"There is very evident absurdity in this." The gnome-like Wybrow, whose trade was English textual criticism, looked round the wine-table by way of carefully collecting attention for what he judged would be an annihilating stroke. "No sense can conceivably attach to the proposition that there was a man in Miles's *cat*. Cats do not admit of the reception of men. But you would be aware of no difficulty whatever, were I to inform you that there was a man in Miles's *hat*. For, even though it is admittedly true that a *hat* is no more capable of containing a man than is a *cat*, yet the idiom is a perfectly common and comprehensible one. I therefore judge, sir"—and Wybrow smiled blandly across the table at Ourglass—"that your report must be the issue of imperfect hearing and insufficient reflection."

The Provost's guest spoke. "That won't really do. It misses out Stuart, who also said something about a man in a cat. If Stuart's father thought he heard the familiar voice of his son say *cat;* and if the last speaker, at that time knowing nothing of Stuart's statement, thought he heard a child with whom he frequently talks say *cat,* then the case for *cat* is a pretty strong one."

It was in the slight pause induced by this speech, and before the textually-minded Wybrow had taken leisure to frame a suitable reply, that Kolmak turned with a polite bow to Bultitude.

"An inordinate love of cats," he said carefully, "distinguished my Uncle Nikolaus."

8. This dauntingly inconsequent remark had the effect of bringing general conversation to a close, the majority of those present plunging hastily into *tête-à-tête* and leaving Bultitude to it. Ourglass took the opportunity of addressing Birkbeck on the subject of which he was pre-occupied at this time. "Bultitude," he said, "was good enough to suggest a little conference about my nephew, Geoffrey. I am most distressed that he should not have returned to Bede's at the beginning of term. And that he should not have written to your Dean, or to yourself as his tutor, is quite incomprehensible to me."

"A letter may have gone astray in the post." Birkbeck, who judged it not easy to overestimate the typical undergraduate's capacity for negligence, was at the same time humanely anxious to say whatever might explain away the present unfortunate instance of this trait. "Or your nephew may have been taken suddenly ill—not gravely ill, of course, but *suddenly*. I hope we may hear from him any day with an explanation that the Dean may be able to accept. He's the most promising pupil I've had in years."

Ourglass's dejection was visibly mitigated by this praise. "Bultitude has formed the curious notion that Geoffrey may be writing a play."

Birkbeck considered this carefully. "But," he asked at length, "might not a play be written in Oxford?"

"That is very true." Ourglass was dashed again. "As a matter of fact, Bultitude has an alternative hypothesis. He supposes that Geoffrey may be—um—preoccupied with a woman. Perhaps he will discount that suggestion, however, when he learns that Geoffrey is, in fact, engaged to be married. And the girl, Geoffrey will have told you, is actually up at Oxford." Ourglass glanced across at the Provost's guest. "And—do you know?—I could almost persuade myself—"

At this moment the Provost, who was generally accounted an amiable man of reserved manners, favoured Birkbeck with a ferocious grimace. There was nothing out of the way in this; it was his regular means of intimating that his enjoyment of his colleagues' hospitality had now continued long enough, and that he would welcome a removal to the adjoining room for coffee. The move failed to abrupt Kolmak's confidences to Bultitude on the subject of his Uncle Nikolaus's cats; indeed this appeared to be proving unexpectedly absorbing, since it was to be observed that Bultitude, with unwonted familiarity, had now draped a massive arm over Kolmak's shoulder. It occurred to Ourglass, seeing his host thus preoccupied, that here was a fitting opportunity to pay his respects to the Provost. Balancing his coffee before him, therefore, and making his way across the room, he found himself greeted with some urgency.

"Ah, Ourglass, how are you? I'd hoped Birkbeck would have put us next to each other in there. Now—look—let me introduce my guest. But where is he? Ah—getting a cigar. John, come back here! This business of your nephew, you know, Ourglass—we must get it settled up. And John, as it happens— But here he is. Ourglass, let me introduce Sir John Appleby. John, this is Dr. Ourglass, the young man's uncle."

Sir John Appleby shook hands. "How do you do," he said. "May I say how much I enjoyed your last paper in the Journal of Ancient Geography? It appears to put Cambremer's discoveries in quite a new light."

Ourglass bowed, much gratified. "I thought when we sat down in Hall that I recognised a likeness. Am I right in supposing . . . ?"

"Quite right, quite right!" The Provost, who had at all hours of the day a great air of being engaged in the rapid transaction of business, nodded briskly. "Appleby, who is an old pupil of mine, is our young woman's elder brother. And he has come up because she has sent for him. It seems that your nephew's silence is now worrying her very much. And quite properly. It begins to look decidedly queer. But John, of course, will clear the matter up."

Ourglass, while endeavouring to hint civil satisfaction that the brother of his nephew's betrothed was of responsible and presentable appearance, wondered why he should be regarded as having particular qualifications for finding the missing Geoffrey. But this enigma the Provost illuminated at once.

"A policeman, you know. Many of my old pupils have passed into the hands of the police, I believe. But Appleby is the only one who did so in the special sense of *becoming* one. And now he's gone back to the metropolitan people as an Assistant-Commissioner."

"Dear me!" Ourglass, although impressed by this peculiar career, was somewhat dismayed. "Does that mean what they call Scotland Yard?"

The man called Appleby nodded. He had a pleasant smile, but the nod was unnervingly incisive. It made Ourglass feel as if he were a short and simple communication that had been rapidly run over and snapped into a file for possible future consideration.

"I haven't met your nephew," Appleby said, "and I hope you will tell me something about him. Your view is likely to be a more objective one than my sister's."

"I am as much worried on Jane's behalf as my own. If I may say so, she has stood up to this disconcerting and alarming incident very well. She appears to be a strong-minded girl, and I consider Geoffrey as most fortunate in having gained her affections." And Ourglass, having discharged himself of this preliminary civility to his satisfaction, peered at the Assistant-commissioner much as an anxious relative might peer at an eminent consultant physician straight from the bedside. "Do I understand, Sir John, that you take a serious view?"

"I have insufficient information upon which to form a view either way. As a mere matter of statistics, there are two chances in five that your nephew has suffered a nervous breakdown with total amnesia, one chance that he is in gaol under an assumed name, one chance that he is concealing a course of conduct that is either illegal or immoral, and one chance that he is dead."

"Dear me! Have you told your sister of these chances?"

"No, I haven't told Jane."

Ourglass was confused. "But of course not. You would naturally—"

"There was no need to. She will certainly have looked them up for herself."

"Bless my soul!" Ourglass respected the instinct to look things up; he admired persons with the ability to do this in out-of-the-way fields. Nevertheless the thought of his nephew's chances of survival being investigated in this manner by a fiancée troubled him. "This is very shocking," he said vaguely, "very shocking, indeed. But your sister is, as I say, strong-minded. There is some comfort in that."

But this was a line of reflection in which Sir John Appleby appeared to see no special utility; he looked at his interlocutor in a silence that was presently broken by the Provost.

"I had young Ourglass to dinner in his first term. He didn't seem to me the suicide type—nor any sort of loose fish either."

"Did it strike you that my nephew might want to write a play?"

The Provost ignored this incomprehensible interjection. "Adventurous, I should say—and even perhaps rash. I got the impression that he had done a lot of courting danger in his time, and found difficulty in doing without it. That's a common enough type with us here at present. Not that he struck me as a common type. I had a feeling that he was rather remarkable." The Provost's eyes fell on the elder Ourglass as he spoke, and some fresh aspect of the matter seemed to strike him. "Odd—eh? But that's how he struck me." He turned to Appleby. "And he's not a boy, you know, John. Older than this young sister of yours by a good way."

"I've gathered as much." Appleby looked from the Provost to Ourglass. "What was that you said about writing a play?"

"It was something put in my head—perhaps without great

seriousness of intention—by Bultitude, there. We were taking—um—a stroll together this afternoon. And when I told him that Geoffrey had last been glimpsed in the country—"

"Now that's very important," the Provost briskly remarked. "That's the last thing about this young man of ours that we have to go upon. It appears that a friend of Ourglass's—*this* Ourglass, that is to say" and the Provost thrust a finger without ceremony into Dr. Ourglass's stomach—"saw the young man in a car—"

"In the back of a *large* car," Dr. Ourglass supplemented, "and with several other men—"

"Driving rapidly through some small village called, I think, Milton Porcorum."

"Precisely. If my informant is to be believed, Geoffrey was last seen in Milton Porcorum. And Bultitude suggested—"

"In Milton Porcorum!"

All three men turned round. The interruption came from Kolmak. He had been standing behind them in the somewhat perplexed reception of much affability from Bultitude. But evidently he had been paying more attention to their conversation than was in the circumstances altogether proper, and now he was staring at them in some obscure but violent agitation.

"Someone has disappeared—*nicht wahr?* And in Milton Porcorum?" Kolmak enunciated this last word in a fashion so Teutonic as to add substantially to the bizarre effort of his interposition.

"Well, yes. We were talking—"

But as the Provost, looking mildly surprised, began to frame this civil reply, Kolmak appeared to convince himself that he had behaved with marked impropriety. He flushed and rapidly clicked his fingers. *"Ich bitte mich zu entschuldigen!"* he exclaimed, and bolted from the room.

"Now, that's a most extraordinary thing." The Provost contemplated his vanishing back in some astonishment. "Kolmak is commonly a quiet, retiring sort of creature, very difficult to draw out. I sometimes think that his understanding of English is negligible, and that he puts odd misinterpretations. . . ."

"But Kurt is a very good fellow, all the same." Bultitude advanced, with a tread that made all the coffee cups in the room tinkle. "I become uncommonly fond of Kurt. Kurt's uncle—"

"Kurt?" The Provost was puzzled. "I never heard you, my dear Mark, call him that before."

Bultitude looked injured. "Kurt Kolmak and I, Provost, have been on terms of increasing intimacy for some time. A very nice fellow, as I say. I don't know what bit him just now. Of course he had been through a great deal of stress. There was a period when, positively, he had to tighten his belt." Bultitude, as he made this harrowing announcement, accomplished a reassuring exploration of his own waist-line, contriving with an effort that the tips of his fingers should just touch over his watch-chain. "His people were liberals, and at the same time members of the old Hungarian nobility. Indeed Kurt's uncle Nikolaus, as I was about to observe, was the cousin of a very dear friend of mine, the old Gräfin Szegedin. Did you ever know the old lady? I recall her once saying to me . . ."

The Provost of Bede's assumed a resigned expression, and Dr. Ourglass one of polite interest. But Sir John Appleby, less socially complacent, lingered only to give Bultitude a professionally analytical glance. Then, murmuring a word in his host's ear, he slipped from the room.

PART FOUR

BODLEY BY DAY

Many books
Wise men have said are wearisom.

PARADISE REGAIN'D

1. A complete alphabetical list of the resident members of the university of Oxford with their addresses is unquestionably the most useful publication of the multifariously active Oxford University Press. This work Sir John Appleby paused to consult in the Bede's porter's lodge; he then emerged into Beaumont Street and proceeded to move northwards at a leisurely pace. It was six minutes after nine o'clock. Christ Church, following its immemorial vespertime custom, was in process of asserting its just hegemony of the lesser academic establishments clustered around it by the simple expedient of uttering a hundred-and-one magistral peals on an enormous bell. Abstraction grew upon Appleby as he walked. He was doubtful of the whole enterprise to which he had agreed to lend himself.

He was much attached to his youngest sister—only the more so because of the wide disparity between their ages. And Jane, very understandably, was in great distress over the disappearance of the young man to whom she had recently engaged herself. But Appleby had never met Geoffrey Ourglass, and he had a professional distrust of people who vanish. Follow up the sort of person who disappears and you will seldom come upon anything either very exciting or very edifying. Frequently you will be performing no kindness to those whom he has disappeared from.

And Appleby was equally doubtful about having come in upon the matter himself. Already, and from afar, he had seen to it that much in a quiet way had been done—so much, indeed, that the continued complete blank that Geoffrey Ourglass's fate presented had begun to take on an aspect of beguilement, of technical challenge, that he had, quite simply, found it very hard to resist. It had been reasonable enough to come up and stay for a night or two by way of fulfilling a promise to his old tutor, now the Provost of Bede's. And it was equally reasonable to employ the occasion for finding out a little more about Jane's young man. But he rather regretted the drift that the affair had taken in common-room that evening. A fairly substantial acquaintance with the academic classes had not altogether freed him from an early persuasion that dons are by nature so many gossiping old women. And he foresaw the Ourglass affair as possibly gaining more notoriety than he was at all inclined to welcome either on his sister's behalf or his own.

On the other hand— And now Appleby quickened his pace. For it was just possible that he had come upon something of real significance right at the start. It was just possible that this Geoffrey Ourglass was authentically the victim of something other than his own weakness or folly. For Jane's sake Appleby hoped that it might be so. And, after all, he had nowhere come upon any suggestion that the young man was either foolish or weak. These were not characteristics that would attract his sister. Moreover the qualities which the Provost had suspected in the young man had been those of adventuresomeness and rashness. It was perfectly conceivable that these might have led him to press into some situation more hazardous than healthy, and to do this from motives that were wholly reputable. And Appleby thought of a certain graph—one of many graphs in a file that never left his desk in New Scotland Yard. It bore a curve that required explaining. Perhaps he was walking in the direction of an explanation now.

And this must be the place. He had turned down a side-road, passed through a small garden and presented himself before a tall and narrow house of which the arched and carved windows were just visible beneath the night sky. He rang the bell. After rather a long wait a light flicked on above his head, the door opened, and he was confronted by a silver-haired old lady swathed in the faded magnificence of a large Paisley shawl. Appleby took off his hat. "Is Dr. Kolmak at home?" he asked.

The old lady found it necessary to give this question a moment's consideration. "Dr. Kolmak *came in,*" she said, "a few minutes ago. But whether he is *at home* it is not, of course, for me to say."

"Ah," said Appleby.

"Dr. Kolmak is my tenant. Or rather he is my sister's tenant. We had thought of a system of bells"—and the old lady made a vague gesture into the darkness—"that would make the position *quite* plain."

"An excellent idea. It would save you inconvenience."

"Precisely." The old lady appeared delighted with the perceptiveness of this reply. "But tradesmen are so difficult nowadays. Lady Bronson has a system of bells. They were installed, however, by her nephew, who is interested in electricity and magnetism. I *ought* to have such an interest myself"—the old lady was apologetic—"since my dear father was a close friend of Professor Farraday's."

"That is most interesting."

"Yes." The old lady seemed a little doubtful on this point. Her communicativeness, it seemed to Appleby, was occasioned less by a preoccupation with the history of science than by uncertainty as to the correct technique for dealing with Dr. Kolmak's visitors. It was to be presumed, therefore, that these were of comparatively infrequent appearance.

But now the old lady had an inspiration. "The name?" she said interrogatively.

"Sir John Appleby."

"Please come in. These things are a *little* difficult. Lady Bronson finds them *very* difficult. But then *her* tenants are *undergraduates.*"

"Ah, yes—a different matter."

"Precisely. Dr. Kolmak—who is of very good family—has

recently been appointed to a lecturership at Bede's. We hope that he may be elected into a fellowship quite soon. There is *one* step."

Appleby successfully negotiated the step and found a precarious foothold on the excessively slippery tiles of a dim, high hall. It was furnished with a number of impossible chairs designed to turn into suicidal step-ladders, and embellished with large photographic views of the Roman forum.

"The Kolmak domain—or should I say demesne?—is at the top of the house. Do you know that dear Frau Kolmak's pianoforte had to be taken in through the roof? She is an exquisite *artiste* and her playing is a great delight to us. Except, that is, when it clashes with my sister's Devotional Group. Will you please to come upstairs? I am afraid that the carpet is a little *tricky* in places. To be quite frank, there are *holes* in it, and no doubt it should be replaced. But my sister and I are too attached to our dear, shabby old things to be at all willing to part with them."

Appleby contrived a murmur indicative of the conviction that such sentiments are the prerogative of highly-bred persons of fine tastes. "The Kolmaks, then," he asked, "have not been with you long?"

"A *little* less than two years."

"And besides Dr. Kolmak himself there is just Frau Kolmak?"

"Just so. And you no doubt know that she is really a *Baronin*. But since coming into *exile* she prefers the simpler title. It is indicative of her exquisite *Gemütlichkeit*." The old lady produced this word with a fine confidence which quite made up for its being not wholly apposite. "We are even fonder of Dr. Kolmak's aunt than of dear Dr. Kolmak himself."

"But you have never met other members of the family?"

"I have not had that pleasure. There was some question, indeed, of our receiving another member of the family—a female." The old lady paused significantly. "I must confess that my sister and I were a *little* anxious. The lady's relationship was, somehow, never very clearly *defined*. And with foreigners—particularly, I fear, *aristocratic* foreigners—one is never quite—" The old lady paused again, and evidently decided that this sentence had better be left in air. "But the proposal seemed to 'fade out' (as Lady Bronson's nephew is fond of saying) and I think some other arrangement must have been made. *One* more flight, and then I can simply *set you on your way.* . . . But here is my sister."

On a landing of modest proportions but lavishly mediaeval suggestion there stood another silver-haired old lady in another faded Paisley shawl. Appleby's conductress paused. "My dear," she said, "let me introduce Sir John Appleby, a friend of Dr. Kolmak's. Sir John, this is my sister, Miss Tinker."

Miss Tinker bowed to Appleby. "May I introduce you to my sister, Miss Priscilla Tinker?"

Appleby suitably acknowledged the propriety of these proceedings. The landing was small and cluttered on one side with an enormous carved chest and on the other with a row of *prie-Dieu.* These latter had something the air of cabs waiting in a rank, and were no doubt brought into requisition during meetings of the elder Miss Tinker's Devotional Group. Meanwhile, they made things decidedly cramped. And this effect was enhanced by walls crowded with large Arundel prints themselves illustrative of uncomfortably populous fourteenth-century occasions. Perhaps it was the Gothic suggestiveness of the *décor* that gave Appleby an alarmed sense of the immateriality of the Misses Tinker. They were crowded up against him, and he felt that a single incautious step might take him clean through one or other of them. This would be interesting, but distracting—and he had better concentrate on the matter in hand. He therefore edged politely towards the next flight of stairs.

"I hope that you may not find Dr. Kolmak unwell." It was the elder Miss Tinker who spoke. "He came in only a few minutes ago, and I happened to pass him on the stairs. We had not the few words of conversation that commonly pass between us. He appeared to be in some distress. I hope it is not an infection. There is not at present any epidemic in Oxford. But we heard only this afternoon that there is a great deal of bronchitis in Bournemouth."

Appleby was now climbing. "Please don't trouble yourselves further," he said. "I'll go straight up." And he mounted, two steps at a time—aware of the Misses Tinker watching him still from below, like disappointed sirens whose singing has had only a momentary effectiveness. He realised that they would certainly be there when he came down again.

On the next landing there was a door apparently enclosing an upper staircase. Appleby knocked, but without result. He opened it and climbed higher. There was another doorway, at which he knocked again and waited. From within he could hear strains of music—a faint and uncanny music. If this was the *Baronin* discoursing on the pianoforte that had to be taken in through the roof then there could be no doubt that she in her turn would prove as ghostly as the old ladies below. The door opened and he was confronted by a handsome woman, old but very erect, who it was safe to guess must be the aunt of the man he was after.

"Good evening," he said. "Is Dr. Kolmak at home?"

The woman eyed him steadily for a moment without reply. Then she opened the door wider and in a manner that invited him to enter. The music came from an Aeolian harp set in a window.

"My name is Appleby, and I was dining in company with Dr. Kolmak this evening. He left before I had an opportunity to talk with him, which I am very anxious to do."

The woman inclined her head. "My nephew," she said, "is unwell."

"I am very sorry." Appleby's tone was mild and conventional. Then suddenly he rapped out: "You are alone with him here still?"

The unlikely shot went home and the woman's eyes momentarily widened in alarm. But she spoke composedly. "If you will come into my *salotto,*" she said, "we will talk together." And she led the way from the tiny landing on which they had been standing into a massively furnished attic room. "Please take place," she said.

Nehmen Sie, bitte, Platz. . . . Frau Kolmak, like her nephew, appeared to preserve a good deal of native idiom. Appleby sat down. But his hostess for a moment remained standing. "Are you, too, of the police?" she asked.

"Yes." Appleby was startled, but saw no occasion for prevarication.

"Then, if you will excuse me, I must put on the kettle."

"I beg your pardon?" Appleby supposed either that he had not heard aright or that, this time, Frau Kolmak's English had gone very markedly astray.

"Not on many days has one the pleasure of twice making tea for the English police . . . it is Mr. Appleby?"

"Sir John Appleby."

"*Ach!* This afternoon it was Detective-Inspector Jones—which sounds much grander, does it not? But you too shall have tea, Sir John."

And Frau Kolmak applied herself to a spirit-lamp. Appleby, unresentful of mockery, watched her composedly. She had considerably more address, he reflected, than her nephew. "You are very kind," he said. "I shall be delighted to have tea."

Frau Kolmak set a kettle on the lamp and turned back to him. "It would be difficult to express to you," she said, "the charm of giving tea to a policeman; the charm—to put it in another way—of being in no expectation of being kicked by him."

"I see." Appleby looked at his hostess soberly.

"The officer who came this *Nachmittag* had a routine task. Unlike my nephew, I am legally of Hungarian nationality. It makes, at present, some difference in the formalities. But you, I judge, have nothing to do with that. You, who are of *die bessern Stände,* have come to control the police from the army, *nicht wahr?*"

"Oh, dear me, no." Appleby was rather indignant. "I joined the police as quite a young man, and right at the bottom."

"That is most interesting." For the first time Frau Kolmak

looked faintly puzzled. Her urbanity, however, remained unflawed. It was, Appleby judged, too unflawed altogether. Frau Kolmak was really under considerable strain. Nevertheless her hands, as they busied themselves assembling what was evidently her formal tea-equipage, were perfectly steady. And presently she spoke again. "Kurt talks very well—when his shyness is overcome, that is to say. So I am not surprised at your seeking his conversation. You, too, are interested in the art of the *trecento?"*

Appleby considered. "It is an interest of my wife's," he said conciliatingly. "I'm afraid I myself know very little about it."

"Nevertheless you have followed Kurt home for the sake of his talk—knowing that he is *von grosser Unterhaltungsgabe?* What you have in mind is a purely social occasion?" Frau Kolmak quietly poured tea.

"I want your nephew's help in an investigation—a police investigation, in point of fact, although my own interest in it is personal and not official. It is a question of somebody's having disappeared."

The small silver strainer which Frau Kolmak was manipulating tinkled against a tea-cup. "Of a man's having disappeared?" she said.

"Yes, a young man—and, as it happens, an undergraduate at your nephew's college."

"A young man from the *Studentenschaft* at Bede's? But how can Kurt—"

"Guten Abend, mein Herr."

Appleby turned round. Kolmak was standing in the doorway—pale, and agitated to the point of being unconscious that he had spoken in German. Appleby put down his tea-cup and rose. "Good evening, sir. I think you will recognise me, although we were not actually introduced."

"Sir John Appleby." Frau Kolmak had folded her hands in her lap and was looking at them. "He has come to speak to you, Kurt, about somebody—a man—who has disappeared."

Kolmak bowed stiffly. "I am afraid I can be of no assistance to you, sir, on that score. There must be a mistake."

"That is perfectly possible, and if it is so I shall owe you, and Frau Kolmak, an apology." Appleby judged it tactful to do a little bowing himself. "Nevertheless I hope you will allow me to explain myself."

Frau Kolmak's eyes travelled from her lap to her nephew's face, and thence to a chair. Kolmak sat down. "I cannot well do otherwise," he said coldly, "to a guest of our Provost's. Please to proceed."

"I think you overheard something of this matter in common-room just before leaving it—and although it concerns somebody at Bede's I believe that it was news to you. Very briefly, a young man called Geoffrey Ourglass, who ought to be up at Oxford now, has vanished. He is, as it happens, engaged to be married to my sister Jane, who is an undergraduate at Somerville. My own concern with the situation is solely on account of this connection."

Kolmak again bowed frigidly. "We express our regrets," he said. "Our sympathy is extended to your sister."

Frau Kolmak slightly flushed. "Kurt," she said drily, "you seem quite to have guessed that Sir John is connected with the police."

"The police!" Kolmak appeared not, in fact, to have guessed the fact, for he now sat up very straight in his chair.

"Please remember that his colleagues have always been friendly to us as well as courteous."

"Tante Lise, you do not understand the danger—"

"I have understood many dangers, Kurt, *liebling,* for now a long time. I shall say nothing more, but my advice to you is as it has been."

During this enigmatical interchange Appleby conveniently occupied himself with his tea. Now he tried again.

"About this young man's disappearance we have only one approach to a clue. He is believed to have been seen in a car, driving through a small village in the Cotswolds. It is so out-of-the-way that it is very tempting to believe that his destination must have been a local one. Enquiries, however, have produced no result. I have been prepared to believe either that Ourglass was, in fact, passing through to a remote destination, or that the identification was a mistake."

Kolmak had ceased to sit back stiffly on his chair. He had leant forward, and his head was now buried in his hands.

"And now, Dr. Kolmak, I must be quite frank, and come to my sole reason for calling on you. This evening you heard the story. Or rather you heard the fact of somebody's disappearance associated with the name of this village—Milton Porcorum. You at once evinced sharper interest and marked agitation. You were so aware, indeed, of having betrayed a peculiarity of behaviour that you abruptly left common-room, and hurried home, feeling ill. Please understand that I should be altogether lacking in my duty to my sister and to this young man—who may well be in some situation of great danger—if I failed to make the most earnest attempt to persuade you to an explanation."

There was a long silence. Then Kolmak looked up abruptly. "It is your sister's lover," he said, "—her *Verlobter*—who has disappeared?"

"It is, indeed."

Kolmak passed a hand wearily over his forehead. "If you were but a private gentleman!" he exclaimed.

"If you have something to reveal, you ought to reveal it. Here is a young girl in cruel suspense and a young man in unknown danger."

"As if I had no cause to feel it!" And Kolmak looked quite wildly round the room.

"I appeal to you, sir, as a scholar—as a scholar and a humanist." Appleby too had stood up.

"Come back—come back to-morrow morning." Kolmak appeared to be swaying uncertainly on his feet.

"To-morrow may be—" Appleby checked himself. Out of

the corner of his eye he had seen Frau Kolmak make him an almost imperceptible sign. "Very well. I will call immediately after breakfast—say at nine o'clock. And, meantime, thank you for listening to me." Appleby moved to the door and from there bowed to his hostess. "And thank you, very much, for entertaining your second policeman to tea."

2. The Misses Tinker were on the landing below, tiptoeing about with rubber hot-water bottles. Appleby sustained their conversation in some absence of mind. Their brother, it appeared, had been Junior Proctor some time in the eighteen-eighties and had been a distinguished advocate of higher female education in the University. Their father had visited Germany as a young man, returned under the novel persuasion that dons ought to engage in research, and in this cause conducted sundry heroic skirmishes against both the obscurantists of Christ Church and the utilitarians of Balliol. At a more convenient season Appleby would have derived a good deal of entertainment from ladies who appeared to regard themselves as contemporaries of Mrs. Humphry Ward. As it was, he contrived to withdraw through the barrage with civil words. The elder Miss Tinker showed him out. As she opened the front door he fancied he heard Kolmak in colloquy with Miss Priscilla above. Perhaps he was explaining to her that he expected his visitor again at an unconscionably early hour.

North Oxford was already sinking into slumber. Appleby walked through the quiet streets lost in thought. The disappearance of Geoffrey Ourglass was linked—tenuously, it was true—with an unimportant place owning the picturesque name of Milton Porcorum. Between Ourglass and Kolmak there was virtually no reason to suppose any connection whatever. Kolmak had nothing to do with the teaching side of life at Bede's, and he had not the appearance of one who cultivates the social acquaintance of undergraduates. Unless there were one or two historians of art among them—and young Ourglass's interests were certainly remote enough from that—they would be no more to him, in all probability, than vaguely recognisable faces. What had interested and agitated Kolmak was not the disappearance of Ourglass, but the linking together of the concept of *disappearance* and the name of *Milton Porcorum.* It was not necessary to stare at this fact for very long before forming a hypothesis. Only the most slender observation, it was true, lay behind it. Still, it was worth holding on to and testing out. *When people disappear, one hears talk of Milton Porcorum.*

Beguiled by this odd proposition, Appleby turned a corner. Why Milton Porcorum? It was a place without significance or marked attraction, offering no unusual facilities for either a life of anonymous beneficence or a period of covert vice. From the insignificance of Milton Porcorum could there be inferred—hazardously indeed but perhaps crucially—another conclusion? *Persons whose disappearance is associated with Milton Porcorum have not been attracted into the void. They have been pushed.*

Appleby had arrived so far in this decidedly uncertain ratiocinative process when his attention was abruptly recalled to the outer world. He was making his way back to the centre of Oxford by certain quiet roads which were very familiar to him, and for some little way he had passed nobody except a single elderly man belatedly exercising a small dog on a lead. But now another figure was approaching him—or rather (what was the occasion of abrupting his train of thought) had faltered in doing so and was rapidly disappearing up a side-road a little way ahead.

That falter was well known to Appleby. He had encountered it often enough during the couple of years he had spent with a helmet and a bull's-eye lantern long ago. Instinctively he quickened his pace and turned the corner. Only a little *cul-de-sac* presented itself. And in this, dimly visible beneath a single lamp, a meagre and apprehensive man stood at bay.

Appleby was amused. It had never occurred to him that he

might still give to a practised criminal eye the appearance of a plain-clothes officer on duty. At a guess, the man was a known burglar, with tools for breaking and entering now on his person, and in thinking to give Appleby a wide berth had taken this unlucky cast down a blind alley.

But at the same time Appleby was puzzled. If he carried his tools with him, the fellow ought not yet to be abroad. The night was still too young by far. Appleby took another look at him, and became aware at once of two facts. They were facts that fitted together. The man was not merely scared or nervous; he was in very great and naked terror. And he was Stuart Buffin's rabbity fellow with the scratched face. He had been up a telephone pole and—more mysteriously—"in Miles's cat." Stuart had not been romancing. He had veritably encountered a sort of museum specimen of that grand stand-by of the popular cinema, the hunted man.

Rather as if to repudiate the charge of craven orthodoxy in this rôle, the man in front of Appleby began to scream. It was an effect that Appleby did not recall having witnessed. The man did not, it was true, scream very loudly, being temporarily afflicted, it appeared, with some hysterical constriction of the vocal cords. Nevertheless the performance was extremely displeasing, and Appleby could see no better way of ending it than by turning on his heel and marching out of the picture. This simple plan he proceeded to put into effect.

But as he walked away he found himself uneasy on two quite distinct scores. The first proceeded from a habitual sense of responsibility for public order. This wretched little man was nothing to him; nevertheless he was either in some real danger or so far gone in lunacy as to be himself dangerous to others. Perhaps therefore he should be tackled and controlled at once, however much he screamed, and whatever indignation the proceeding aroused among disturbed residents in the district.

Appleby's second uneasiness was more obscure. He had a queer feeling that the man *was* in some way part of his direct concern. Yet he could assign himself no shadow of reason for this belief. Appleby snapped his fingers in vexation—and in the same instant was in command of the hidden connection he sought. Kolmak! It was not once but twice that Kolmak had broken into other people's talk earlier that evening. The second occasion had been the notable one concerning Milton Porcorum. The first had been upon the mention of Stuart's rabbity fugitive as having a scratched cheek. And Appleby could recall now that both these interjections had possessed precisely the same quality.

He was on the point of emerging from the *cul-de-sac*. The man had stopped screaming. Appleby turned and saw that he was endeavouring to scale a wholly impossible brick wall. He watched him for some moments until he fell back panting and exhausted; then he spoke quietly down the length of the *cul-de-sac*.

"I'm not your enemy. Try to think. You are unarmed and helpless. If I want you, I've got you."

The man had turned and was standing immobile, his arms spread-eagled against the wall. He was one, Appleby fleetingly thought, who had unconsciously a sense of style, an actor's instinct. It would make an effective shot.

"There would be no sense in my standing talking like this until, perhaps, the police came along and I had to clear out. So you can see you're in no danger with me."

The man straightened himself, but said nothing.

"I do, as it happens, know something about you. You've been up a telephone pole. And you've been in Miles's cat."

The man made a sudden dash for where, in the brickwork by which he was imprisoned, he had belatedly glimpsed a green-painted wooden door. He shook it furiously. It was locked. He turned again, and spoke at last.

"You're one of them." His voice was at once high and hoarse. "You're one of them, or you couldn't know that."

"Nonsense." Appleby got out a pipe and proceeded to fill it. "One of the children told about it. The one that helped you. And look here: *he* knew about the telephone pole, but your enemies didn't. Isn't that right? If I was one of them, I wouldn't have tumbled to that yet."

"They're clever enough."

"And a lot too clever to stand jawing like this. Where are you trying to get to?"

The man hesitated. "Into Oxford. But I lost my way. I want to get into a crowd."

"Come along, then—we'll go together."

The man didn't move.

"You're in a trap there, if this *is* a trap; and you can't make matters worse by coming out. Look, I'm crossing over to the other side of the road. You can come up here and see that there's nobody else about. And then we can get you where you think it's healthy."

Appleby suited his action to his words. The road was still quite empty. And presently the meagre man cautiously emerged into it. He looked about him warily but dully, and then crossed over. "I wouldn't have believed that the old professor was one," he said. "But he was."

Appleby realised that the man beside him was played out in both mind and body. Perhaps he needed food. And certainly he needed sleep. "If we go by Walton Street," he said, "we can get a cup of coffee still at a place quite near this end."

The meagre man was glancing swiftly from side to side as he walked, like a creature moving through the jungle. But Appleby doubted whether he retained much power to descry, let alone to ward off, danger. That dash down the *cul-de-sac* had been a pitifully feeble move. The man was approaching, in fact, a state of somnambulism. His response now, although designed as truculent, was ineffective. "Who are you, anyway?" he said. "Nobody asked you to come interfering with me."

"Well, we do sometimes get what we don't ask for."

A car went by, close to the kerb, as Appleby spoke. And the meagre man's whole body quivered. "They've got a van out," he said, "and cars too. Smashed one great car, they did—and two of them ought to have broken their ruddy necks. But there's none of them dead yet, worse luck. None—see?"

"I see. None of them dead."

"The law should get them." Suddenly the meagre man's voice sharpened. "What are you, anyway? That's what I ask. Are you the police?"

"Yes—I *am* the police."

What might have been either a curse or a sob broke from the meagre man. He stumbled—lifting a knee queerly, as if he had made a wholly futile attempt to run.

"Here you are. Hot coffee, and a sandwich if you want it." And Appleby steered his captive—if he was that—to a table in the small café he had had in mind. "Your head will feel clearer, you know, when you've had that."

He fetched coffee from the counter, glancing about him as he did so. There was nobody in the place except a sleepy woman presiding over the stuff stewing in the urns, and a man and a girl in a corner, staring at each other silently and in heavy-eyed misery. It was not very cheerful. But Appleby doubted whether a more festive atmosphere would much have encouraged his new acquaintance.

"Here you are. Sugar in the saucer."

The meagre man took the coffee in two trembling hands, stirred, and drank. A couple of mouthfuls appeared to give him sufficient strength to take matters up where he had left them. "I never had anything to do with the police," he said. "They've no call to come after me."

"They haven't—not so far as I know." Appleby put down his pipe and produced a packet of cigarettes. "Smoke?"

The meagre man reached forward and took a cigarette as an addict might snatch an offered drug. "Thanks," he said. It was a word the enunciation of which appeared to afford him peculiar difficulty.

Appleby faintly smiled. With this customer he was on familiar ground enough. A little twister who could put up a genteel show among the simple, and get away with a pound note on the strength of one plausible tale or another. Appleby had often seen them, and often seen them scared—of six months, or two years, or perhaps a thrashing from some dupe's brawny husband. But he had never seen one as hard-pressed as this. Stuart's rabbit with the scratched cheek had been out in deep water. And he didn't like the feel of it.

"No," said Appleby, "I don't suppose the police have any call to come after you. But perhaps you have a call to go after them."

The meagre man looked up quickly. "I don't know what you mean," he said.

"I rather think you do. The only way out of some tough spots is through the police station. It's a bit bleak. But it's as safe as Buckingham Palace." Appleby paused. "Even," he said, "if they keep you for rather a long time. Safety. Quiet and safety and all found. . . . Safety . . . *safety.*"

The meagre man's head was nodding. "You're a devil," he whispered, "a clever devil." With an effort he looked straight at Appleby, raised his cup and drained it, let it clatter back into the saucer. "See here," he said—and his voice strove again for truculence. "What sort of policeman are you, anyway? You don't *sound* to me like a policeman. Too much the bloody gentleman, you are. A bloody gentleman up to something dirty—that's you. Well, don't come to me."

"Shall I get you another cup of coffee?"

The meagre man shook his head. His eyes were filling with tears of helplessness and rage. "Policeman, indeed!" he pursued. "How'd you like to come to the mucking station and see what they say? Oxford cop, eh?"

"Not Oxford. London."

With the effect of some tiny mechanism starting into motion, one of the meagre man's cheeks began to twitch. "You mean you're from the C.I.D.?"

"One of my duties is to look after the C.I.D."

"Christ!" The meagre man looked at Appleby for a moment with all the sobriety of conviction. Then—totally unexpectedly—he smiled. It was not a very pleasant smile, but neither was it malignant. It was a smile, Appleby knew, of suddenly gratified vanity. The little twister endeavoured to square his shoulders in their cheap padded jacket. Then he leant forward. "I'll tell you something," he whispered. "I'll tell you something to surprise your ruddy highness. I'll be bigger than you one day . . . bigger by a long way. I'll give your C.I.D. its orders—see? Yes, and the ruddy Government too."

Coffee, fatigue and a little applied psychology, Appleby reflected, will sometimes do the work of large charges of alcohol. "Well, why not?" he said. "A man can always have a bit of luck."

"You need more than luck. You need guts."

"Ah—to grab what's there for the grabbing."

"What d'you mean?" The meagre man made a spasmodic movement of his right hand towards his breast. "I haven't grabbed anything. So you needn't think it."

"Nobody said you had." Appleby rose and went over to the counter for a second cup of coffee. In his jacket pocket the fellow had something he set store by—and something he had grabbed.

"I've lost my wallet." The man spoke quickly and defensively as Appleby returned to the little table. He tapped his chest with a hand that trembled. "Left it in a pub where I got some supper. Cleared me out."

"Bad luck." He had some command of his wits still, Appleby thought. He had realised the betrayal in that involuntary movement, and he had thought up this yarn to cover it. Only—what was rather odd—he had made the yarn sound as if it were true. Possibly it *was* true. "You mean," Appleby asked, "that you haven't a penny?"

"Not a mucking farthing. And it's damned unfair." The man's voice rose in a disagreeable but convincingly authentic whine. "It means I'm helpless against them, just when it all looked like coming my way."

"It sounds just too bad." Appleby applied himself to stirring his fresh cup of coffee. When he looked up it was to see his companion glancing furtively and apprehensively first out into the darkened street and then at the lovers sitting glumly over their silent quarrel in the other corner. "About that cat—" Appleby said.

The meagre man's head swung round as if at the blow of a fist. His face was ashen. "What do you know?" he said hoarsely. "It wasn't me! The cat got on his shoulder and he tripped. The gun went off—" He fell back in his chair, and both his hands went to his throat as if to choke words that it would be fatal to utter.

"There was a gun in this affair of Miles's cat?"

"You're making me mix things." The voice was now no more than a whisper. "It's not evidence. It's against the law. The judges don't allow it."

"Never mind the judges, Mr.—?"

"Routh."

Appleby looked at his companion curiously. He was certainly pretty well through; he had handed over his name as if drugged. It was the moment for a shot that was wholly in the dark. "Routh," he asked sharply, "when were you last in Milton Porcorum?"

It was a hit. The man calling himself Routh uttered a strangled cry and made a futile effort to get to his feet. "You *do* belong to them," he whispered. "You must. You know."

"I am a policeman. I know a good deal, but I am a policeman, all the same." Appleby's voice, low, slow and clear, was like a hypnotist's addressing a man in trance. "The cats, Routh. Miles's cat. The other cat. They are both out of the bag. But you are safe with the police. Safe. We'll go to the police station and you can tell me just as much as you want to. Or they'll give you a bed. They always do, if you've lost all your money. A bed where the biggest gang of crooks in England couldn't get at you. Come along."

And Appleby got Routh to his feet and out of the café. It was like handling a drunk. The night air was chilly but the man scarcely revived in it; his feet scraped and stumbled on the pavement; his head turned from side to side blindly in an empty convention of vigilance. He would be an unsuitable guest to introduce into the Provost's lodgings, for he would provoke too much curiosity on the part of anyone who set eyes on him. Yet Appleby was determined to hold on to Routh. In some undefined way the man was a link in the chain—tenuous but perhaps vital—that bound together Ourglass and Kolmak and Milton Porcorum. The police station, then, was the thing. If Routh had no great crime or misdemeanour on his conscience, then tact, a square meal, warmth, the law in its benevolent aspect of a powerful protector, would in all probability get his story from him. Alternatively, there was the fact that he was without visible means of support and had been loitering in a manner suggesting wrongful intentions; on the strength of this the poor devil could be charged, and his background and movements rapidly investigated.

But it was a considerable distance to police headquarters in St. Aldate's, and Appleby remembered that there would still be cabs in the rank in St. Giles'. He turned left down a side-street. "Come along," he said encouragingly. "We'll cut down here and get a taxi."

Routh hesitated. "It's dark," he whispered. "And lonely. I don't like it. They may be waiting in it."

The little street was certainly deserted and poorly lighted. Appleby took a side glance at the dim silhouette of his companion, wondering what queer adventure had reduced him to this state. "I don't think we need worry about that," he said. "We're in Oxford, you know; not Cairo or Casablanca."

He took Routh's arm and gently impelled him forward. The man moved on beside him, unsteadily, but without resistance. Appleby felt satisfied. This was an odd and unexpected evening's work. But he had an instinct that it was getting him somewhere, and that he had at least a fringe of his problem under control.

At this moment Routh gave a weak cry, and for a fraction of a second Appleby was aware of himself as surrounded by figures that had sprung up apparently from nowhere. Then something was thrown over his face, and his head swam. He heard the engine of a car coming up the deserted street behind him. He smelt what he recognised as chloroform. He was fleetingly aware of having made a mistake—some ridiculous mistake. And then consciousness deserted him.

3. Like Pericles in the play, Appleby came to his senses to the sound of music. For what appeared an infinity of time it was a music of obscurely sinister suggestion. It set a problem with which his mind seemed to wrestle down long corridors. It reminded him of some careless and fatal error. For this he hunted through long stretches of labouring hours. And then it came to him. He had, through some absurd vagary of the mind, imagined himself in Oxford when he was, of course, in Cairo. This music witnessed to the sober geographical truth. It was like no music that is familiar to western ears. Rising and falling fitfully, it passed from harmony to discord and from discord to harmony . . .

Memory stirred abruptly in Appleby. He opened his eyes upon a small room into which daylight was filtering through a light-coloured blind. He was on a bed, partly undressed, and warm beneath a feather covering. Frau Kolmak was standing beside him with a coffee-pot. And from just outside came the low music of the Aeolian harp.

"Good morning, Sir John. I believe you are none the worse of your adventure—no?" Frau Kolmak set down the coffee, turned to the window, raised the blind, and appeared to take an appraising glance at the roofs of North Oxford. "Kurt will be here *augenblicklich*—in a moment. He is shaving. The possession of a bathroom is a great satisfaction to him."

Appleby sat up. "Does your nephew commonly go about the streets at night, chloroforming people?"

Frau Kolmak laughed. "You are confused. He will explain. I too am confused. It appears that Kurt has said something to the driver of a cab—something that in Oxford he judged it not possible to say. He is pleased." Frau Kolmak lowered her voice. "There are matters of which I hope that he will speak to you." She glided from the room.

Appleby sat up and drank the coffee. It seemed to him extremely good. But it always does, he reflected lucidly, when provided by persons with continental associations. Preponderantly, it must be a matter of suggestion. He looked up and saw Kolmak standing before him.

Kolmak bowed. In his prized private bathroom he had evidently shaved with the greatest nicety; he was dressed with some formality in a black jacket and striped trousers; this, Appleby conjectured, was a civil tribute to the presence in his household of a high official of the police. "Good morning," Kolmak said. "I hope, Sir John, that you are not too badly shaken—"

"I'm not shaken at all. Where is Routh?"

"Your companion of last night? He is in the little room"—Kolmak made a gesture indicating some far corner of his domain—"and still asleep. I had not realised that he was your colleague."

"My colleague?" Appleby stared, and then—a little painfully—smiled. "Well, we'll talk about that presently. Will you tell me first how we got back here?"

"With the man you call Routh there was no difficulty. He is of slight build. I got him upstairs myself. But you, Sir John, presented a more serious problem." Kolmak paused and clicked his fingers. He appeared confused. "But how clumsy I am in expressing myself in English still! I do not mean to suggest that you are a *heavy* man. Your figure, if I may say so, might reasonably be described as a spare one—is not that the word? But your height—"

"Quite so. But do I understand that you really managed to

haul me up all those stairs while unconscious? It's unbelievable."

"The difficulty was not insuperable. My aunt helped. And the Misses Tinker too."

"God bless me!" Appleby drained his coffee and swung himself off the bed. "Didn't they think it a little out of the way?"

Kolmak nodded with some solemnity. "I ventured to suggest to them that matters of state security were involved. They will be models of discretion. And discretion appeared to me to be most important. I knew, Sir John, that your position in the police did not necessarily mean that you wished any of your colleagues to be officially associated with you at the moment. This consideration guided my course of action from the first."

"I congratulate you." Appleby looked at his host in some astonishment. "And may I ask just what *was* your course of action from the first? So far as I can make the thing out, this fellow Routh and I were waylaid and kidnapped by an uncommonly bold gang of criminals. And now—here we are, hoisted up to your delightful flat through the efforts of your aunt and the Misses Tinker. If you feel at all like it, I should welcome an explanation."

"By all means. When you left us last night I was agitated, I was uneasy. The thought of your sister's anxiety was very distressing to me. There are reasons why I should feel for her. After only a little hesitation I followed you downstairs, meaning to invite you back, or perhaps to have some conversation with you on your walk to Bede's. But one of the Misses Tinker held me in talk—it is the habit of these *Damen,* as you will have remarked—and by the time that I got out of the house you were some way ahead. I hesitated, and followed you irresolutely for some way. Then you disappeared down the *Sackgasse*—how do you say it?"

"The cul-de-sac."

"Aber! How wise you English are to enrich your already expressive language from the French! In Germany our purism in such matters— But that is not the point. I waited and heard voices. I was nervous—unaccountably nervous—and I concealed

myself. When you appeared again it was with this man. For a second I saw him clearly under the street-lamp. It was a shock to me. You must understand—" Kolmak hesitated.

"That you had had certain dealings with Routh already?"

"Ja—wahrhaftig! I was startled that you should be associated with him. It was something that put me at a loss. I followed you at a distance until you disappeared into the little café. I lingered nearby, wondering whether to join you. You will judge, Sir John, that my conduct by this time was quite irrational. But I continued in doubt, and when you came out I followed you again. It was thus that I was near by when the attack was launched upon you."

Appleby smiled. "It seems fortunate that they didn't chloroform you too."

"I was much disposed to sail in." Kolmak paused, apparently pleased with his command of this English idiom. "But there were four or five of them, and it seemed unlikely that I could improve matters. It was very well timed, and they had you both in the van in an instant. No sooner had they done so, however, than there was the sound of a car approaching from the far end of the street. At once they scattered, and the van drove off. But now I come to the odd thing."

"To what you found it possible to say to a taxi-driver?"

"Ganz richtig! What approached was a taxi—and empty. In Oxford—I cannot tell why—one may not hail all taxis, but only certain taxis. It is a system I do not understand. But this taxi I hailed. It stopped. I jumped in and said 'Follow that van.' "

"It was most resourceful of you, Dr. Kolmak."

"The man did so—without hesitation! We drove some way—I think it must have been down Little Clarendon Street—and were presently in St. Giles'. I had a further thought. I said 'Pass it before we reach Carfax.' He was a most understanding man. He ignored the traffic lights at Broad Street—this, I hope, will not get him into trouble—and was well ahead as we approached the cross-roads. I called to him to stop, thrust a note into his hand, and jumped out. My hope was that the lights at Carfax would be against the van. And they were! I was waiting as it drew up. I stepped into the road. There was nobody but the driver, and the window on his near side was open. I thrust in an arm, switched off the engine, and withdrew the key. He was immobilised."

Appleby laughed. "I am tempted to say that you have missed your true vocation."

"There was a constable, as there commonly is, on the farther kerb. But I was uncertain of the wisdom of inviting official intervention. I therefore said to the driver 'Get out and go away; otherwise I will summon the constable.' He obeyed, for plainly he had no choice in the matter. I at once took his place, put back the key in the ignition, and drove on. The constable may have thought that the engine had failed—what is the word?"

"Stalled."

"Thank you—stalled. But he was aware of nothing further. I took the route by Pembroke Street and St. Ebbe's, and drove home."

"You still have the van?"

"No. When I had broken into it at the back, and the two of you were safely here stowed in the flat, it occurred to me that the van might well betray your whereabouts, supposing that those people were prowling the streets again. So I drove it to the car park near Gloucester Green and left it there."

Appleby was putting on his jacket. "I am extremely grateful to you. And so should this fellow Routh be too. By the way, I think we'd better go and have a look at him."

"You are sure that you are quite all right?"

Appleby smiled a trifle grimly. "I've had to recover from worse knocks before now—and a good deal more quickly. Moreover I shall feel a bit of an ass until I've caught up with this whole queer racket. It comes back to me now that, seconds before they caught me out, I was paying myself smug compliments on getting along very nicely."

"Like many of your countrymen, you surprise me, Sir John." Kolmak moved to the door. "In Germany—even in Austria—you would be a very strange policeman. I remember— Why, Tante Lise, *was ist's?*"

Frau Kolmak had entered the room in some precipitation. *"Was ist's?"* she repeated expressively. "But he is gone—the other one! *Da liegt der Hund begraben.*"

Kurt Kolmak sat down on the bed and threw up his hands in despair. "That I should not have thought to keep watch! And here has been Sir John complimenting me as one deft in such matters!"

"You mean that Routh has gone?" Appleby spoke sharply. "They have got him?"

Frau Kolmak shook her head. "He has gone—but freely. Nobody could have come to him. Our door was secured inside, and so was the house-door below. He too, after his adventure, slept through the night. An hour ago I took him coffee. Then, only a little after, I heard sounds of a door closing. *Leider,* I did not think! It must have been this man stealing out."

"Then, for the moment, we have lost him." Appleby smiled. "He must have managed it uncommonly quietly to escape the conversation of the ladies below. Particularly after the excitements to which you introduced them last night. They must be all agog. Have you a telephone?"

"It is a thing impossible to obtain. But the Misses Tinker—"

"Then I think I will go down and beg the use of it. Your nephew was very wise to feel that we should avoid publicity. But this is now a matter for the local police, all the same. The fellow Routh must be found. So must that van. And one or two other things must be investigated as well. Then, Dr. Kolmak, if I might borrow your bathroom and a razor—"

Kolmak beamed. "But certainly! You will find the bathroom, for a household of this modest character, exceptionally well appointed."

Appleby hurried out. The Aeolian harp was playing softly on

the little landing. Through the open window it pointed at the Radcliffe Observatory on the sky-line, as if its operation depended on perpetual cupfuls of air tossed to it by the whirling anemometer. Appleby gave the instrument a glance of some affection as he passed. Cairo was well enough. But it was satisfactory to be back in Oxford.

4. The Misses Tinker were below, crowned with mob-caps and equipped with feather-dusters. Appleby much doubted whether their discretion would long be proof against the charm of retailing to Lady Bronson and their other North Oxford acquaintance of the same kidney the sensational events that had lately transacted themselves beneath their roof. By the time that his telephone calls were made and his shaving in the Kolmak bathroom accomplished, Frau Kolmak had provided in her *salotto* a breakfast for one, impeccably presented after the most orthodox English fashion. Appleby sat down to it very willingly. "I got on to the Provost," he said to Kolmak, "and told him that I had domesticated myself here for the night. He remarked that my comfort could not be in better hands than those of your aunt."

"Kurt has a communication to make to you." Frau Kolmak spoke with a trace of nervousness, as if she could not be quite sure of her nephew's communicativeness until he was launched upon it. "But I know that at breakfast the English have the custom of reading the *Times*. It is at your elbow, Sir John; and if we might perhaps leave you—"

"Decidedly not." Appleby was emphatic. "Quite soon I must go out and see my sister, and get going on a number of other things as well. It is most desirable that we should have this talk at once."

"Then I will explain to you." Abruptly Kolmak sat down at the opposite side of the table. "My aunt has a daughter. Or rather—" He hesitated. "How the English flies out when a little emotion, a little distress, comes in! This daughter, this Anna, *verstehen Sie,* is *ein angenommenes Kind—"*

"I understand. An adopted child."

"Also! Anna is a highly educated woman—an *Ärztin,* skilled in the treatment of children."

"A doctor—a children's specialist."

"Ja doch! And she has herself a child—a fine boy of five."

"She is a widow?"

Kolmak hesitated. "In fact and law, no. But, morally, yes. Anna's husband has left her. He too is a doctor, and he long practised in Breslau—a city to which some ridiculous new name has lately been given. Now, he is in Leningrad, directing some *wichtig*—some important—medical research. But his wife and child he would not take with him, although it would have been permitted. His motive I shall leave undiscussed. It was not reputable. Anna, with her child, was stranded. We strove that they might come here. But there were difficulties."

"Anna is legally this Russian doctor's wife?"

"Yes."

"I see." Appleby had a long and saddened familiarity with tangles of this sort—the private aftermath of Europe's public follies. "Then there might certainly be difficulties, as you say."

Kolmak nodded gloomily. "And then the matter was taken out of our hands. You must understand that Anna was very anxious indeed to come to England."

"She had some compelling reason?"

"But naturally." It was Frau Kolmak who answered this, and in some haste. "I had brought her up. She wished that she and the child might be with me here."

Kolmak straightened himself in his chair. "There was a further reason. We are deeply in love."

"It seems a very good reason." Appleby looked gravely at the man sitting stiffly before him. "And then something decisive happened?"

"Anna came."

"She managed to get into England in some irregular way?"

"She did. She was impatient—and she is resolute and able."

"And the child?"

"She brought the child too."

Appleby smiled. "I think," he said drily, "that Anna must be decidedly able. And then?"

"She was in London. We were much distressed. We hoped that permission might yet be gained, and that she could come to us here. But there seemed no way to begin. It was a *Stillstand*—an impasse."

"Matters certainly weren't improved."

"It was decided that she must leave the country as she had come, and that we must begin again. But it would be yet some weeks before that could be arranged. Anna, who knows English well, decided to go into the country. There were difficulties, you understand, about remaining in one place. So she bought a bicycle, with a little seat for the child, and with a rucksack she set off. She passed through Oxford, going west, and almost every day we had a letter. But the letters stopped. For a time we were not alarmed. A week passed, and we worried. But I had no means of making enquiries. Then, one day, I received this."

Kolmak produced a pocket-book and from it drew something which he placed before Appleby. It was a plain postcard. On one side, written in a clear, foreign hand, was Kolmak's name and address. On the other, in the same hand, was the message:

Both unharmed. Do nothing. A.

For a moment Appleby studied this in silence. "When did it come?" he asked at length.

"Three weeks ago to-day. And it was despatched, you will see from the postmark, in the little place called Milton Porcorum."

"And without a stamp."

"Yes, indeed. The Misses Tinker, who take in our mail, had to pay when it was delivered. That is one of the puzzling things."

"Does Anna usually write in English?"

"No. But on a postcard she must have thought that it would be less noticeable."

"Her English, you say, is good? It is good enough for her not to write 'unharmed' when she meant, simply, 'well'?"

"Assuredly."

"When travelling, we sometimes send messages reading 'Arrived safely.' So there is a shade of difference between 'Both safe' and 'Both unharmed.' She would be aware of that? You are aware of it?"

"Certainly. You must understand that, although our conversation is imperfect, our understanding of English is fully literary. 'Unharmed' seemed strange to me at once. It was the reason of my venturing to disobey Anna's injunction. We were gravely concerned. Difficult as Anna's position was, there was nevertheless something altogether strange in this message."

"You are quite sure that it is in her hand?"

"Both my aunt and I are certain of it."

"How did you disobey this injunction? You didn't go to the police?"

"Certainly not. I was assuredly not entitled to do anything of the sort. But I went down to Milton Porcorum. It proved to be a small village with nothing remarkable about it. I felt that I must not so far disregard Anna's message as to go about asking questions. So I learnt nothing. In the afternoon I sought for aerodromes near by. The idea had come to me that Anna might have found at such a place a friend willing to fly her straight out of the country. But I was wasting my time, and I knew it. Anna's message did not—did not cohere with such a thing."

Appleby nodded gravely. "I agree with you."

"So I returned to Oxford. Then evil thoughts came to me. It is painful to speak of them. Tante Lise, you must explain."

Frau Kolmak had been sitting quite still by her piano—the same, Appleby conjectured, that had come in through the roof. But now she turned to the two men. "Kurt thought that Anna might be saying good-bye to us—that she might be shaking us off. He was ill with the strain of this anxiety, Sir John, and these ideas visited him. Some offer of security and affluence made by a powerful man—a protector, you understand?—had tempted her." Frau Kolmak gently smiled. "This was a most foolish notion, for my daughter is a very honest woman. It was a brief sickness of Kurt's, however, which we must mention, since it serves to explain how he came to make his discovery."

"His discovery?" Appleby swung round on Kolmak. "You *know* something?"

"Indeed I do. With these certainly foolish thoughts in my head, I went back to this little village several times, and I endeavoured to explore the whole neighborhood. I took field-glasses. What I was interested in now was great houses—the homes of wealthy people of the kind to which might belong, I fancied, Anna's seducer. These are horrible words to speak."

"But your discovery?"

"For a time I was almost mad, and I went about with my field-glasses like some unhappy man constrained to spy upon the privacy of others. And one house in particular tormented me, since it lies in the greatest seclusion. I came upon it, in the first instance, early in my search, since it is quite close to the village itself. It is, in fact, the historical manor house of both Milton Porcorum and Milton Canonicorum. There is a park surrounded by a high wall; and plantations and the lie of the ground make the house and all that lies near it virtually invisible from any public road. But my concentration was such that I found one spot—a small hillock to the west—from which I could just bring into focus the corner of a formal garden. I studied it intently for a long time—perhaps more than an hour—and saw no one moving in it. Then something caught my attention in that part of the park that lay nearest to it. The park, I should say, is in places oddly subdivided by high wire fences, as if the owner, perhaps, keeps several species of animal that he desires not to mingle. What I was looking at was a small field so enclosed—do you not call it a paddock?—and lying, I judged, quite close to the invisible mansion. There were small animals moving in it. They might have been rabbits or hares. And a child was feeding them. It was Anna's child."

Appleby drew a long breath. "You are sure of that?"

"I am certain of it."

"Let me remind you that you were a good deal upset. For an hour or more you had been concentrating with your binoculars upon what was scarcely a rational scheme of observation."

"I know it. But there was no mistake."

"And the little boy cannot, in the circumstances you have outlined, be at all intimately known to you." Appleby was gently insistent. "Can you be so certain that this was not an aberration? May you not have thought you saw what you expected to see?"

"I have asked myself these questions many times, Sir John. And, although the child vanished almost at once and did not reappear again, I am quite confident that it was Rudi."

"Did you take any action as a result of this discovery?"

"First, I should say that I was for a time a little easier in my mind. Is not this a strange thing, now? The mere sight of the little boy through my field-glasses destroyed at once the bad thoughts which I had been nursing about Anna. And they have not come back to me. But I was, of course, anxious still. It came to me that Anna might have left Rudi in this place—perhaps some sort of children's home—the better to carry out some plan of her own. She is devoted to the child. But at the same time she is a woman of intellectual interests, deeply concerned by the world's political and social problems. When this possibility came to me I made enquiries about Milton Manor. It is not for children but for adults—a large, private *Kurort* or *Klinikum*. I do not know the word—"

"We used to say nursing-home or sanatorium. But we have started saying clinic too. Did you find out anything more?"

"Nothing. I still felt not at liberty to ask questions openly, or to pay a visit. And in secret it appears impossible to make any approach. There is this high wall; there are these fences. But the establishment is large and must employ many people. I have thought to disguise myself, perhaps, to seek an engagement—"

Appleby smiled. "That is very resourceful, but perhaps the time has come for other measures."

"There are yet two matters of which Kurt has to tell." Frau Kolmak was sitting at her piano rather as if she proposed to provide a musical *coda* to these final revelations when they came. "First, there is his adventure with the guest who has just left us."

Appleby nodded and turned to Kurt Kolmak. "You are aware of some connection of Routh's with this place near Milton Porcorum?"

"Wahrscheinlich! But it is only from yesterday that this small piece of knowledge dates. Early yesterday morning I set out again on a further *Rekognoszierung*—a further spying. I walked all round the park. The circuit was almost completed, and with nothing gained, when I saw the *sogenannte* Routh approaching down a lane. He was staggering slightly, as if drunk or ill. There appeared to be blood on his face. I was very wary. It was not my wish to be seen by anybody at all at this prowling and spying. There was still Anna's injunction. Therefore I slipped behind a hedge and through my glasses studied this man. He turned along the road bounding this mysterious estate with which we are concerned. And then, as my glasses followed him, another figure came into view—one who had just appeared, it seemed, through a small door in the high wall of which I have spoken. I was excited. It was the first time that I had seen anybody appear from the place. And this figure—a man with high shoulders and of some presence—had an air of authority. His clothing was rural but elegant. He might have been the *Landjunker*."

"The Squire?"

"Also! We ourselves employ the word. *Nun!* This man remained standing by his small door until Routh went by. No gesture, I believe, passed between them. But then he called Routh back. Routh appeared to hesitate, and then retraced his steps.

The two engaged in conversation. It was my impression that there was some sort of dispute. And then I was interrupted. I had climbed a gate, you understand, and was in a field, crouched behind the hedge through which I was peering with my binoculars. Suddenly there was a farm-labourer in the field behind me, calling out to demand what I was doing. No doubt he suspected that I was a poacher or a thief or a deranged person, since my posture was not one that an innocent man would adopt."

Kolmak paused, slightly flushed, and clicked his fingers. "I see now my situation as comical. But at the moment I was humiliated and confused. I got up and ran away."

"Eine dumme Geschichte!" Frau Kolmak laughed softly. "But there is more of it to tell."

Kurt Kolmak nodded. "I gave no further thought to what I had seen. And this was because, when I recovered from my confusion, a new thought had come to me. Perhaps Anna was willingly a patient in this clinic. Perhaps she had suffered a nervous illness. She was, after all, virtually a fugitive—and one with a child to care for. Such a situation must involve a great strain. She might, then, have found this place, where Rudi also could be, and have determined not to communicate with us—apart, that is, from this single card, written, it might be, in a disturbed state. What, in that event, was my duty? I found it hard to decide, and I spent the rest of the day tramping that countryside and endeavouring to wrestle with the problem. It thus came about that I returned to Oxford by a circuitous route, changing buses eventually at Abingdon. Imagine my surprise when I saw, getting off the same bus at Gloucester Green, the man whom I had last seen in conversation with the owner, as it might be, of Milton. There was, of course, no mistaking him. This was the man whose face had been bleeding; the scratches were still visible on his face. I determined to track him to his destination. If I knew where he lived, then I might be able to take thought and find some means of gaining valuable information from him."

"I see." Appleby, who had finished his breakfast, was listening intently to this recital. "You started to trail Routh. Did he seem scared?"

"Assuredly he did."

"He had the appearance of a man who believes himself to be pursued?"

"That was my impression."

"Before he had any opportunity of knowing that *you* were on his track?"

Kolmak considered. "But yes! As soon as he got off the bus he made his way to one point and another about Gloucester Green —and always looking uneasily about him. This, I am sure, was before he ever set eyes on me. Presently he went into a small hotel. I waited. He was there long enough, I should say, to get a meal. When he came out, our eyes met. Very foolishly, I had waited directly in front of the place. I know that instantly he suspected me of spying on him. He proceeded at once to put the matter to the test. My following of him was very clumsy and obvious. And quite soon he got away from me, boarding a bus that I was unable to catch."

"A bus coming out to North Oxford?"

"Nun ja! It was a Number 2. And here was an end of my playing the detective—the secret agent! Only how surprised I was, on going out to call you back last night, to find you conversing with this man."

"I should much like to converse with him again. But there is still something further you have to tell me?"

"Yes." Kolmak's face took on an expression more anxious than any it had yet worn. "There has been another message from Anna. It, too, has arrived by post—this morning, while you were still asleep. You have it, Tante Lise?"

Frau Kolmak nodded, and rose from beside the piano. There was something in her movement that betrayed the fatigue of long anxiety; and Appleby saw that she was an older woman than he had supposed.

"Here it is, Kurt. I fear it occupied my thoughts to the exclusion of other matters. Had it not been so, Herr Routh would not have slipped away from us so easily."

Appleby shook his head. "Don't worry about that, Frau Kolmak. It may give him a chance to make some interesting contacts. Perhaps he will be found with them by my Oxford colleagues. Routh is decidedly their main interest at the moment, and they are a highly efficient body of men."

"Sir John, here is Anna's second note. Again it is unstamped. And the material seems not designed for the post."

"It certainly does not." Appleby was looking at a slim piece of cardboard, about four inches by three. Medially on one of the longer sides, and near the edge, there was punched a small circular hole. "It's clearly meant for use in a card-index. Addressed in the same way as the first, and posted in Milton Porcorum in time for the 4.15 p.m. sorting yesterday." He turned the card over and read its message in silence:

> *Do not be hurt that I do not write. I am not a free agent, and there is danger in the attempt. To-day or soon there is a crisis. Do nothing. But be by your telephone every day from 10 to 11 a.m.*
>
> *A.*

Appleby sat so long in thought before this enigmatic missive that Kolmak stirred uneasily beside him. "Sir John—it suggests something to you?"

Appleby shook his head. "This about the telephone. I don't understand it."

"In my room at Bede's there is an instrument. And Anna has the number."

"But of course—stupid of me." Appleby nodded absently. "What Anna enjoins upon you is rather a nerve-racking routine, I am afraid. But you had better be off to it. The time is nearly half-past nine now. Incidentally, I must go down and make another call from the Misses Tinker's machine."

Kolmak rose as if to open the door. "That will be to your colleagues, arranging that my line in Bede's be tapped?"

"You are very acute—again the secret agent in the making!"

"I am inclined to wish that I had told you nothing." Kolmak was very pale.

"And that you had left me in that van?"

"Aber nein!" Impulsively, Kolmak took Appleby's hand. "You judge Anna to be in danger?"

Appleby inclined his head. "I do." His voice was grave. "She says so herself—and it appears that she is a level-headed and capable person."

"She is indeed!" Frau Kolmak had come forward. "My daughter has a good brain and great courage. Can you, Sir John, whose experience must be so great, form any conjecture as to her situation and Rudi's? If so, I beg you to speak, however black the picture may be."

"There is no scope for conjecture yet. Your daughter is almost certainly in some sense a prisoner. But she has been able at some risk to send you a couple of notes, and at a pinch she believes she can command a telephone. She might have stated her precise whereabouts and has refrained from doing so. Twice she has said 'Do nothing.' She has made no appeal for help, but at any moment she may do so. At the moment, that is about as far as we can get. Except, of course, for the parallel situation of Routh."

"The parallel situation?" Frau Kolmak looked bewildered and rather displeased. "Surely you see no similarity between my daughter and that man?"

"Certainly I do. Routh too, I suspect, has been in the hands of this mysterious organisation. And Routh too has been fighting back. That is all to the good, since I suspect that we are very definitely in the presence of something to be fought against. But Routh and your daughter may prove to have something else in common."

Kolmak was looking at his watch. "Please do not speak in riddles," he said. "Please explain."

But Frau Kolmak laid a hand on her nephew's arm. "I think I understand," she said quietly. "I considered the little man with attention, and when I gave him coffee I exchanged a few words with him." She was growing visibly paler as she spoke, but she stood very upright beside her piano. "We will not go further into this now."

Appleby moved to the door. "There is, as you know, another person who must be fitted into the design."

"The *Verlobte* of your sister—Mr. Ourglass?"

"Yes. He too, from what I hear of him, would fight back. But, in that other particular, he offers no parallel to Routh and your daughter."

Frau Kolmak considered. "Might the young man be freakish, adventurous—and affect—what you have in mind?"

"That is a very shrewd suggestion. And now I must be off—and you too, Dr. Kolmak, to that telephone." Appleby turned back to his hostess and bent over her with some formality. *"Auf Wiedersehen, gnädige Frau."*

On the little landing the Aeolian harp was still uttering its muted music. Appleby wondered what Routh had made of it. He wondered, too, what he ought to make of Routh.

5. Jane Appleby left Somerville College at nine-fifty, thus missing her brother by five minutes. It was her intention to proceed to the Examination Schools and there hear a lecture by the Stockton and Darlington Professor. In spite of her engagement to Geoffrey Ourglass, or perhaps because of it, Jane had now been, for more than a year, in general sequacious only of the more severe intellectual pleasures. This particular weekly occasion she invariably found wholly delectable. For many of her fellows it was an hour of furious activity—and indeed it has been calculated that more young women are constrained to buy fresh notebooks after the discourses of the Stockton and Darlington Professor than after any other learned occasion whatsoever.

Jane, however, was accustomed to sit in a still repose throughout. The substance of what the Professor had to say had, in point of fact, been bequeathed to her by an aunt who attended the lectures in 1925; and Jane was thus in the fortunate position of being able to sit as in a theatre and enjoy the finer points of the performance, without anxious thoughts of the likely bearing of such inactivity upon her examination prospects.

But now that Geoffrey's fate—or could it be behaviour?—had got her down (and to herself, at least, Jane now admitted that it had done this) Jane found herself, week by week, taking less and less delight in this particular facet of the pursuit of knowledge. The plain fact was that if she were not to be miserable she must give her mind more active and tough employment than any that the proceedings of the Stockton and Darlington Professor could afford. She was very little disposed to sit and mope; she had been determined that her work was not going to suffer on account of the miserable and bewildering turn which her affairs had taken; and when she had come up at the beginning of term to an Oxford still void of Geoffrey she had signalised this determination by extracting from her tutor, for work in a college examination, the portentous mark known in Oxford as a pure Alpha. But since then she had been finding it progressively difficult to avoid making an ass of herself, and she had found that her best weapon in this struggle lay in the more stretching forms of mental exercise. It thus came about that, half-way down St. Giles', Jane decided not to hear the Stockton and Darlington Professor after all.

If this decision was of momentous public importance (as may, indeed, presently prove to be the case) the public showed no consciousness of the fact. Around and about that secondary hub of Oxford upon one border of which stands the College of the Provost and Scholars of the Venerable Bede, and upon another the miniature churchyard of St. Mary Magdalen, both Town and Gown continued undisturbed upon their familiar occasions. Regius Professors, visibly bowed down beneath their weight of erudition, pottered about, buying cakes and pies. Heads of

Houses, upon whom even more evidently reposed heavy burdens of administrative care, absently exercised dogs or companioned their wives through a morning's brisk shopping. Outwards towards the Banbury or the Woodstock Road an unending stream of battered sports cars bore cohorts of male undergraduates, discreetly concealed amid golf clubs, shot-guns, and riding kits. Inwards towards the lecture-rooms and libraries of the University rode an answering army of young women on bicycles bearing large baskets bulging with massive volumes, as if they were the delivery service of a community given literally to devouring books.

It was as one in the main stream of this literary movement that Jane Appleby had now reached the lower end of St. Giles'. On her right the reposeful statuary on the Taylor Institution—unknown whether mythological or symbolical, allegorical or historical—stared impassively across the hubbub to where Balliol, Trinity and St. John's expire in a complicated embrace. Before her was the Martyrs' Memorial. To the right of this was Bede's. Jane took one glance at the college of her vanished beloved and decided that the prime need of the morning was arduous thought. She would make her way not to the lecture of the Stockton and Darlington Professor but to the upper reading room of the Bodleian Library, where there happened to be reserved for her a work of very sufficient intellectual difficulty. She would wrestle with this until noon and then hunt up her brother. To this resolution Jane had come when she saw that somebody was waving an umbrella at her from the corner of Beaumont Street. It was Geoffrey's uncle, Dr. Ourglass. She signalled her intention of joining him when she could, and presently threaded her way at some hazard across the street.

"My dear, I am very pleased to see you, and I was delighted to meet your brother yesterday evening. I was dining in Bede's as the guest of Mr. Bultitude, whom I am glad to be able to introduce to you."

It had been Jane's hurried impression as she dodged the traffic that Dr. Ourglass was standing beside a large barrel awaiting delivery to the Bede's buttery. She now realised that she had been in error. The barrel was bowing to her with gravity. It was, in fact, the celebrated Mark Bultitude. "How do you do," he said. "I am afraid we divert you."

As Jane had been aware of an element of the ludicrous in the conjoined appearance of the gentlemen before her, she found this ambiguity disconcerting. "Oh, no," she said hastily, "I wasn't going anywhere important; only to the Bodleian."

Mark Bultitude directed a faint smile upon Dr. Ourglass, as if calling upon him to remark the delightful fatuity of the young. "In that case," he said, "we can make this small claim upon your time with a clear conscience."

Jane, like most people of her age—and even a few quite mature ones—disliked detecting herself saying something silly. "It's not time wasted at all," she said. "One ought to meet the really interesting people." She contrived to let her eyes rest, rounded in admiration, upon Bultitude. "Yesterday I managed to talk to that funny old woman who peddles bananas."

"You have the right instinct. You will end by collecting all of us Oxford worthies. We are a diminishing band, after all. For one thing, there are now so few openings." And Bultitude looked comfortably around him, as if seeking some enormous aperture through which he might edge himself.

Dr. Ourglass thought it well to change the subject. "It appears," he said carefully, "that Mr. Bultitude is acquainted with a number of Geoffrey's—and my—distant relations; and he has become interested in this distressing thing that has happened. He is very anxious to help. He even suggests that he and I make an expedition."

Jane received this communication with mixed feelings. She liked old Dr. Ourglass, although she had no high opinion of his practical acumen. And she was spontaneously and instantly grateful to anybody—even this terrible great fat *poseur*—who expressed concern and a willingness to help in the horrible matter of Geoffrey's inexplicable and now long-continued disappearance. At the same time she hated figuring as the young woman who had mislaid a young man. She was well aware that all sorts of low, sinister, or facetious constructions could be placed on such a situation, and she was only the more sensitive to these because none of them had ever been even faintly obtruded upon her. "Thank you," she said. "I am quite desperate, you know. Geoffrey simply *must* be found. He may be terribly ill—so ill that he doesn't even know his own identity."

Bultitude nodded soberly. "An able and well-connected young man," he said. "With everything before him here at Bede's—and a further tie of which I am now very well able to estimate the force. I am extremely shocked. Birkbeck ought to have been altogether more vigorous in the matter. He cannot, poor fellow, afford to lose good pupils right and left. Ourglass tells me that your brother is taking the matter up. I was sorry not to have any conversation with him last night. But we shall meet. We shall undoubtedly meet. I have never, I believe, known anybody in the police. But my uncle Hubert once had command of the Yeomen of the Guard."

Jane felt that the conversation in which she had become involved was somewhat lacking in direction. Dr. Ourglass appeared to have the same feeling, and again changed the subject with unusual abruptness. "Jane," he asked, "has Geoffrey ever shown any disposition to *write*—for example, a play?"

"I never heard him speak of such a thing." Jane was puzzled. "Geoffrey is simply a straight-out, tip-top scientist. And they don't usually write plays. Of course Geoffrey is fond of acting, but that's a different matter. Why do you ask?"

"Mr. Bultitude had a notion that a long-continued retirement and—um—neglect of one's friends is sometimes to be accounted for by absorption in a literary task."

"I see." Jane thought this decidedly a poor idea. Nor did Bultitude seem pleased at its being aired again. Perhaps Dr. Ourglass was innocently labouring something that had really been one of his companion's obscure jokes. Anyway, she was not going to stand any longer at a street-corner gossiping like this. "I think," she said, "I'd better go off and do some work."

Bultitude nodded benevolently, as if here were another of the touching frailties of the young. "Quite right," he said. "What sort of acting?"

For a moment Jane was at a loss. "I beg your pardon?"

"What sort of acting is the young man fond of? Has he taken part in any plays here in Oxford?"

"Oh, I see. No—Geoffrey hasn't, I think, done any acting in a regular way since he left school. I just meant that he likes putting on turns. He can dress up a bit, and then pass himself off in a pub as pretty well anything. It's a sort of freakish amusement that he gets quite a lot of fun out of from time to time."

"Impersonations, in fact."

"I suppose it may be called that." Jane found herself obscurely resenting the word. "Only not of individuals, you see. Just of types."

"Quite so. Impersonation, one might say, on the Theophrastan model. It doesn't sound a particularly dangerous hobby. The hazards ought not to extend much beyond a black eye."

At this Jane felt really cross. "You'd have to be quite tough, Mr. Bultitude, to take to punching Geoffrey. He'd be back and finding a soft spot or two in no time."

"Capital—capital. Young men are too neglectful of those manly accomplishments nowadays. Have you ever joined in these impersonations, Miss Appleby? And has the young man any favourite turns?"

Jane ignored the first part of this questioning. "He can do dons. And bewildered foreigners. And—let me see—yes, young clergymen, and down-and-outs."

"Young clergymen!" It was Dr. Ourglass who spoke, and he was apparently a little shocked. "I had no idea of this—and in a person of high academic promise!" He paused as if looking for a more reassuring view of the matter, inoffensive to his nephew's betrothed. "Versatility," he pursued, "is a wonderful endowment. I am all too conscious of being sadly without it myself."

But by this time Jane had turned her bicycle. A momentary break in the stream of traffic could be made the civil occasion, she felt, of a tolerably brisk farewell to her interlocutors. "Sorry," she said suddenly. "Here's my chance." And at that she darted away.

Although it had been accompanied by her best smile, Jane was not altogether happy about this manoeuvre. It was perhaps neither mannerly nor courageous; and she had only an obscure sense of why the encounter thus rather abruptly terminated had rattled her. When safely on the farther side of the road, therefore, she turned her head for a moment, intending to locate her companions of a second before and impart what cordiality she could to a parting wave. It was a movement involving her in a mishap which just escaped being serious.

Dr. Ourglass and Mark Bultitude appeared to have moved off, and Jane's eye continued to search for them a fraction of a second longer than was compatible with wary cycling. In the same instant a man stepped blindly off the kerb in front of her; there was a bump; and Jane found herself in the unpleasant position of lying flat on the road, with the wheel of a bus hurtling past her head.

She knew, however, that she was unhurt, and she scrambled hastily to her feet. It is bad to have been within inches of death. But, when one is young, it is almost worse to have made a fool of oneself, and to see a little crowd gathering, most of whom have just observed one come down hard on one's behind, and to expect at any moment a policeman, solemnly insistent upon making copious notes. Jane therefore hastily grabbed her bicycle and looked anxiously at the man with whom she had collided. He too, blessedly, was on his feet. If he were only unhurt and disposed not to make a fuss—

He was backing away through the little knot of people whom the incident had collected. Jane stared at him in surprise. He was a little rat of a fellow, shabby and unshaven, and—what was the odd thing about him—in a state of palpable terror. And it was not, Jane could see, what *had* happened that was the occasion of his miserable state; it was what *might* happen. The man as he tried to back out of the crowd glanced about him in vivid apprehensiveness; when he knocked into somebody he drew back as from a blow; his complexion was of an alarming pallor which emphasised his possession of one badly scratched cheek. That, Jane supposed, had been her fault—as must be also the sadly dusty and crumpled state of the man's attire. She moved forward at once, wheeling her bicycle. "I'm most terribly sorry. It was entirely my fault. I hope—" Jane paused, disconcerted. The man's eyes had swept past her quite blindly; his unscarred cheek was twitching; his tongue went rapidly over his lips with an effect that was reptilian and repellent. Suddenly he turned, ducked, dodged, and ran. Jane was addressing her apologies to empty air.

Or rather she was addressing them to a small group of people uncertain whether to be puzzled or amused. The handlebars of her bicycle had got twisted, and to this a couple of undergraduates were attending with expressions so solemnly solicitous that Jane suspected them of concealing coarse amusement at the unlucky manner of her tumble. The one bright spot in the picture was the absence of any bobbing policeman's helmet. "Thank you very much *indeed,*" she said. Her intention was to speak with an awful and freezing coldness. Unfortunately much of the breath appeared to have been knocked out of her body, and the words emerged with a panting effect proper to an adoring maiden chivalrously rescued from a ravisher or a dragon. She took the bicycle and thrust its nose not very gently into the crowd. Now, thank goodness, she was clear, and had edged into Broad Street. She mounted, settled herself rather gingerly in the saddle, and put this deplorable *contretemps* rapidly behind her. But the consciousness of having been vastly idiotic remained with her oppressively. The oddity of the terrified man's behaviour went entirely out of her head. So too did her encounter with Mark Bultitude and Dr. Ourglass, and the latter's unexplained suggestion that they were going to make an expedition.

6. The upper reading room of the Bodleian Library is frequented in the main by persons occupying a middle station in the elaborate hierarchy of Oxford learning. In a university, as in the republic of literature, extreme longevity is a prerequisite of the first eminence; and in Bodley (as the great library is compendiously termed by its frequenters) those in whom extreme fulness of years and exceptional depths of erudition are thus naturally conjoined commonly inhabit studies, niches, carrells and (it may be) cubicles of superior distinction in other parts of the building—notably in what is known as Duke Humphrey's Library and the Selden End. These latter, although not places of the highest antiquity, are very, very old; and the pursuit of learning has for so long transacted itself within them as to have generated not only a peculiar aura but also an indescribable smell. As long as this smell endures Oxford will endure too. If its undergraduate population were dispensed with, Oxford would not be very much changed. If its bells, even, fell silent, something would be left. But if this smell evaporated it would be a sign that the soul of Oxford had departed its tenement of grey, eroded stone, and that only its shell, only its tangible and visible surfaces, remained.

It is normally only for the purpose of consulting the great catalogue of the Library that these ancients of the place repair to the upper reading room; and this they (and they alone) may do by means of a lift—a lift the nether terminus of which is a jealously guarded secret, and from which egression at its upward limit is almost equally mysterious, since none of the sages is ever observed actually stepping from it, being invariably first remarked advancing down the reading room with measured tread against a background of unbroken lines of books.

Nor do the young largely frequent the upper reading room, since for them, in sundry dependent libraries, judiciously selected books, independently catalogued, are provided in what, to their large innocence, appears inexhaustible abundance. It is only occasionally that—like those stripling cherubs who, in the first stainlessness of this terrestrial world, were drawn by curiosity to take a peep into Eden—undergraduate members of the university toil upwards to this unwonted sciential eminence. Those who do not take the lift to the upper reading room must mount a flight of sixty-four steps, involving twelve right-angled turns. It was to this that Jane Appleby addressed herself shortly after her misadventure hard by Bede's College.

There is surely something unique, if indefinable, in the atmosphere generated in the reading room of a great library. So many minds intently employed in divided and distinguished worlds; black men beside yellow men, and yellow men beside white; shoes and ships and sealing-wax all being studied in a row; the vision of that mysterious Goddess, alluring within the multitudinous and inexplicable folds of her sable robe, who at once unifies the spectacle and makes it possible: all these make a library a solemn place to an exploring cherub of twenty-one. No doubt Jane Appleby came in order to master a book that she knew to be confined here. But she came, too, for the smell of old leather and vellum and wood that permeated the approaches to the place; for the sound, strangely magnified in the stillness, of a fly buzzing on a window-pane, or for the muted clanking of the Emett-like contrivance which, behind the scenes, drew its continuously moving train of books up through secular darkness from crepuscular repositories below. She came, in short—an unconfessed tourist disguised as a scholar of Somerville—for atmosphere. But if Jane came for sensations, she certainly did not come for sensation. She was not at all prepared for the spectacle that was presently to be afforded her.

The reading room appeared to be less frequented than was common at this hour. Nobody occupied the desk where Jane's book was waiting, and she settled down to it at once. Or rather she endeavoured to do this—and with no expectation of difficulty. Her mind was well-disciplined, and the constant sub-acute anxiety in which she now lived did not (as has already been remarked) seriously interfere with her working. And as for the upper reading room as atmosphere—that, she was convinced, was something that came to one most exquisitely as a faint wash of surface awareness when the greater part of the mind was plunged deep in its task.

But, this morning, Jane's mind proved reluctant to plunge at all—reluctant (as she told herself fretfully) even to wet its toes. Surface awareness turned out to be her sole stock-in-trade. She buried her nose in her book—which was a very big one—and peeped guiltily over its upper margin at the world about her. This, persisted in, was conduct so monstrous, that she positively expected some dramatic consequence to ensue. A bell might ring loudly, the little door magnificently labelled Protobibliothecarius Bodleianus open with an ominous creak, and hitherto unsuspected attendants, garbed in a Byzantine splendour congruous with that resounding inscription, seize her and bind her in every limb. She would be delivered into the maw of the Emett-like machine; that machine—unprecedentedly—would be thrown into reverse; and she would be conveyed to the icy embrace of some subterranean Oxford Bosphorus. Come to think of it, Oxford *did* have at least one underground river. Her brother had told her that, as an undergraduate, he had once traversed it in a canoe. . . .

Jane felt a sudden chill. It was a feeling none the less horrid for being familiar—for being a sensation that gripped her whenever chance brought any occasion of danger into her head. She remembered now that just this thought had come to her half an hour before, when the rumbling bus had gone by within inches of her nose. Perhaps Geoffrey, having unaccountably strayed in the vacation to some outlandish place, had been inches less lucky. Or perhaps he had thought to make the solitary exploration of that hidden Oxford river, and his canoe had struck a snag, had pitched him—

Abruptly Jane emerged from the dark, dank tunnel into which her fearful imagination had carried her. Without her being at all aware of what it was, something in the actual and present world around her had plucked at her attention. It was not—deplorably—the printed page before her. It was not the neighbour on her right: a grey-haired woman copying from a book the size of a postage-stamp—bating Geoffrey, Jane thought, myself forty years on. Nor was it that picturesque Oxford figure, old Dr. Undertone, on her left. For Dr. Undertone, surrounded by eighteenth-century theology, had sunk, with closed eyes, into that species of profound cerebration, to a vulgar regard deceptively like simple slumber, which is not unfrequently to be observed in the upper reading room. It was neither of these people. It was, in fact, the man with the scratched face.

He was still only on the threshold of the room. Subconsciously, she must have become aware of him the instant his pale—his curiously haunted or hunted—face appeared at the door. But, if Jane saw him, nobody else appeared to do so. Very few people in the upper reading room ever sit peeping over the top of their books.

The man had no business in the place. She was, somehow, quite certain of that. But he had not, apparently, been asked if he were a reader. This was not surprising, for it is only very infrequently that any official of the Library murmurs to anybody a courteous enquiry of the sort. Nor, really, did he look at all out of the way. He was shabby, but scholars can be shabbier than anybody else in the world. He was grubby, but that is not absolutely unknown among the learned. He was harassed to what was quite evidently the point of nervous collapse, and he had the appearance of one whose mind is bent with maniacal concentration upon the solution of some single, urgent and ever-present problem. But this is not uncommon among those who pursue the historical Homer or the origins of the Sabellian heresy, or who are hounded by urgent conundrums concerning the comparative phonology of the dialects of the upper Irrawaddy.

The man was completely at sea about the sort of place he had landed in. An unsensational explanation of his appearance would be simply that he had taken a wrong turning when searching for the picture-gallery. But if, to a gaze once bent upon him, he had not the air of a man concerned to read old books, neither did he very convincingly suggest any interest in old portraits. He was looking neither for knowledge nor for aesthetic delectation. He was looking for refuge.

To this conclusion Jane was, of course, assisted by recalling the man's odd behaviour when she had collided with him in the street. He had simply got up and bolted. Either, then, he was mentally deranged (which was the most likely explanation) or he was in actual fear of pursuit and apprehension. He was alternatively either a bit of a lunatic or a bit of a criminal.

Jane's mind reacted with no special interest to either of these notions. Although much given to reading—and over large mugs of cocoa discussing solemnly with her friends—the most recondite psychopathic aberrations chronicled by Freud or Stekel, her conviction was that at the casual sight of such distresses peeping out from some individual, good manners and natural instinct combine to make one look the other way. Nor did crime remotely interest her; she left that to her brother John. Despite all which, she now bent a steady but covert observation upon the fugitive. Between them, after all, was a common bond: they had lately almost delivered one another to death on the high road.

The man had now realised that he was in a library. He glanced over the rows of bent figures and made as if to sit down. But in the upper reading room every desk is commonly loaded with books reserved for one reader or another, and although it is the convention that one may take any place not actually occupied at the time, a stranger will always be likely to feel that there is standing room only.

For a minute or so the fugitive stood. In this there was nothing that was likely to call attention to him. The walls between the square Tudor windows are lined with books and bound journals supposed to be in common use, and before these, scholars will stand for hours on end, either running through the pages of one and another volume or simply studying their spines with an air of profound research. The man plainly hesitated to take a book from the shelf, but he contrived to let his eye run over several rows as if in search of some specific work. In this, even if it had been generally detected as a subterfuge, there would have been little to excite remark. For it frequently happens that scholars, seized suddenly as they are walking past by some irresistibly enticing train of speculation, and being brought to an abrupt halt thereby, avoid (what would be odious to them) the appearance of any singularity of conduct by going through just this conventional inspection of whatever shelves are nearest to hand. From these, nothing much distinguished the man with the scratched face save this: that every few seconds his gaze ran furtively along the stretching lines of books to the door of the reading room.

Several people wandered in, and Jane believed that she could see the fugitive quiver each time. The Emett-like conveyor belt behind the scenes emitted one of its faint clankings, and the man gave a sort of jump as he stood. Nevertheless, he was demonstrably getting the hang of the place. He had now boldly taken a volume from the shelf, opened it, and turned round so that he could survey the room over the top of it—a technique, in fact, closely approximating to Jane's own.

Seen full face, he looked very tired as well as frightened. Jane remembered that free libraries of the municipal order are frequently the resort of the homeless, who will sit with an unmeaning book before them for the sake of shelter and a meagre warmth. Perhaps even this august chamber had been put to not altogether dissimilar use on some occasion or another. But this man was not minded to shelter from the elements. He was sheltering from his own kind.

At this moment somebody else entered the room. He was a man with high, square shoulders, and his appearance was eminently orthodox. His features held the mingled stamp of intelligence, authority and mild enquiry. His clothing was so quiet as to lend positive assertiveness to an extremely faded Harrovian tie. He carried a sheaf of papers yellowed with age, and under his arm was what appeared to be a mortar-board—more correctly known as a "square"—and a crumpled M.A. gown. He was, in fact, the very type of the consciously busy don, dropping into Bodley to order a book before hurrying off to lecture.

The man with the scratched face had been scanning the readers with some particularity. And now the entry of the donnish person, from whom he was momentarily concealed, seemed to touch off in him a spring of activity. His eye had been on Jane. He thrust the book he had been holding back on the shelf and came straight towards her.

Jane experienced a second's ridiculous panic. There came to her an intuitive understanding of what the fugitive was about. He had recognised her. And—just because she was the only person in this strange reading room not absolutely unknown to him—he was going to direct at her some urgent appeal. Nothing could be more irrational. But the man had reached a breaking-point at which only instinctive responses were left to him.

And then he faltered. Jane wondered, with a quick compunction, whether she had shown herself overtly hostile to his approach. However this might be, the man halted not beside her desk but beside Dr. Undertone's. He had been feeling in a pocket. Jane saw that he now held a paper in his hand.

The quintessentially donnish person was scanning the room. If it was the man with the scratched face that he was seeking, he had not yet located him. And now the man was leaning over Dr. Undertone's desk. Dr. Undertone took no notice. Since his eyes were still closed in meditation, and since he was ninety-six, there was nothing surprising in that. Nor did anybody else except Jane appear to pay any attention either. As books but not desks are reservable in the reading room it is necessary to do quite a lot of prowling round other people's property.

The man with the scratched face thrust the paper he was carrying into one of Dr. Undertone's books and walked straight on across the room.

7. It was, as the vulgar say, a new one on Jane Appleby. And before she could decide what action, if any, was required, her attention was riveted upon the next act of the drama being played out covertly before her.

The donnish person had seen the fugitive and was advancing upon him. Between himself and this advance the fugitive was concerned to put a barrier. And one obvious barrier was available to him. Beginning at that end of the reading room which is nearest the door, and extending in two parallel lines down a substantial part of its length, run low, double-fronted cases containing the major portion of the great manuscript catalogue of the Bodleian Library. To move round these massive islands is to circumambulate a brief record of the entire intellectual and imaginative achievement of the race. And this is what the two men—pursuer and pursued—were doing now. They were playing a sort of hide-and-seek round this monumental guide to universal knowledge.

Jane watched, fascinated. It must, she realised, be some sort of symbolic comedy, arranged expressly for her benefit, although she had not the key of it. This weird ballet was being danced for a stake somehow commensurate with the tremendous character of its setting.

And nobody else noticed. For the strangest behaviour, Jane perceived, can pass undetected in the most sober places. To any one not persistently attentive to the whole sequence of events she was witnessing, nothing in the least out of the way had occurred or was occurring. That one man should be patently pursuing round the catalogue of Bodley another man who as patently fled, was a phenomenon offering in itself no difficulty whatever to a casual analysis. There are always in Oxford colleagues prone to engage with one at unseasonable times; there are always legitimate lengths to which one may go in side-stepping their approach. In Bodley the right-thinking greet only with the most distant nod (if at all) their fathers, mothers, sons, daughters or most intimate friends. But there are always those who default upon this convention: fellow-workers importunately desirous of learned communication, sociably disposed persons thinking to give (or receive) an invitation to dinner, deans and senior tutors allowing so exaggerated a regard to administrative affairs as to be willing even here to whip up a vote or debate a college by-law; there are all these, and there are plain bores as well.

Had the donnish man and his quarry positively broken into a run, or had the former offered to vault the long breastwork of enormous manuscript volumes standing in his way, this open breach of decorum would doubtless have been visited with the severest censure on the part of the assembled body of readers. But nothing of this sort was in question. The pursuit here in progress was a pursuit in slow motion. Presently it was to strike Jane that this was a very odd circumstance indeed. For the moment she was absorbed in watching it.

Half a dozen people were moving about the catalogue—lugging out a volume here and there, hoisting it by its leathern loop to the desk-like top of the long case, finding some desired entry and copying it upon a slip, replacing the volume and moving on to hunt for something else. Both the man with the scratched face and his pursuer were making some show of doing the same thing. Nevertheless their actual preoccupation was clear. The one was concerned to edge up and the other was concerned to edge away. This went on for some time. It was like some crazy sequence in a dream.

And that was it. There was an element of the hypnotic or the hypnoidal in the affair. And it was only in a minor degree that the donnish man was concerned physically to corner his victim.

That, indeed, he had in a sense done already. What was now in question was an obscure battle of wills. The object of the pursuer was to compel the other man to leave the reading room, to walk quietly out of the library. And his weapon was this: that his person, or personality, was so repulsive to his victim as to make it physically impossible for the latter to bear any approach to contiguity. As the donnish person advanced, in the same measure was the man with the scratched face irresistibly obliged to withdraw. Watching the two of them at their covert manoeuvring around the catalogue was like watching some ingenious toy. Or it was like watching a child forcing one piece of magnetised metal jerkily across a table by nosing towards it the answering pole of another.

For Jane there was a moment of queer horror in this discovery of a sentient human being reduced to the condition of an automaton. And the donnish man was gaining in authority—was gaining in repulsive or expulsive power—as the unnatural game progressed. She wondered if her own collision with the fugitive had borne any part in the apparently fatal breaking of his nerve. And perhaps it was he who was presently to be dropped through a trap into some chilly Oxford Bosphorus. . . . Jane jumped. Close to her, the door round which she had been building that foolish fantasy quietly opened. But no guard of janizaries was revealed. All that emerged was Bodley's Librarian—an elderly man with a high, domed forehead, quite bald, on which were symmetrically disposed several tiers of spectacles. Bodley's Librarian lowered one tier of spectacles to his nose and mildly surveyed the reading room at large; then he elevated these again, brought down another, and consulted his watch; finally he substituted a third pair, glanced at the people more immediately around him, and moved slowly down the room. Occasionally he paused to pat a reader benevolently on the back, for he took a fatherly interest in his flock. Among others, he patted the donnish person as he edged along the catalogue—an attention which the donnish person received with every symptom of restrained and learned pleasure. He glanced into the apartment concealing the Emett-like engine—at which the engine gave a subdued clank by way of respectful greeting—and then drifted out of the room.

A long, low wheeze, as of air let gently out of a bicycle tyre, made Jane glance to her left. Dr. Undertone had opened his eyes and was looking at her in great astonishment—rather as if, on returning to his immediate surroundings, he had discovered himself seated next to a studious walrus or erudite dromedary. This was disconcerting to Jane, but, upon reflection, not at all surprising. During a large part of Dr. Undertone's reading life, it had to be remembered, women—and particularly young women—must have been an unusual sight in Bodley. Dr. Undertone's eyes went back to his book—to that one of the small litter of books on his desk that lay open before him. He looked no younger than his years, and he seemed to Jane tired and ill. But he also seemed very dogged. There was a story that on his ninety-fifth birthday he had been discovered at his tailor's demanding to be shown a good, hard-wearing cloth. And now with a claw-like finger he was tracing out the words on the page in front of him. Jane wondered with what coherence and cogency they reached his brain, and what large labour of research he was embarked upon. . . . She turned her head. Both the man with the scratched face and his pursuer were gone.

So now she could get on with her book. The comedy which she had been watching had come to the indecisive and obscure conclusion which comedies of real life—or for that matter tragedies either—are always likely to exhibit. But was it a comedy? If so, it had the quality of leaving its audience obstinately uneasy. Jane's book was no more attractive to her than before. The woman on her right—Jane forty years on—was unattractive. Dr. Undertone was an uncanny old creature, uncomfortable to sit beside. The upper reading room, usually so dear to her serious mind, had gone spectral and insubstantial around her. What was important was not the slow march of intellect going forward invisibly but irresistibly at these rows of desks, but the physical pursuit of that wretched little man by a spurious don—a pursuit now, presumably, continuing below, or outside the building. Jane thrust aside her book and rose. Dr. Undertone gave her a glance of grim satisfaction. She hurried as briskly as decorum permitted from the reading room.

The staircase upon which she presently found herself was deserted. Provided one has the agility necessary for cornering neatly as one moves, its shallow wooden treads admit of a considerable turn of speed. Jane found herself going down hell for leather. If her progress brought her full tilt into collision with the Vice-Chancellor, slipping upstairs to snatch half an hour's fearful joy from a book, it just couldn't be helped. It had come to her that she was involved, personally and deeply, in something very urgent indeed.

She reached the open air. It was now possible to take several routes. She might make her way by the entrance to the Divinity School—obscurely known as the "Pig Market"—in the direction of Broad Street. Or she might move in the same general direction by way of the Clarendon Building. Or, again, she might take the little tunnel or passage on her right that gave immediately upon Radcliffe Square. She chose the last of these courses. And in a moment she knew that she had guessed right.

A small crowd had collected. It was very like the sort of crowd of which she herself had been the centre an hour before. Only this time there was a policeman. And this time the person who had drawn the crowd together didn't get up.

It was the man with the scratched face. He lay just off the footpath, supine on the cobbles of the square. As backcloth he had one of the great buildings of Oxford—the rounded magnificence of the Radcliffe Camera. In such a setting it would have been possible to feel the prostrate figure as something too insignificant for pathos—a mere piece of crumpled or deflated, of pashed and pounded, organic matter. But Jane's heart contracted as she glimpsed him. She shoved to the front. It wasn't difficult, for the crowd was no more than a knot of people—some standing, some doing no more than linger for a moment as they passed. Nothing sensational was happening. It was possible to suppose that the man was dead—dead of heart failure, or something of that sort—if one didn't notice that a cheek—the unscratched cheek—was twitching faintly. And he seemed to be lucky in having gained medical attention quickly.

For close by, at the corner of Catte Street, stood a large black car, with a chauffeur sitting impassively at the wheel. Out of this must have stepped the figure now kneeling, stethoscope in hand, beside the fallen man. He was dressed in a dark coat, and on the ground beside him he had laid a Foreign Office hat and a pair of immaculate yellow kid gloves. It looked as if, by some odd chance, the accident had attracted the notice of some very grand doctor indeed. And then this reassuring figure glanced up. In the same moment, as if his doing so had been a signal to them, all the bells of Oxford fell to chiming the hour. For Jane Appleby it was a moment of chaos, and she could not have told whether the jangling was inside her own head or out of it. For this dignified physician was the identical donnish person of the late drama in the upper reading room. He had in some degree changed his spots, but he was discernibly the same leopard. And he had made his kill.

Almost without knowing what she did, Jane pushed forward once more and dropped on her knees beside the hunted man. He had opened his eyes. Now he moved his head slightly and looked at her. She saw that he recognised her—or perhaps that he took her for somebody else. His lips trembled, but no sound came. Then his glance went to the man kneeling opposite, and Jane saw his eyes dilate. She knew that it was in terror. Something moved at his side. It was his hand, groping towards Jane. "Mummy," he whispered, "darl—" His voice faded into a faint, thin wail.

Jane turned. She had remembered the policeman. But the policeman was briskly waving people to the footpath. To the accompaniment of an urgent little bell that had been quite lost amid the chiming all around, an ambulance had driven up, halted and backed, and was now standing with its open doors within a yard of the prostrate man's head. Attendants were getting a stretcher out. A sense of desperate urgency seized Jane. She scrambled to her feet and caught the policeman by the arm. "Stop!" she cried, "I want to tell you—"

But the policeman shook himself rather roughly free. "Just a moment, miss," he said brusquely. "Plenty of time when we've got him in."

The stretcher, with the man on it—the hunted man—was being lifted into the ambulance. "You don't understand," Jane cried. "It's a trick! These people—"

From behind her she heard again the hunted man's thin wail. She was irresistibly impelled to turn back to him. He was just disappearing. Their eyes met. His head moved slightly in a sort of agony of impotence, "No!" he whispered. "You can't do it to me . . . not . . . not to Milton—"

The door of the ambulance slammed. The policeman was by the bonnet, shouting to people to keep clear. The ambulance moved. The policeman opened the door beside the driver and stepped inside. In a second's swift acceleration the ambulance had swung out of Radcliffe Square and was gone. Jane turned round. The black car, with its spurious doctor, had gone too. The little knot of spectators was dispersing. To rush at one of them with a cock and bull story would be completely futile. It was the first downright adventure of her life. And she had been roundly defeated.

But there was something more than that. She stood where the hunted man had lain—stood fighting for recollection, for clarity, for what she knew was a single supremely important perception. She had a sudden irrational wish to be in open country, to be in a quiet room. All around her was a massive apparatus of learning: cliffs of books in the Camera, in the Codrington, in the Bodleian—and even beneath her feet, she knew, more and more learning, profound, unfathomable, in subterranean chambers deep below the cobbles on which had been flung by some horrible and surreptitious violence the wretched little man who in his agony had called out to her as to his mother. . . . Jane laughed aloud, in incipient hysteria. It was like being very thirsty on a broad, broad ocean. All that knowledge—and she wanted one single elusive fact alone.

She dug her nails hard into her palms. They were nails inadequately prepared to be very effective in this way, but she contrived to make them hurt. The man had whispered something just as he was whisked away. It was something idiotic, meaningless . . . something about a poet. . . . *Not to Milton* . . . that was it. But why—

And then Jane understood. The sudden, full wash of lucidity over her brain was like a plunge into cold and reviving waters. Milton was not a man but a place. And the poor devil's last gasped word had been an agonised cry against being swept off to it.

And now he had vanished. And it was through a Milton—Milton Porcorum—that somebody had reported seeing another man being driven. Another vanished man. . . .

For a moment her whole body felt very cold; it was as if she had indeed been plunged in icy water for a long time. But she knew she could run—and she ran. She ran through the Bodleian quadrangle, careless of its violated quiet, and through the gap between the Clarendon Building and the Sheldonian Theatre. There was no car for hire—as she had hoped there might be—in the rank between Turl Street and the gates of Trinity. But she had only to go on to the foot of St. Giles' to be sure of finding one. She might have got there quicker on her bicycle, but she had forgotten all about that.

At the most, it would take a little over an hour and a half. . . . Struck by a sudden thought, she stopped and turned, panting, into the Broad Street post office. She was out of it within three minutes and running up Magdalen Street. It was just here that she had had that idiotic collision. But not so idiotic, either. She would never have noticed what was going on in the upper reading room had she not earlier knocked the man down in the street. And she wouldn't have done *that* had she not been in such a hurry to get away from poor old Dr. Ourglass and that ass Bultitude. So even fat and famous dons had their utility. . . .

She tumbled into a waiting and reasonably powerful-looking car. The driver, a young man in an enveloping duffel-coat, received her instructions with unobtrusive respect—with a respect *so* unobtrusive, indeed, that Jane took a second look at him. If the morning's events had not made her sensitive to the notion of imposture, she would probably have held her peace. As it was, she spoke out boldly and with frank suspicion. "Didn't I use to see you at lectures?"

The young man's eyebrows raised themselves slightly in mild reproach. "Madam," he said, "must I always be reproached with my past?"

Despite the turmoil of her thoughts, Jane still had some area of her mind available for the sensation of feeling a fool. "I'm sorry," she said. "It just surprised me. Will you please—"

Her speech was cut short by a sudden and astonishing commotion all around her. It was rather like being incontinently in the middle of a flock of starlings. This commotion wheeled on the car as on a pivot and disappeared down Beaumont Street. The young man was startled too. "That's odd," he said. "What on earth can the little creatures—" Then it seemed to occur to him that a taxi-driver should be a man of few words. He shut the door on Jane, jumped in in front, and took the wheel. The car moved smoothly off down Magdalen Street and the Cornmarket. It had turned at Carfax and was nearing the railway station when the young man spoke over his shoulder. "I know fares sometimes don't like it," he said, "but do you mind if I make an observation?"

Jane compressed her lips. The world—or certainly the world of Oxford—is full of tiresome young men. "Not in the least," she said coldly.

"Well, it's about those lectures. I was carried away by presumption. It wasn't me you saw. Your question prompted me to claim a higher station in life than I am rightfully entitled to. I hope you will forgive me."

"Stuff and nonsense. It was certainly you. You came from Balliol."

The young man gave a low moan. "Then it has happened again—this humiliating, this intolerable confusion."

"I don't know what you're talking about."

"It was my brother."

"Your brother?"

"My *legitimate* brother, Herbert. I'm just 'Enry."

Jane lost patience. "For goodness sake, shut up. And get a move on."

The road ahead was clear. The young man who was pleased to call himself 'Enry cast a swift backward glance at his passenger. "In a hurry?" he asked.

"Yes."

There was that in Jane's voice that the young man took a moment to digest. "Life or death?"

"Quite honestly—just that."

The young man thrust at his accelerator so that the car seemed to punch Jane in the back. "If I lose my licence," he said, "and—mark you—it's all that stands between a poor bastard boy and the gutter, I am wholly yours. They say these things will touch eighty."

Jane set her teeth. "Then," she said, "touch it."

8. The play had been timed for the eve of the half-term holiday. This avoided complications over home-work. And the play had been quite a success. But this served only to lend the morrow a tiresome air of anti-climax. Stuart Buffin, having improvidently made no arrangements whatever for its expenditure, felt this with peculiar force. The sensation, however, was pervasive throughout North Oxford that morning. Had this not been so, things might have turned out very differently. To begin with, Jane Appleby and her driver 'Enry would not have experienced that startled moment at the spot which has now for some time been the hub of our narrative: that corner, to wit, of St. Giles' and Beaumont Street the dominating feature of which is Bede's College.

Stuart's sense, moreover, of having brushed adventure on the preceding evening was another important factor. And—further to this again—was his indignation that this sense of having brushed adventure had itself been brushed rudely aside. His father, lingering for a few moments in benevolent if absent contemplation of the frugal family supper before going off to dine in Bede's, had received the story of the hunted man without enthusiasm. He had even made a derogatory remark about the effects of too much Superman—a quip that had offended Stuart as much by its *passe* quality as by its injustice. The world, Stuart considered, was not so pervasively dull and securely ordered a place as long years of comfortable dining in Bede's and similar establishments led elderly persons to believe. Things *did* happen. Only, when they began to happen, authority was prone to take one firmly by the ear and lead one into inglorious security. That was what had occurred during the war, when substantial numbers of future Tigers had been bundled off to America. It was what had happened when the gym caught fire and they had been indecently herded into the middle distance much as if the fire-engines had been a force of hostile tanks. *They* would always nip in and cut you out of things if given the chance.

These and other dark thoughts had disposed Stuart Buffin to make a most belated appearance at breakfast that morning. They disposed him, when he realised that his mother wanted to get the table cleared, to sit owlishly over this repast, nibbling his way through toast and marmalade at the steady rate of one slice every twelve minutes. This recalcitrance, however, was visited with its just penalty, and Stuart found himself implacably roped in to help with washing up. By the time that this tiresome operation was accomplished and he had emerged into the hall the clock was striking ten. He wished that he had fixed something up with Martin or Miles or Dick or Malcom. As things were, he addressed himself gloomily to climbing the stairs, being persuaded that nothing lay before him but a morning's communion with his stamp collection. And stamp collecting, he was rapidly coming to feel, was a nauseating practice. . . . It was at this moment that the telephone bell rang.

Stuart's mood being not at present co-operative, he at first felt disposed to ignore the instrument. His father had already left the house. If his mother had to hurry in from coping with the hens in order to answer the thing, or if Mrs. Sparks emerged from her soap-suds to deal with it and got the message hopelessly muddled—well, that was just too bad. Stuart, however, was really a child tolerant of—indeed, amiably disposed towards—those with whom fate had directed that he should live. Partly because of this, and partly because the call was probably from one of his father's pupils, tiresomely wanting to change the hour of a tutorial—in which event Stuart would give himself the satisfaction of replying to the great lout with the most awful and freezing courtesy—he decided to answer the summons after all. He moved over to the telephone and picked up the receiver. What he heard was a low voice with a foreign accent. What he believed this voice to say was "Stuart, is that you?"

"Yes." Stuart growled this reply with a good deal of moroseness. He had jumped to the conclusion that some silly ass of his acquaintance was having him on.

"This is Anna." The voice was really a woman's—and it was tense and vibrant. "The place is called Milton Manor, near Milton Porcorum. The danger is now too great. And it is to the boy." The voice grew suddenly yet more urgent, so that

Stuart felt a queer pricking in his spine. "Come at once, Kurt. Bring—"

And then the voice broke off. It broke off with a sharp, interrupted cry and a smothered gasp: it was as if powerful hands had closed round the speaker's throat. There was a thump—a very horrid thump—and then the click of a receiver being set down. The line was dead.

Stuart . . . Kurt. It had been a wrong number—they were always happening—and he had got a message not meant for him. Stuart Buffin found that he was trembling and wet all over, as if he had tried to break the record in the school quarter mile. He found that he had sat down—and it was only because of this, he realised, that he was not rushing to his mother for all he was worth. For he was not in the slightest doubt about the kind of thing with which he had been in contact over some unknown distance. It was violence . . . danger . . . evil. And suddenly his eyes rounded. It was more even than that. It was the proof of what he had known: that things *happen.* He took a deep breath. He glanced in quick stealth about the hall, listened for footsteps, for any sound in the nearer rooms. There was nobody about. He picked up the telephone again and swiftly dialled a number. And when he got an answer his voice was as urgent as the woman's he had just heard.

"This is Stuart Buffin; please may I speak to Miles? . . . Miles, it's Stuart. Ring round and get everybody to your place *now.* I'm coming straight across. . . . *Everybody.* . . . Miles, it's something sticking out . . . it's tremendous. . . ."

He banged down the receiver and dashed upstairs, taking the steps three at a time. When he came down again a moment later he was wearing his dark blue blazer with the crouching tiger on its pocket and its peremptory injunction: *Symmetry.* In the pockets were his purse, his torch, his big clasp knife.

Stuart's mother, returning from her hens, was just in time to see the boy disappearing on his bicycle. For a moment she was sharply anxious. But he was safely past the cross-roads—the quiet one, which she was convinced could be so treacherous. Thank goodness, she thought, Stuart seemed to have found something to do. It had looked like being a sticky half-term.

9. Miles never did things by halves. There was a formidable gathering of Tigers in the hut, and soon debate ran high. The red-haired Tigers—known throughout Oxford to be the most temerarious and terrible—were on the side of Stuart, and of Miles who was their natural leader. But (as in the great consult in Satan's Pandemonium) there were other voices that urged caution. Of these the first was Dick's—that cool intelligence who, as Dick Whittington, had maintained so lofty a port amid answering confusion the evening before.

"I think it's too far," Dick said. "We *could* make it. But look at that hilly terrain." His finger went down with a staff officer's decision on the map spread before him. "It might take up to three hours." He shook his head sombrely. "A good many of us would never get back."

"I don't see why not." Miles was obstinate. "Coming back, a lot of it will be downhill."

"I know that, idiot. But we'd have a head-wind against us."

"A head-wind!" Miles was rash and eager. "How can you tell that?"

Silently, Dick moved his finger first to the pocket-compass by which he had set the map, and then to a window through which it was just possible to see a neighbouring weathercock. Everybody was impressed. Stuart saw that things were going badly. "But the wind's sure to change," he said. "It nearly always does, in the afternoon."

"That's right!" Several Tigers, mostly red-headed, immediately took up in all innocence this mendacious statement. "Stuart's right. The wind always changes. Ask Malcolm. Malcolm knows."

And Malcolm, the scientifically minded child who had been

somewhat overborne by the complexities of theatrical lighting the evening before, nodded gravely. "Of course," he agreed. "It has something to do with the cooling off of the central land mass. But I'm not *quite* sure about the details."

"I bet you're not." Dick was quite angry. "And there's another objection. We'd have to leave some sort of word. We can't all just go off. And if we once let parents and people know—"

But this was a mistake, and was at once cried down. "Rot!" "We can all go off till supper time." "That's only the kids." "Just say it's a picnic." "And so it would be if we took some sandwiches." "Leave some sort of message to be found later."

"Very well. I agree we could go—if we could make the distance." The lucid Dick was quick to abandon an untenable position. "But there *is* the distance. And there's another thing. I think it more important. Stuart says this may be frightfully serious. That means we ought really to speak out about it. Probably to the police."

"And what good would that do?" Miles advanced into the centre of the assembly. This delay infuriated him, and his face was growing increasingly pink beneath its mop of red hair. "Everybody would say Stuart had been dreaming—or sogging himself in flicks. One never *does* get things like that believed."

"Here, here!" "Miles is right." "They'd laugh at it." "They'd laugh at it—and then keep an eye on us." "No good." There was now clamour from all over the hut, and most of it was in the form of a demand for action. A crowd was milling round the map, disputing fiercely. Dick walked away from it moodily—rather as Napoleon might have withdrawn himself from the burdensome society of a group of excited Marshals.

"Why not go by train?"

Everybody turned and stared. There were several girl Tigers in the gathering, and it had been a small and very red-headed one who spoke. Dick turned round. "Nonsense. Go and look at the map, Marty, I've been through this Porcorum place by car.

It's miles from a railway station."

The girl called Marty thrust her way close to the map, and with some difficulty got her nose above the level of the table. "I thought so," she said. "We can put our bikes on the eleven twenty-five, and be in Bourton-on-the-Water an hour later. And from there we can *strike.*"

There was a moment of awed silence. Of Tigers it is particularly true that the female of the species is more deadly than the male. The small person called Marty was challenging the gathering with flashing eyes and dilated nostrils. Dick was clearly wavering. But a new and solid point occurred to him. "And what about the fares?" He ran his eye over the assembled crowd. "It would be an enormous sum. And bicycle tickets, too. We wouldn't have anything like it even if we pooled all we've got."

"We've got the money for the Dumb Friends from last night. It came to pounds and pounds. Martin has it. He was treasurer."

Again there was a hush. Before this female ruthlessness the predominantly male assembly was momentarily speechless. Then a serious-looking boy spoke from the back. "Isn't that," he asked, "what's called embarrassment?"

Yells of mirth from the better informed greeted this unhappy malapropism, mingled with urgent demands for Martin and the money-box. Dick, like the Homeric hero hither and thither dividing the swift mind, and seeing that the issue was in fact decided, instantly took the course necessary to maintain his predominance not only of the gathering as a whole but of the insurgent and triumphant faction of the red heads. "All back here with bikes in fifteen minutes," he shouted. "Sandwiches, chocolate, macs, compasses, and all useful weapons. Proceed by Banbury Road, St. Giles' and Beaumont Street. Roll-call at the station, and Martin and I buy all the tickets. Nothing to be said at anybody's home except that it's a picnic." He raised his voice against a swelling chorus of excitement, "And I hope—you silly twerps—you won't make all that row if we have to go into action. You might be a crowd of howling Chinese."

Without paying much deference to this tart remark, the crowd hastily dispersed. Stuart Buffin and his crony Miles, wild with joy at having carried the day, dashed for their bicycles. But before they could leave the hut they were cornered by the unremittingly clear-headed Dick. "Look here," he said, "trying to talk sense to these silly asses is no good at all. But I'd better tell *you.*"

"What do you mean—tell us?" Stuart was suspicious. "This is jolly well my affair. It's for me to be telling you."

"Forget it." Dick frowned at hearing himself drop into this vaguely transatlantic expression. "All I want to say is this. Before that train goes out I send a telegram from the station—see?"

"Who d'you want to send a telegram to?" Miles was quite as wary as Stuart.

"I couldn't care less." This time Dick seemed to take satisfaction in the raciness of the expression. "The police, your father, my father, the Prime Minister: you can take your pick. But to somebody I send back word of just where we're going. No reason why we shouldn't keep in touch. We're not bandits, you know. We're part of the law." He took a quick glance at Stuart and Miles, uncertain whether he had hit on a line that would appeal to their childish intellects.

"Very well." Miles was pink and furious. "But if we find a couple of country bobbies at this Bourton-on-the-Water place, told off by telephone to pack us off home, I'll—I'll scrag you."

"You're welcome." And Dick went briskly out. A little Secret-Service-Boy stuff, he was reflecting, had its amusing aspects. There was no harm in giving the young a day out with Biggles—provided that one kept, for one's own part, the realities of the situation in mind. Riding off to collect his sandwiches, he began composing his telegram. It looked like being quite a long one.

But presently, and as he furiously pedalled, his serious air relaxed. There was nobody to see him. He grinned broadly. For even this serious child had a proper streak of fantasy. He looked forward to the confusion at the railway station when a small army arrived with bicycles and insisted on loading them on the sleepy little train for Bourton-on-the-Water. After that, there might, or might not, be adventure in the thing. He had an open mind. He always had.

PART FIVE

NEMESIS AT MILTON MANOR

And they, so perfect is their misery,
Not once perceive their foul disfigurement.

COMUS

1. Appleby made a final jotting on the pad in front of him. "Thank you, Superintendent. The facts seem to be pretty well as I remembered them. But there's one more thing—about the place Milton Manor. . . . Yes, I know it's that. What I want is something much fuller. Get on to the General Medical Council. These concerns must be registered, and you can get a bit of a line through that. Who sends people there, and why—you see? . . . Yes, of course they're often sticky. If there is delay, ask the Commissioner to be good enough to tackle somebody high up at once. But remember the time-factor. I don't want a bulging file next Friday; I want what you can get by noon. . . . And—Superintendent—one more thing. You've spotted this place on the map? Good. Well, if you don't hear from me between two and three o'clock, carry out Instruction D. . . . You needn't sound so surprised. . . . Yes, I *did* say *D*. . . . Thank you—that's all."

The Provost of Bede's knocked out his pipe into the comfortable fire glowing in his study, and waited until Appleby had put the receiver down. "Well, well," he said; "and to think that all those meditative essays you used to read to me were leading to this. . . . You are become a very brisk fellow, my dear John."

"They weren't meditative; they were merely thorough." Appleby smiled rather absently, and walked across the long room to stare out of the window. "As for briskness, since you became the Head of a House, you are a model of it yourself."

The Provost reached for a decanter. "I attribute the still comparatively unclouded state of my faculties to the observance of one single rule. I have taken to nothing but solitary drinking. Drink does no harm if you are in a position to give your mind to it. Moreover the habit is very inexpensive. Two glasses of brown sherry—or, for a change, of light hunting port—consumed slowly between eleven a.m. and noon: I do all my work on it." The Provost raised the decanter. "But, for this once, I will have somebody join me. Perhaps I may convert you."

Appleby took the glass held out to him, and shook his head. "The prescription is useless to me. My hours of labour are not so agreeably contracted. Frequently I work right on into the middle of the night—only to be hit on the head in a quiet Oxford road and carried away in a van. If many of your guests are served in the same way, it will positively give the place a bad name. I think you ought to take the matter up with the Proctors."

"It will be simpler, John, that you should take it up with the criminals. And that is just what you have rather the appearance of being engaged in." The Provost took the poker and gave a vicious thrust at a sluggish lump of coal. "Look here—I wish you'd tell me what all this is about. Is this tramp, or whatever he was, that you hit up with last night—Routh, did he call himself? —really connected with our missing undergraduate?"

"I think there can be small doubt of it." Appleby's voice was grim. "For my sister's sake, I wish it wasn't so."

"You think the young man was once hit on the head and put in a van, too?"

"No, I don't. Because I don't think Routh's adventures began that way, either. Nor Miss Kolmak's."

"Miss Kolmak? Who on earth is she?"

"Well—that's not, come to think of it, her name. She's Mrs. Something-or-other—some name with a decidedly farther-side-of-the-iron-curtain twist to it, I imagine. And she is the adopted daughter of your Kurt Kolmak's aunt. She, too, appears to have been kidnapped, together with her small son."

"God bless my soul! Do you mean to say, John, that such outrageous things happen in this country?" The Provost, who had been about to set down the poker, appeared to think better of it—much as if a handy weapon might be needed at any moment.

"It seems they do." Appleby made a wry face. "Unexplained vanishings do from time to time occur. And lately some have occurred in a way that has set us thinking."

"You mean that this queer and disgraceful business here somehow hitches on to a situation you have been investigating already?"

"I think it just possibly may. And, while I'm waiting for a little more data, I propose to tell you about it—just as I used to bring you philosophical problems that were too tough for me."

The Provost, while receiving this analogy with evident scepticism, abruptly put aside the poker and sat down. "Good," he said.

"Well, then—here is the first problem I'd put to you. Suppose Provost, that you are to all appearances a law-abiding Englishman—one engaged, indeed, in some wholly beneficent profession—"

The Provost grinned. "You always did begin, my boy, with some wild hypothesis."

"Don't interrupt. Suppose that, although your way of life is entirely blameless, you yet keep a Minotaur in your back yard. This creature must have its regular tribute of youths and maidens. Not a vast number, for this is a small and abstemious Minotaur. Still, its appetite is steady, and must be satisfied. How would you do the catering?"

The Provost considered. "I should keep an eye open for the *filius nullius,* the *filius terrae*—"

"While avoiding the *filius honesto genere natus.* Precisely! In other words, it would be foolish to make away with persons of established position so long as you could conveniently find waifs and strays."

"I see what you're getting at." The Provost stretched out an arm for his second glass of brown sherry, appeared to think better of it, and thrust the decanter out of reach. "But it doesn't seem quite to fit last night's proceedings. Assistant Commissioners of the Metropolitan Police are neither strays nor waifs."

"That was a different matter. My guess is that they were endeavouring to recover an escapee, and that they just had to take me while they were about it. Although there may well have been another reason, too."

"Are you going to tell me who 'they' are?"

"I wish that, with any certainty, I knew. But let me stick to a proper order. Some time ago there was a curious case of a fellow who was released from prison after serving a long term on account of a big robbery. He hadn't a relation or acquaintance in the world, and he took to drifting about, getting a labourer's job from time to time in one town or another. Nobody ought to have had the faintest interest in either him or his movements. But—as it happened—the Bristol police had. There was stuff that had never been recovered, and they thought that eventually he might make for it. So an eye was being kept on him, without his knowing it. He vanished."

"Smart of him, I'd say."

"Perhaps. But there have been one or two other cases that have come, you might say, within the same general category. Waifs and strays who turned out to be not quite absolutely *filii terrae* after all. They vanished and—what nobody would have suspected from their circumstances—were enquired about."

The Provost frowned. "Interesting, no doubt. But, unless the numbers were quite considerable, I don't see that you could build much—"

"They grouped on the map."

The Provost sat up abruptly. "And this place we keep hearing about—Milton Canonicorum—"

"Porcorum."

"This ridiculously named place is well in the picture?"

"It is. Not plumb centre. But decidedly there."

"And it's dawned on you that you now have a new crop of relevant disappearances?" The Provost had suddenly assumed an expression of sombre melancholy, suggestive of a rational being condemned to pass long hours in the society of more primitive forms of mental life.

Appleby smiled. "You haven't altogether lost your old touch. And the point's fair enough. But remember that I came up thinking simply of this young man of my sister Jane's. And he's a bit out of series, as you probably already see. But there's the first fact: people have in a mild way been tending to disappear within a certain area. People like this chap Routh."

"A tramp?"

"Routh is not in the least a tramp—and, I'd say, nothing like half so honest. But he is definitely a lone-wolf type. Probably he's proud of it, so that it would emerge pretty well at a first brush with him. Well, I think he went to feed the Minotaur."

"And was disgorged again?"

"And escaped from the labyrinth. I'm not sure it wasn't with blood on his hands. And he certainly carried something that he believed valuable off with him."

"Not an Ariadne?"

"Something much more portable than a young woman. He had it in the inside breast-pocket of his jacket." Appleby had risen and was pacing the room—his eye, every now and then, straying expectantly to the telephone. "Well, he got away. Then they got him again, plus me. Then we were both rescued by this astonishing Kolmak of yours, about whom I must ask you presently. Then, in the early morning, and while I was still oblivious, he beat it."

"And is now?"

"I only wish I knew. And I have my fears, as you can guess. The local people have a net out for him—but I don't much like the way the half-hours are going by without news. . . . Where in Oxford would you hide, Provost, if you felt yourself to be a fugitive both from lawlessness and the law?"

"In Bodley." The Provost had no doubts about it.

"I hadn't thought of that. Do you think the local men—"

"It certainly won't be quite their first thought either."

"Well, we must give them a little more time. Now, consider the woman. Her name is Anna, and she has managed to smuggle both herself and her child into England. Her position was irregular, and her past was no doubt a long history of senseless persecution. Probably she was inclined a little to dramatise her predicament. She and her boy were fair food for the Minotaur."

The Provost stirred uneasily. "I begin to believe in it. And I don't like it—particularly the bit about the child."

"Quite so. But here we come to an odd thing. It is quite clear to me that this woman, with her little boy, was carried off and put under some sort of constraint. But not an absolute constraint. She twice managed to elude the vigilance of her captors—I think we may call it that—and communicate covertly with Kolmak. On each occasion she could have declared her whereabouts. And on each occasion she deliberately refrained. The second message spoke of danger, and of the possible need to send an urgent telephone summons for help. That second message was sent off yesterday afternoon. Kolmak is waiting beside his telephone now. And, of course, it is being checked. If his number is called, any conversation will be recorded."

The Provost, who had been sitting with closed eyes, momentarily opened them. "What about a wrong number?"

"What's that?" Appleby was startled.

"Suppose this woman's danger is suddenly precipitated. She's in a great hurry to send out a telephone-message—secretly. Quite likely, you know, to get through to the wrong number."

Appleby frowned. "Then it will depend on a time-factor. The County people will be arranging to tap the telephone—or telephones—in this Milton place. But, technically, it will be a bit of a job."

"Just an idea." The Provost's voice was so vague and apologetic that Appleby found himself grinning a most juvenile grin.

He remembered very well what this meant. The old boy was really thinking.

"My impression is this. The woman called Anna feels that she is on the verge of discovering something. She judges it so important that it is her duty to continue courting danger—danger not only for herself but for her boy. She didn't want Kolmak, the police, rescue, and so forth. What do you make of that?"

"Has she a profession?"

"She's a doctor."

"Would you say, John, that Minotaurs find female physicians particularly toothsome?"

"I think I'd say that her profession made her something of a special case. Perhaps there was some idea of making her less a victim than an attendant."

"And, correspondingly, her professional knowledge would give her a special interest in—and perhaps penetration about—the activities of the establishment."

"Quite so. And now come to young Geoffrey Ourglass. He is clearly to be bound in somehow. He too vanishes—long before either of these other two—and is last seen being driven through Milton Porcorum. But at once—or almost at once—his uncle, his fiancée, his tutor, and no doubt plenty of other people too, start enquiring about him. So you see what I mean by his being out of series."

The Provost nodded. "The point is hardly an obscure one. Far from being a *filius terrae,* this young man is highly prized by the world and shortly due to scoop the pool: a First in Schools, a secure and probably highly distinguished career, an admirable wife and an irreproachable brother-in-law—" Abruptly the Provost's eyes came open again, fixing themselves on Appleby as if he suddenly felt obliged to verify this last statement. "But—great heavens!—now that I come to think of it—"

The telephone at the farther end of the room gave a low purr. Appleby leapt to it. "Yes," he said, "yes—I am Sir John Appleby. . . . An accident? . . . I see. . . . And what about that van? . . . Thank you." He put down the receiver and turned to the Provost. "Routh was still in Oxford just after ten o'clock. A constable saw him bolting down Broad Street."

"Saw him! Then why the dickens didn't he go after him?"

"Because it was only when he got down to Carfax that the word about Routh was passed to him by the next man. You must remember they've been on the job only a couple of hours. But seeing a fellow rather the worse for wear making off down the street, the constable took a good look at him. And a passer-by told him there had just been some sort of accident with no great harm done—this fellow having bumped into a bicycle, or something of the sort. But, so far, a hunt in that district has produced nothing more. Incidentally, the van that operated so drastically against Routh and myself last night, and that was driven away and parked by Kolmak, has vanished. The enemy must have retrieved it."

"Enemy seems the right word, John. I get the impression that you are confronting quite a crowd. But there was something I was going to say. It's a story about young Ourglass that Birkbeck told me, but that didn't strike me as relevant until this *filius terrae* business sprang up. To begin with, Ourglass, as you probably know, isn't really so very young. He's in the last batch of our actual war-service men, and he must be a good many years older than your sister."

Appleby nodded. "He's twenty-seven."

"Well, the point is this. Although not a *filius terrae* in actuality he did on one occasion put up a very good show of being one. And the story is so much to his credit that I am sorry it didn't reach my ears earlier. I don't very effectively get to know our men before the end of their second year, and I'd have been glad to make this fellow's acquaintance earlier. But perhaps you know about him from your sister?"

"I know very little. Jane has been rather close about the engagement, and so far to-day I've failed to contact her." Appleby glanced quickly at the Provost. "You know, the more

I've thought about this business in the last few hours, the grimmer the view I've been inclined to take about the young man's chances of survival. The mere length of his disappearance looks pretty bad. But I'm not sure you're not going to tell me something hopeful."

"I hope I am. At least young Ourglass appears to be—or to have been—a person very well able to give a good account of himself. The facts are these. He has a flair for acting of sorts. Character-turns and sketches—and an ability to take on the colouring of the people he's living among. Moreover, he's a bit of a linguist. Well, in the last couple of years of the war he was spotted doing that sort of thing—simply to amuse himself and his friends—in Italy. He could do an Italian peasant to the life. So he was parachuted either into Germany or German-occupied territory—I'm not sure which—and managed to get himself rounded up as a D.P. worker and clapped into an armament factory. Before the show ended, it seems, he got one or two pretty useful bits of information out. A pretty gallant job. And I've an idea that his subsequent delay in getting up here may have been due to some rather similar assignment. It might be part of your picture—eh?"

"It might, indeed. And it's odd that nothing of this came through to me. The young man must be even closer than Jane."

"Presumably he is. I had this from Birkbeck only after you left common-room last night."

"And from whom did Birkbeck have it?"

"From Bultitude."

Appleby frowned. "Bultitude! You mean your fat scientist?"

"That is a very cavalier way, my dear John, to speak of Bede's only celebrity. Bultitude had it from somebody terribly high up in something. He likes altitudes, you know."

"So I gathered." Appleby was silent for a moment. "Great carcass of a man, isn't he? How did they use him in the war—as a barrage balloon?"

"Biological warfare."

"Sounds horrid."

"Quite unspectacular, I believe—or at least the parts of it that ever got going. Thinking up insulating materials that wouldn't be devoured by bugs in New Guinea and Malaya. . . . Would you care for that second glass of sherry?"

"No thank you. Nothing more for me until luncheon in Milton Porcorum."

The Provost nodded. "I wondered when you'd be going out there."

"I'm leaving at noon. But first I want to catch Jane, and also get more reports from the local people and the Yard. . . . Ah, there they are."

The telephone had purred again, and Appleby sprang to it. "Hullo, is that— Oh, I see. . . . This *is* Sir John Appleby speaking. . . . Yes, go ahead. . . . What's that word? . . . s-u-a? . . . I've got it. Go on. . . . Thank you. Yes, send the confirmatory copy to me at the Provost's Lodgings." He put down the instrument and turned to the Provost. "Well, I'm dashed."

"Telegram from London?"

"No. It was from Jane, here in Oxford. Listen." Appleby glanced at the note he had made. "Man weedy scratched face first observed upper reading room now being taken non sponte sua in ambulance to Milton stop left Radcliffe Square 11 a.m. stop am following in hired car investigate." He threw the paper on the desk. "And it's signed 'Jane.' What do you think of that?"

"That your sister has the rudiments of the Latin tongue. Though why she should break into it—"

"She felt that to say in English that a man had just been carried off against his will from Radcliffe Square might provoke questions and hold her up. Well, these people have got Routh again. And they may presently have this impetuous sister of mine as well. I'd better be off."

"I agree." The Provost rose. "Does it occur to you that they must know you *know?*"

Appleby nodded grimly. "It certainly does. Of course the only positive fact they have is that I have talked with Routh, and they probably suspect nothing of our having tumbled upon other evidence pointing their way. They may reckon now on extorting fairly reliably from Routh just what he did tell me. But—unless we have the whole picture wrong—Milton Manor now contains a large and quite ruthless criminal organisation, who have been up to heaven knows what, and who now confront a state of emergency. In fact, they are preparing to pack up. And that's what I don't like."

"I don't see why not. It means that, even before you know what their game is, you've got them on the run."

"No doubt. But people driven to hurried packing sometimes decide to travel light. They even scrap things."

The Provost pursed his lips. "I hope you return in time to dine. And if you bring back our missing undergraduate—well, his dinner too awaits him—such as it is."

2. Just short of Witney, it occurred to Jane that the young man styling himself 'Enry might eventually find her behaviour odd. She had very little to go upon. Indeed, all she could do was to poke about Milton Porcorum enquiring for an ambulance. And that must be a proceeding that would strike anyone as a little out of the way. She had better, therefore, do some explaining. On the other hand it would not do to explain too much. If she announced that it was her aim to track down and interview a number of men who had just carried out a highly criminal abduction, he might suppose her to be mad or at least unwomanly. He would probably suggest applying to the police. But she had done that—she was sure in the most effective way possible—by sending John the telegram; and now it was a point of honour to push straight in herself. If the ambulance led to Geoffrey, and to piercing the dark veil that had made a nightmare of her life week after week for what seemed an eternity, she must follow it at any hazard whatsoever, and with all the speed that a hired car could muster.

Jane determined to reopen communications. She therefore leant across the front seat. "May I explain a little?" she asked.

"Does a romantic secret cloud your birth too?"

Jane ignored this. "What I'm looking for," she said, "is an ambulance."

"Isn't that a trifle pessimistic? I'm quite a careful driver—although you *are* making me go at a fair lick."

"It's impossible to talk to you."

"Not a bit. I'm attending. And I'll find you an ambulance if I possibly can. Any particular sort?"

"I want to *trace* an ambulance. It left Oxford—Radcliffe Square to be exact—at eleven o'clock, and I think it's going to this Milton Porcorum, or to somewhere near there. There is somebody in it that I want to keep in contact with. Only I wasn't told just where it's bound for."

The young man received this in silence. But he had the air of giving the matter a good deal of thought. When he did speak, it was with some appearance of irrelevance. "My name is not 'Enry."

"I didn't think it was for a moment."

"My name is Roger Remnant. I *was* up at Balliol. And doubtless you and all your acquaintance *did* see me at lectures. I didn't think much of them."

"I'm sure my acquaintance would all be very much upset if they knew."

"Not your acquaintance—the lectures. That was the trouble. I didn't manage to see much in the lectures, and eventually the chaps giving then weren't able to see much in me. Fair enough. But I thought I'd like to stop about Oxford for a bit, so here I am. Who are you?"

"My name is Jane Appleby. I'm up at Somerville."

Roger Remnant bowed gravely towards the wind-screen; he was driving much too fast to take his eye even for a moment from the road. "How do you do."

"How do you do." Jane judged it discreet to comply with this fantastic observance of forms.

"Our association is now on an entirely different basis." The late 'Enry made this statement as if he wholly believed it. "And we had better get back to this ambulance. You say it left Oxford at precisely eleven o'clock. We left at eleven-ten. There would be a point at which it was no more than two miles ahead. But it would increase that lead when it got into more or less open country and we were still nosing out of Oxford. An ambulance can get away with a lot. I'm afraid we're not likely to catch up with it. And, of course, it may have gone out of Oxford by the Woodstock Road. I reckon Witney and Burford to be best, but I can see that there's a case for Chipping Norton and Stow-on-the-Wold."

"I see." Jane was impressed by this professional clarity.

"So it looks as if our best course will be simply to enquire for it when we get into the neighborhood you think it's making for."

"That's what I think." Jane was relieved. Roger Remnant appeared disposed to take it as all in the day's work.

"Is it really an ambulance, or is there something queer about it?"

Jane jumped on her swaying seat. She hadn't expected this swift perspicacity. "It—it's something queer."

"I expect we'll find it. Do you know the country?"

"Not very well."

"There are some maps in the pocket on the door on your left. You'd better sit back and do a bit of work on them."

The map that looked most hopeful was an ancient one on a scale of eight miles to an inch. Jane learnt what she could from it. Finding the area involved, she ran to earth, despite the jolting of the car, a small black point marked "Milton." Towards this, and from a secondary road some miles away, an unobtrusive scratch moved indecisively before petering out. The place must be decidedly in what is called the heart of the countryside. She looked about her and saw that they were already in rural solitude. There was an empty road before them, with nobody in sight except two trudging women with rucksacks. It was good walking weather. The autumn day was like a great cup of sunlight. She thought of the wretched little man shut up in the near-darkness of the bogus ambulance, of the sinister power that had edged him out of the security of the upper reading room, of the alarming efficiency with which he had then been dealt with in what could have been no more than a few seconds free from public observation. And she suddenly felt cold. The Cotswold air, perhaps, was chilly despite the clear sunshine.

The drive seemed endless. But eventually she was aware that they had left the high road, and were plunging down what was no more than a lane between high hedges. The proximity of these magnified her sense of the speed at which the car was travelling; sometimes a projecting branch whipped its sides with the effect of a momentary hail-storm; she wondered what would happen if they met a farm wagon, or a straying horse or cow. Roger Remnant took a right-angled turn almost without slackening pace, so that the racing wheels and strained chassis gave a squeal of protest. "No call for alarm," he said. "Tyres just a trifle in need of air. . . . Here's another one." They cornered again by a small, half-obliterated sign-post that Jane failed to decipher. It had a look of local enterprise, and suggested recesses of the region so obscure as to be beyond the interest of any county authority. They rounded a bend and a scattering of cottages appeared before them. "My guess," Roger Remnant said, "is that this is it." And he brought the car to a halt.

The place consisted of no more than six or eight cottages. Jane jumped out. The car had been travelling so fast that her feet for a moment felt unsteady under her.

"There doesn't seem to be much life." Roger Remnant too had got out and was surveying the hamlet. "And we're too early for tea—or two late by about twenty years." He pointed to a board, depending by one remaining nail from the side of the nearest cottage, which forlornly announced the presence of this facility. "Not a tourist centre. Nothing ye olde. But there's a school farther down the lane. That means there are probably other little places like this round about." He sniffed. "It *smells* of pigs."

Jane moved to the side of the lane and peered into the garden of the cottage with the superannuated sign. It was a wilderness of weeds from which protruded, like wrecks in a fabled Sargasso sea, the rotting remains of a few home-made tables and benches. "It's a sort of shop," she said. "And a post office as well. I'll go in."

"Give a shout if you want help." Remnant spoke humorously —but Jane, looking at his eyes for the first time, saw that they were grey and serious. "Now or later."

"I will." She walked to the front of the cottage and pushed open the door. A small cracked bell feebly tinkled. There was a little room with a counter, and a surprising variety of wares exposed for sale. These latter all contrived to look thoroughly dreary. The place was so dismal that it was possible to feel the dismalness seeping even inside the tins. And there was still a smell of pigs.

The bell had been without effect. The little shop was untenanted. Jane tapped on the counter. Presently there was a response to this from some interior recess: the sound of an unwieldy body moving low on the ground, accompanied by a loud and displeasing snuffling.

Jane had a moment of panic. Milton Porcorum. . . . Perhaps she was really in the middle of a nightmare, and it had brought her to the land of the pigs. The whole hamlet would prove to be veritably inhabited only by Pigling Blands—by little pigs going to market, and little pigs staying at home. She would find nothing but a dumb and bestial rout . . . mute inglorious

Miltons with trotters and curly tails. Or perhaps she had come to the land of Circe and her swine. . . .

"Yes?" The old woman who had appeared in a doorway was lumbering and stout; she snuffled; and she had a mottled and unwholesome complexion, definitely suggestive of a Gloucester Old Spot. But at least she was endowed with speech.

"Is this Milton Porcorum?"

"It be." Any faint suggestion of cordiality that might have been read into the old woman's expression decidedly faded. "You'll have lost your way." She spoke with sombre conviction, born, no doubt, of many similarly unremunerative tinklings at her bell and tappings on her counter. "Just go straight on."

"But," said Jane, "if you don't know where I want to go—"

"Go straight on."

It was like something particularly exasperating in *Alice in Wonderland*. Jane tried again. "I'm not quite sure of the place I want. But it's where the ambulances go."

"I never heard of any ambulances. We're all healthy here."

"I'm sure you are." Jane hastened to disclaim any reflection upon the salubrity of the Milton Porcorum air.

"It's at Canonicorum you'll find folk going sick. They've an ill wind at Canonicorum."

"Canonicorum?"

"Milton Canonicorum." The old woman enunciated the words with perceptible distaste.

"I see. But I'm thinking of ambulances that bring people—patients—from quite a long way off. Is there some hospital—"

"There's nothing of the sort here. Canonicorum's the place for carryings-on. There's talk of a cinema."

"You don't happen, in the last hour or so, to have *seen* an ambulance? An ambulance with—"

"You'd better try Canonicorum."

Jane decided that it was hopeless. "Very well," she said. "I *will* try Canonicorum. But how do I get there?"

"I've told you, haven't I? Go straight on."

The old woman turned and vanished—snuffling, as she had come. Jane had for a moment the disordered fancy that she heard a rustling of straw.

3. She left the little shop and the bell tinkled behind her. She was baffled, and for a moment felt discouraged to the point of hopelessness. The ambulance had vanished; there was no more to it than that; and she might as well return to Oxford. But at least she could go on to Milton Canonicorum first. Not that she had any faith in it. Just as Milton Porcorum contained nothing but porcine old women, so would the answering village be populated exclusively by monkish and uncommunicative old men. They would have nothing to say—except that there was an ill wind at Porcorum, and that she should go straight on.

She returned to the car and reported her lack of success to Roger Remnant. He listened attentively. "The old lady sounds a rich type," he said. "If you don't mind, I'll have a go at her myself." And he walked over to the shop.

Jane looked about her. She ought to make her enquiry of anybody she could see. But Milton Porcorum seemed the next thing to a deserted village. The few remaining cottages constituting it were unpromisingly blank and silent; the only sound was a distant, shrill shouting from the school some way on; the only wisp of smoke, even, was from a farmhouse a couple of fields away.

Remnant was back again. "She'd farrowed," he said.

"Don't be absurd."

"Nothing but a small, fat, sucking-pig of a child. She said that granny had been taken poorly. The shock of doing no trade with you has sent her to her bed. But I did a bit of trade myself. It's all I got out of the place. A much better map. The one-inch Ordnance Survey."

Jane took the map and they climbed into the front of the car together. "We'd better try Canonicorum," she said. "And I'll have a squint at this as we go." She spread the map out on her knees. "What a tremendous difference this makes. One feels one could really find one's way about with it."

"If we knew where to go, Miss Appleby, it would take us there in no time. As it is, we'll try Canonicorum, as you say. They may have quite a line in ambulances, after all."

"It's about three miles ahead, and this lane curves right round to it, skirting a big green patch."

"That's a wood."

"Only mixed up with the green there's a lot that's uncoloured, and dotted with little circles."

"Park and ornamental ground. There ought to be a seat in the middle."

"A seat? Oh—I see. And so there is. It's called Milton Manor."

"Milton, thou shouldst be living at this hour. But, actually, it will be quite dead—or dead so far as the old squirarchal spirit is concerned. Here's the wall bounding it. Pretty formidable, isn't it? But there'll be nothing inside except a district headquarters of the Coal Board, or perhaps a high-class private loony-bin. . . . That wall would keep anybody in." The car was now racing past a seemingly interminable curve in masonry. "Look at that sinister little door."

"Stop!" Sudden and unaccountable certainty had flashed upon Jane. "It's the place."

Remnant threw out his clutch and applied his brakes. "The place where the ambulance has gone?"

"It must be." Jane was peering at the map. "But go on. I've seen where there must be gates and a drive. In about a quarter of a mile. A black spot and then a double line of fine dots through the park."

"That will be a lodge and a drive, all right." The car moved on again. "Are we going to pay a call?"

"Yes."

Remnant said nothing. But he was frowning slightly.

"You don't mind, do you? I don't expect I shall be long."

"I don't mind a bit. But, you know, you've managed to import an atmosphere of melodrama into this. Yet you don't look a romancing type. It seems to me you may be running into something uncomfortable. . . . Here we are." The car had stopped again at a point where the high wall was pierced by double iron gates. "I wish you'd tell me what this is about, and how it began."

Jane hesitated. The gates were flanked by massive stone pillars supporting eroded and obscure heraldic animals; there was a lodge immediately inside; and from it a well-kept drive curved away through a gloomy belt of woodland. She had never supposed herself to be very sensitive to impalpable things. But even the outer defences of Milton Manor had an atmosphere she greatly disliked. "Well, as a matter of fact, it began—or more immediately began—in the Bodleian this morning."

"The Bodleian!" Remnant's tone might have been elicited by a mention of something as remote as the Taj-Mahal. "You mean the place where they keep all the books?"

"Precisely, Mr. Remnant." Jane looked at the younger man suspiciously. But his innocence appeared entire and unflawed. "I don't suppose that your occasions ever drew you there."

"Not at all." Remnant was indignant. "I once took an aunt of mine there. She wanted to see something called King Alfred's Jewel."

"Don't you think that was the Ashmolean?"

"Aren't they the same thing?"

It was borne in upon Jane that the young man, although doubtless not of a studious temperament, was decidedly not a fool, and that this idiocy was his way of expressing a profound scepticism as to her proceedings. That this wild goose chase was authentically the consequence of anything that could have happened in Bodley was really too much for him. And small wonder, Jane thought. But she could hardly sit back and try to tell him the whole story now. "Look here," she said, "do you mind if we just get out and nose around? Perhaps I'll try explaining presently."

He jumped out, came round the bonnet of the car, and opened the door for her. "Very well," he said impassively. "Provided we nose together."

They crossed the road and peered through the high iron gates. The lodge showed signs of being tenanted, but there was nobody stirring. Jane shook the gates cautiously, and tried turning a large wrought-iron handle. They were certainly secured. "What does one do," she asked, "when visiting the gentry? They don't seem to demean themselves by having any sort of door-bell."

"Blow the horn, I suppose—and wait for the vassals to come running out, touching their forelocks." Remnant's distrust of their proceedings seemed to have increased, and his voice for the first time held a hint of impatience. He really *did* believe—Jane thought resentfully—that she was a romancing type, after all.

She spoke almost at random. "It can't be empty," she said. "Everything's very tidy."

"Except for a bit of litter outside." Remnant had stooped and automatically picked up a scrap of crumpled paper from just beside the gates. He seemed to be summoning resolution to speak his mind. "Now, look here . . . well, I'm damned!"

Unthinkingly he had smoothed out the piece of buff paper in his hand. It was a blank book slip from the Bodleian.

4. "He saw people filling in slips from the catalogue. And he pretended to be doing the same thing—so as not to attract attention." Jane spoke absently. She was still staring, wide-eyed, at the small oblong of paper.

"For goodness' sake, woman, explain yourself. Who did?"

Jane paid no attention. "And he must have had this one, crumpled in his hand—when it happened. And then—well, when the ambulance stopped for those gates to be opened, and he knew he was on the threshold of the place, he managed, somehow, to thrust it outside. In the desperate hope that it would act as some sort of sign. . . . And it has."

"I can see that it's a sign, all right. Do you mean that somebody has been taken in here against his will?"

"More than one person. I'm sure of it now! This wretched little man that I saw for the first time this morning, and—and somebody that I know much better . . . who is very important to me."

"Nothing to do with—with being quite lawfully taken charge of by doctors who believe—rightly or wrongly—that they are insane?"

"Nothing to do with that."

"Good!" Roger Remnant spoke with decision. "Then the whole thing is simplified. Here they are. We're morally certain of it. And now we just have to get them out again. We go straight in, Miss Appleby."

She turned to him gravely. "You mean that? You're helping?"

He answered her gravity with sudden extreme merriment. "My dear young woman, *you* are helping. Bulldog Drummond is on the job—but of course you can stand in the corner and hold the sponge and the towels. Incidentally, unlike the bone-headed Bulldog, we don't go *quite* straight in. That might be unhealthy. We send some word of our intentions into the outside world first. That's sense. *Then* we go right in. That's what, in the circumstances, a chap—and even a lass—must do."

This judicious admixture of prudence and personal honour was something that Jane found she highly approved of. "As a matter of fact," she said, "I've done that already. I sent a telegram to my brother before I picked you up."

Remnant grinned. "Do you always telegraph your brother before you—"

Jane was mildly confused. "Don't be an ass. And he'll have got it by now. He's in Oxford."

"An undergraduate?"

"No, he's much older than I am. He's a policeman."

"Excellent. We now approach something like social equality."

"He's an Assistant Commissioner at Scotland Yard."

"Snubbed again." Remnant's cheerfulness, however, suffered no appreciable diminution. "And that suggests something. How do we stand to one another when we do barge in? Great lady and her chauffeur?"

"You don't look a bit like a great lady's chauffeur, Mr. Remnant."

"I'm not very sure, for that matter, that you look like a chauffeur's great lady. What about brother and sister?"

"Very well."

"And what's our business?"

Jane hesitated. She hadn't considered this. "We should really know," she said, "what the place *is*. I mean, what it *pretends* to be. They must know in Canonicorum. Shall we drive on there first, and ask?"

"Certainly not. I wouldn't call that going right in. Come on—into the car, face the gates, and sound the horn like mad. Childe Remnant—and faithful page—to the dark tower came."

"And trust to luck?"

"We haven't much else to trust to, have we?"

Jane said nothing, but climbed into the car.

Remnant backed, swung round to face the gates, and gave a blast on his horn. It was a very loud horn—or here in the silence of the country it appeared so—and he made prodigal use of it.

"I say," said Jane, "perhaps you'd better not be so—"

She stopped as she saw a door in the lodge open and a man come out. He walked briskly but without hurry to the gates, and immediately unlocked them and drew them open.

Remnant drove in and stopped. "Sorry to make such a row," he called cheerfully, "but we've got an appointment, and we're a bit late."

The man had every appearance of respectability, and might have been a retired N.C.O. in the employment of his former colonel. "Yes, sir. With the Medical Superintendent or the Assistant Director?"

"The Medical Superintendent." Remnant's voice held not a hint of hesitation.

"Very good, sir. Will you drive straight up to the house?"

"Right—thank you." Remnant prepared to let in the clutch.

"One moment, sir. Have you been here before?"

"No. This is our first visit."

"Then I'd better mention, sir, that there's an inner fence right round the park. It's because of the animals, sir; and as some of them are very valuable, the gate across the drive is kept locked. I ring through to the house, and a man comes down at once to open it. You won't be delayed more than a couple of minutes, sir." The man stepped back smartly—the air of the old regular soldier was now unmistakable in him—and turned to close the gates.

They drove on. "We're in," Jane said.

"We're in—and that reliable retainer is now locking the gates behind us. Presently the same thing is going to happen at an inner barrier. It's not hopelessly out of the way—but it's not quite what I'd call natural. . . . Well, we now know that the establishment is a medical one."

"That it *pretends* to be that."

"Nothing on this scale could be a hundred per cent bogus. You just couldn't get away with it. We'll find this is a perfectly pukka sanatorium, or something of the sort, with the dirty work neatly confined to the back stairs."

"Perhaps so. And I don't in the least know what the dirty work is. I only know that they kidnapped a helpless looking little man from the heart of Oxford this morning, and that weeks and weeks ago they kidnapped somebody I'm going to marry. And he's not at all helpless."

"Then they're crazy." Remnant still spoke with the same composed decision. "Listen. We may find ourselves up against what looks like a very formidable set-up indeed. I don't know—but it's a guess. Master criminals. Some deep design. A powerful and ramifying organisation. The whole bag of tricks—see?"

"Yes." But Jane wasn't quite sure that she saw.

"But it will be paper-thin. We just have to put a fist through it and it goes. Just remember that we approach the job in the light of that knowledge."

"Very well." Jane didn't at all know whether she was listening to wisdom or folly. But she realised that Roger Remnant was a heartening companion.

"Here's the fence—and the valuable animals."

The fence, constructed of a stout wire diamond mesh, ran off on a convex line on either side of them, and in that arc of it which was visible, the gate now immediately before them appeared to be the only aperture. Just beyond it, a herd of deer, unfamiliar in appearance, was peacefully grazing. The park behind them was dotted and streaked with clumps and groves of trees, amid which there was still no sign of a house.

They were silent for some minutes. The man at the lodge seemed to have underestimated the time they would have to wait here. And the wait was unnerving. Knowing what they did, they were bound to look somewhat askance at the sort of large zoological enclosure into the sinister security of which they were about to deliver themselves.

"Have you got a plan?" Jane found that she had uttered the words spontaneously and without premeditation. They seemed to represent a very definite handing of what was, after all, entirely her affair to the young man beside her.

"Certainly not. Nothing could be more hampering. And you're not going right in if you have a plan."

Jane found the *mystique* of this difficult. "You mean you just charge head down?"

"Nothing of the sort. I mean that it's only useful to think of the current move. Try thinking ahead, and you only clog your mind with preparations for situations that are not, in fact, going to turn out at all as you imagine them. . . . Here the fellow comes."

"I don't at all know about that." Jane eyed rather apprehensively the figure now hurrying towards them from the farther side of the fence. "For instance, there's this. We told the man at the lodge that we had an appointment. Probably he has reported that on the telephone. And we *haven't* an appointment."

Remnant chuckled unconcernedly. "If there's anything in all this at all, my dear woman, we shall meet rather more considerable embarrassments than that. . . . Good morning. We're very sorry to trouble you in this way."

"Not at all, sir. Sorry to keep you waiting." The man now throwing open the wire gates was as respectable as his fellow. "It's this particular herd, sir. We have orders to lock up when it's grazing this section of the park. Very rare, I understand these deer to be. It makes things awkward for visitors. But it's better than having the deer stolen for a black market in venison. You'd hardly believe it, sir, but it's happened here two or three times."

"Kidnapping—eh?" Remnant shot out the question abruptly.

"Exactly, sir." The man was certainly not disconcerted. "Will you drive straight on? You can't miss the house. And the entrance to the clinic is by the main door, under the portico."

They drove on. Remnant gave Jane a triumphant nod. "There," he said, "you see? We pick up the facts as we go. Our visit is to the Medical Superintendent of a clinic. What *is* a clinic?"

Jane considered. "I think it's becoming a fashionable word for a grand sort of nursing home—the sort that has one special line. If the rich want to slim, they go and live on roast beef and orange juice in the appropriate clinic."

"Perhaps that's it. Perhaps that's what the deer are for. One vanishes into the kitchens daily in the interest of a high-protein diet." Remnant swung the car round a bend in the drive. "Here we are."

A large house had appeared before them. Its form was irregular and rambling, so that it might have been very large indeed; but the aspect which they were approaching was dominated by a graceful white portico, now glittering in the sun. They looked at this curiously. "It must take an awful lot of paint," Jane said.

"About as much as the Queen Elizabeth. I suppose it gives the right effect: cheerfulness and antisepsis hand in hand. There's a garden over there with quite a lot of people."

"They must be ambulatory patients."

Remnant slowed down. "You do have a fine stock of words." His glance was moving swiftly over the whole scene. "What sort of patients are they?"

"The sort, oddly enough, that don't need an ambulance."

"Well, they certainly don't look as if they had been kidnapped in one. Do you think we drive under this portico affair? I think we do. Nothing like a confident approach to the dark tower."

"Yes, drive right in." Jane found that her heart was beating much faster than usual. But it was only sensible, she reminded herself, to feel a bit scared. Unless she had made a colossal ass of herself—and that would really be almost worse than anything else—they had embarked on an enterprise of very actual danger.

They got out in front of a short flight of steps and mounted to a door painted in brilliant vermilion. There was a large brass bell-pull, brightly polished, and a small brass plate, equally brightly polished, on which both their glances fell at once. It read:

MILTON MANOR CLINIC
REGISTERED OFFICE

As Jane read this she was aware of a first twinge of mere misgiving as momentarily replacing her alarm. The little notice was somehow both unobtrusively and monumentally respectable. She had a vision of imminent fiasco—of a reception at first puzzled, and then successively amused, annoyed, frigid. . . . But Remnant appeared to have no doubts. His hand had gone out unhesitatingly and given a brisk tug at the bell-pull. This proved to be attached to one of those genteel contrivances which simulate a miniature carillon. They stood for a moment listening to the brief cascade of musical notes releasing itself somewhere inside. Before it had died away—or, Jane reflected, they could turn and bolt—the door was opened.

They were aware of an interior that was all cool, clear colours and polished floors. Standing before them was an immaculate nursing sister. "Good morning," she said.

"Good morning." Roger Remnant in his old duffel coat, Jane noted, had somehow taken on the appearance of springing from the most privileged and opulent class of society. "I am Lord Remnant." He paused as if this must be a very sufficient announcement in itself. The nurse seemed suitably impressed, but her features contrived, at the same time, to suggest the need of further information. Remnant's eyebrows elevated themselves slightly. "My sister and I have an appointment with the Medical Superintendent."

"With Dr. Cline?"

"I'm afraid I have no idea. His name hasn't been given to me. The appointment was made by my aunt—or at least she intended to make one. But it is just possible that she failed to ring up. She is very distressed—has been very hesitant about the whole matter."

"I *quite* understand." The nurse's voice might have been described as oozing comprehension. "Will you please come in? I am afraid that if there has *not* been an appointment you may have to wait a little. Dr. Cline is having a terribly crowded morning. But I will let him know at once."

They entered a large hall with panelled walls and a broad staircase, all of which had been enamelled in light greens and greys. At one end was a bright fire, vying with the sunshine that poured in through tall windows giving upon some broad court at the back. The other end was a mass of chrysanthemums disposed behind and around a small fountain. Two silver-haired old gentlemen of distinguished appearance were coming down the staircase, surrounded by a group of spaniels. As they reached the bottom a manservant appeared and encased them in hats and coats. They turned down a broad corridor, apparently intent upon a stroll in the gardens. Jane had an enhanced feeling that it was all too true to be good—to be at all good for what was surely the utterly extravagant hypothesis she had formed. High blood pressure, or chronic disorders of the liver, looked like being the only sinister revelation Milton Manor had to offer.

They sat down to wait. By way of intellectual beguilement there was a choice between *Country Life* and *The Field*. It was all too depressing for words.

The wait, however, was brief, for the nurse returned almost at once. "Will you come this way?" she said. "The Superintendent can see you now."

They were led for some way through the house and shown into a room of moderate size, furnished with consistent sobriety as a study. Dr. Cline was a rubicund man of buoyant manner who came forward with a frank smile. "Lord Remnant?"

Roger Remnant bowed. "My sister, Lady Jane," he said gravely.

"How do you do. I understand that your aunt— But I am afraid it is a little chilly here—and really a little gloomy as well. I suggest that we go out to the sunshine of the terrace." And Dr. Cline led the way towards a pair of french windows. "After all, there is much to be said for a cheerful atmosphere when discussing these things. Whether the Clinic is efficient is a matter of statistics. But that it is a reasonably gay sort of place you will presently see for yourselves."

The Medical Superintendent, it was evident, had no hesitation in getting briskly down to sales-talk. And he had all his wits about him. Jane had a sudden and horrid conviction that, before admitting them, he must surely have made a grab at Who's Who or Debrett. But of course, for all she knew, Roger Remnant might really be a lord. He might even have a sister called Lady Jane. . . . They had emerged on a flagged terrace. It was liberally provided with garden furniture, but untenanted. Perhaps it was reserved for the Superintendent's private use. For on a second terrace, immediately below, was a scattered group of some half-dozen people. They were for the most part elderly, and engaged in reading, conversing, or simply gazing into the gardens. An air of waiting, somnolently but pleasurably, for what could confidently be anticipated as an excellent luncheon, was pervasive among them. The only pronounced activity visible was on the part of a small boy of about five years of age, who was wandering restlessly from individual to individual. . . . At this small boy Jane, as she sat down, took a second look. And it flashed upon her that he represented what, so far, was the only discordant note about the place. For he did not look at all a gay or cheerful child. On the contrary, there was something strained and tense about his whole bearing. And when he glanced towards the upper terrace for a moment it was with eyes that it was not at all comfortable to become aware of.

But Roger Remnant was talking—and with the most complete assurance still. "You will understand, Dr. Cline, that this is an entirely tentative enquiry. And my aunt—who is naturally very distressed—has felt quite unequal to coming down herself. She is afraid that—"

"Quite so, Lord Remnant, quite so." The Superintendent was eminently willing to meet this half way. "There is always the dislike of talk—of gossip. But I assure you that it is a matter which we handle with a good deal of acquired skill—of *finesse,* I may say. Residence at Milton Manor can be *entirely* confidential. Take correspondence, for example, from the patients' private friends. That can go to an address in London, from which it is brought down daily by private messenger."

"That," said Remnant, "is very important." He smiled amiably at Dr. Cline. "It makes one begin to see one's way more clearly." And his eyes, although quite expressionlessly, moved fleetingly to Jane's.

"Precisely." Dr. Cline looked understandingly at his visitors.

Then—and rather as if it were something that had just come into his head—he suddenly assumed an appearance of mild professional reserve. "But I must point out," he said, "that, in the first instance, it would have to be your—um—uncle's personal medical advisor—"

"We perfectly understand that. But I must repeat how tentative this is. Nothing has been suggested to my uncle, and his doctor is not yet really aware of—er—how bad the position has become. What has happened is simply this. My aunt confided her anxieties to Lord Polder, who is a very old friend."

Dr. Cline, at the mention of this most august of medical names, bowed gravely.

"And Lord Polder mentioned the possibilities of the Milton Clinic. He, rather than the family doctor, you know, would be the best person to take on the difficult job of broaching the matter to my uncle. They regularly shoot together. And of course they are constantly meeting in the Chamber."

Jane wondered whether the Chamber was really what very grand people called the Lords. Anyway, it sounded well. It all sounded incredibly well, indeed. And this fashionable little medical parasite appeared to be eating out of Remnant's hand. She speculated on what atrociously disreputable disease the noble peer under discussion—whether real or imagined—was about to be plagued with by his ruthless nephew. . . . But now Remnant had gone off on another tack.

"There is one thing that makes my aunt rather uneasy. She has been told about the research. Of course, my sister and I understand very well that research is always carried on in a leading institution of this character. But my aunt would want to be assured that there was no risk—"

With a gesture perhaps a shade more theatrical than professional the Medical Superintendent of the Milton Clinic raised two protesting hands. "But quite so! And I can assure you that nothing of the sort would at all impinge upon your uncle during his residence here. The research is, of course, of the utmost importance. We are making constant gains from it on the therapeutic side—constant gains. But, of course, nothing is embodied in our regular treatments that has not abundantly proved itself when employed in the case of—um—patients otherwise circumstanced. The research establishment, indeed, is entirely separate. The Director and I, needless to say, are in the closest co-operation—the most intimate scientific touch. But the two establishments have no contact, so far as patients and—er—inmates are concerned. The inmates—who come on *very* reduced terms and who are *most* helpful to us—are a completely detached community. We have fixed them up very pleasant—yes, *very* pleasant—quarters in the old stables."

Remnant looked much relieved. "I see," he said. "Guinea-pigs, what?"

Dr. Cline did not let his wholesome respect for the aristocracy prevent him from looking slightly shocked. "It might be better, my dear Lord Remnant, to express it—"

But Remnant had turned to Jane with an air of brisk decision. "Well," he said, "I think that about settles it—don't you, Jane?"

Jane nodded, and spoke for the first time. "It all sounds very satisfactory—and hopeful for poor uncle. And, for poor aunt Emma's sake, I shall be so glad if it puts things right."

"Quite. Well, we must book the poor old boy in, and then get Polder to apply the heat." From this slangy excursion, proper in addressing a sister, Remnant turned with renewed gravity to Dr. Cline. "You could manage it at any time?"

"Well, hardly that—hardly that, I fear. But the wait would not be long. And it will, of course, be perfectly correct that Lord Polder rather than a family physician should refer your uncle to us."

"I think we'd better have a firm date, if we can. Nothing like going straight ahead once these things are fixed upon." And Remnant looked firmly at Dr. Cline. It was evident that, for his distinguished family, waiting-lists simply did not exist. "In fact, I think it had better be Monday."

"It is just possible that it could be arranged." For Dr. Cline, seemingly, this was a game that had to be played out according to the rules. "But I shall have to take a look at the book. And as my secretary is away for the day, it will be necesary to go across and consult it in the other wing. Will you excuse me?"

And Dr. Cline bowed himself off the terrace. Roger Remnant took a long breath. "And now," he said, "now, my dear sister Jane—where do we go from here?"

5. Jane was watching the small boy. He had been becoming increasingly restless and irritable. In fact he might have been described as trailing his coat, for it was his evident desire to make himself sufficiently tiresome to the elderly people around him to stir them into drastic action. It must, Jane thought, be a poor sort of life for a child amid these comfortable invalids or valetudinarians. They did not appear to take much interest in him, but what interest they took was wholly benevolent. Children need an occasional rumpus. They find an adult world that never turns aggressive on them extremely frightening, for it makes them feel their own aggressive impulses to be something wicked and out of nature. The small boy—he appeared to be a foreign small boy from fragments of his speech that drifted to the upper terrace —was decidedly in this state. He was longing for a clip on the ear. And nobody seemed at all disposed to give it to him. . . . Jane turned to Remnant. "Where do we go now? It depends on how much we feel we've really found out. What is this place, anyway? What is it going to cure our uncle of?"

Remnant chuckled. "Obesity, I should say—to judge by that great fat man who appeared a minute ago."

"A fat man? I didn't see any fat man."

"He simply popped round the corner of the terrace for a moment and vanished."

"Probably he was one of the doctors—grown sleek on the job. I don't think it's obesity. It may be rather comical to be fat, but it's not indecent. And apparently to make it known that you're taking the cure at Milton Manor just isn't done." Jane's eye went again to the people below them. "Besides, just look at that lot. You can't say that their garments are beginning to hang loose upon them. Rather the reverse, if anything."

"True enough. And, in point of fact, I don't think we need be in any doubt about the place. Our poor uncle's danger is D.T.'s. And this clinic—ostensibly, at least—is nothing more than a high-class drunks' home. The alcohol habit cured in six weeks. Utmost privacy assured. Fee, five hundred guineas."

"And something else goes on behind?"

"Something else goes on behind." Remnant paused. "Unless, that is, we're barking utterly up the wrong tree."

"You think I'm making a fool of both of us."

Remnant shook his head decidedly. "I certainly don't think that. But you must admit that, so far, there's precious little evidence of dirty work behind the curtain. If only— Good lord, look at that boy!"

The boy's desire to plague his companions had increased yet further. He had gone up to an elderly lady apparently engaged upon a cross-word puzzle and insufferably snatched her paper from her. The lady had merely smiled and made a small, resigned gesture. And at this the boy had lost control of himself. Darting forward again, he had dealt her a stinging blow across the face. And—once more—the lady simply smiled.

This was the startling incident that had attracted Remnant's attention. But it was not concluded. The boy had drawn back. He was very frightened. He looked from face to face of the people scattered around him. Some of them had seen his act; others were preoccupied. But nobody made any move. He gave a choking cry and rushed at a tall man with a pipe in his mouth who was sitting in idle contemplation of the garden. The boy knocked the pipe to the ground and clawed, battered at the tall man's face. The man smiled, slightly shook his head, got up and moved to another seat. Most of the people were now watching. They watched as if nothing abnormal was occurring. But this was itself the only abnormal thing about them. They conversed, smoked, looked up from or returned to their books with every sign of reasonable mental alertness. The boy threw himself down on the terrace and sobbed. At this the lady whom he had first struck rose and bent over him solicitously. Others showed a similar kindly concern. And then from a door farther along the terrace a nurse hurried out, picked up the weeping child, and carried him away. The whole incident vanished. Everybody was completely composed. It was like seeing a wet sponge being passed over a slate.

Remnant had got to his feet. He and Jane looked at each other. wide-eyed. Without a word passed between them, they knew that they were agreed. They had witnessed something unutterably shocking. A child's temper-tantrum had betrayed the presence of abomination—there, in the clear sunlight, only a few yards away. It was something obscure, and at the same time instantly clamant. They had witnessed the fruit of some horrible violation of human personality.

Jane heard Remnant catch his breath and saw him move in half-a-dozen swift strides to the lower terrace. He looked quickly round the people assembled there and picked out a man in a somewhat different category from the others. He was younger and of fine physique, with a strong mouth and jaw; he might have been a professional soldier. Remnant stepped up to him and slapped his face hard. The man jerked back his head. Remnant could see pain—perhaps two sorts of pain—in his eyes. Then he too smiled, rose, walked quietly away.

Remnant returned to the upper terrace. He was very pale. At the same moment the nurse who had carried off the boy returned with a second nurse somewhat older than herself. They moved about among the group of people, speaking to them briefly. Each of those so spoken to nodded, smiled, rose, and moved off. They betrayed no consciousness of awkwardness or discomfort, but went off in a group—either conversing placidly or glancing still at their open books. Within a few seconds the lower terrace was empty.

Jane was aware of something wrong with herself. She realised it was a sense of brute, physical nausea. But she could just trust herself to speak, and she opened her mouth to do so. Then she became aware that Dr. Cline had come back. He was carrying a large diary.

"I see that we can just manage it." He sat down, glanced at the empty lower terrace and then at his visitors. "Ah," he said, "I am afraid that you have been obliged to witness one of our little hitches. I assure you that they occur very infrequently. And I think I had better explain the system to you."

Remnant nodded—and Jane noted with admiration that he did so very pleasantly. "Yes, Dr. Cline, we should very much like to hear about the system."

"Our patients are divided into messes—into progressive messes. It is rather like the successive forms in a school. You must realise—and it is the reason why our treatment sometimes has to be of rather long duration—that alcoholic addiction is merely one form of addiction to drugs. It cannot be broken at once. The process must be gradual. Consumption is reduced in stages—stages, of course, that go hand in hand with the progress of our psychiatric and other treatments. And here let me emphasise that what we aim at eventually is *total* abstention. Experience has compelled us to conclude that a return to moderate indulgence is psychologically impracticable. It is a thousand pities—for, after all, a glass of wine is both a civilised and a wholesome pleasure."

"But with former addicts it doesn't work?"

"Precisely!" Dr. Cline tapped the book on his knees with measured and impressive emphasis. He was well launched on his sales-talk once more. "Our patients go out drinking *no* alcohol—and our figures show that in eighty-seven per cent of cases the cure is permanent and absolute. Perhaps—on the psychological side—the decisive factor is this: that we never antagonise them. There is a positive transference from the first."

Dr. Cline paused on this weighty technical term. His smile was amiable, Jane thought, but his eye was wary. Remnant broke in smoothly. "I see. The patients, in fact, just love all they get?"

Dr. Cline appeared gratified by this interpretation of the tenor of his remarks. "I think I can say that they are very well contented from the first. And now, about the messes. On arrival, most patients go into—well, what one might term the Lower Third." Dr. Cline permitted himself a mild laughter at this scholastic pleasantry. "It is, of course, entirely a matter of the amount of wine and so forth served at table. In the Sixth—shall we say among the prefects?—there is none at all." He paused admiringly. "Not even a light cup; not even a glass of cider!"

"Remarkable."

"I think I may say that it is. But of course it is necessary that intercourse between the various messes—and I need not tell you that each has its own dining-room—should be minimal. Otherwise a certain amount of friction and jealousy is apt to be engendered. The people we saw just now belong to a mess that ought not to be in this part of the grounds. Some mistake had been made. But I need hardly say that—such unfortunate slips apart—nobody here has ever the slightest feeling of being dragooned, of being ordered about. . . . And now I will just mention some details about the fees, and so on. But perhaps we might go into that more conveniently indoors. And no doubt you will wish to go over the Clinic, so as to be able to give your aunt a full description of it."

Remnant nodded. "We should certainly like to see," he said, "whatever can be seen."

"Which is everything!" And Dr. Cline smiled quite brilliantly as he led the way back into his study.

6. It seemed to Jane Appleby that matters were now at something of an *impasse*. They might be shown a great deal of Milton Manor Clinic. But nothing more would transpire that was at all to their purpose. They could get away, and then think again. Or presumably they could get away. For the Medical Superintendent appeared not in the least to suspect their *bona fides,* and there was no reason to suppose that the respectable and respectful persons who had unlocked gates upon their arrival would not unhesitatingly perform the same service for them when they signified a wish to depart. Yes, they could clear out—and consider themselves thoroughly lucky in doing so. Perhaps their account of the very odd thing they had seen would be sufficient immediately to procure a radical investigation of the whole place. But meantime she had seen or heard nothing of the fate of Geoffrey—which was the single and overwhelming concern with which she had come. She had seen only a brief, enigmatical horror which filled her with the deepest fears for the man she loved. And to go away hard upon that sinister and imperfect revelation seemed to hold something craven in it that she did not like.

The Medical Superintendent had sat down comfortably at his desk, opened his large diary, and produced a beautiful gold fountain pen. "I am bound to say that you are very wise," he murmured. "In these cases quite a short space of time may be important. Monday, I think you said, Lord Remnant? Excellent! What can be more satisfactory than decisive action?"

"What, indeed?" And Remnant, leaning across the desk, slapped Dr. Cline hard across the right cheek.

The man scrambled to his feet and staggered backwards, his mouth feebly working. It did not appear that he was either a very courageous or a very quick-witted person. He stood staring at them helplessly with watering eyes. Then he made a dive for a drawer in his desk, emitting at the same time the enraged snarl of a cornered animal.

But Remnant was before him, and slung him across the room. "Reactions very poor," he said. "Definite signs of resentment. Needs a spot of the cure himself."

Cline regained his balance and dashed for the fireplace, his hand stretched out in front of him to press a bell. Remnant stepped forward and hit him on the jaw. Cline made a half turn on his heels and dropped to the floor. He struggled to his hands and knees and rose, staggering. His mouth was streaming blood. He opened it and let out a feeble attempt at a yell. Remnant hit him again. He went down and lay quite still.

These were proceedings that Jane Appleby had never before witnessed except in the cinema. She stared at the inert body of the Medical Superintendent and felt her head swim. Remnant had stepped to the closed door and was listening. "No sound of alarm," he said.

"Is he dead?"

"Good lord, no." Remnant looked down impassively at the figure supine on the carpet. "But it's not a bad knock out. Do you know, for a moment I thought I had mistimed it? Getting a bit rusty, I'm afraid, at this sort of thing."

Jane's head began to clear. "I suppose you *haven't* mistimed it? I mean, it was the best thing to do?" She was far from clear what their next step could be.

"I told you, didn't I? When you meet a thing like this, you put your fist straight through it. And it's obvious enough now. These people are kidnappers, just as you said. And they use their victims —the little man you saw to-day, those people outside, your own young man if they've caught him—for some filthy sort of experiment. The only thing to do is to keep on hitting them hard."

"I see. Well, whom do you hit next?"

"I'd say that this just about concludes our concern with the clinical side. It's not of much interest, and I expect that this precious swine hasn't all that importance in the set-up of the place. What we're looking for is the research. . . . Will you do something?"

"Whatever you say."

Remnant cheerfully grinned. He was reflecting, perhaps, that these were not words which this young woman frequently addressed to her male contemporaries. "Then cut out to the car. Don't be in a hurry to offer explanations to anybody you see about. Remember you belong to a class of society accustomed to going its own way unquestioned."

"Thank you very much."

"Yank up the front seat. There's a leather bag, and there's a bottle. Empty the bag, put in the bottle, and bring it back here. I'll give you four minutes. Then, if you're not back, I'll change plans and come and find you. Understand?"

"I think I do." Jane took a deep breath, opened the door, and walked out of the room.

The broad corridor was deserted. So was the hall with its foolish little fountain and its massed chrysanthemums. But in the vestibule was one of the manservants she had seen earlier. She fancied he looked at her curiously. Jane walked to the front door and halted—with the air of one who very seldom has occasion to open doors for herself. The man jumped to the door-handle and let her out. "I'm returning," she said briefly, and walked across to the car. She managed to do as Remnant had instructed her—and probably, she judged, without the precise nature of the operation being observed. She turned and mounted the steps, the bag in her hand. The man was waiting, with the door held open. He bowed impeccably and closed it behind her. She thanked him and walked on.

Remnant was sitting on the Medical Superintendant's desk, examining a revolver. He looked quickly up as she entered. "Good girl," he said. "Now we get cracking again."

Jane looked about the study. "Where's Cline?" The Medical Superintendent had vanished.

"I've lugged the guts into the neighbour room." As he delivered himself of this stray fruit of his former frequentation of the lecture-halls of Oxford, Remnant slipped the revolver into his pocket. "This is what he was making a grab for in the drawer. I don't like the things. Noisy. But you never know what will come in handy."

"Mayn't he recover quite quickly?"

"I've tied him up, gagged him, and put him in a cupboard. Useful that they taught us all those dirty tricks. Got the bottle?"

"Here it is." Jane set the bag down on the desk. "What are you going to do now?"

"About Milton Manor?"

"Yes—of course."

"Burn it to the ground."

"Burn it! You can't—"

"Never believe it." Remnant had brought out the bottle. "Capital stuff, petrol. And this room is pretty well ideal. Panelled walls, bookshelves, massive desk, all those curtains—give us a splendid start, believe me." He uncorked the bottle. "Just pass me that big waste-paper basket, will you?"

Jane gasped, but did as she was told. "But what about Cline?" she said. "Didn't you say he's in a cupboard?"

"Cline? Oh—I see what you mean. Well, they say it's not really bad. The suffocation knocks you out before the actual roasting. Quite humane, really." Remnant was going composedly about his fire-raising operation.

"But—but it would be murder."

"Just stand back a bit, will you?"

Jane's head was decidedly swimming again. "You don't know what you're doing! You can't murder—"

"Much worse than murder going on here, if you ask me. Whole place over-due for the everlasting bonfire. I say, what an anti-climax, my dear woman, if I haven't got a match."

"I devoutly hope you haven't."

"Here we are—box of vestas. I think you should have the fun of starting it off. Your show, after all."

"I'll do nothing of the sort. I think you must be—"

"Just one lighted match, please. Into the waste-paper basket. And then we go out by the french window."

Jane glanced unbelievingly at Remnant. He was looking her straight in the eyes. He might be crazy, but he was certainly not mad. She took the box, got out a match, and struck it. It was like being a hangman and giving a tap or a pull to whatever worked the drop. She threw it into the waste-paper basket and there was a great leap of flame. Remnant grabbed her and they bolted through the window.

Remnant chuckled. "I never had a girl commit murder for me before. You mayn't believe it—but it's the honest truth."

Jane's head was still misbehaving, and she felt that at any moment her knees might misbehave too. "Look here," she said, "couldn't we just—just get him out of that cupboard and drop him into a flower-bed?"

"How pity runs amok in gentle heart." Remnant was looking rapidly about him. "Or have I got that one wrong?" Abruptly his manner changed. "I say," he said, "I'm sorry. As a matter of fact the whole place isn't going to burn down—worse luck. A fire started in the night like that might get sufficient grip to do it. But not now. Your match hasn't started much more than a pretty good diversion. And that's what we want."

Jane gave a long gasp. "Then let's make the best of our chance."

"Capital. Excellent girl. You know, until we winkle out this young man of yours, and until I get back to my wife and twelve kids, you and I make not a bad team."

7. Jane became aware that they were hurrying with considerable purposefulness along the terrace. "Where are we going now?"

"It's like this. I reckon that in the excitement of our little fire, you and I will be forgotten for a bit back there. And that gives us our chance of finding the other side of the place."

"The research side?"

"Exactly. The real devilry is there. What we want is the boys in the back room. I expect there will be quite a number of them. And—for that matter—I expect they're really at the back. Did you notice the structure of the place as we drove up? There seems to be a lot of new building—much less dressy than all this—stretching out behind. . . . Round this way."

They turned a corner of the main façade of the house, and as they did so heard shouts behind them. Jane quickened her pace yet further. "Are they after us?"

"Not a bit of it. They're after the fire. No doubt in a remote place like this, with a big staff, everybody has a job when it comes to fighting a blaze. That means that we turn their own efficiency against them."

"I see. And I'm not really surprised you didn't care for those lectures. You must have found the dons' wits a bit on the slow side."

"Steady on. There's a chap coming." Remnant laid a hand on her arm and brought her to a leisured walk. "New patients—understand?"

Jane nodded. The man approaching them was clearly some sort of servant or attendant about the place. He had almost the look, indeed, of what might be called a guard, for he had the measured pace of somebody on a regular beat. Remnant raised a hand and beckoned him forward. "The sort of patients we are," he murmured, "don't mind mentioning a disastrous fire in passing. But they preserve a lofty demeanour, all the same."

The man had quickened his pace and was eyeing them suspiciously. "One moment," he said; "are you residents in the Clinic?"

Remnant frowned. It was evident that he was one very little disposed to be questioned in this way. "Certainly, my man. But I signed to you to tell you that you are needed at the front of the house. There appears to be a fire."

Audible corroboration of the truth of this was now available. Somewhere on the other side of the building a shrill bell was sounding; there was shouting and a calling of sharp words of command; it was even possible to hear an ominous crackle of flames. The man hesitated, took a bunch of keys from his pocket, made as if to turn round, and then hesitated again. "Not through the red door, please," he said sharply. "Some of the Director's animals are out, and they're not to be disturbed." Again he looked them over in quick scrutiny. Unlike the servants they had so far met, he had only the most perfunctory semblance of a respectful bearing. The shouting increased, and this appeared to convince him where his most urgent business lay. He went off at a run.

They resumed their brisk pace. "You see?" Remnant said. "They always hand you your next move on a plate. We find a red door and go straight through. It looks as if he's meant to keep it locked, but thought he was hardly going to move out of sight of it. . . . How peaceful all this is."

Jane was not very confident that she agreed. But she had come to recognise that with Remnant one had an exhilarating sense of going just where one wanted to go. There was now nobody near them. Only on somewhat higher ground on their left, and beyond the formal gardens, a scattering of people—patients presumably—were strolling and pausing before what appeared to be a series of enclosures cut into the slope of the hill. Jane glanced at these as she hurried forward. "It's very odd," she panted, "but it looks rather like the zoo—a private zoo."

"Nothing more likely. All guinea-pigs needn't have only two feet. And that fellow said something about animals through the red door. . . . How this place goes on and on."

They were still skirting the main building on their right. But it had now changed its character, and presented a long line of mullioned windows separated by heavy buttresses which had nothing much to support. There was something decidedly uncomfortable upon passing each of these in turn, for they seemed almost constructed for the sake of affording lurking-places.

"But here we are." The mullioned windows had given place, for a score of paces, to blank walls. And now, between two of the buttresses, they came upon a wide archway, so high that one could have driven a double-decker bus beneath it, and closed by vermilion-painted double doors. Inset in one of these was a wicket. Remnant gave this a thrust and it opened; they went forward as if through a short tunnel, and presently emerged in a broad courtyard. On their right was some sideways aspect of the main building. The three other sides of the court were formed by a miscellaneous but continuous jumble of stables and offices.

"Quick!" Remnant took Jane's arm and drew her like a flash behind the shelter of half-a-dozen piled bales of hay close by where they had emerged. There were three or four men on the farther side of the courtyard, hard at work trundling a small fire-fighting wagon from a shed. They brought it across the yard at the double; the doors beneath the archway were flung open; they disappeared towards the front of the house.

"Another riddance of bad rubbish." Remnant drew Jane from their hiding-place and glanced around. "Nobody else in sight—and no animals. We'll go through there." He pointed to a narrower passage-way that seemed to afford an egress from the courtyard immediately opposite where they stood. "And I think we'll go at the double too."

They dashed across the yard and up the passage-way. When they emerged it was to run full-tilt into a man standing stationary in the open air at the farther end. He stepped back, at the same time whipping something from a pocket. It was a revolver. This time, there could be no doubt whatever about what they were in contact with.

"Come on, then!" Remnant had shouted over the man's shoulder—and with so convincing an urgency that the elementary trick worked. The man spun round apprehensively and Remnant sprang at him. In a second he had gone down with the same sort of thud as had the Medical Superintendent. Remnant knelt beside him, and then glanced up at Jane. "Go on," he said sharply. It was a tone of command more absolute than any he had used before.

She walked on. She felt a sudden fierce excitement—and at the same time wondered how much more of this she could stand. He was with her again within seconds. She saw that, once more, he was very pale. It was a moment to hold her tongue, but she was physically unable to do so. "What did you do to him?" she asked.

"Nothing pretty. He'll be the worse of it for weeks. But it gives us the time we need. He's behind a bush. . . . And there are the animals."

They had continued at a run along a narrow lane between high wooden fences. On their left this fence continued to shut out any view, but on their right it now turned off at a right angle, and their path was bounded instead by a plantation of fir trees. Among these a number of small pig-like creatures were routing. Jane recalled her queer thoughts at Milton Porcorum. They seemed, somehow, less queer in this setting. It was possible to believe that these snuffling and grunting little creatures had lately been small boys and girls—and that they were themselves approaching the very hall of Circe. . . . She brought her mind back to what Remnant had been saying. "What time *do* we need?" she asked.

"Not much. If we manage anything at all, it must be soon. Within an hour or so the whole place will be packing up."

She looked at him incredulously. "Packing up?"

"Certainly. Keep a clear head. Didn't I say that one has only to put a fist through an affair like this and it crumples? No matter how cleverly the sinister side of the place has been insulated and hidden away, it is almost absurdly vulnerable. Whatever it is, it's a thoroughly top-heavy piece of villainy, and the chaps who run it must be prepared to fade out at very short notice indeed. And the moment they discover I slugged that fellow behind us, or that I punched poor old Cline on the jaw, they'll know their hours are numbered. You see, they won't dare to reckon we broke into their filthy hideout without leaving a word or two behind us. Presently they'll be on the run. We want to trip them up in the first hundred yards. . . . There seems to be a building through the trees. We'll make for it."

They plunged into the little wood. The small pig-like creatures scurried out of their way. Jane thought of the forbidding outer wall, the high wire fence, the men who seemed to prowl the place with guns, the sinister suggestion of inner recesses of the building given over to the perpetration of unspeakable things. She remembered the terror of the little man in the upper reading room. . . . But Remnant treated the whole impressive structure as so much papier mâché. She hoped he was right. The plantation was no more than a narrow screen of trees, and they now found themselves before a long, low, blank building that ran off indefinitely on either side. Remnant glanced to his right. "Seems to run out from the back of the house. Lit by skylights let into the flat roof. All the windows and doors—and perhaps a corridor—on the other side. Much what we're looking for, if you ask me. Let's see if we can get round it on the left." They turned and hurried along the blank surface of the building. It would not be a pleasant spot to be brought to bay against. "Well, I'm blessed!" Remnant had come to a halt. Before them was a sheet of water, and into this the end of the building dropped sheer. "Take a look at that."

Jane looked. Before them was a small lake, its banks thickly wooded. Near the centre was an island, almost entirely occupied by a large circular temple of somewhat bleak design. The walls of this were entirely blank, and recessed behind Doric pillars supporting the curved architrave; above this was a somewhat inelegant and incongruous dome. But the odd feature of this not very successful ornamental venture was its being joined to the building they had been skirting—and joined by a drab and utilitarian enclosed wooden bridge. It was like a Bridge of Sighs run up in a drearily functional age.

"Quite a strong-point, in a quiet way." Remnant was looking at the temple with a sort of reluctant admiration. "Ten to one, it's the nerve-centre of the whole bit of voodoo we're enquiring into." He glanced at Jane, and she saw that his face was set in new and grim lines. "All hope abandon, ye who enter here."

She felt herself turn pale. "You think it looks horrible?"

"Well—my guess is that it could do with a little airing. And now we go up this apple tree."

Jane stared. Here at the edge of the little lake there was the ghost of an orchard, and one gnarled and sloping old tree grew close to, and overhung, the building beside them. "You mean we get on the roof?"

"Just that. Then we can either drop down on the other side,

where there may be doors and windows, or take a bird's eye view of things through the skylights. I'd like to know just how the ground lies in this long building before we tackle the island and that temple. We'll do our final clean-up there, I don't doubt; but we'll just have a look at this first." Remnant was already on the flat roof, and in a moment he had hauled Jane up beside him. "It's rather raked by the windows of the house. But that can't be helped." He walked to the nearest skylight, knelt down, shaded his eyes and peered in. "I can't see the whole room. But it looks like a small bedroom—and not exactly luxurious. We'll move on to the next."

They were unpleasantly exposed, Jane thought, to anybody who was prepared to take an interest in them. But excitement sustained her; she felt a mounting certainty that they were really coming nearer to Geoffrey; and if he, and others, could be rescued at all, Roger Remnant seemed very much the man to do it. He had dropped down beside another skylight, "Different cup of tea," he said. "Rather like Cline's study over again. Leather chairs, handsome books, bathing belles by some lascivious old Italian over the mantelpiece. What about its belonging to Cline's opposite number on the research side? . . . Move on to the next. . . . Looks like a lab. It *is* a lab. . . . And so is this one. As far as I can see all these rooms intercommunicate—and they open on a passage on the far side as well. The set-up is pretty clear, wouldn't you say?"

Jane too was peering into a laboratory. "Well, it looks like research, all right. But as for the set-up—"

"The main building, as we've seen, is pukka clinic. Wealthy drunks faithfully attended to. Perhaps used as guinea-pigs at times, but only a quiet way. Move a bit in this direction and you come to the research outfit. Has all the appearance of being pukka too. Enquiry into the physiology of alcoholic addiction, or some such rot. Some advanced drunks, perhaps, as cot-cases. You can always be a little bolder in experimental treatment with 'no-hope' patients—particularly if they come from the humbler classes of society. Move a little farther and perhaps you come to more fundamental research. But by that time, if you ask me, you're over the bridge and on the island. And just what you keep isolated there, the world simply doesn't know. Suppose a high-class patient, strolling in the grounds, hears some rather nasty noises from that direction. Why, our talented research scientists are doing something useful to one of these dear little pigs."

Jane found her breath disposed to come and go in shaky sobs. "If half of what you're imagining is true, it's—"

"Quite so. But don't forget it now has only about half an hour to go. We're right on top of it." Remnant stamped his foot on the flat roof. "And now we drop."

"Five minutes is too long. If we can drop, let's drop quick. But how?"

"If we dropped down on the other side, we might be able to force a door or window giving on the corridor. But this"—and again Remnant stamped—"is still, remember, no more than out-works. We want to get straight at the brain-centre. And the dividing-line, I'd say, is that handsome room with the bathing nymphs. Beyond that, there's a change of atmosphere—that little bedroom, for instance. A more honest word for that would be a cell. And close after that there's the bridge. I wonder if one could get along the top of it? Let's see."

They retraced their steps. Jane stopped by the first skylight at which Remnant had paused, and herself peered down. She drew back her head hastily. "There's somebody there," she whispered. "A woman. She's lying on a little bed."

"She must have been in another corner when I looked." Remnant in his turn peered down. "Seems the moment to take a chance." He put his foot through the skylight.

The crash of splintered and falling glass seemed terrific. But Remnant thrust at the thing with his foot again and again. Within seconds the skylight was a wreck. The woman below had sprung up and was staring at them. "Friends," Remnant said. "We're breaking up this whole racket. Sorry to startle you."

"Aber!" It was less a word than a hoarse cry. "You are truly friends? *Gott sei Dank!* You may be just in time. They have taken my boy. They have taken my boy to the island. Never have they done that before."

"We'll have him back to you in no time."

"But you cannot get in! Look—between us still there are these bars and that strong mesh."

Remnant knelt down. The skylight had been as flimsy as such things commonly are. But there remained, at the level of the ceiling of the cell-like apartment below, a barrier of the sort the woman had described. Remnant nodded. "I see. But don't worry. You couldn't do much with it from below. But from up above it may be a different matter. Please stand right back." Remnant rose, retreated a dozen paces, and ran. A yard before the shattered skylight he leapt high in air, and then went down with his feet rigid under him. There was a resounding crash. Jane ran forward and looked down. Remnant was on the floor below, scrambling to his feet from amid a debris of twisted bars and tangled wire netting. He looked up. "Did I say you put a fist through it?" he called. "A foot's even better. Now then, down you come. Imagine you're making one of those thrilling midnight climbs into college."

With what she felt was a dangerous approach to hysteria, Jane laughed aloud. Then she scrambled over the edge and dropped. Remnant caught her. "Good girl." He turned to the woman. "We know a good deal. Explain about yourself. As quick as you can."

8. "I am Anna Tatistchev, a doctor." The woman's eyes were wild with anxiety, but her speech was collected. "I was persuaded—it is now a month almost—to come here with Rudi, my small boy. I was to be shown work of medical interest in which I might assist—living quietly for a time, as it was necessary for me to do."

Remnant nodded. "You mean you were hiding from someone?"

"From the English police. Rudi and I ought not to be in England. So I came. For a time the work seemed indeed interesting and honourable. Then I suspected. There were patients—experiments too—that I did not understand. Or not at first. Then my position was difficult. They had chosen well. An outlaw is helpless."

Remnant had walked to the single door of the room. He held up his hand for silence, and listened. He shook his head, came back, and smiled. "Isn't 'outlaw' pitching it a bit steep?" Anna Tatistchev looked at him uncomprehendingly. "Never mind. Go ahead."

"I found that my so-called employment was almost imprisonment. I have known prisons, but this, for me, was a new kind. But I came to know that it was that. Twice only I found a way to send out a message to my friends. I did not yet wish them to come, for I believed that there was much evil here of which I might discover the secret. Evil so great that my own safety must not be counted. No—and not even that of my boy. Twice I slipped notes deep in a pile of letters that I knew would be taken, without more examination, to the *Ortspostamt*—the little post-office. And there was a telephone from which I believed I could send a call for help if some crisis came. And yesterday—it came."

"And you managed to telephone?"

"This morning—yes. And I hoped that my message got through. But I was detected as I was speaking. So my imprisonment was made strict in this small room."

"They know that you got this telephone message out—giving the address of this place?"

The woman nodded. "They know that."

"Then they must certainly be packing up. But why did a crisis come yesterday?"

"It is obscure. But there have been several misfortunes—calamities. One is very technical, and I have been able to find out little. But some preparation of great intricacy—one vital to what goes on here—has become impure, and so is nearly all gone inert. The little that is left will be similarly useless in a day or two. And there is even some hitch in starting the long process of synthesising it again. I suspect that some—how would you say?—*entscheidend*—"

"Crucial," Jane pounced on the word at once.

"—that some crucial formula is not available. Then, there was a death. One of the Assistant Directors—the only one with whom I have had dealings—died. It is my thought that he was killed."

"Capital." Remnant nodded briskly. "One less to deal with."

"And the man who first persuaded me to come here—a man called Squire—has been in trouble. I believe it is thought that more than once he has acted rashly in finding people who might be obliged to stay here—to stay here and to submit to things. And I think too that there was an escape. It may have been an escape of such a person."

"It sounds a pretty full day. And the result is that something is being hurried on?"

"I fear that it is so. There are to be two or three swift experiments. It is a matter of using quickly, and while it is still potent, the substance—"

"I understand." Remnant was dragging a small table to the middle of the room and perching a chair on it. He was clearly determined that action should begin again without delay. "But what *are* these experiments? What does the whole thing aim at?"

"It is a scientific conspiracy. They call it Operation Pax."

"Operation Pax?"

"The aim is to find a means of neutralizing the combative—the aggressive—component in the human personality, and perhaps of spreading this, like a disease, through whole populations. They call that the General Pacification."

Remnant received this in silence. But Jane spoke up at once. "*Would* that be a bad thing?"

"It is the question I asked. At first it seemed to me that here was something perhaps of great benefit to mankind. I soon saw that it was the intention of these men to use their achievement in evil ways. They planned the means of making whole peoples —whole nations—helpless, impossible to arouse. These would be mere cattle—mere sheep—while others would remain wolves, lions, beasts of prey. And they would sell this instrument of power. More—they would *be* this power. For somewhere in this organisation, in some inner circle to which I have not penetrated, there is a lust for power, an unlimited ambition, that is very terrible."

Remnant was testing his means of climbing again to the shattered skylight. "Certainly a very considerable project," he said. "What we call a tall order, Dr. Tatistchev. But, only half an hour ago, we have seen it under way ourselves. Now we're going to stop it."

"But surely—" Jane hesitated. She was struggling for clarity amid the fantastically vast issues which had suddenly opened around her. It was like being a swimmer unexpectedly submerged deep in a whirlpool to escape which it was vital to strain every nerve and muscle. "Surely it is like the other great discoveries of science—very powerful for either good or evil? Surely it is matter of how it *would* be used?"

Anna Tatistchev nodded gravely. *"Fraulein,* so I too thought. But it is not so. *Gar nicht!* For the process is not a modification, but a destruction. It would create not another sort of men, but something less than men."

"Quite right. It's pure devilry." Remnant spoke absolutely. He sounded not at all like a man whose intellectual vigour had been inadequate to support the discourses of the Stockton and Darlington Professor. "Every creature born into a world like this needs every scrap of aggressiveness, or whatever you call it, that he can summon up. Most of us might use it better than we do. But the thing itself is ours; it's a need and a birthright; and the chap who'd steal it must have it turned against him overwhelmingly. That, as it happens, is our job now. I haven't over-much of it myself, but—"

Jane again found herself laughing. But this time it was not in the least hysterically. "What you have will do to be going on with. And we'd better *be* going on with it. Let's climb out."

"Then out we go. But there's something more to find out first." Remnant turned to Anna Tatistchev. "Do you think they have other places besides this?"

"I think they have."

"Well, now—they must be packing up, you know. They simply must. That escape, your telephone-message, things we've done this morning if by now they've discovered them: these things are their marching orders. But you think the active villainy is going on still?"

"I am sure it is. There are two reasons. One is the using to the best advantage of what little remains of the substance of which I have spoken. And that is why I fear for Rudi. It was only early yesterday that I came to suspect this of a child's being required. It is believed that with a child certain effects may be more lasting and complete than any achieved so far. And they have taken my boy to the island! I beg that you and your friends should act quickly."

Remnant nodded in brisk reassurance. "As it happens, we haven't any friends here yet. But we, ourselves, are going to act now."

"*Gott sei Dank!* Then you will be in time. It was only within this half an hour that they took him. And they will have put him to sleep. There is a certain harmless drug which must act—I think for perhaps an hour—before the thing is done. . . . But you must hasten very much, because of the other."

Jane caught her breath. "The other?"

"A young man. For him too I think they intend the injections. And then, if they had to abandon this place, they would take them both away. For these are crucial experiments. And it might be a long time before the substance is prepared again."

"Have you seen this young man? Do you know his name?"

"His name—no. He has not told it to me. But I have seen him and two or three times spoken. He is tall and fair, and his complexion—I do not know the word—"

Jane was trembling all over. "You mean—"

"It is *sommersprossig*."

"Freckly . . . it's Geoffrey!"

The little prison-like room swam round Jane, and she sank down on the bed. Remnant strode across to it and gave her an uncompromising shake. "Steady on. This is the best news we've had yet. The chap's alive. And we'll have him joining in the kicking in no time."

Anna Tatistchev too had come over to Jane and taken her by the hand. "He is your husband?"

"He is going to be."

"Nothing has yet happened. He is well. His danger too is great, but your friend will save him."

"It's horrible—abominable!" Jane sat up straight. "He has been kept here for weeks in this frightful peril, and nothing has been done." She turned to Remnant. "For God's sake, put your fist through the rest of the place—quick!"

"Come along, then. Up we go."

Jane climbed on the table. She hesitated. "You spoke to him? Did he speak of how he came here, or of—of things outside?"

"I was told that he was a very bad dipsomaniac, segregated here, and for whom there was little hope. Then I suspected that he was really imprisoned. Several times we spoke through a door before I had a glimpse of him. He told me that he had come here disguised, and for adventure—pretending to be homeless and friendless—because he had stumbled on the suspicion that the clinic was criminal. And they held him. I told him of how my own suspicions had grown, and of how I too now knew all the evil. We have talked hurriedly—secretly—of the danger, and of some plan. But then they took him to the island."

Remnant jumped on the table. "Well, we're going there now."

He picked up Jane as if she had been a child, mounted the chair, and gave her a vigorous hoist that sent her scrambling out on the roof. He turned to Anna Tatistchev. "I think three may be too many at the moment. Is anybody likely to come in on you here?"

"I think not."

"Then, just for a time, you'd better stop. We've started a distraction at the front of the house that must be keeping the bulk of these people busy. With luck Miss Appleby and I can break in to this place on the island and take whoever is on guard there by surprise."

"You are brave people. Have you arms? . . . Yes? Then go. I will wait, since you ask me. But there is one other thing of which I was to speak. It is the second reason why they will press on with what they have wished to do, even if they feel that soon they must abandon this place. It is the active evil spirit . . . I do not know the words for it."

"I think I see."

"Since yesterday I believe it has become a madness, a fury. Such a plan as theirs aims at wealth and power. But it springs simply from an illness of the mind, a compulsion to destroy. And if things go badly, and their ambitious plans are checked, then they will destroy blindly, rather than not destroy at all. So they are very dangerous."

Remnant nodded. "In fact there's a strong case for getting in on a little destruction first. That's just my notion." He put his hands up to the shattered skylight and heaved himself to the roof. "We'll be back in no time."

Anna Tatistchev nodded. *"Gott gebe!"* She sat down quietly on the side of the bed.

Jane Appleby was already at the extreme end of the long roof. Remnant hurried after her. Fortune, he thought, had thrown him up against two very good sort of women for an affair of the sort on hand.

9. Jane was staring at the temple. It had a sufficiently forbidding look. "Ought she not to have come with us? She's the child's mother, after all."

Remnant shook his head. "For the moment, only business considerations count. We've got two guns—the one from Cline's drawer, and one I took from the chap I slugged. . . . Got a pocket?"

"Yes."

"Ever fired a revolver?"

"Quite often. But only at targets, I'm afraid."

Remnant grinned. He seemed to have leisure to regard this as a capital joke. "Good enough. Here you are." He handed Jane Cline's weapon. "Right shoulder if you want to be humane. Tummy if you're feeling nasty."

"I see." Jane shivered slightly. "I can imagine circumstances in which I shall feel very nasty indeed."

"They won't happen. We're a step ahead of all that. Things are going along quite nicely. It's a matter of impetus, you know. First thing they teach you about assault."

"And I can imagine other circumstances in which I should find you insufferable, Mr. Remnant. . . . How do we go?"

"Straight across the bridge, Miss Appleby. Take your shoes off."

Jane obeyed without asking questions.

"Good woman. We go across the lid, so to speak. And it's tin. Don't want to make a row. Twenty fires in that highly respectable drunks' home wouldn't draw the whole high command away from this affair in front of us. So follow me, and don't speak until you're spoken to."

Jane compressed her lips. There were moments when she found Roger Remnant very hard to take. His own shoes were off and strung round his neck. From the roof on which they stood to the upper surface of the tunnel-like bridge was an easy drop, and he made it in absolute silence. Jane dropped down beside him. They went forward on tiptoe. The surface was of corrugated iron. Walking delicately, it was not easy to keep a sure balance. But in less than a minute they had reached the other end.

Remnant came to a halt and stood quite still, frowning. Jane saw that the next problem was a hard one. On either side of them the sheer wall of the temple went off in a blank, smooth curve, and below them it dropped clean into the water. Remnant's voice came softly in Jane's ear. "No good taking a swim. Bad splash. Bad for the guns. We don't know what's on the other side. This is perhaps the only entrance—and it may be sheer like this all the way round." He paused, rapidly appraising again the whole situation. "Have to go up."

Jane looked up. The proposal seemed blankly impossible. What confronted them was a steeply pitched pediment—presumably an ornamental feature crowning the doorway now concealed by the bridge—which rose until it almost touched the curved cornice of the building. Remnant put out his hand to it. "That or nothing," he murmured. "We can just get on the outer face of the pediment; it's not too steep to crawl up—at least I don't think so. How to get off it and on top of the cornice is the headache. But there isn't sudden death below; only a filthy ducking. I think I can take you. Follow me." He edged himself on to the pediment, belly downwards, and crawled up its smooth incline. "Not bad," he whispered back. "Pediment projects beyond the cornice a good six inches. And there's a lightning-conductor to help. We can do it. Come on."

Jane came on. Her head was clear, but her recollection immediately afterwards confused. Somehow they had done it. They were lying in a sort of broad lead gutter behind the cornice. Beyond this again rose the curve of the dome.

"We're perfectly hidden here. Lie still. I'm going right round." Remnant breathed the words in Jane's ear and set off at a crawl. He had become, she realised, suddenly very cautious. He disappeared round the curve of the dome, keeping wholly prone in the gutter. His progress in this fashion could not be rapid; to Jane it appeared an age before his head and shoulders emerged from behind the answering curve of the dome on her other hand. She thought inconsequently of Sir Francis Drake, home after circumnavigating the world.

"The temple doesn't cover the whole thing. There's quite a bit of ground on the other side, and the island runs out in a little tongue, with a much smaller temple at the end of it. That means there's probably another entrance to this big one, facing that way. But, ten to one, it's pretty massively locked up. I'm going up again. Better do it from the other side, where there's less chance of being seen."

This time they both crawled half round the dome. Peering over the cornice, Jane presently saw the vacant stretch of island that Remnant had described. The second temple was very much smaller: an oblong affair, again with Doric columns. Jane, a severely educated child, at once saw that it was a miniature version of the Theseion at Athens. But Remnant was paying more attention to what was above him. "Only a step up to the drum," he said. "But the first part of the dome's more difficult. However, it's ribbed. I'll go up and have a look." He rose, spread-eagled himself between two of the ribs to which he had pointed, and worked himself upward. As the ribs converged and the pitch lessened the going got easier. Presently he set himself astride a single rib and kneed himself to the top. Within a minute he was sliding down a rib and had come to rest beside her again. It was an expert roof-climber's job, and Jane guessed that if he was unfamiliar with the lecture rooms of the colleges of Oxford he was tolerably familiar with their towers and pinnacles. "Any good?" she whispered.

"What have you got on under that skirt and jersey?"

By this time Jane was schooled into finding nothing that Roger Remnant said at all odd. "Nylon."

"A lot of it?"

"Well, quite a lot." Jane was apologetic. "It's getting on in October."

"Stockings?"

"Nylon too." This time Jane was yet more apologetic. "Economical, really."

"I want the whole lot."

"The whole lot?"

"Listen—it's as I thought. The lantern up there screens a circular opening at the top of the dome."

"An eye."

"Very well—an eye. And it looks straight down on a sort of small circular hall—"

"A cortile."

"—with rooms opening off all round. I think we can make something that will take me down."

"If you mean out of my nylon, then I'm going down too."

"We'll see about that. Look—I'll nip round here a bit and see what I can contribute." Remnant grinned. "Not that I can really compete. But a pair of braces will give us a final useful three or four feet."

He was gone. It was not a commodious spot in which to undress, but Jane made no bones about it. The garments when lying in a heap at her feet seemed absurdly tenuous. She picked them up and crawled with them farther round the drum. The sensation of a skirt and a woollen jersey next to her skin was mildly disconcerting. Remnant was waiting for her. He took the things one by one. "Absolutely splendid. Marvellous stuff. Take an elephant. Unfortunately it needs a bit of time. You can fill it in by finding your way about that gun."

Jane obediently found her way about the gun. Remnant worked with concentration and extraordinary care. Every drop of impetuosity seemed to have evaporated from his personality. She suddenly knew that her confidence in him was complete.

He had finished. "You saw how I went up?"

"Yes."

"Could you do it?"

"Yes."

"Then up you go first. If you slip, go slack and spread-eagle.

You won't come really fast, except right at the end here. And —listen—when you do get up and peer over, the floor will seem the hell of a long way down. But it isn't as far as it looks."

"I understand that."

"Then off you go."

The woollen jersey tickled horribly as she sprawled and kneed her way upwards, and the scratching of the tweed skirt was worse. But the climb itself was a good deal easier than she had expected, once the first thrust of the dome was conquered. In a few minutes she was under the lantern with which this freakish building was surmounted; and a moment later Remnant was beside her.

"A bit conspicuous up here, so we don't want to waste time. And there won't be much of this admirable rope to spare, so we mustn't waste that either. . . . But here's the lightning-conductor again. Saves us a couple of feet. There—it's fixed. You can go up and down ropes?"

"Yes."

"Then you may follow as soon as I've touched down. If it bears me it will bear you."

"In that case wouldn't it be better—"

"Be quiet. The stuff's all right. It's the knots. But I've worked each one just all I know how. Well, this is the dangerous bit—see? Every way the dangerous bit. After this the clean-up will follow."

"I believe you. Go ahead."

Remnant swung himself over the eye. "As it happens, I go down a bit fancy. But you come plain—feet, knees, both hands. No bright girl of the gym—understand?"

"Agreed."

Remnant drew the revolver from his pocket. He still had his appearance of extraordinary concentration. And then he was gone—so quickly that whatever was fancy in his method quite eluded Jane's analysis. Whatever it was, it took him down the improvised rope like an express elevator, and with the revolver poised ready in a free hand. He was safely on the floor—a marble floor, Jane suddenly saw—and standing quite still. He did not look up. That, she realised, would have made this yawning and suddenly horrible chasm seem somehow much deeper. He would betray no anxiety about her. His attention was absorbed in studying the circle of closed doors surrounding him. A gentle draught of air came up. It was a very chill air, and it stirred the crazy dangling thread that, minutes before, had been no more than a thin and diaphanous sheath round her own body. It looked now as if it would scarcely bear the weight of a small plummet at the end of it. But it had borne Remnant. She realised that it was now or never—both for this, and for ever looking herself in the face again. She went over and down—hand over hand, carefully, as she had been told.

She had done it, and the marble floor was very cold on her bare feet. Remnant's hand came out and touched hers. It was a gesture commanding absolute silence. The little cortile, with its cupola and lantern above, could be a dire acoustic trap. A mere whisper, incautiously pitched, would echo and re-echo round it, until the reiterated and amplified sound was like surf breaking on a beach. Jane strained her ears. She could hear only a low, intermittent sighing, now rising towards a whistle and now sinking to a moan. It was the wind, she thought, playing through the lantern and washing round the chill concavity of the dome.

Remnant moved his other hand slightly. It was the one holding the revolver. She understood, and drew out the weapon in her own pocket. She gripped it firmly, imagining the clatter it would make if it fell. She looked downwards. The marble was white and faintly veined, like her own feet that rested on it. She looked around. There were five closed doors. Two of them were symmetrically placed on either side of a vaulted passage leading, she guessed, to the main doorway and the bridge, and the fifth was directly opposite this.

She heard her own heart. Remnant's left hand let go of hers and described a small circle in air. She understood him instantly.

It was like having a twin brother with whom no speech was necessary. He disliked the way the closed doors surrounded them. Let the wrong one open, and for a fatal second they could not help being taken unawares. His finger moved, and she knew that they were to stand back to back. With infinite caution he took a step sideways. She did the same. It was like ceasing to be man and woman, and becoming a monstrous crab. They moved towards the vaulted passage, holding the doors covered on either hand. She still heard faintly the sob and wail as of invisible wind. They had traversed the breadth of the marble floor. It was patterned in concentric circles, and their slow progress had been like that of a pawn on an unfamiliar board. The open archway was now above their heads. The length of the corridor on which it opened must correspond to that of the surrounding rooms.

She was touched lightly on the shoulder. It was her job to stand guard alone. Remnant had gone. A moment later she heard the first sound that either of them had occasioned. It might have been the scrape of iron on stone. Remnant was back and standing beside her, his revolver in front of him and his glance circling warily from door to door. His left thumb went over his shoulder. She was to make the same inspection that he had just carried out. The passage proved to be no more than eight paces long. At the far end were massive double doors, sheathed in bronze, and with their handles gripped in the jaws of bronze lions. A key stood turned in a powerful lock. And a stout steel bar, pivoting at the centre, had been swung round and engaged in niches in the surrounding stone. It had been the sound of this forced home that she had heard a moment before. Remnant had made very sure that they would not be surprised from the direction of the bridge.

So they were shut up with the enemy, lurking in some or all of the surrounding rooms. Jane thought of those gruesome pictures, beloved of persons who fabricate history-books for the very young, depicting martyrs in the arena, awaiting the release of the wild beasts from their cages. She returned to Remnant.

He was not—as the analogy might suggest—engaged in prayer. Nevertheless he had something of the same rapt quality. And he appeared to be listening with all his ears. It came to Jane in a flash that there was something ominous in the silence of the place. Remnant had been very sure that this whole hideous organisation must be aware its hour had struck. What if it had already vanished to some other lurking-place, some emergency headquarters—taking its crucial victims with it? There was nothing but dismay in the thought. A thousand times better than that would it be for every one of those five sinister doors to open simultaneously and pour the whole filthy gang upon them. Which means—thought Jane dispassionately—that at least I haven't got cold feet. . . . But that wasn't true in a physical sense—for now both her feet and calves felt icy at the creeping chill of the marble.

Remnant signed to her to stay where she was. He began to move—more rapidly now, but with absolute noiselessness—round the circumference of the circular hall. She was unable to follow him continuously with her eye, for it was her business to keep all five doors under observation. And this was the best position from which to do that. The curve of the building put even those most immediately on either hand all but simultaneously within her vision. She wondered if she was to shoot at sight. The revolver was perfectly steady in her hand, and she knew that at this range she could do what damage she was minded to. . . . Remnant was stopping at each door, intently listening. She had a sense that he was inwardly perplexed—perhaps even that some doubt was growing in him. He paused longest at the door directly opposite. He crouched down by it, and she saw that he was licking his left hand. For a moment the effect was weirdly feline. Then she saw that he was passing the moist hand close to the floor, and then at a right-angle up the edge of the door. . . . Presently he moved on and completed the circuit. She glanced swiftly at his face as he came up to her. His eyes seemed to have gone darker. There were beads of sweat on his forehead. He pointed back at the door straight ahead of her. She knew that they were to go through it.

They moved straight across the floor, brushing as they went past it the tatter of nylon that had brought them here. Remnant paused, pointed to himself, raised one finger; he pointed to Jane and raised two; he stepped for a moment in front of her and made a gesture from his back to the space on his left. She understood that he was to go in first, and that as she followed she was to place herself on his left hand.

He was reaching for the handle. He must be proposing to take a chance that the door wasn't locked. The faint sob and whistle she had already heard was louder. Perhaps the wind was rising. . . .

Remnant flung back the door. It was of abnormal thickness, and bedded in rubber. What Jane had heard through this insulating medium was a human voice, screaming in agony.

10. Something whined past her ear and smacked against a wall far behind her. She knew that it was a bullet; that with formidable swiftness of response the enemy had met the assault in its first moments. Then she realised that she was again on the wrong side of the door. At that first shot Remnant had thrust her back and half closed it on her. Her impulse was to thrust at it furiously. But his shoulders were hard up against it, and she saw that to push might be to endanger rather than help him.

The screams of agony had mercifully ceased. Or perhaps they had only disappeared behind a curtain of more deafening sound. So confounding was the uproar that for a second she lost all clear understanding of its occasion. She recovered herself and knew that it was a gun-battle. The number of shots actually fired was not, perhaps, so very many all told. But the reports chased each other wildly round the domed hall to which she was still, infuriatingly, confined, and the noise was so great as to shut out every other sensation and perception. She looked quickly round to see if anybody was emerging from the other rooms. If reinforcements did come from these she would have a part to play yet. When she turned again Remnant's shoulders had gone. She had a horrible fear that he had been hit; that he would be lying crumpled on the floor. She pushed at the door. It swung back freely and she entered the room.

The place reeked of powder, and of queer smells she could not identify. There was one further shot. She saw a white-coated figure in the middle of the room dive head foremost to the floor like an acrobat and lie still; and in the same instant she was aware of two similar figures dashing through a door straight in front of her and slamming it behind them. Remnant was on his feet still; he leapt at the door through which the figures had retreated, and locked it. Then he turned round and saw her. "Go out," he said.

She found herself trembling with anger as she looked at him. "I'll never forgive you—never!"

"Go outside." His voice was low—but it fell on her like a strong hand. She turned and walked unsteadily into the circular hall, her temples hammering. Things that she had momentarily glimpsed and instinctively refused to acknowledge the meaning of swayed before her inward vision, and she felt, like an actual physical thing, an icy and invisible hand on her heart.

"Jane—please come back now."

She turned again and re-entered the room. "I'm sorry," she said.

Remnant raised the ghost of a smile. "We're getting on pretty well. I think the child's all right." And he pointed to a corner of the room. Jane took one look and ran to it. Rudi Tatistchev, the small boy whom they had already glimpsed once that morning, was lying there, curled up, his face stained with tears, and apparently in a deep sleep. She knelt beside him and took him in her arms—with a surge of deep feeling such as she had never known.

"He really is all right. They hadn't got going on all that." Remnant had come up beside her. "They were busy instead with your poor devil from the Bodleian."

"They wanted to experiment—"

"No—not that." Remnant's voice was very quiet. "They were trying to get something out of him. He's been pretty filthily handled. That was why I pushed you out the second time. I wanted to tidy him up a bit. He'll be quite all right—in time. I've put him over on that bench."

Jane set the sleeping child down gently and turned round. The battlefield—for it was like that—was a large, wedge-shaped room that had been turned elaborately into an operating theatre. It was lit by sundry impressive electrical contrivances, and the only daylight—as presumably with all the rooms in the temple—was from shallow windows high up under the architrave. There was blood now all over the place. In the middle of the floor, huddled on his side, the man she had seen fall there lay in a pool of it. He was alive; his body was spasmodically twitching; when it did this it emitted noises that were not human but merely mechanical or hydraulic; and his face was hideously grey behind a neatly trimmed red beard.

Her eye passed swiftly on, very fearful of what it might next see. But there was now only one other figure in the room: the little man into whom she had so fatefully bumped upon leaving Dr. Ourglass and the inquisitive Mark Bultitude. Fate had decreed that he should be one of Nature's meaner and more insignificant creations; man had lately seen to it that he should be much less even than this. He half lay, half sat on a bench by the wall where Remnant had shoved him, wrapped in a sheet patched with blood. His eyes were open, but it was impossible to tell if they saw.

"Stay here and keep an eye on things—and particularly for anybody coming to monkey with the door." Remnant was moving across the room again. "I'm going to make sure there's nobody lurking—of his own will or otherwise—elsewhere in the building."

She watched him go out, understanding very well the meaning

of his move. They had rescued the little man she had seen kidnapped in Radcliffe Square—or at least they had rescued what was left of him. And—what would have been worth crossing the world for—they had rescued the little boy. But of her lover whom she had set out to seek there was still no sign. . . . She looked at the shambles about her—the product of the heat of battle and partly of madness and cold cruelty—and her whole body shivered as if in ague. The resources of the desperate people amid whom destiny had brought her appeared endless. Perhaps about England, about Europe, they had half a dozen places like this; and perhaps they were already hurrying to one of them now, bearing Geoffrey with them.

Remnant was back. The chill of the ghastly place seemed mitigated as he entered. "Nobody and nothing," he said. "On one side a room rather like Cline's but grander, and with a laboratory next door. On the other side a bedroom and a slap-up bathroom. And there's a surprisingly dry cellar used as a store."

"I see." Jane's voice trembled. Her eye fell on the bearded man on the floor. "Can we do anything for him?"

"Unfortunately he's past getting anything *from*." Remnant's tone held a momentary savagery that startled her. "He's going to die."

"Do you think that Geoffrey—"

"Your young man? Don't worry. I'm afraid they're holding him still. But he's in no danger. Or in no danger of—this." He glanced round. Jane saw that, beneath his reassuring manner, he was fighting mad. "We've smashed all that for good."

"They may have the means of starting it up elsewhere."

"Don't be dismal. And they've got something coming to them yet." He looked at the locked door that gave on the farther end of the island, and frowned. "Only we've got to think. . . . I wonder if the poor chap over there can tell us anything."

They both crossed the room. Jane's bare feet were like metal dragged at by some powerful magnet under the floor. With an immense effort she looked straight at the man and walked on. His eyes were still open. And as they reached him his lips moved.

"Others . . . there was a kid."

Remnant spoke clearly. "The kid's all right. He's over there. Was there anyone else?"

"The little place beyond this . . . I didn't see it the first time." The man's face contorted itself with the effort of speaking. "They put me in there first . . . a young chap . . . prisoner—"

"Yes?"

"Asked—" The man gave a deep groan. "But I didn't—" His eyes turned to Jane. "Bicycle," he murmured, with a queer inflexion of recognition. And his eyes closed.

Jane looked at Remnant. "He means the little square temple?"

"Clearly. A couple got away there when they'd had enough of the shooting game here. And there might be one or two more. You say you sent a telegram to this top-ranking policeman brother of yours?"

"Yes." Jane looked at her watch. "And he must have got it well over an hour ago."

"Of course they don't know about that. But it seems they *do* know that Anna What's-her-name got out a telephone call. So they can't reckon on much more grace. On the other hand, they can no doubt communicate with the rest of the gang—those that are real in-on-the-thing accomplices, I mean—who are now milling round our fire. They may have found poor old Cline in his cupboard."

"I suppose those people in the other temple can get away if they want to?"

"Good lord, yes. The lake would be no obstacle to them at all. Ten to one, they're gone by now. They've got precious little motive not to quit. Unless—" Remnant frowned. "I think we'll try a little experiment." He moved across to the door leading to the open air and studied it. "Metal-sheathed too," he said. "So there's not much risk. Come over here." Jane joined him. "Now, listen. While I—"

A high, hoarse scream from behind them froze the words on

Remnant's lips. They whirled round. The savagely man-handled figure, who a minute before possessed scarcely the strength to whisper, had flung off the sheet enveloping him. Bloody and almost naked, he was staggering across the room. In an instant they saw why. The bearded man had got on his knees and was crawling along the floor, clutching in one hand a short, gleaming knife. He glanced sidelong as he moved—and Jane, catching his eye, saw that in his last moments humanity had left him and he was become a beast.

"Not the kid!" The little man, as he screamed the words, flung himself upon the insane creature on the floor. Rudi Tatistchev, in his deep drugged sleep, lay no more than a yard away, and the bright surgical knife had been poised in air. There was a second's violent struggle as Remnant rushed forward. The two figures on the floor were a tangle of flailing and twitching limbs. Then there was a single deep groan. Remnant took the bearded form by the shoulders and flung it aside. It lay quite still. The little man turned over on his back with a low wail. The knife was buried in his breast.

Jane dropped down at his side. He opened his eyes on her and his lips moved. "Your kid," he whispered. "Your kid's safe . . . across the . . . weir. . . . They can't . . . can't pull the plug on him. . . . Dar—" His lips became motionless, and his eyes closed.

Remnant moved from one inert form to the other. "Both dead." He looked down at the torn body of the little man whose name was unknown to them. "I don't suppose he ever got high marks as a citizen," he said soberly. "But he wasn't a bad chap."

It was an unexpected epitaph on Albert Routh.

11. A mile short of Milton Manor, Appleby overtook and cautiously passed a small horde of children on bicycles. Almost immediately afterwards, and as he turned into the side-road on which the entrance to the estate must lie, he just saved himself from head-on collision with a powerful car swinging out at a dangerous pace. The two vehicles came to a stop, bonnet to bonnet, with a scream of brakes. Appleby was preparing to speak in his frostiest official manner when he became aware that the driver of the other car was known to him. It was the fat Bede's don, Mark Bultitude.

Without attempting to back, Appleby climbed out. "Good afternoon," he said. "We nearly did each other a good deal of damage."

For a second Bultitude, who had not stirred from his wheel, stared at him blankly. Then his face broke into a smile. "Dear me," he said. "Sir John Appleby, is it not? I was sorry not to have some conversation with you last night. We are undoubtedly here on the same errand."

"Except that I am coming and you are going."

"Precisely. You remember Cumming who was always going, and Gowing who was always coming? Too few people now read that immortal diary. . . . You are looking for news of the young man Ourglass?"

"At the moment, I am looking for my sister. It is she who is looking for him—with some rashness, possibly."

Bultitude raised his eyebrows. "I was being introduced to your sister a few hours ago in Oxford. If I may say so, I thought her a delightful girl, who never says anything silly, and who looks particularly charming when she thinks she has."

"Thank you."

"It was meeting her that put this expedition into my head. . . . Good gracious—what a mob of brats!"

The children on the bicycles had swept past. They were shouting and arguing hotly as they disappeared in a cloud of dust. Appleby watched them absently. "It was through meeting my sister that you came out here?"

"Actually, I had suggested to the young man's uncle—I think you met him when he was my guest last night—that we should come and do a little exploring together. But he finally excused himself. Not that he isn't genuinely anxious about his nephew. But I believe that I offended him deeply—although almost, perhaps, without his conscious awareness—by making one or two unfortunately facetious suggestions when he first told of the matter. Anyway, I came straight out myself."

"I see." Appleby, who a few minutes before had been in a tearing hurry, produced a pipe and filled it slowly. "You've become interested in this young man?"

Bultitude considered. "It appears," he said gravely, "that this Geoffrey Ourglass is an *Ourglass*. I had no idea. One is naturally interested in a well-connected youth."

"Naturally." Appleby looked hard at the fat man. Bultitude, he thought, must have had a motor-car body more or less built round him.

"And if in addition to that he has brains—as this Geoffrey apparently has—then he is a *rara avis* indeed. No exertion should be too great if he can be brought back to Bede's."

"A very proper collegiate feeling." Appleby lit his pipe. "And you came out this way simply because you had heard the story of young Ourglass's having been seen driving—or being driven—hereabouts?"

Bultitude's arms began to flip about his person with something of the helplessness of the wings of a penguin. It presently appeared that he was in search of a cigarette-case. Appleby produced matches. When this exigency had been adequately met Bultitude picked up the conversation as if it had not been interrupted. "No, Sir John. I had a further reason—an acquaintanceship in these parts."

"At Milton Manor?"

"My dear Appleby—if I may so address you—how thoroughly on the spot you are. At Milton Manor, as you say. A certain Dr. Cline, who runs the place. Or who runs one side of it."

"That is most interesting to me, Bultitude. A close acquaintance?"

"Dear me, no. My intimates, such as they are, move in other

classes of society. A former professional contact—no more. But it struck me that it might be worth consulting him."

"How very odd."

Bultitude pondered, as if resolved to accord this response fair consideration. "Yes," he said. "I agree. It *was* odd. It was a queer idea. Less an idea, indeed, than an intuition."

"A successful intuition?"

"Unfortunately not. At first Cline was engaged, and then they couldn't find him. Moreover there was a fire. By now the whole place may be burnt down."

"Burnt down!"

"Would it be so regrettable?"

This time Appleby looked at Mark Bultitude very hard indeed. "Am I to understand that you have formed an unfavourable opinion of this clinic?"

Bultitude smiled his most brilliant smile. "I should conceive it—upon reflection, but quite recent reflection—to be highly dangerous and probably highly criminal. . . . Dear me—how late it is! I really must be pushing on."

Appleby seemed not altogether disposed to take this hint at its first offering. "It seems likely," he said grimly, "that my sister is in this highly dangerous and probably highly criminal place now. I shall be there myself in five minutes—"

"I am delighted to hear it. The matter—if I may be allowed to say so—will be in most competent hands."

"And unless certain coded instructions are given to the contrary, there will be a very considerable force of police there—well, a little later on."

"How much I wish I could stop. Unfortunately, most important business calls me back to Oxford . . . *most* important business, my dear Appleby. And now, if perhaps I were to back a few yards—"

"That is most obliging of you, Bultitude. It is really my car that ought to be moved."

"Not at all, my dear fellow—not at all." By what was, in him a remarkable acrobatic feat, Bultitude contrived to raise an arm in a condescending and dismissive gesture. "By the way—-was it just the old story of Ourglass's being seen hereabouts that has brought *Miss Appleby* out this way?"

"Far from it. Last night—although she knows nothing of this—a thoroughly desperate gang of criminals were hunting a small man with a scratched face about Oxford. They captured him. They captured me too."

"That was indeed an achievement."

Appleby smiled. "If I were confronted with them, I would be the first to offer my congratulations."

"It would be handsome of you. But proceed."

"We both escaped—or rather were rescued. Then this little man faded out. My sister saw him this morning in the upper reading room in Bodley."

Bultitude raised his eyebrows. "How very interesting. It is true that highly criminal proceedings are frequently conducted there—but on what must be termed, conventionally, the intellectual plane."

"Then she saw him being kidnapped from Radcliffe Square, and somehow learnt that the destination of the kidnappers was Milton."

Bultitude's engine started into life, and his car shot alarmingly backwards. It then advanced, clear of Appleby's mudguards, and stopped again, with the engine ticking over. The bulk of Bultitude deflected itself by some inches from the perpendicular. In a common man the attitude would have been that of leaning affably out to bid a friend farewell. "This has been a most enlightening conversation, Appleby. I have missed a luncheon party, but I am really very glad that I came out, all the same. There are times when one must cut one's losses—in the interest, of course, of greater ultimate gains."

"Yes, indeed. It is a generalisation one must bear in mind." Appleby stepped clear. "I hope your important business in Oxford will go well."

"And I, in my turn, am most anxious about the issue of yours, here in Milton. And who knows"—Bultitude let in his clutch and his car glided smoothly forward—"that we may not meet and compare notes later?"

"In your common-room to-night?"

Bultitude smiled. "I wonder," he said—and drove on.

12. The cyclists had not got far. Appleby passed them again round the next bend, scattered over a grassy knoll in a sort of irregular bivouac. Some were eating sandwiches or apples; some were disputing hotly; the greater number were listening to an impassioned harangue by a small, red-haired boy. Perhaps they were unable to agree on whether their expedition had taken them far enough. Appleby was not inclined to give the matter much thought. He had other things to think about.

At the lodge of Milton Manor he was nearly involved in a second collision. The gates were open, and a couple of heavy covered lorries were just swinging out. Drawn into the side of the road with his engine running, Appleby eyed him grimly. Then before the gates could be shut again he drove through them and stopped. A respectable-looking man at once hurried up. "I'm very sorry, sir. But no visitors to-day."

Appleby shook his head. "I'm not a visitor. I'm a fireman."

The man looked startled. "Sorry, sir. My orders are—"

"Don't you know the place is on fire?"

"Yes, sir. I've had it on the house-telephone. But my—"

"Then don't be a fool, my man." Appleby was suddenly brusque. "I always come out ahead of my brigade, as you very well know. The engines will be here within a minute. Leave these gates open, and see that nothing gets in the way."

"But you won't get through the fence." The man was puzzled and worried. "And I've orders—"

So there was another barrier. It was something, Appleby thought, that one might have guessed. "But surely," he said, "you keep a key here?"

"No, sir. I telephone up to the house." The man was apologetic. "It's the animals, you see. Very valuable, they are."

"No doubt. And I suppose the house itself is of some value too. And it's burning. See that you telephone at once." Appleby let in his clutch again and shot forward. As he did so he fancied he heard, far off and faintly from behind him, the chirming of a great many bicycle bells.

Driving fast, he rounded a bend and saw a tall wire fence in front of him, running away on either side of equally tall gates of the same material. If he waited, perhaps somebody would come and unlock them. Or perhaps somebody would not. No buildings were as yet visible, but from beyond a belt of trees a thin column of smoke was rising. It did not look as if the fire reported by Bultitude was in fact very serious. He took his foot from the accelerator, meaning to slow down and consider his best course of action. As the roar of the engine died, he thought for a moment that he heard the crackle of flames. Then he realised that the sound was of rifle or revolver fire. He compressed his lips and peered ahead, trying to estimate from a distance the strength of the barrier before him. There really was no help for it. He pressed down on the accelerator hard. The car had still been travelling at a good pace. He felt in his back the sudden thrust of its eight roaring cylinders. One did this in the circus. Only there the barrier was of paper, and the vehicle a discreetly cantering horse. . . .

The gates went down with a crash—and with a flash of brilliant blue flame. Appleby's body tingled all over; there was a queer sensation in his scalp; for a moment an unaccountable smell of singeing filled the car. By the time he had taken a guess at what had happened he had rounded another bend and glimpsed Milton Manor straight before him.

There was a crowd of people out on a lawn—patients, he supposed, because several nurses appeared to be attending on them. At a little distance from these a man in a white coat was lying back in a deck chair, with the appearance of being assisted or revived by two more nurses. Farther on, he could see a red fire-tender and a tangle of hoses. He cut off his engine and heard another shot. It came from somewhere beyond the house. The drive forked and he swung left. It curved towards the house again, and in front of him he now found a tall archway that appeared to lead into a courtyard. He drove straight through.

13. "And now for our experiment."

Remnant was coolly ripping a strip of cloth from the white linen coat of the corpse with the red beard. Some yards back from the door that pointed towards the tip of the island he had already built a formidable double breast-work out of the stainless-steel equipment with which the place was lavishly provided. Now he advanced to the door with his improvised rope—the second he had constructed that day—in his hand. He tied it to the handle, unlocked the door, and retreated, gun in hand.

"You'd better be inside this too. And bring the boy. It will be the safest place if there really is shooting and things begin to ricochet."

Jane Appleby did as she was told. "You think they're still there?"

He grinned. "I'll be pretty surprised if they are. But we'll take no chances. . . . Ready?"

Jane nodded.

"If anything does happen, take your time. I got the lie of the land pretty well from the roof. They've no chance of rushing us, even if they've been reinforced from the house. And—by that same token—we have no chance of advancing against them. . . . *Now!*"

Remnant pulled firmly at his rope and the door swung open. In an instant a bullet rang past above their heads.

Jane's heart leapt. They were still there—which meant that Geoffrey was still there too. "Roger Remnant," she murmured in her companion's ear. "His first bad guess."

Remnant's reply was lost in a second rattle of fire. The bullets ripped harmlessly overhead. She heard a click of metal beside her. Remnant was fiddling with a long forceps and a couple of mirror-like stainless-steel plates. "First-rate periscope," he said. "Keep down, whatever you do. I'll give you a full report in a tick." He shoved up the forceps with one plate gripped in it, and manoeuvred it to an angle. "O.K. Perfectly clear. Temple has pillars all round. And a couple of fellows are lurking there to keep us back. I'll just touch them up a bit. Show them we're quite lively." He suddenly thrust out an arm and fired.

"Perhaps they can't get away?"

"Unless we already have friends on the spot, I don't see that that's possible, worse luck. They must have a punt beyond the temple—or something of that kind. I'd say they're holding what's a strong position until they get a car round from the house. Then they'll be off, all right."

"I wish John would come."

"That your brother? So do I. We could do with every Appleby—male and female—your family can raise." Remnant's voice was not, Jane considered, altogether convincing. He's a vain creature, she thought ungratefully, and just loves it being all his show. He'd like to beat them off his own bat. And I wouldn't put it beyond him. . . .

Her thought was scattered by the sudden roar of an engine starting into life somewhere beyond the square temple in front of them. Remnant scowled. "There they go," he said. "But keep down still. I'm going to have a proper squint. . . . Hullo—what's that?"

From somewhere out in the park a new sound came to them: that of racing cars, a low, almost continuous penetrating horn, and behind that a single urgently-chiming bell.

Jane gasped. "It's John . . . it's the police—and an ambulance. . . ."

Remnant had got on his knees. He fired a couple of shots at the farther temple, waited a second, and stood up. "Gone," he said.

The engine beyond the temple was still roaring. Suddenly above it they heard a single shrill call—a call for help. The sound brought Jane to her feet in an instant. "Geoffrey!"

For a second she saw nothing except a row of Doric pillars and a dark doorway beyond. Then a single figure emerged flying—the figure of a young man in ragged trousers and a torn shirt. His hair was matted and his face was a dead white streaked with grey. Two men—one in a white coat—pounded after him.

"Jane—Jane!" It was a cry like a child's—and as he uttered it the young man thrust out blindly, gropingly, an appealing arm that seemed bruised and blackened in its torn sleeve. "Help!"

She took the breast-work at a bound and ran. She heard Remnant curse and leap after her. There was a hail of bullets, and she heard Remnant give a cry, spin round and fall. But she herself was untouched. Geoffrey was no more than five yards away. She was nearly there. She was nearly touching him— Suddenly from the lake on her left a dark, dripping figure rose up, took her in a flying Rugby tackle and then, with almost no loss of impetus, went rolling with her across the narrow tongue of land and into the lake on the other side. The water closed over her head just as she heard another fusillade of shots.

For a moment she thought that she would never come up again—that she was down at some great depth in the grasp of a drowning man. Then—ludicrously, tragically—she found that she was struggling upright in some four feet of muddy water. Her head was out; she shook it; her eyes cleared—but in her ears there was still a great roaring. The square temple was straight in front of her. And above it hung something monstrous, out of nature: a vast and hovering insect. She shook her head once more, and knew that the roaring noise was not inside her own brain. The noise came from the insect. The insect was a helicopter. . . . Even as the realisation came to her the machine climbed, hovered again, and moved off on a lateral course.

"They certainly seem to keep a trick or two up their sleeve."

She swung round. The man who had carried her headlong into the lake was standing breast-high in the water beside her. It was her brother John.

14. She was sitting on the bank. The skirt and jersey that had been her only garments lay heavily on her in sopping folds. Her hair was soaking. The shoes still slung absurdly round her neck were two small buckets of water. Only her eyes were dry—dry and bitterly angry.

"John, why did you do it—*why?* It was Geoffrey—he's alive!"

"Which is more than you would have been in another five seconds." Her brother, who was binding up Remnant's right arm, spoke grimly and without turning round. It dawned on her that he was quite as angry as she was. "Do you think, sir"—he was addressing Remnant—"that this was a proper affair in which to involve my sister?"

"Yes, I do—or I wouldn't have done it." Remnant in his turn was angry and uncompromising. "She has what it takes—and I don't know that there's any other test." He smiled wanly. "Besides—if I may say so—she rather involved me. I apologise, all the same."

"How dare you apologise!" Jane had jumped to her feet, at once dripping and blazing. "I think—"

"Easy, easy." Her brother was now smiling at the two of them. "I apologise too. We needn't quarrel. After all, we're doing pretty well."

Jane felt the blood going to her head. "Doing pretty well! With Geoffrey—"

"Use your head, Jane."

She gasped for breath. John was every whit as intolerable as Remnant. "I *do* use my head."

"Very well—just consider. Those people in the helicopter are some sort of criminal I haven't got the hang of. Perhaps you two have. Something pretty bad, no doubt. But, likely enough, nothing can be proved that would positively hang them. But if you hadn't gone in the lake, my girl, you'd have gone in your coffin. And then they *would* have been murderers—every one of them, regardless of which did the actual shooting. You'd have gone. And your young man would have followed."

"By jove—that's right!" Remnant, struggling with considerable pain, looked up sharply. "As it is, he's tolerably safe. The devilry's over; we cooked that goose. And if they're not murderers yet, they're unlikely to commit gratuitous murder now."

"It's what the man with the red beard meant to do." Jane still spoke hotly. "Sheer gratuitous killing of that child."

"He was off his rocker. But the fellows who got away like that"—and Remnant jerked his head skywards—"have all their wits about them still. If you ask me, they'll land young Geoffrey in the next county—"

"He's not young Geoffrey. He's a lot older than you are—and very much more—"

"Be quiet, Jane." Appleby had stepped to the edge of the island and was scanning the park. "By and large, your friend is right. . . . Now, where have all those police come from?"

"Those police?" Jane opened her eyes wide. "Aren't they yours?"

"Quite impossible. I did arrange for something of the sort in certain circumstances. But a good deal later in the afternoon. . . . And what the dickens is all that yelling?"

"I shouldn't be surprised at a bit of yelling." Remnant spoke drily. "This place is on quite a big scale. Jane and I have more or less smashed it. But you'll find, sir, that there's a fair amount to clear up."

"I find no difficulty in believing you there." Appleby was still scanning the grounds. "It isn't . . . it isn't by way of being a children's home? I could swear those were children's voices."

"Dear me, no—nothing of the sort." Remnant had got to his

feet. "I see you haven't got your bearings at all. But if I may lend a hand—"

"Thank you—I think I can manage." Appleby was still inclined to treat with some asperity the confident young man whom he had found involved with his sister in a shooting match. "You came here by car?"

"By taxi. I am a taxi-driver."

"Then I hope you drive, sir, with rather less impetuosity than you fight." Appleby frowned, seemingly feeling that this had come out with rather more of complimentary implication than he had intended. He turned to his sister. "Can *you* drive a taxi?"

"I don't think, John, that I have the right sort of licence."

"Bother the licence. I don't think that that wound's serious. But it had better have medical attention at once—and not precisely of the sort they seem to keep about here. Put this young man in his cab and drive him to Oxford at once."

"But, John, couldn't we—"

"At once. Drive straight to Casualty at the Radcliffe. When you've got him comfortably settled, dispose of his precious cab where you please. Then go back to Somerville and stay there. Perhaps you can find some dry garments in this barn of a place as you go. I shall."

"Couldn't we—"

"Listen. I shall bring you definite news by midnight. That's a promise."

"Visitors can't come in after—"

"Don't worry. I'll get in, even if I have to rouse the Principal from her bed. Now, get moving, or you'll catch a chill. I'm off to get a line on all this uproar. It needs calming down."

Remnant pointed to the big circular temple behind them. "If you go through there—"

"Thank you. It will be quicker to go as I came." And Appleby took a shallow dive into the lake and vanished.

15. Hard after riding through the shattered wire gates the expedition had split up, obedient to tactical dispositions laid down by Dick. Stuart Buffin found this an excellent plan; it meant that he and his friend Miles were on their own with a small group of like-minded Tigers, and that they could forget Dick and his unremittently asserted High Command. Piling their bicycles, they had made a wide detour to the left of the drive. Now they had climbed to the brow of a low hill, and the chimneys of the house could be seen below them.

"It *is* on fire!" A lanky boy ahead of the others pointed dramatically to the dark column of smoke rising from the house.

There was an immediate babel of voices, not very conformable with the idea of a military force moving up to a surprise attack. "The place is on fire. . . . It's burning down. . . . Rot —that's a potty little fire. . . . Anyway, there's a fire-engine. . . . Only the kind people keep themselves. . . . It's the crooks. . . . Why should the crooks burn down their own place, you silly twerp? . . . I don't believe there are any crooks. . . . Shut up and come on. . . ."

"Listen!" Stuart's voice asserted itself above the hubbub. "I hear something else. Be quiet."

The chatter dutifully stilled. Round the part of the building that was on fire orders were being shouted, and on a lawn at the side of the house a collection of elderly and harmless-looking people were huddled in a group talking. But over and above this there was certainly another sound. It was like the sound that an axe will make across a valley in frosty weather. Only this sound came in short bursts, with nothing of the regularity of axes being set to a tree.

"It's shooting." Stuart spoke with sudden conviction—and also considerable relief. "I was right. They *are* crooks."

"Crooks don't spend their time shooting." A sceptical voice spoke from the back. "In this country they don't often shoot at all."

Stuart swung round. "Well," he demanded, "*isn't* it shooting?

Don't you know the sound of a gun going off, you idiot?"

"Probably somebody out after rabbits."

The confusion of voices grew again. "The crooks are shooting. . . . There's a man out after rabbits. . . . They're shooting at the crooks. . . . Somebody says there's shooting. . . . What rot. . . . Listen, I tell you. . . ."

"Look!" Miles's arm had shot out. "Those buildings in the middle of the lake. You can see the flashes. It's a battle. Come *on,* you asses!"

"Here's the fire-brigade!" The cry was raised by a shrill voice on a flank. "Golly, they're coming at a lick."

"That's not a fire-brigade. All fire-engines and things are red." Stuart was staring down at the drive. "These cars are blue."

"The fire-brigade's come. . . . It isn't the fire-brigade. . . . There's a bell. . . . That's an ambulance bell. . . . Rot. . . . I tell you it is. . . ."

Stuart was frowning. "The cars have something on their roof."

"It's the police!" Miles gave a shout of excitement that was quickly echoed by everybody. "It must have been to the police that Dick sent his telegram. They'll join the shooting, with any luck. Run!"

The whole party tumbled down hill. Suddenly the lanky boy, who was still leading, dug his heels hard into the ground, slithered, and came to a stop. He had almost hurtled over the lip of a small precipice. The Tigers halted beside him, and stared down unbelievingly. What lay below them was a sort of den, gouged out of the side of the hill. And it contained half-a-dozen tigers.

"It's a zoo. . . . There are tigers. . . . It must be Whipsnade. . . . And lions farther along. . . . Masses of wild animals. . . . You large idiot, Whipsnade's miles away. . . ."

"It *is* a zoo—a sort of private zoo." Stuart had begun to skirt the upper edge of the series of dens. "They're all barred in front, and then there's a terrace to walk along. Let's get down."

"Wait a minute." Miles did not approve of the way in which the adventure looked degenerating into a mere visit to the zoological gardens. "I can just see something going on in a sort of yard behind the house. Chaps loading a lorry in a fearful hurry. I expect—"

"There's a helicopter going up!" It was the young scientist, Malcolm, who eagerly called attention to this new sensation. "Look—from behind that square temple, where they were shooting."

Everybody stopped and stared. "It's going up. . . . It's moving away. . . . Why does its nose point down? . . . Why has it got a little propeller too? . . . That's because of the torque, idiot. . . . It hasn't much speed. . . . Yes, it has—wait and see. . . ."

"Look out!" Miles' voice was urgent, quelling the chatter. "There's a man coming up that path on a motor-bike. What a lick! and he's coming this way. He's coming along the terrace with the dens. . . . Take cover."

They flung themselves on the ground. The motor-cycle had screeched to a stop at the end of the line of dens and the rider had leapt off. He was in a tearing hurry; and as they watched he began to run along the terrace, stopping every twenty yards and doing something that resulted each time in a heavy metallic clang.

"He must be the keeper." Miles was whispering in Stuart's ear. "He's opening all the doors between the dens and turning them into one."

"It's the crook!" Stuart's voice was tremulous with excitement.

"What?"

"The crook I saw chase the little man out of the house."

"The little man who was in my cat?"

"Yes, you idiot. The little man shinned up the telephone-pole, like I told you, and this fellow came running out after him. With a gun—I saw it. He's got queer shoulders. I'd recognise him anywhere."

"They must be all the same crooks—that lot and the people holding the woman who got the wrong number—who wanted somebody called Kurt— *He's letting them out!*"

The children all sprang to their feet. For there could be no doubt of what the man with the queer shoulders was now up to. He was heaving back a gate in the last den of all—a gate that opened on the bare hill-side. And in the den were lions.

Miles picked up a flint and hurled it. His aim was perfect; it took the man on the side of the face, and he staggered back. Miles and Stuart charged down the hill. The other Tigers, very little aware of what was happening, charged happily after them, whooping joyfully. The man looked up and saw the racing children; he hesitated, and then dashed for his machine. Some of the lions were roaring, and this was taken up by the other wild beasts farther back—beasts that were now padding and leaping into each other's dens. As Miles reached the terrace the first lion emerged and paused uncertainly, waving its tail. The children behind, still unknowing, gave another yell. The lion retreated just inside the den and crouched. Miles flung his whole weight on the gate and it shut with a clang in the instant that the lion sprang at it. The creature fell back with a snarl, and then there was a moment of complete silence. The Tigers stood, solemnly staring through bars at a congeries of beasts of prey that would have done credit to Noah's ark.

"Do you think they'll fight each other?" Malcolm, always intent upon natural knowledge, glanced mildly round his companions. "They are usually aggregated, after all."

"Segregated, you silly stinks-merchant." Some more lettered Tiger spoke with proper scorn from the rear. "Let's poke them up a bit and see."

The man who had attempted to free the wild beasts was gone; they could just hear his engine in the distance. There being no prospect of pursuing him, the suggestion just made had clearly considerable attraction for the younger and less responsible Tigers present. But at this moment there was a further diversion.

"I can see the others." It was Stuart who spoke, and he pointed across the park. "Better join them. It's different, I expect, now the police have come. And the shooting's stopped."

"They've got hold of something." Miles's face under its mop of untidy red hair lit up at the prospect of further excitement. "Come on. Let's cut across and see."

They ran the length of the terrace and out across the open park. The group approaching was certainly in some commotion; and it was contriving to make even more noise than their own group had done. It dropped on to a path as they drew near it; and in doing so it parted and revealed what was occasioning its clamour. In the midst of the children padded a large, tawny beast. Stuart gave a gasp of horror. "It's one of the lions!"

"We've got a lion! We've got a lion!" The small red-haired girl called Marty was walking beside the beast, her arm plunged deep in its mane, and she was shouting at the top of her voice. "We've got a tame lion—it's just like Miles in his cat!"

The lion was not, in fact, so very like Miles in his cat—for the simple reason that it was not nearly so aggressive. It shambled uneasily amid its new companions, looking now to one side and now to the other in a sort of amiable self-disparagement. It looked a very unhappy lion.

The two groups had begun to shout questions at each other, and were on the point of merging, when the motor-cycle engine was heard again. They turned and saw the machine hurtling towards them. The man with the queer shoulders had failed to get away on the path he had planned. Now he was having another shot—and it was evidently a desperate one. He rounded a bend at suicidal speed and very badly—he did not appear to be a good rider—and as the Tigers scattered they could see his eyes glaring and his mouth working convulsively. Hastily they scrambled to safety on either side of the path. But not so the lion. The lion turned and lumbered off down the path in front of the motor bike. It behaved just like a rabbit caught in the headlights of a car at night—without the wits to get off the path on one side or another. . . .

It was all over in a flash. The man was almost up with the lion. The lion, increasingly terrified by the roar of the engine, slightly changed direction. The man swerved—far too wide and uncontrolled a swerve for his purpose—and the lion tried to turn. The front wheel struck the lion a glancing blow on the flank; the machine staggered; and the man went over the handle-bars. The machine tumbled over and over, and came to rest with its front wheel spinning. The man lay quite still, with his head tucked oddly under him. The lion lay down at his side.

Some of the children moved uncertainly forward—including Dick, who had returned from some foray or reconnaissance ahead. But as they did so a man appeared before them as if from nowhere, for they had been so absorbed by the accident that none of them had seen his approach. His clothes were dripping wet. But he stopped them in their tracks with a single gesture of authority. "All right," he said. "Stay where you are." He walked over to the motionless figure of the man with the queer shoulders, stooped over it for a moment, and then came back, looking them swiftly over.

"Can we help, sir? Can one of us take a message?" It was a subdued voice speaking from the middle of the group.

The man in the soaking clothes shook his head. "No," he said gently, "you can't give any help here. . . . Anybody in command of your lot?"

There was a moment's hesitation, and then some shoving and pushing. A boy rather taller than the rest stepped forward. "Would you please," he asked politely, "say who you are?"

"I am Sir John Appleby." The man looked gravely at the children as a group, but addressed the tall boy. "I belong to the Metropolitan Police. I come, that is to say, from Scotland Yard."

There was a moment's silence that spoke of absolute awe. Even the tall boy appeared to have to think twice. But when he spoke it was with composure. "My name is Richard Martin," he said. "How do you do?"

"How do you do." Sir John Appleby was looking at their blazers. "You all come from Oxford?"

"Yes, sir."

Sir John Appleby turned for a moment and looked at the house, now cordoned by police. "And is one of you responsible for this remarkable turn-out of the County Constabulary?"

Richard Martin answered without hesitation. "Yes, sir. I sent a telegram."

"I see."

"I hope, sir, it was all right."

"It saved the situation." Appleby's eye had again strayed in a certain wonder to the mass of blue uniforms in the middle distance. "It's an effect that I doubt if I could have achieved myself. You must be a natural master of the electric telegraph."

This time Richard Martin violently blushed. But his voice maintained its composure. "I gave the wording some thought," he said.

"Always a good thing to do." Sir John Appleby smiled, and glanced over the whole group. "Thank you," he said. "The police are much obliged to you all. And now you had better cut off home. Can you get a train part of the way?"

"Yes, sir."

"Good. You might meet a head-wind." Appleby nodded briskly. "Good-bye."

"Good-bye, sir."

Appleby turned away, and the Tigers moved off obediently in search of their bicycles. But a moment later a voice spoke at Appleby's shoulder. "Sir, may we ask a question?"

Two of the boys had remained behind. One was red-haired and his eyes were still shining. But it was the other who had spoken.

"Go ahead."

"My name is Stuart Buffin."

"I've heard of you. And I begin to understand. But what's the question?"

"May we talk about this?"

Appleby appeared to consider this question with a good deal of grave deliberation. "Even if you don't," he said, "I suppose the younger ones would be bound to?"

"I don't think so, sir. We have them pretty well in hand."

"That's an excellent thing." Appleby smiled. "But I think you can talk. Everyone his own story at tea. It's a good part of the fun, after all."

"Yes, sir!"

Wreathed in smiles, Stuart Buffin and his companion hurried off after the other Tigers. Appleby walked back down the path. The lion was still lying close by the man. They were covered with the same dust. The brute looked at Appleby apprehensively, and sheepishly licked its paws. It looked a very harmless lion. Nor would the man now couched with it ever do any harm again.

PART SIX

BODLEY BY NIGHT

Unwounded of his enemies he fell.

SAMSON AGONISTES

1. Roger Remnant's headlong drive to the demesnes of Milton Porcorum et Canonicorum, involving as it had done much fast cornering, resulted in trouble during Jane Appleby's much more cautiously conducted return journey. A tyre blew out just before Eynsham. And as Jane took some pleasure in debarring her companion from attempting to assist her in any way, and laboriously but effectively contrived to substitute the spare wheel herself, it was nearly five o'clock when she reached the Radcliffe Infirmary. There she handed over her charge, answered such questions as the mildly sensational nature of his wound made necessary, and then drove back the few yards to Somerville. Such clothes as she had hastily commandeered from Dr. Cline's deplorable clinic by no means became her, and the frailty of her sex obliged her to get out of them at the earliest possible moment. She changed quickly, resisted the conversational attempts of several interested friends, and returned to the car. It was her intention to return it to the rank where she had so fatefully picked it up, and then to retreat hastily into college without answering any questions. There she would await news from John with whatever patience she could muster.

The first part of this project went smoothly. She drove down to the end of St. Giles' and saw that there were no other taxis waiting in the rank. This was decidedly to the good. Remnant, presumably, had colleagues, and if one of these was about he might prove tiresomely inquisitive. She had just swung the car round to bring it out of the line of the traffic when she heard a vigorous hail from the pavement opposite. "Taxi!" Since it did not occur to her that she might herself be the object of this shout she paid no attention. *"Taxi!"* This time the shout was a bellow. She looked up and saw, first the silver knob of an elegant cane being brandished peremptorily in air, and then—beneath it and spread out far on either side, the massive figure of Mark Bultitude.

Jane was feeling both exhausted and grim. She had been the occasion that day of at least two notable acts of deliverance from evil; and these she regarded with deep and honest satisfaction. But the one thing that she had set out to accomplish—the one act of deliverance that lay nearest her heart—she had failed in, and her final desperate attempt to achieve it had resulted only in the wounding of a total stranger who had stood by her that day like the staunchest friend. Geoffrey had been snatched from her—almost literally from her grasp—with what had been in effect the very maximum of cruelty. The situation now was worse than it had ever been, since she at last knew the quality of the people who held her lover in their hands. And despite her long-standing faith in her brother, and her almost equal faith in Roger Remnant, she found it very hard to take comfort from the reassurance they had tried to give her. That John would very quickly run to earth such of that evil gang as yet remained alive—that she would indeed receive news of this before the end of the day—she certainly believed. But she had been at too close quarters with the horrible madness underlying the criminal conspiracy she had uncovered to have anything but the direst forebodings as to what might be Geoffrey's fate if he was no longer of any utility to it alive.

All this being so, Jane had very little use at the moment for any further encounter with Bultitude. She had come to the conclusion earlier that day that he was a foolish and rather offensive figure, who had displayed a purely impertinent interest in her troubles. So now she let her gaze pass him stonily by, and prepared to step quickly from the car and march off without explanation.

This, however, proved to be impossible. Bultitude had recognised her; for a moment his features expressed extreme but seemingly genuine astonishment; then he launched himself into St. Giles' with all the resistless momentum of a hippopotamus taking to the water. A Number 4 bus swerved violently away from him much as it would have done, Jane thought, upon the sudden materialisation before it of a Centurion tank. And a moment later Bultitude was at her side.

"Excellent!" he said. "Excellent! In the morning the keen young student off to Bodley, and in the afternoon the resolute and emancipated bread-winner. But—my dear Miss Appleby—have you had the Proctors' permission to follow this laudable avocation?"

Jane, who hadn't thought of this one, eyed him askance. "I am putting it away for a friend," she said. Her tone was icy.

"Then the misfortune is mine. I had hoped to hire you to take me to Trinity."

"To Trinity!" Jane could have thrown a stone into the nearer precincts of this venerable place of learning from where she sat.

"Certainly. I missed a luncheon party there and had intended to present my apologies to my host. However, that can be deferred."

"I expect there will be other taxis turning up here presently."

"No doubt. But not other young ladies with whom I have a strong impulse to converse."

Jane, who could think of no polite reply to this—and who was determined to be polite, since she suspected that earlier in the day she had been rather rude—said nothing.

"I have already had some conversation with your brother, Sir John—on my way back from Milton."

"From Milton! You mean that you made your—your expedition, as you called it?"

"I went to Milton Manor, decided that it was a very shady place indeed, and came back to think about it. Probably I should have decided to contact your brother in any case. I am not fond of policemen investigating the vagaries of Bede's undergraduates, and I had—indeed, still have—some notion that I might clear the business up myself. Would you advise me to try?"

"No—certainly not." Jane still spoke coldly. But Bultitude's more direct manner of speech was making her look at him with new interest. "We have discovered that it was full of criminals, practising abominable scientific experiments upon people kept there by force."

"I must confess, Miss Appleby, to being not altogether surprised by what you tell me."

"I don't see how you can know anything about it. And, if you did, it was your duty—"

"It is the business of scientists—those few of them who are *not* engaged upon experiments abominable in one way or another—to put two and two together as rapidly as may be whenever queer appearances come their way. And that—since yesterday—is what I have been doing. And I may say that I mean to have Geoffrey Ourglass back at Bede's." Suddenly Bultitude looked Jane very straight in the eyes. "Where is he?"

"They have him still. They got away with him at the last moment."

Bultitude gave a moment to studying the silver knob of his cane. "I'm sorry," he said.

"John thinks that they are unlikely to do him any harm now. Perhaps they will let him go."

"I see. . . . I wish I could help." Bultitude tapped his cane on the ground. "And perhaps I can. The scientist sometimes remembers the importance of very simple things. When did you last have a meal?"

Jane stared. "Why—well, it was at breakfast."

"Then come and have some tea."

Jane hesitated. She was coming to believe that she had misjudged Mark Bultitude. "Thank you very much. But John said I was to go back to college and wait."

"He hopes to have news?"

"Yes—before midnight."

"That is rather a long time off—and tea can be consumed with a moderate approximation to civilised custom in something less than half-an-hour. I should like to hear a little more of your day's adventures—and tell you a little more of my own. Incidentally, I have some quite good Orange Pekoe."

Jane decided to go. Bultitude puzzled her. He seemed to have his own slant on the affair. Perhaps if they pooled what knowledge each possessed something really helpful would emerge. It was a long shot, but a shot worth taking. And the invitation was certainly an entirely harmless one. It was also subtly flattering. For Mark Bultitude was commonly reputed not to care for young women at all. "It's very kind of you," she said. "I'd like a cup of tea."

"Then come along. There is only the breath of Beaumont Street to negotiate, and we can walk straight into my parlour. I need hardly tell you that the rooms I keep in Bede's are on the ground floor. My philosophy of life, such as it is, is nothing if not *ventre à terre*."

2. The apartment into which Jane was presently ushered by her host would have been described by an unfriendly critic as overwhelming. It was large, and everything in it had the appearance of being very valuable. Bultitude, dispensing his Orange Pekoe from an equipage that had appeared with miraculous speed, gave his young guest a charming smile. "I see," he said, "that you are looking at my Battle of the Centaurs."

"Oh—yes." Jane was not aware that she had been looking at anything in particular.

"It is, in fact, a Caravaggio. I bought it of the Gräfin Szegedin—you know the dear old Gräfin? I was speaking of her to somebody only last night—a good many years ago. It gave the poor dear a helping hand."

"That was very nice of you." Jane took her tea and spoke without much enthusiasm.

"And the little hunting scene is by Uccello. Dear Bernhard—you know Berenson?—prefers it to the one in the Ashmolean. The Rembrandt was picked up for me by Bredius—or was it Borenius? I really forget—just before the war." Bultitude looked about him with what was either complacency or a good imitation of it. "Nothing but odds and ends, of course, but I think they hang together not too badly."

"I suppose it's a very nice room." Jane, who was much depressed again, realised that this was not altogether a happy choice of words. "I mean—"

"They tell me that my pupils call it Toad Hall. Undergraduates have an extraordinary faculty for hitting the nail on the head."

Jane stared. Bultitude, she divined, was rather a complex person.

"And the name is the more apposite since I bought a very large car. Perhaps it was the pleasure of driving it that really drew me out to Milton this morning."

He had plunged back to the point. For some reason it was not easy for him. He was pausing, as if searching for words, and Jane had suddenly the impression of being in the presence of some large, masked anxiety. "But you really knew something," she asked, "before that?"

"I wonder if I did?" Bultitude frowned. "But won't you have a muffin?"

Jane suspected that the fat don was going to be evasive, after all. His attitude was coming to puzzle her very much. There was something baffled in it—as if he was helpless in knowing where to begin with her. . . . But now he was trying again.

"This place in Milton is in the hands of the police?"

"Yes."

"So far, so good. I suppose you already know the things your brother told me."

"John said very little. Our talk was hurried—no more than a scrap. I think he was anxious to get me out of the place and begin clearing it up in a professional way. I'd meddled, I'm afraid."

"If you did, the circumstances make it very natural." Bultitude had one of his odd drops into simplicity. "Then you don't know—no, your brother told me you didn't—that last night this gang of criminals was hunting a man—a little man with a scratched face—about Oxford?"

"I know that they were hunting him this morning. I saw them at it in the upper reading room, when I was reading there."

"Sir John told me something of the sort. Who else was working there at the time?"

"I don't think I noticed them, very particularly. But I was sitting between old Dr. Undertone and Miss Butterton."

"They actually chased him about the reading room? It seems unbelievable. Surely they'd have been stopped?"

Jane shook her head. "It wasn't quite like that. There was only one man in chase. The little man kept edging away from him. He came quite close to me. And then his pursuer seemed to force him out of the room by something like sheer will-power. It was rather horrible. . . . But not so horrible as what happened later, at—at Milton."

Bultitude laid down an unbitten muffin and again frowned. He appeared to have less and less liking for a conversation which he had himself insisted on initiating. "That happened . . . to this same little man?"

"Yes. They got him, you know. And—and I think he knew something they wanted to know. When I arrived there—with the young man to whom that taxi really belongs—"

"A young man?"

"His name is Remnant. I don't really know him. He's in the Radcliffe. He got hurt—not badly. He's just had to go to Casualty. But I was saying that when we got there, and broke in—"

"You broke in?"

"Well, this Mr. Remnant did, and I followed. We found that these people had—had maltreated the little man very badly. He's dead now. But that's rather another story. He saved a child."

"Saved a child—from these people who were conducting abominable experiments?"

"Yes."

Bultitude—who did so many things with ostentation—slipped a handkerchief from his pocket and gave a covert dab at his brow. "I can see," he said, "that everything has been worse even than I thought. It is quite wrong to make you talk about it so soon. I apologise."

"That's all rot." Jane did not at all know whether she was grateful or impatient. "And I thought perhaps that you had something to tell me?"

"There are one or two things that I can mention." Bultitude—and the action, it occurred to Jane, was as incredible as that of the man in a circus who ties himself into knots—Bultitude had stooped down to the lowest of an elaborate system of trays by which he was flanked and grabbed a plate of excessively creamy cakes. But the action had not absolutely excluded from her view a look of swift calculation such as she imagined herself to have seen on his face before. He raised himself, puffing and blowing. "Won't you have one of these?"

Jane took a cake. She was young, and could eat automatically and unknowingly when her body required it. "You can mention—?" she prompted.

"I can mention—well, that during the war I had a good deal to do with one or two rather special lines of enquiry. The physiology—and also the psychology—of fear and bravery, endurance and the liability to crack up, aggressive and passive responses to stimuli—things of that sort. For instance, I knew a man called Cline. Later I heard that he had taken a place in the country and was developing new ways of treating drunks. It was a laudable but not very exciting activity. And it didn't quite fit in with what I remembered of Cline. Naturally, I didn't think much more about it. Then I gathered that he had associated with him—ostensibly in this blameless species of social medicine—several people whom I also knew. The question of why they came together again as crusaders of scientific temperance was a real one, which I found myself turning over from time to time. . . . Those little ones with the cherry on top are excellent."

"No more, thank you." Jane had set down her cup and was leaning forward on her chair. "And then?"

"I believed myself to have found the explanation. It was an explanation which meant that the whole affair was no business of mine. And so I put the matter out of my mind. It was only yesterday, when the sinister nature of your *fiancé's* disappearance was brought home to me, and I learnt from his uncle that he had been seen near Milton, that I saw I must make a crucial enquiry. As you have doubtless heard"—and Bultitude gave a brilliant if rather strained smile—"I have a great talent for knowing all the right people. I rang up a friend in town, and learnt confidentially that my explanation of the holding-together of Cline and his group was wrong. I had supposed that they were doing work on a secret list; and that the drunks' home, and the researching into alcoholism and so on, were genuine and reputable activities serving at the same time as measures of secrecy—secrecy dictated by national security. Now I learnt that nothing of the sort was in question. What they were up to, they were up to on their own account. And I didn't like it. For some of them had quite patently been persons of altogether impaired moral perceptions."

Bultitude as he produced this orotund phrase again mopped his brow—but this time openly. There was a moment's silence. "And . . . about Geoffrey?" Jane asked. "Can't you say anything about him?"

"I can say this—that as soon as his uncle said something connecting his disappearance with Milton Porcorum I recalled an element in the conversation of one of these people I have been talking about."

"Cline's friends?"

"Yes. He was not a scientist but an administrator; an able—and yet again in some ways rather stupid—person, called Squire.

This fellow used to praise"—Bultitude hesitated—"used to praise those civilisations, if they are to be called that, which delivered over felons, captives, slaves and the like, alive, to the uses of science. He used to say that it was the way to get results. And there were others who used to back him up. I thought of it as idle talk without substance. But now we must—"

"Mr. Bultitude—tell me." Jane had sprung to her feet. "Were they—when you knew them—mad as well as bad? If things go wrong with them, and their plans crash, and there are—are people who are no more use to them, will they . . . would they—" Jane found herself unable to finish her sentence.

"No." Bultitude had also risen. "In my opinion—not."

"They won't . . . kill Geoffrey?"

He looked at her strangely, and for a moment was silent. She suddenly saw that he, too, was indeed a scientist. The fat *poseur,* the University Worthy, the celebrated snob had all faded out of him. Instead of these—little estimable but yet human and intimate—there was only something aloof and very cold. He made as if to speak, and then hesitated again. She believed that—out of the sheer instinct of the scientist—he was seeking for words which he could believe an exact representation of the truth as he saw it. "Miss Appleby, Geoffrey Ourglass is in grave danger. It would be foolish to pretend otherwise. Yet I think I see something which would mean that he is safe from them. But I may be very, very wrong. . . . You must go?"

Jane nodded. She was very pale. "I think I'd better go. John may come."

Bultitude bowed, moved to the door and opened it. "Thank you for coming to tea," he said gravely. "I hope you will come again—not alone, but in very much happier circumstances. Let me walk with you to the lodge."

"No—please no!" Jane was agitated. "I am going to hurry. I mean—"

Very faintly, Bultitude smiled. "And hurrying is not my line? But you are perfectly right. Good-bye."

"Good-bye." Jane stepped into the open air, and turned to reach the lodge. As she did so, her eye went uncalculatingly to the window of the room she had just left. Level evening sunlight was pouring into it, and in this illumination she had a final glimpse of her late host. He was in movement—very rapid movement—across his gorgeous room. Then he stopped. She saw his face unnaturally large, framed in the centre of Caravaggio's struggling Lapithae and Centaurs. He was talking urgently into a telephone.

3. There was no message from John. Jane took from the shelf that notebook in which her aunt had bequeathed to her the lectures of the Stockton and Darlington Professor, efficiently abridged. But this afternoon the volume had no charm. Recognising that she was unable to work, she fell to pacing her room. But this was not very satisfactory either; there were too few paces to take, and too many things to step over in taking them. Presently she discovered that her restlessness had a more specific cause than the general anxiety under which she lay. In her encounter with Mark Bultitude there had been something missing. He had failed to say something that he ought to have said. Or *she* had failed—

One of her immediate neighbours was giving a polite tea-party to relations and dons. The murmur of talk from this reminded her that she had been invited. She paused, oddly seized in the midst of her grim situation by purely social dismay. It was frightfully uncivil to have forgotten all about the thing. She had better still appear, with whatever apology she could think up. . . . As she moved to the door she remembered—remembered something which, either by inadvertence or some wholly obscure design, she had not told Bultitude. And as she remembered this she forgot about the tea-party; it vanished into the oblivion from which she had fished it a moment before. She left her room and once more hurried out of college. She had told Bultitude something of the affair in the upper reading room which had been the first occasion of her adventures that day. But she had missed something out—and until a moment before she had missed it out of her own thoughts too. The little man who now lay dead at Milton Manor had *hidden* something in the upper reading room. He had thrust something into a book on old Dr. Undertone's desk. And what he had there hidden must surely be what his captors had sought. Moreover, there was something further that could safely be said. The hidden paper—for it had been that—if it at all came into the picture in this way, was important. The unrelenting manner in which the pursuit of the hunted man had been carried out was surely proof of that. Only the fantastically rapid series of events in which she had been involved could have made so significant a point slip her mind. . . . Emerging into the Woodstock Road, Jane turned right and set off hurriedly for the Bodleian Library. The paper, whatever it was, must be retrieved and given to John. As she gained St. Giles', she almost broke into a run. It had become her accustomed way of moving, that day. But Oxford people are often in a hurry, and nobody paid any attention to her. Had they done so, they might have remarked that something like a procession was involved. An unobtrusive person was, in fact, following Jane Appleby down the street. But this was not all. A second unobtrusive person was following the first.

4. In the upper reading room the long day's task was almost done, and learning had turned to packing up for the night. The unashamed were yawning, the reflective were finally sorting out their musings, the industrious were gathering up sheaves of notes. In its hutch in one corner the Emett-like conveyor-belt moaned with a suggestion of weariness stoically borne; in another corner Bodley's Librarian was amiably assisting an Ethiopian to decipher a manuscript, and for this purpose and superimposed three pairs of spectacles each upon the last. A broken light still struggled through the broad Tudor windows, and sent long, soft shadows exploring across the littered, or ordered, desks. The people continuing here and there to get up and go were commonplace and familiar; at the same time it was possible to feel them as growing shadowy and insubstantial—a race of middle spirits, grown half ethereal with long feeding on books, and presently to be succeeded, as the dark came down, by other spirits wholly transmuted—the veritable ghosts to whom the tremendous place most truly belonged. Bodley at midnight, Jane thought, must be the strangest of all places ever reared by mortal hands.

Miss Butterton—Jane Appleby forty years on, Jane Appleby as she would be if the transmuting years were to wash over her here—was gone; her tiny duodecimo and decimo sexto volumes were marshalled in disciplined ranks, as if waiting to stand guard through the night. And Dr. Undertone was gone too. But his desk was empty.

Jane paused for a moment, disconcerted. Then she turned away and retraced her steps down the reading room. There was an assistant sitting at the table near the great catalogue. She went over and spoke to him. "Has Dr. Undertone finished with all his books, do you know?"

The man nodded. There was nothing out-of-the-way in the enquiry, for in Bodley people are always mildly hunting one another's volumes. "Yes. As he went out at lunch-time he said that he would need none of them again. So they were cleared."

"Simply all put back on the shelves?"

"Yes. Dr. Undertone spoke quite decidedly—in fact curiously so. I'm afraid it will be too late to get anything back for you now."

"Thank you." If Jane had been disconcerted before, she was now nonplussed. But she asked one more question, although she already knew the answer to it. "There wouldn't be any record of the books he's been using?"

"Oh, no." The man was surprised. "The books go back on the shelves and the slips are destroyed."

"Yes—I see." Jane moved away. An understanding of the extreme queerness of what had occurred came to her fully as she walked towards the door. If in all the wide world the little man has sought an inviolate hiding-place for his scrap of paper he could scarcely have found a better than he had done. For the paper now lay between the leaves of one among several million books. If old Dr. Undertone's present studies were markedly off a beaten track—and with so immensely learned a person they almost certainly were—it might be a generation, or even a hundred years, before—quite fortuitously—the thing was again held in human hands. It was Dr. Undertone alone who could now abbreviate this process.

So struck was Jane by this strange consideration that she stopped dead in her tracks—thereby just avoiding, as it happened, being bumped into by a hurrying figure now entering the reading room. She stood aside, gave the figure an abstracted glance, and saw that it was Geoffrey's uncle, Dr. Ourglass. Her heart sank a little. He was certainly the most harmless of men. But—just at the moment—she had no list for a further colloquy with him. In a moment, however, this apprehension turned out to be groundless. Dr. Ourglass had not noticed her. He hurried down the reading room with a purposeful air not altogether common in him. No doubt he wanted to verify a reference before the place closed. When Jane last glimpsed him he had stopped, disconcerted, before an empty desk. So he, too, had been balked of some book. . . .

It had been Dr. Undertone's desk. Jane was half-way down the sixty-four steps, and had taken six of the right-angled turns, when this fact confronted her. Her head whirled—much as if she had been taking the right-angled turns much too fast. Then she turned and ran upstairs. When she reached the upper reading room again it was to find Dr. Ourglass departed. Exercising some lofty privilege, he must have gone down in the lift.

5. Jane came downstairs again—slowly, this time—and in the Bodleian quadrangle stopped to think. One or two

readers came out and passed her; a nondescript man was examining the Pembroke statue; another nondescript man was staring at the effigies on the ornate East Tower. Jane turned to her right and emerged into Radcliffe Square. It was just here that they had got him. . . .

Again standing still, and absently watching through the great arched windows of the Camera young persons for the time more studious than herself absorbed in the reading of law or of English literature, she firmly dismissed the behavior of Dr. Ourglass as coincidental and distracting. Old Dr. Undertone was her quarry. She knew that he was a Fellow of St. Gregory's. And, almost certainly, he was a bachelor and lived in college. Even at ninety-six, only a bachelor could have looked at her quite as he had done that morning—as if she had been a camel or a crocodile. And, remembering that look, Jane hesitated. Better leave it to John. Dr. Undertone might decidedly not welcome the visit, close upon his dinner-hour, of a beast of burden or a creature of the mud claiming the status and consideration of a member of the University.

But Jane Appleby—at this late stage of our narrative it can, like some other things, no longer be concealed—was a girl of impetuous and even headstrong disposition, lightly disguised by an air of learning. She ought to have been in Somerville; she had been told to remain there by an admired brother greatly senior to herself; nevertheless her legs were now taking her rapidly in the direction of St. Gregory's College. There are no long distances at Oxford, and in five minutes she had passed through the gates. "Can you tell me," she asked the porter, "which are Dr. Undertone's rooms?"

"Number five staircase in the next quadrangle, madam." The man had hesitated before replying. Probably the enquiry was unprecedented; in all Dr. Undertone's seventy-odd years at St. Gregory's no female had ever enquired for him before. But Jane marched on. The second quadrangle was small and high and dark and damp; its walls—like many stone walls in Oxford—

tettered and peeling; evening mist was beginning to thicken in it and lie in almost palpable folds, as if nature were concerning herself with the weaving of a shroud.

Jane found number five staircase. The stone treads were worn and hollowed; the walls were grimy and flaking; there was an indescribable smell—the smell of centuries of food and wine and sweat and polished leather. Dr. Undertone had rooms on the first floor. Jane climbed. The whole quadrangle was very silent. She stopped on the landing and listened. There was no sound. Dr. Undertone's oak was not sported and she knocked at the door. There was no reply. She knocked again, without result. Perhaps he was a bit deaf. Indeed, he well might be. And he would have several rooms, and perhaps be in a farther one. . . . Jane knocked a third time and waited. Perhaps she should go down again and find the scout who worked on the staircase. Probably Dr. Undertone kept a personal servant who might be discovered in some dungeon decanting port or counting claret. . . . Jane gave a fourth and perfunctory knock, opened the door, and peeped in.

The room was large, lofty, and completely surrounded with books. The only light was from a single candle, set in a candle-stick with a reflector to it. This had probably been a bold innovation of Dr. Undertone's in the Eighteen-eighties. He must have turned conservative before the spread of gas or the invention of electricity. There was a dull glow from an open fire which had been allowed to go almost out. It played upon the surface of a large, shabby desk, piled with disordered books and papers. Everywhere the books overflowed from the walls into the room; they were piled on chairs, on occasional tables, on decaying horse-hair sofas, on the threadbare and ragged Turkey carpet. On other chairs—since there was no wall-space for them—pictures were propped with the air of having been set down there many decades before: photographs of athletic groups fading into mere yellow stains, as those they represented must, for the most part, have already crumbled into dust; photographs, equally ancient, of dead and buried St. Gregory's dons assembled round dead and buried royalty; copies of Raphael Madonnas and Murillo saints such as mothers used to give to undergraduate sons with injunctions to attend the sermons of Dr. Pusey. Over the mantelpiece was a portrait of Archbishop Tait, and directly under it a small shield displaying the arms of Rugby School. On the desk, in a silver frame, was the photograph of an early Victorian lady. All Dr. Undertone's life was concentrated in this room. But Dr. Undertone himself was absent.

To go farther would not be decent. She must try—Jane decided—to find a servant and enquire when Dr. Undertone might be able to receive a visitor. But as she was about to close the door softly, and explore the situation downstairs, another door opened at the far side of the room. It was a manservant. Perhaps he had heard her.

Jane took a step forward. "Is Dr. Undertone at home?"

"Yes, miss." The man closed the door behind him. "Never more so, if you ask me."

Jane hesitated. "Do you think he can see me?"

"Yes, miss."

"Then will you tell him—"

"I can't tell him anything, miss. He's dead."

6. Jane felt rather queer. She was seeing and hearing too much of death to-day. "Dr. Undertone has died—this afternoon?"

"Just after luncheon, miss. When he came back from the Bodleian he wasn't looking at all well. And I think he knew it was coming, for he ordered an extra chop."

"An extra chop?"

"Yes, miss—for his luncheon. 'Finch,' he said, 'two chops'—just like that. And he ate them." The man paused. "Ate them right down to the bone, the Doctor did." He spoke with a good deal of pride.

Jane considered. "I hope I shall be able to do that."

"That's right, miss." The man nodded approval. "And he drank a couple of glasses of burgundy. Then, when I came into clear, he flew into a terrible rage."

"A rage?"

"A terrible rage, miss. It was fearful to watch. 'You rascal,' he said. The Doctor often addressed me like that, miss. He was a good honest-spoken gentleman of the old school. 'You rascal,' he said, 'when did you uncork that wine?' And he stood up, all swollen and purple in the face. 'How often have I told you,' he said, 'that burgundy must breathe?' And then, miss, he fell dead. It was what you might call a very peaceful end."

"I suppose it was."

"I've seen worse, miss, by a long way. For instance—" The man checked himself. "But such talk isn't proper to a young lady. I don't expect, miss, that you'd ever have seen death?"

Jane smiled rather wanly. "I have—as a matter of fact."

The man's serious face lit up. "Then perhaps, miss, you'd care to view the body? Very fine, it is. Just like a baby."

"Thank you . . . but I think I'd rather—" Jane scarcely knew how she got out of the room and into the air, now turned more damp and raw, of the little quadrangle. It was still very silent, and this time she knew why. . . . From somewhere on the other side a wafer of eaten stone detached itself from the wall and fell with a dull, small explosion. Change and decay, she thought, in all around I see. And she hurried from St. Gregory's. Nothing, she was sure, would ever bring her back there.

Moreover she should be in college. A sense of urgency so possessed her that she took a taxi, pausing only to scrutinize the driver. He was elderly and quite uninterested.

A telephone message was waiting for her. It said simply "Ten o'clock—John." Which was something—but she disliked its brevity. She looked at her watch. In a few minutes she would have to go into hall and dine with some two hundred of her kind. The prospect rose before her as unusually depressing. Her mind had ceased to work, either anxiously or eagerly, on the problem of Geoffrey's peril, the chances of saving him, what John would prove to have done. She felt simply that she had come to a dead stop, that all the wishes and fears left in her were very small and very futile, that life was bad and Oxford worse. But her body was shockingly tired, and perhaps it was only for a time that it was dictating this craven line of thought. The only sound resource was to find the next thing to do, and do it. But there wasn't anything. . . . And then she remembered that there was. She had a duty to walk round to the Radcliffe Infirmary and enquire about Remnant. Perhaps they had been able to send him away. On the other hand, they might have had to clap him into bed.

She ran into him under the archway by the lodge. After the manner of Oxford males preparing for a foray into unknown regions, he was making a cautious survey of Somerville in the gathering darkness. His arm was in a black silk sling. But he had managed to change, and was now dressed in an immaculate dark suit, like a fashionable undergraduate prepared to go up to town. The effect needed only a hard hat and an umbrella to be complete—and it was disconcerting. Jane felt that he was a stranger, after all. But Remnant smiled, and she realised that she had guessed wrong. "Come along," he said. "We need dinner badly."

"Are you all right?"

"Perfectly all right, thank you. But hungry—as I say."

"And do you often dress like that?"

Remnant nodded his head seriously. "Only change I have. That and a pair of pyjama-trousers. Everything else gone up the spout to support the wife and little nippers. . . . Any news?"

"Yes and no. No news from John—nothing about Geoffrey. But I have found out something queer myself."

Remnant looked at her, she thought, with momentary apprehensiveness. "Something to tell?"

"Oh, yes. And John's coming in to see me at ten."

"We can eat quite a lot by then. Where would you like to go?

Mitre? George?"

"If the family is right down on the bread-line like that, Mr. Remnant, you oughtn't to be thinking of going anywhere at all."

Remnant made no reply to this. Argument indeed was unnecessary, for they were already walking down the Woodstock Road. "The Radcliffe's not a bad place," he said. "I got a cup of tea and bun."

"And I got Orange Pekoe and some out-size cream-cakes from Mark Bultitude."

He gave her a quick sidelong glance. "Like him?"

"I don't think I know. But he's in on all this in some queer way."

"He's the enormous great fat man at Bede's?"

"Yes."

"Well, listen." Remnant hesitated. "*He* was the fat man that I caught a glimpse of on that terrace when we were waiting for Cline."

Jane nodded. "That doesn't surprise me a bit. He told me that he'd been out there this morning, doing a little quiet investigating. He'd been suspicious about the place for some time."

"I see." They walked for some way in silence, and when Remnant spoke it was abruptly. "Here we are. In we go."

Their dinner at first showed some signs of being rather a laboured affair. But Roger Remnant made no attempt to be more entertaining than the continued crisis in Jane's personal affairs warranted. He was as hungry as he had said, and he managed to make Jane feel hungry too. As she ate and drank she ceased to find a good deal of silence burdensome. She ceased, too, to feel that her sallying out like this had perhaps been in rather feeble taste. Remnant had now the manner of a civilised business man, with matter of substance to come to that must yet wait until dining is over. And thus they arrived in decent comfort at coffee and cigarettes. He eyed her gravely. "What is the queer thing you have found out for yourself?"

"It's not so much something I've found out as something I've remembered. And you'll think me an utter ass for not remembering it before. When the little man was in the upper reading room this morning he *hid* something—a paper."

"And has anybody found it?"

"Almost certainly not. And now it seems possible that all chance of finding it is gone. It's like this." And Jane told the story of the late Dr. Undertone and his books.

Remnant heard her through in silence. "Good riddance," he said at last.

"Of poor old Undertone?"

"Lord, no. He sounds a decent stick. But of that paper. If it was something your little man had stolen from our Milton friends, then, ten to one, it's better vanished. Some secret trick of their dirty game—that's what it must be."

"Yes—I think it must be that too. But it hasn't disappeared in any absolute sense. Some other reader in Bodley may come on it to-morrow."

Remnant was frowning across the room. He started. "Sorry! I was just thinking there was somebody over there that I've knocked up against not long ago. . . . Whatever it is, your new reader isn't likely to make head or tail of it. He'll chuck it in the waste-paper basket—I suppose there are such things in Bodley?—and that will be that."

"I think it's important."

He looked at her curiously. "It's hardly the centre of your problem, Jane."

"It might be. It might be the key to it." Jane, who less than an hour before had been feeling that she had no more fight in her, was again quick and eager. "To begin with, it must be important to *them*. They did so much to get it back that—"

"I agree. But still I don't see how, directly, it's going to help."

"If *we* had it, it might be a card in our hands."

"You mean a bribe, a bargaining point, a hostage—something

like that?"

"That against Geoffrey."

He looked at her with yet fuller gravity. "These people can't be bargained with. They are outlaws. It would be futile, immoral, illegal. You couldn't give them back—"

"Of course I know that. But if we had it the thing might be a bait, a trap, *something.*" Jane's voice was suddenly urgent and appealing.

"Very well. The thing, whatever it is, would certainly be better in our hands than simply lost. It may be the key to something that has potentialities for good as well as evil. But how do we get it?" Jane could see that Remnant's mind was beginning to work swiftly and in a way she knew. "You are sure nobody could have spotted the actual book the little man thrust it into? What about the person on Undertone's other side?"

"There wasn't anybody."

"Then on *your* other side? Somebody might just have got a squint from there."

"That was Miss Butterton. She might conceivably have seen that the little man was fiddling with Undertone's books. But she couldn't have seen that it was this particular book or that."

"Certain?"

"Absolutely."

"Then we come back to the start. There's only Undertone himself. Short of a *séance,* we can't ask him. . . . What was his line of country?"

Jane considered. "He was an ecclesiastical historian . . . no, that's wrong. I remember! He retired ages ago from the chair of Pastoral and Homiletic Theology. And he's been compiling an enormous history of that ever since."

Remnant grinned. "Remember," he said, "that I stopped off from all that lecture-stuff. Do you mind telling me just what that rigmarole means?"

"It means something more impossible than I can say. His work in Bodley consisted in reading all the sermons that were ever published."

"And have a lot been published? I don't think I've ever seen any."

Jane laughed a little desperately. "Far more of them than of anything else in the whole world."

"Well I'm blessed! I'd never have thought it." Remnant stared at her with the utmost naïvety—but his next question was sufficiently shrewd. "Do you think Undertone would have a collaborator—work hand in hand with some other old person who would share the burden?"

"I'm pretty sure he wouldn't. Part of his legend is his extreme aloofness and isolation."

Remnant had paid their bill. "Up you get," he said. "We'll take a walk on this. It needs thinking out."

There was now a thick mist shrouding Oxford—the Thames' valley mist which is not quite a fog, but which gets in your throat and eyes all the same. Jane thought walking through this a poor idea and not likely to clear the brain. But she had got in the habit of obeying Remnant. They set off. Tom, the great Christ Church bell, had not begun the tolling that would announce five past nine. She still had plenty of time in hand if she was to be back in college with half an hour to spare before her brother's arrival.

"I suppose we couldn't get in?" Remnant's voice spoke from the uncertain darkness beside her. "I mean into this old man's rooms in Gregory's?"

She was rather shocked. "The body's there. They'll have sported the oak by now to leave it in decent security. And we couldn't possibly ask."

"You can't think of a story that would get us in? Nephew and niece? Illegitimate but sorrowing children hurrying to Oxford at the news?"

"Of course not! I think you are the most unscrupulous person I've ever known. And—anyway—it wouldn't be the least good."

Remnant said nothing. They continued to walk in silence.

Either their footfalls were producing a queer echo in the mist or somebody else was walking this inclement evening behind them. Jane lost her bearings. Presently Remnant spoke with an air of casual surprise. "This *is* Gregory's," he said. "Never been in it. Have you—before to-day? Low college."

"We can't all go to Balliol."

"True—true. And we can't even, all of us, stop there when we make it. They're very keen, at Balliol, on a chap's going to those lectures." Remnant's voice was extremely absent. "Where about are that poor old chap's rooms?"

"Number five staircase in the second quad."

"Well, I believe this is the second quad we're skirting now. . . . On this side?"

"Yes—on the first floor, at the corner. You can't see in this stuff—or I can't. But they must be those rooms just above our head now."

"Interesting." Remnant did not sound as if he was at all interested. "Mind if I just step behind this archway to light a pipe?"

"Not a bit." It was a chilly night, Jane felt, to hang about. But she owed Remnant a good deal more than permission to smoke. She waited. Suddenly—and utterly without rational occasion—she felt panic grip her. It was as if danger had suddenly reached out hands at her in the dark. . . . "Roger!" Her call was low but urgent. There was no reply. *"Roger!"*

"Yes, Jane?" The mist was playing odd tricks with sound. His voice seemed to come from straight overhead. "Don't worry. Keep quiet. Even with only one arm it's pie. I'll be back in two ticks."

She understood—she understood and trembled. But she did not call out again. Aeons passed. Once she was certain that she heard whispering in the darkness—an angry and dissuasive whispering. There was a further effluxion of almost infinite time. She knew that—for the first occasion in her life—she had lost her nerve and her wits. So she must keep still. If she only kept still nobody—not even Remnant—need ever know. More time went by—enough time for whole solar systems to emerge from mere vapour, spin, and perish. . . . Suddenly her right hand was taken in a strong clasp. She knew that she could scream. Fear sometimes kills the power to do that—but with her it had not done so. She kept silent. Remnant's voice spoke in her ear. "Good girl." He took her arm and moved her forward through the mist. "A bit more walking. Say as far as Magdalen bridge. This still needs thinking out." They went on in silence. It seemed incredible that only a minute or two before she had been scared out of her wits. . . . "I say"—Remnant's voice was unwontedly diffident—"what would *perlegi* mean?"

For a moment she was puzzled. Then she understood. *"Perlegi?* It's Latin for 'I have read through.' "

"I guessed as much." The voice was now triumphant. "Then we've got it."

"You actually got into Undertone's rooms?"

"Quite easily. I went up the rustication and in at the bedroom window. Roof-climbing used to be one of my things, rather."

"I see. . . . You said the *bedroom* window?"

There was a quick chuckle in the dark—and then Remnant's voice, swiftly repentant. "I'm sorry if it shocks you. I've had times that rather blunt one to all that. . . . And he's dead, all right."

"You—"

"I made sure. This is so queer a business that you can take hardly anything on trust. . . . And then I got it—this *perlegi* business. A fairly fresh piece of paper on his desk, with a lot of book-titles in Latin and French—and then after all but the last two this word *perlegi* and a date. The last date was to-day's. Oh—and there were a lot of letters and numbers against each book. I copied them down too."

"The case-marks."

"What are they?"

"Where the books live on the shelves—all over Bodley. They're very complicated, and only the Bodley people understand them. You copy the case-mark from the catalogue, and that tells them where to find the book for you."

"Don't you go and get it yourself?"

"Of course you don't, you idiot. But I suppose you're pulling my leg."

"No, I'm not." Remnant sounded aggrieved. "Just not been my line. If you roof-climb, and that sort of thing, then you just can't expect to sit in libraries too and have people bringing you books. It wouldn't be reasonable. You must see that."

Jane was silent. She knew by this time that when Roger Remnant talked such ineffable nonsense as this his mind was likely to be hard at work in its own effective way.

"Aren't a tremendous lot of the books underground?"

Jane started. She had been thinking that she again heard footsteps. "I believe so—although, of course, readers don't go down. I've been told that it's quite tremendous—miles and miles of it. But of course that must be an exaggeration."

"Well, now—don't they arrange the books in a sensible order —alphabetically, or something like that?"

"My dear boy, you just haven't got the scale of the thing. There are *millions* of books. Some are kept together in great collections, more or less as they were given to the place. Others are arranged I just don't know how. The commonly-needed books —the sort of book *you* would ask for if you ever went in— are kept together and handy; and a lot of them are on open access. But the sort of stuff old Undertone revelled in is probably all over the place. And the catalogue—or those case-marks you've copied—is the only clue. And it's only a clue, as I say, to one of the library people."

"I think it's quite absurd." Remnant was honestly exasperated. "You mean to say that you and I couldn't find these things? That if we broke into this Bodleian place—"

"Broke into Bodley!" Even although she knew she was being absurd, Jane's voice was stiff with horror.

"Why ever not?"

"You just don't understand. Besides, you're talking nonsense. We've found what we want. The thing is certain to be in one of those books. And it's certainly safe there till to-morrow. John must see about it."

"I hate to say it—but I think John might be a bit behind the times."

"John is never behind the times."

"Well, we don't need to argue about that. I'm sure he's a good sort of stick." It was evident that Sir John Appleby's manner at Milton that afternoon still a little rankled. "The point is that I'm not at all sure about the thing's being safe there till to-morrow. . . . Did you think I took rather a long time over my burglary?"

"Well"—Jane was cautious—"yes, I did."

"It was because I had to join in the queue."

"Whatever do you mean?"

"There was somebody before me, jotting down those books. I had to lurk in the bedroom quite a bit."

"It's impossible! I'm sure nobody in the reading room understood what was happening, besides me. . . . Did you see who this person was?"

In the darkness Remnant seemed just to hesitate. "Yes."

"Somebody we know?"

"Yes. At least you know him. And I know him by sight."

Jane gave a gasp. "Was it Mark Bultitude?"

"No. It was your young man's uncle, Dr. Ourglass."

"Dr. Ourglass! He's the most harmless—" Jane gave a little cry, and groped for Remnant's arm. "But that's what I said to myself, when I saw him— I forgot. I haven't told you. I saw him in the upper reading room this evening, peering at Undertone's empty desk—just as I had been doing myself. I thought it could be no more than a queer coincidence."

"Well, it wasn't."

"Surely old Dr. Ourglass hadn't climbed—"

"Good lord, no. He had plainly been brought into Undertone's room, as official as anything, by some great panjandrum at Gregory's."

"I can't understand it."

"No more can I. But it doesn't make me feel that this needle in your absurd haystack of a Bodleian is particularly safe. . . . Hullo—I wonder where we've got to?" They had been walking seemingly at random, and now Remnant was peering about him in the dark. "How very odd. Do you know, it looks like Radcliffe Square?" Suddenly he turned his head, as if listening.

Jane's heart sank. She had experienced just this technique a little too recently to have forgotten it. "Now, look here, Roger Remnant, I simply will not—"

Reaching out in the darkness, Remnant suddenly put his fingers on her lips. She fell silent—and found that, like her companion, she had frozen into immobility. The mist was now very thick, and the few lights in the Square made little impression on it. One could see no more than the vaguest outlines even a couple of yards ahead. His voice was in her ear. "Sorry, young woman. Getting into melodramatic habits. But I've had a feeling that there's somebody interested in us."

"So have I. I had it when you were doing your climb into Gregory's."

"Well, we're old hands at all that. And it's probably imagination anyhow. . . . We'll scout round here."

They were somewhere out in the Square, for she could feel cobbles under her feet—the identical cobbles on which the little man had been lying before they bundled him into the ambulance. Then she lost her bearings. Far away she heard a train hoot, and nearer at hand there were some young men calling to each other in the mist. But the voices might have come either from Brasenose or from Hertford, and her sense of disorientation was complete. The street lighting was going dimmer and more yellow. Straight ahead of them, nearer the ground, they saw a dull red glow. Remnant moved towards it. She realised that he was reconnoitring the terrain of some proposed operation. Again she felt misgivings. She ought to be back in college, waiting for John. . . . The red glow came from a charcoal brazier. Some building was going on, and in a little shelter before the fire a night-watchman was settling in to his job. They went on, and were presently in complete darkness. Again Remnant spoke softly in her ear. "About roof-climbing—"

"I'm not going roof-climbing, and neither are you. You can't possibly—not with that arm."

"Listen—and don't be so quick to make irrelevant remarks." Remnant's tone held its old assurance. "It's a principle of Oxford roof-climbing that there is no natural feature known to climbers of which there is not a pretty fair artificial equivalent in the buildings of this city. And the principle has been worked out very fully."

"I haven't the slightest doubt it has."

"Do you know about the Mendip caves?"

A dim and horrid light began to dawn on Jane. "No—I don't. And, what's more—"

"They form a very extensive system of underground caverns which it is possible to get into here and there—with a very tight squeeze. *Really* very tight. Not a game, for instance, for your friend Bultitude. Well, like everything else in the world, the fissures that take you down there have their equivalent here in Oxford. Or rather have *one* equivalent. You're standing beside it now."

"You mean—?"

Roger Remnant laughed, very softly. "I mean that you and I, Jane, are about to enter the world's greatest library."

7. Somewhere at her feet Jane heard a muted clang, as of a metal plate or grid forcibly displaced. For a fraction of a second a torch flashed on in Remnant's hand, and she had a glimpse of what appeared a very small circular aperture flush

with the ground. Then the darkness was again entire and Remnant was once more whispering.

"Listen carefully. This is important. As it happens, I've never made this expedition, for a reason that I can tell you about later. But I have the facts. First, there's your clothes. People commonly strip."

"Thank you—no. I've lost quite enough perfectly good clothes to-day already."

"Good enough. But they absolutely mustn't bunch up. Can you grip your skirt between your knees?"

"Yes."

"That should do. Your measurements are pretty fair."

"Thank you very much."

"You go down feet first—legs together, hands palm downwards on your thighs, wrists in the pit of your tummy, all quite rigid. Can you feel your heart beating?"

"Yes." Jane was tart. "I can."

"Let it count five for you as you go down. Then begin to pull up. That means you jack-knife ever so slightly. Behind down and knees up. You may lose a bit of skin. But it's perfectly all right, unless you start slowing down too suddenly and too soon."

"What happens then?"

"The confidential character of our mission fades out. I fetch the police, the Fire Brigade and the University architect. Sappers are sent for from the nearest garrison town."

"I see. I don't think it's a thing to think about very much."

"Then down we go—me first. Don't worry. It's not half as bad as that crazy nylon rope."

"I'm not worrying. I just want to say—"

Remnant had vanished. For a moment Jane thought that he had stepped behind her. "Roger," she said softly.

There was no reply. Her sense that there was any longer somebody near her must have been illusory. He had really gone —had vanished down that small hole that now lay invisibly at her feet. He probably has the disadvantage, she suddenly thought, of not having the sort of heart that makes itself heard. . . . For a second she hesitated. What she had meant to say was that her appointment with John made this underground proposal impossible. And he had known it well enough. His cutting her short like that—his simply vanishing like the bad fairy in pantomime—had been typical Remnant unscrupulousness. . . . Jane found that she had sat down on very chill stone—and that, as once before that day, her legs were dangling in nothingness. The shaft, chute, or whatever it was, felt quite desperately narrow, and she had a sudden vivid sense of what it must be like to be the lead in a pencil. But Remnant had gone. And his shoulders must be far broader than her hips. Jane went too.

She certainly lost some skin, but there was more of indignity in the thought than painfulness in the sensation. Her brain worked with extraordinary speed. As she fell she guessed what the particular hazard of this journey must be. The chute must have a kink in it, or must somewhere flatten out like a section of a big dipper. If you gained too much momentum there would be a nasty crash at the end. If you checked it too soon you simply came to a stop in a spot too tight for wriggling. She felt that she had never had a nastier thought. . . . She was suddenly in empty space, and Remnant had caught her and set her on her feet.

Her knees were unsteady, and she felt the need of something to say. "It was absolutely horrible. Miles worse than the nylon rope. But just your cup of tea. Why have you never done it before?"

"Because I like shaving at half-past seven and having breakfast at eight."

"What has that to do with it?"

"Well, of course it's one-way traffic. You couldn't go *up* that, could you? There's a bit of Latin I once knew—"

"Facilis descensus Averno—quite so. I knew some spark of learning would be struck out of you sooner or later, Mr. Remnant. But I don't see—"

"And there isn't any *other* way out. The whole place is locked up at night as strongly as a bank. I suppose the books must be valuable."

"I suppose they must." Jane was alarmed and angry. "Do you mean to say that we have to stay here till morning? John—"

"Bother John."

"I won't bother John."

"Bless him, then. The normal situation is this. Chaps coming down to the Mendip caves simply have to lurk until the place is opened up, and then dodge their way out. The few people who have made the attempt have got away with it so far. But—"

"Of all the perverted and idiotic uses to which to put—"

"—a great library? I'm quite sure you're absolutely right. But, as I was saying, to slip out when things open up is desperately difficult. Sooner or later, somebody will be caught, and there will be a fearful row—far worse than over roofs and towers and things—and the Mendip caves will just cease to be a feature of Oxford life. Which will be a great pity, in my opinion."

"Can't we get up to ground-level?"

"I think not. We're inside a vast, well-ventilated safe. Look at it that way." Remnant fell silent for a moment. They were standing in complete darkness. "I have got an idea, all the same. When we've found this paper—"

"I don't believe we can possibly find it."

"Don't be dismal, girl. When we've found this paper, it occurs to me that we might rustle up a telephone. The place must be stuffing with them, and one of them may be connected with the city exchange. In that case, we'd just ring up the old boy who runs this place—"

"Bodley's Librarian?" Jane, who thought that she had already touched the uttermost verge of horror, felt her blood curdle in her veins.

"I don't see why not. He could come along with a key and let us out. Glad to assist the course of justice, and so on. I'd ask him to keep dark about the caves, of course."

"To keep—" Jane found herself speechless. At last, with a struggle, she found words. "We'll tackle that problem when it comes. At the moment, the point is that we don't in the least know how or where to find this batch of books. Particularly as we're in pitch darkness."

"A point well taken. But here you are." And Remnant snapped on his torch.

The beam fell on books. This, at least, was reassuring; Remnant had not been wildly out in his calculations and landed them in a sewer. Jane remembered the odd fantasy she had indulged that morning of being precipitated through some hidden trapdoor into dark and subterranean waters, deep beneath the foundations of Bodley. It had been, she decided with interest, a clear case of dream-like precognitive thinking. One's actual dreams were said to be full of distorted images from one's own future. . . .

Her eye was following the sweep of Remnant's torch. It was a powerful torch, and its beam had now moved laterally far into darkness. But it was still playing upon books. It swept back, and then off in the other direction. The books ran off, apparently to infinity, in that direction too. It struck her that she had seen something like this not long ago. For a second she was puzzled. And then she knew of what she had been reminded. It was the high and interminable boundary wall of Milton Manor. But that had appeared to lose itself in distance because it was a single great curve—what the old writers on aesthetics liked to call an artificial infinite. The books marched on and on in straight lines.

"I had no notion of this." Remnant—for the first time since she had known him—seemed impressed. He also seemed puzzled. "Do they keep all the *old* ones?" he asked.

Caught unawares, Jane laughed aloud. And her laughter pealed and rolled through vaulted immensities, to come echoing back to her, deepened to a sort of stage thunder. "They didn't always," she said. "At one time they had rather a knack of selling things. But not much goes out of the place now."

"It's very depressing." Remnant's reaction was decided. "I've never before been made so powerfully aware of life's utter futility. All those chaps scribbling away, persuaded that fame and immortality were just round the corner. And now nobody so much as remembers their existence, except this old fellow—what do you call him?—Bodley's Librarian. It's the sort of thing that makes one look round for a drink. Sorry to be such a barbarian."

"You're not terribly singular. A great library made Dr. Johnson feel much the same. . . . But now you see that it *will* be rather difficult finding what we're after."

"It's just a matter of time. And we've got all night for it." Remnant was dogged. "Good Lord—look at that!"

He had turned the torch upward, seeking the roof. But as its beam climbed and climbed it still met books—although books now in part obscured by open-work cat-walks of cast iron, by vertical ladders and spiral staircases, and by a criss-cross of supporting girders. Jane felt slightly giddy. But she managed to speak firmly. "Try downwards."

The beam swept down. They were standing on just such a catwalk as they had been observing high above their heads. Below them was another infinity of books.

It was like something, Jane thought, by Piranesi—a dream–architecture cunningly devised to suggest at once the reach and the impotence of the human mind. But Remnant's response was now severely practical. "It all seems reasonably orderly. You made it sound, you know, quite cock-eyed. But there are all the books—"

"Nothing like all the books. This is just a place that was dug out forty years ago to hold a million or thereabouts. There are stacks and stacks elsewhere: in Bodley itself, in the New Bodleian, in the basement of the old Ashmolean—"

"I see. Well, this will do for a start. But the point seems to me to be this: the more books there are, the more efficient must be the system of running them to earth. All that case-mark stuff can't be an absolute abracadabra. What sort of people actually find the books?"

"Quite small boys, I've been told—although one hardly ever sees them. Some people say it has to be either boys or dwarfs, so that they can wind their way between some of the stacks. Rather like children in the coal mines long ago. But that's unreliable."

"Any ponies? They have them in mines."

"No. I think it's a matter of mechanisation having been brought right up to the face, so to speak. There are said to be conveyor-belts, and pneumatic tubes, and all sorts of gadgets like that."

"But the crucial point is those boys. No doubt they're bright lads, but they can't all be little Einsteins and Isaac Newtons. The job must be organised so that they get a grip on it fairly easily. There may be this collection and that collection, as you say. But there must be over-all order, and a key to the whole thing. We can certainly puzzle it out in time. The trouble is"—Remnant hesitated—"that there may be others on the scent who understand the system already. I expect most dons do."

"Dons?"

"My dear girl, we can't ignore the fact that we know two of them to be mixed up in this affair in a rather unaccountable way."

"But we're in and they're out." Jane felt very clear-headed. "*They* can't get in until Bodley opens up. If we could find the telephone you spoke of and put up a sufficiently convincing show, we could make sure that those likely books were searched officially before anybody else was allowed to lay hands on them. And surely that's our best plan."

"Good girl—*fairly* good girl." Remnant had begun to move cautiously forward, shining his torch before them. "But about others getting in—getting in any time now—well, I just don't know. Think of that Gregory's business. I got in there just as we have got in here. And there was old Ourglass already, almost scooping the pool. And—mind you—I expect the sort of people who run places like this are pretty guileless. Other-worldly, and all that. Suppose a plausible and unscrupulous colleague hurried in on this Bodley's Librarian as he was flooring his fourth glass of port—"

"I think you have distorted ideas of life among senior members of this University." Jane paused. "Still, I see what you mean."

"It comes back to this: that the best thing will be for us to win out now. And first, we want lights."

"Isn't that risky?"

"I don't see how it can be. We might be at the bottom of a mine, for all anybody in Oxford can know about it. . . . And —by jove!—here we are." Remnant's hand had gone out to a cluster of switches; he flicked at them rapidly one by one. Clear light sprang up everywhere. What they had hitherto only glimpsed piecemeal they now saw in its entirety. Thus displayed, the vast storehouse was not less impressive than when Remnant's torch had been exploring it. It was this, partly, as being another world from the Bodley that Jane knew. There, the building and its furnishings were heavy with immemorial associations and rich in intrinsic charm, so that the books were no more than an element in the total effect. But here, everything was modern and bleak and functional; the single use of the place was to range in an accessible manner as many books as could be crowded in. There were three main levels; they stood now on the second; and this and the level above them were no more than a system of girders supporting the stacks and the narrow lanes that ran between them and at intervals intersected them. Thus visibly on every side of them, and above them and below them too, were hundreds of thousands of books. It was a striking spectacle, but it was an uncommonly oppressive one as well. The narrow lanes were mere slits or canyons between the interminable and towering cliffs of leather and cloth and vellum. These went so monotonously on and on that one was constrained to fancy some illusion—one, perhaps, whereby a spectacle of less incredible proportions was merely magnified by a cunning arrangement of mirrors. Nor, whether one looked up or down, did the eye and mind gain any relief. For the first time in her life Jane felt that she had some inkling of what it must feel like to be a neurotic suffering from acute claustrophobia. Living in a submarine must be something like this—a Jules Verne submarine as cramped as a real one but as big as a grand hotel. She would have given anything for space to swing a cat.

Remnant was busy with a pencil and paper against the side of the nearest stack. "There you are," he said. "One copy for you and one for me, since we may find it quicker to split up. Title and case-mark of the four likely books. They're as complicated as you said. But I've noticed something about them. They're in pairs. These two differ only in the last couple of figures on the line. And it's the same with those. So we have just two rows of books to find, all-told. There's a start in that."

Jane doubted it's being much of a start, but she said nothing. Certainly Remnant's observation was accurate as far as it went; in two several places in the Library they had to find a couple of books that would be shelved almost side by side. But in the *Library,* she reminded herself grimly; not necessarily in this single vast chamber hollowed out under Radcliffe Square. She looked at the stack nearest to her—one of a thousand identical units in the place—and frowned. "Why is it so broad?" she asked. "Books don't require all that depth."

"I've always been told that some are very deep indeed." Remnant seemed to take considerable satisfaction in this little joke. He was peering at the stack. "Actually, it's pretty cunning—a space-saving arrangement. I wonder if the old boy thought it up himself."

"You have a very primitive notion of the functions of Bodley's Librarian. But how does it work?"

"Can't you see? They all move on rails. That allows you to mass four tiers of books without any space between. It's simply two double-fronted book-cases that move parallel to each other and almost touching. And in every long row of them there's one gap. You just find your place, and, if what you want is behind, you give a shove and get the gap where you want it. . . . Like this." Remnant, as delighted as a boy with a new mechanical toy, gave a thrust at the case beside him. It rolled away, traversed the gap to which he had pointed, and came to rest with a dull thud against the case beyond. "Isn't that enchanting? You could have your gap in the same place on both sides, and be able to dodge through." He grew enthusiastic. "You could have a sort of perpetually changing course, and think up a sort of dodging game with rules. I wonder if the old boy—"

"For pity's sake get to work." Jane was exasperated. "If we have to shove a lot of these things about it easily doubles the job. . . . I wish I had a notion where to begin."

"Haven't you? Look down at your feet."

Jane looked and was abashed. She had noticed that the ends of each stack bore case-marks. She now saw that at every main inter-section the floor was painted with a system of arrows and symbols designed to show what further case-marks must be sought in one direction or another. She studied first this and then the paper in her hand. "I don't think we're burning hot," she said, "but it does seem to me that we may have had the enormous luck to begin not altogether cold. . . . I believe all four really will be in this place, after all. Look—you hunt the two *'perlegi'* ones and I'll hunt the two others."

8. It was perhaps twenty minutes later that Jane knew she had progressed from warm to hot. Not only the case-marks but the titles glinting on the old leather spines told her as much. She had come to that wide field of learning upon which the late Dr. Undertone had turned himself out to grass in his ripest years. *Sure Sanctuary of a Troubled Soul* . . . *Preces Privatæ* . . . *An Explanation of the Grand Mystery of Godliness* . . . *Bowels Opened* . . . The ancient hortatory voices seemed to murmur endlessly on the shelves, as they must have come to murmur ceaselessly in the ear of the dead scholar.

She was on the ground floor of the vast chamber. Remnant's

quest had taken him higher, and into a remote corner. They were like Adam and Eve in the Garden, when they had separated the more efficiently to cultivate its fruits. Jane's mind, drawn to this analogy by the biblical cast of the acres of old print around her, for a moment elaborated the fancy. It was by taking advantage of that rash isolation of our first parents that the serpent—

Suddenly she knew that she was uneasy. But that was foolish. There could be no serpent in Bodley. She brought her mind back to her task. *An Apologetical Narration . . . The Sinner's Mourning Habit . . . A Buckler against Death.* She halted, and gave a low cry. The first of the books she sought was there in front of her. *God's Terrible Voice in the City.* She stretched out her hand to take it from the shelf. The hand trembled, so that she could hardly hold the volume securely. It was the excitement of the discovery, she told herself, that made her tremble. The book was quite small. She opened it, shook it, ran through the pages. There was no lurking paper.

And now for the second book, which she knew could not be far away. Peering at the shelves, she moved along the stack in front of her. *A Large Theatre of Divine Judgments . . . Enthusiasmus Triumphatus . . . The Religion of Protestants a Safe Way to Salvation. . . .* Her excitement must be mounting, for now she was trembling all over. *A Treatise Concerning Eternal and Immutable Morality. . . .* It was not excitement that had taken command of her. It was fear.

It was the same fear that had reached out and seized her in the dark when she had been left alone outside St. Gregory's. And it was fear of something very evil and very close to her. Her senses, she knew, had brought her no report of this presence. But her certainty was entire. She fought against it. She forced her eye to travel over two more books. *Joy in Tribulation . . . An Examination and Censure of False Devotion. . . .* She could hardly breathe. She looked at the next book, and put out her hand to it with a gasp. Then her senses did speak. One of the iron platforms above her head creaked, vibrated. She turned her head, and something moved on the very fringe of her field of vision. She looked up. Danger threatened her—not, as she had irresistibly felt, from close at hand, but from high on a remote gallery. There, framed at the end of a vista of stacks, a man had appeared. He was looking at her directly and fixedly, and she saw that it was not Remnant. The platform creaked again beneath the weight of the man standing on it. He was Mark Bultitude.

At least she must have the book. She grasped it and pulled it from the shelf. Bultitude was raising an arm as if to point at her. She remembered that she could shout.

"Roger!"

As if she had spoken a magic word, the books immediately in front of her moved. Thrust at by an unseen hand on its farther side, the stack glided away on its rails. And in the gap stood a man—a man with a pale, freckled face.

"Geoffrey!"

As once before that day, she stretched out a hand to her lover. And Geoffrey Ourglass too stretched out a hand. But it was not to her. It was to the book.

The movement was a blinding revelation—instantaneous and final. The foundations of Jane's world had crumbled as in some fantastic spectacle on a stage. She gave one protesting cry, and then acknowledged the truth. Geoffrey took a step forward and with horrible dexterity, like a low thief on a race-course, drew the book from under her arm. He stepped back and the stack moved again. In a fraction of time she was once more confronting only a wall of books. She heard a woman's voice calling for help in a strong, clear voice. It was her own.

The place was suddenly full of voices: her brother's, Remnant's, Bultitude's—and another, elderly and authoritative, that she knew to be that of Bodley's Librarian. At the end of the long lane of books in which she was standing she glimpsed one and then another hurrying figure in uniform. The police had come. Over the dark surface of the great horror that Jane confronted, a tiny and momentary horror rippled. It was very shocking that the

Bodleian should be turned over to this sort of thing.

There were now other sounds as well as the shouting: a low rumbling, at first intermittent and then rapidly becoming almost continuous; a succession of dull thuds, with now and then a clash of metal, as one massive and buffered rampart of books came hard up against another. It was Roger Remnant's grotesque game come true. The place had become a vast maze, through which Geoffrey fled and the mustered forces of society pursued. But it was a moving, a protean maze; a kaleidoscopic or mutable labyrinth, changing its form from moment to moment as, now here and now there, one or another gap opened or closed between the stacks. It was like a chase through a surrealist nightmare—a chase down endless corridors in which every yard of wall could become at any moment an opening valve, a sliding door. . . .

They were closing in. They were driving him towards the centre of the great, dimly-vaulted chamber. Jane moved towards the centre too. She had no awareness of what she was doing. Her lover had been a criminal. And now he was become a hunted man.

In the middle there was a small clear space—a sort of well up one side of which a spiral staircase climbed through tier upon tier of books. Geoffrey had leapt out of hiding and was at the foot of it. He started to climb. The book was still in his hand. He went up with incredible speed, so that as her eye followed him the surrounding books seemed to take on a spiral motion of their own. There were two figures pounding after him. He was high—very high. Not far above his head must be the cobbles of Radcliffe Square, where that other hunted man had lain. . . . From somewhere on a lower level she heard a shouted summons, and in an instant two further figures had appeared at the head of the stair. Geoffrey saw them, ducked under the rail, and leapt perilously to the top of a stack. He swayed, steadied himself, prepared for another leap. In the split second before his taking-off the book dropped from his hand. His foot caught on it and he fell.

He fell sheer—and into a great darkness that now flooded up over Jane. But for a second yet her inward eye could see him—

plunging down through a million books, rank upon rank of books, armies of unalterable law.

9. "Thank you." Bodley's Librarian took the book from Appleby, laid it on his desk, and examined it carefully. "The joints are cracked, I fear. But, on the whole, we must congratulate ourselves on getting off fairly lightly." He turned to Remnant. "I suppose," he asked mildly, "that you came in by the Mendip cleft?"

For the first and only time during the events here chronicled, Roger Remnant was staggered. "Yes, sir—we did. But surely *you* don't—"

"My dear boy, I first entered Bodley that way myself. It was what first drew my interest to the Library. So it is very possible, you see, that one day this room will be your own. I had supposed, I confess, that the Mendip cleft had long since passed out of mind. Otherwise, no doubt, I should have felt constrained to have something done about it. As one grows old, you know, one becomes very cautious and curmudgeonly." Bodley's Librarian picked up the book again, adjusted his system of spectacles, and again examined it. "This is now something of a bibliographical curiosity, Sir John. It cannot be often that a book has proved lethal—in a direct physical sense, that is to say. Curious, too, that it should be *this* book. You have looked at the title?"

Appleby shook his head.

"*A Thunderbolt of Wrath against Stiff-Necked and Impenitent Sinners*. . . . Whether the young man was indeed impenitent at the last it is not for us to say. But his persistence in crime certainly suggests that he was stiff-necked."

Bultitude was turning over the leaves of the book. "Not a neck stiff enough to stand that drop. It was broken and he died instantly. . . . And here is what it was all about." He drew from the book a folded sheet of quarto paper, smoothed it out, and laid it on the desk. For a few seconds he studied it silently. "Interesting," he murmured. "And extremely complicated—in fact, quite beyond me."

"There is much that is beyond *me*." Bodley's Librarian was courteous but firmly curious. "You say that this young man had actually succeeded in becoming the directing mind behind a formidable scientific conspiracy?"

Appleby nodded. "He was known to have been a first-rate scientist—as brilliant as we now realise him to have been unscrupulous. His adventures during the war had brought him into the way of conspiratorial activity. We don't know how he uncovered this organisation, or how he managed, within no more than a couple of months or so, to force himself to the top of it. But I suspect the key to his sinister success lay simply in his being very clever. A man may be both able and brilliant without being that. Young Ourglass held all three of these cards."

Bodley's Librarian elevated one pair of spectacles to his ample brow. "In what," he asked, "was this cleverness instanced?"

"Notably in the measures he took to retrieve the mistakes of less intelligent colleagues. There was a fellow called Squire who was inclined to take the bit between his teeth in the dangerous business of kidnapping people or luring them into Milton. Ourglass, who kept himself quite aloof and concealed, had a wary eye on that. Three times he met, or tried to meet, critical situations of the sort by exploiting the flair he had for character-acting. Squire brought in the foreign physician, Dr. Tatistchev, thinking that she might eventually be corrupted into a valuable member of the gang. When Ourglass gathered that she might be unreliable, he put himself in her way as a victim of the place and endeavoured to find out where she stood. Again, Squire brought in the little man Routh, and then let him escape again, with this paper in his possession, and with a corpse, it seems, to his credit. That was the grand disaster. Before Routh was recaptured, he had hidden the paper—as we now know, in *A Thunderbolt of Wrath*. Before licencing more brutal methods, Ourglass seems to have tried the same bogus-prisoner trick. But his most brilliant—and blackguardly—application of it was on the island, after the fight. There was a matter of minutes left to him if he was to get away. And he thought it likely that Routh would have parted with his secret to his rescuers. So he put up a show of making a desperate bid to escape. He knew, you see"—Appleby's tone was grim—"the sort of person my sister is. And he'd have had her—and any secret she possessed—if I hadn't myself nipped in just in time. As it was, he failed—and simultaneously gave the whole show away."

"He almost gave the show away to *me*." It was Remnant who spoke. "You see, I'd rigged up a bit of a periscope and caught a glimpse of the fellows who had been shooting from behind the pillars of the little temple. And I had the impression—no more than that—that the fellow who rushed out as a fugitive had been one of them. It put me in pretty wretched doubt. But I don't see how *you* could have known."

"It was no great feat of detection." Appleby smiled. "He came running from the place, you remember, in a ragged shirt, and holding out his arms. His right arm was blackened right up to the elbow. In other words, this supposed helpless fugitive had been firing with a revolver in a confined space. There was smoke on his face too."

Bultitude began flapping about his person, produced a cigarette-case, caught the eye of Bodley's Librarian, and hastily stuffed it away again. "So you, my dear Appleby, had certainty. I had only suspicion. It was born the moment I heard of this able young scientist's being seen in the neighbourhood where Cline and his queer lot were working. But it was not a nice thing to speak up about until one was sure. I was feeling very cagey—I believe that is the word—when we met this morning. Later, when your sister came to tea and I heard about the incident in the upper reading room here, I saw that I must get all the information about it that I could. I got hold of Miss Butterton on the telephone. She had noticed the little man, and seen him doing something at old Undertone's desk. It was not difficult to guess what he had been up to. Not being of a very active disposition—a fact, Appleby, which your sister has very frankly pointed out to me—I enlisted the help of young Ourglass's uncle. If my suspicions were correct, he was going to suffer a great family humiliation, and I judged that it would be easier for him in the end if he could look back upon having a little helped in the cleaning up. Eventually, and in our own way—much less spectacular than Mr. Remnant's here—we got a list of the books in which the secret, whatever it was, was likely to be hidden. I then sent old Ourglass home to bed—things might well begin to happen which would not be fit for him to witness—and contacted Bodley's Librarian and yourself."

Remnant was frowning. "I don't understand how young Ourglass got after us."

"No difficulty about that." Appleby shook his head. "He still felt that you might have got the whereabouts of the paper from Routh. And he was, of course, desperate about it. Without it, apparently, nothing could be retrieved from the ruins of his organisation at all. Well he got out of his helicopter—I don't yet know where—in time to have Jane trailed in Oxford. Later, he joined in on that himself, and went down your so-called Mendip cleft after you. . . . Only, of course, *I* was having Jane trailed too."

"*You* were!"

"Certainly. I know my sister pretty well. And I didn't quite trust her to stop in Somerville."

Remnant rose. His face had gone very still and grave. "You say you know Jane well. Will she . . . get over it?"

"In time she will." Appleby looked at the young man swiftly. "But I think I understand what you mean. I don't know. Perhaps."

"Ought I to go away?"

Bodley's Librarian too had risen. "I take it, Mr. Remnant, that you are not a married man?"

"No, sir. I put up a bit of a yarn to Jane about the missis and the twelve kids. But I'm not."

"The other side of the world. For a year."

"Write?"

"Picture post-cards every three weeks. A letter from time to time."

"Then I'll be off." Roger Remnant moved to the door. He had the habit of not wasting time. "I suppose, sir, they'll let me out?"

"I am sure they will." Bodley's Librarian dropped a pair of glasses on his nose and smiled. "But I doubt whether they will let you back again." He advanced and shook hands. "If, when you do return to this country, you are minded to pursue your studies here at irregular hours, will you please ring me up? I have a telephone beside my bed. Good-bye."

The door closed. Mark Bultitude looked at his two companions with a light of sudden speculation on his face. "A very good boy," he said. "I wonder, by the way, if he's a *Remnant?* It hadn't occurred to me."

Bodley's Librarian had moved over to a window and opened it. "I don't know how you people feel. But to my mind there's been a good deal in this that needs blowing away with a breath of fresh air."

They crossed the room and stood beside him. A wind had risen and dispersed the vapours shrouding Oxford. Before them were the spires and towers of the city. They looked up, and could distinguish a few stars. Directly below the window there was a dull red glow. It was the night-watchman's brazier, and the night-watchman was sitting beside it, stuffing a pipe. He glanced up at the sky—an old man, unambitious and serene.

The wind was blowing hard, and licked the charcoal to a fuller glow. A puff of it blew through the room; there was a flutter of papers behind them; something white floated past their heads into the open air and drifted towards the ground. Before they realised the significance of what had happened it had come to rest, close by the old man's feet. He stooped to it. Appleby leant out, prepared to shout—and stopped as Bultitude murmured something in his ear. The old man picked up the scrap of paper—it was simply the first thing to his hand—folded it, thrust an end into the brazier, and lit his pipe. Then he tossed the remaining fragment into the flame. He drew at the pipe and again looked at the stars. His face appeared yet more serene than before.

Bodley's Librarian closed the window. "We can go to bed," he said. They left the room in silence, and in silence walked through the immemorial place, empty and yet so tremendously thronged. "I'm fond of Bodley," Bodley's Librarian said casually. "And particularly of Bodley by night."

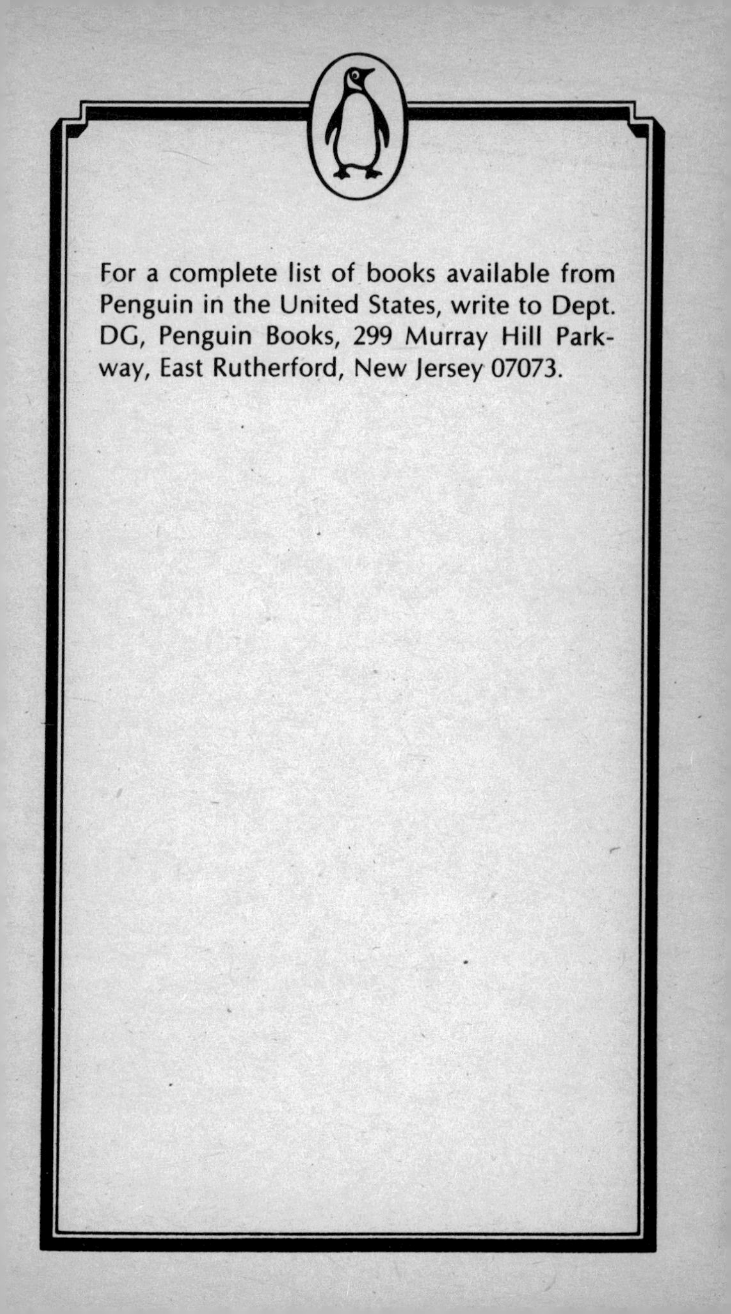